RETURN TO MAGNOLIA BLOOM

A MAGNOLIA BLOOM NOVEL BOOK 1

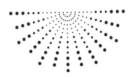

PAULA ADLER

DRAGON DREAMS PRESS, LLC

I hope you enjoy Return to Magnolia Bloom. If so, please leave a review on your favorite sites (Amazon, Goodreads, BookBub). THANK YOU!!

Please sign up for my newsletter to receive my next free novella, updates, and information on all future releases at <u>PaulaAdler.com</u>. Here are links to my author pages at all the usual places: Amazon, Goodreads, BookBub, <u>Facebook</u>

PRAISE FOR MAGNOLIA BLOOM

I can't recommend this entire series enough. By the end, you'll be wanting to visit Magnolia Bloom and rub Penny the Dragon's nose and cuddle with the adorable sheep, Lulu. ~ Penny, Amazon Review

Hallmark Holidays at the Castle, Halloween through Christmas. I would love for PBS to make a mini-series of this series so I could binge watch it! The overall story arc brings many generations together, many secrets become exposed and pain gets soothed and healed. This is an awesome series. ~ GranJan, Amazon review

Strong women and community; struggling together when necessary. Groundbreaking, unhindered my race, gender or religious affiliation. A strong and proud testimony to the human spirit. ~ Molly, Amazon review

Wonderful writing. I couldn't put it down. *Highly recommended!* ~ *Bestselling author Dee Davis*

Deeply emotional and richly imagined, the world of Magnolia Bloom is a universe that captured me and wouldn't let go, long after I turned the final page. ~ *New York Times and USA Today bestselling author Jean Brashear*

Paula Adler gifts us with a multi-generational family saga that combines romance, heartbreak, an honest-to-goodness Texas castle, travels to exotic locales and a cast of characters who'll grab your heart and not let go. The love gluing the MacInnes family together shines through on every page, even when they're dealing with the pain all families experience. So pour a cup or a glass, snuggle into your favorite chair and prepare to become an instant member of the clan! ~ *Bestselling author Merline Lovelace*

I wanna read more! ~ *ElizrdbthSpeaks, Amazon review*

Checks many boxes, contemporary, romance, historical, family saga, southern Literature, and women's fiction. ALL OF MY favorites I will seek out Paula Adler from here on out. ~ *Natalie F., Amazon review*

Get nice and comfortable, (you) won't want to put the book down. ~ *Sofe, Amazon Review*

Can't wait [to] continue the saga. ~ *Lisa G., Amazon review*

It pulls you in and keeps you wanting more. ~ *Sasha, Goodreads review*

CHAPTER ONE

PAIGE – NOW

I LOVE GETTING to my tiny office while it's still dark outside. Avoiding Austin traffic is one perk, but no phone calls and no interruptions rank much higher. Leaving the suburbs at five o'clock in the morning is completely normal and has absolutely nothing to do with avoiding my too-quiet house, my at-least-on-paper husband asleep somewhere in our sprawling one-story ranch, and the sadness engulfing my life.

Clearly, with such an impressive opening statement, I should've been a trial lawyer instead of a paralegal.

A glance out my window, small as it is, tells me I got here earlier than usual. From my vantage point on the eighteenth floor, the morning sun seems to mirror my lethargy, inching slowly over the I-35 side of downtown, the view changing so much it doesn't feel like Austin anymore.

Nothing feels like Austin anymore.

I pick up my Driskill Hotel commemorative globe and shake it. Bats fly around the Texas landmark instead of snow, and there couldn't be a more on-the-nose metaphor for my life if I were looking it up in a book of clichés.

My intercom light goes green before a voice comes through the speaker.

"Ms. MacInnes? It's Molly in Security. I have a Kase Santiago here?"

Kase?

I press the corresponding button. "Thanks, Molly. Send her up."

I hurry to the elevator bank with my keycard, as she'd be stuck in the lobby otherwise. When the doors slide open, my best friend exits in a coordinated tan linen pantsuit highlighting her could-be-a-model figure, dark hair and eyes, and skin turned goddess-kissed by the merest hint of sunshine.

Meanwhile, my Scottish-supplied pigment provides me a breath-taking choice between lobster red or chalk white.

"Hey, you." Not one of my more brilliant greetings, but this is Kase. And it's six-thirty in the morning. "What're you doing here?"

"Meeting with Angelica at seven. She has revised numbers to discuss and I nabbed her first appointment of the day."

Angelica's the senior partner in Mergers and Acquisitions. I'm in litigation and don't visit the M&A side much, but when Kase entrusted the firm with her business, I made sure she demanded our resident cobra in a power suit. With Kase considering selling a portion of her built-by-hand cosmetics company to a big-deal beauty empire, I'm doubly glad Angelica will dissect every line of every email. The line-through-and-revise in the contract will be nothing short of breathtaking.

"If this was supposed to be on my calendar, it's not. Sorry."

Kase offers, and I accept, an eco-friendly coffee cup from our favorite bistro. We both bought into Buy Austin as a mantra, not a slogan, figuring our disposable income should stay local.

I swipe us into my side of the building and lead the way to my office. It's not much more than a cubicle, but it has a door, and it's mine. After twenty-plus years, I've earned it, but it's still a perk for a paralegal.

"Ain't no thing. I don't expect you to keep up with my appointments."

Kase folds herself into one of the Target-quality chairs opposite my desk, a hint of her perfume—not exactly spicy, not exactly floral—floating in the air.

I tip my cup at her. "You're a lifesaver. I haven't made it to the break room yet."

She gives me her signature this-doesn't-make-me-happy head tilt. "I knew I'd find you here at the crack of dawn, but, girl, this is getting out of hand. You look sharp, though."

I glance down to see what I put on this morning. Oh, yeah. My go-to gray sheath dress and black blazer. I flip the end of the herringbone scarf she gave me for Christmas at her. "It's credit to you that the note-takers think I have a semblance of style."

"Clearly, I need to come up here more often. I normally get you in yoga pants and a sports bra with a long disintegrated underwire."

I lift a brow. "But hey, bra."

"Good point." She takes a sip of what I'm certain is green tea with raw honey. "So, spill. You didn't answer last night."

I grab my phone from the desk and swipe the screen awake. Sure enough, I missed a call from her.

"Mea culpa. I went to bed early. Headache."

"Which is also happening too often. Next application you fill out is going to need a box for Translucent under Caucasian."

I probably wouldn't mind if people hypothetically told me I look like a younger, dark-headed Helen Mirren as much as people actually tell Kase she looks like Zoe Saldana. Truthfully, though, I look nothing like the former, and Kase is prettier than the latter.

I wrinkle my nose at her. "Not all of us are lucky enough to have a Nordic-and-Haitian melanin combo, you know. You got the best of both hemispheres."

She gives me the duck lips of confusion. "Did you fail geography?"

"Probably. I don't remember taking it."

"The evidence speaks for itself."

I put my phone down and sit back, my chair the only first-rate thing in my microscopic space. I got approval for the top-of-the-line ergonomic edition, as I spend too much time in it to play games. I make few demands, but I refused the hand-me-down shuffle from the attorney side and won't apologize for this one extravagance. I consider it my bonus for bringing Kase to the client roster.

Kase raps her knuckles on my desk. "Earth to Paige."

"Sorry."

She tosses a nod at the picture on my credenza. "Why, pray tell, do you still have that picture in here? I mean, even I will admit he's crazy-good-looking, but shouldn't it be in a drawer somewhere?"

I look over at my favorite snapshot of my husband, taken just before we broke, so not much more than five years ago on the beach in Roatan. A professional photographer couldn't have done a better job framing the sunset behind his windblown hair, all dark and wavy and begging to be run through my fingers. His smile warm. His eyes teasing, the corners crinkling, his expression all come-hither.

And I hithered.

"Yeah, I guess you're right." I couldn't put it in a drawer yet, but I did turn it face down.

"Sorry, sweetie. I shouldn't have done that to you this early in the morning. So let me deflect by asking what's happening in your pretty head. When you avoid me, all my warning bells go into overdrive."

I don't take the bait and tease her about the mixed metaphor, which probably scares her as much as it does me. Instead, I pick up my mechanical pencil and maniacally click the lead dispenser.

"Apparently, my should-I-file-for-a-divorce teeter-totter has tipped over to yes."

Kase squints at me like she's trying to read the warning label on a medicine bottle without her cheaters. "Are you serious this time, or will you call me later and tell me it was a Benadryl hangover talking?"

I find a smile. Not a good one, but a close approximation. "I deserve that. I've flip-flopped more than a politician in an election year."

"Understatement, but the question is, what caused the totter?"

I take a long draw from my cup to stall, but also for a needed hit of go-juice. "Maybe it's because all these years I thought my instincts would give me a definitive answer, and as long as I had doubts, it wasn't time." I spend a moment making sure my cup is precisely in the center of the coaster, as if the world will stop turning if it's a degree off. "The doubts are gone."

"Wow. Color me stunned."

"I know I frustrate you, but I finally realize that instead of hating him, which was what I was sure would be my sign, I don't feel anything at all."

She launches forward like there's a spring in her chair. "Oh, honey." She reaches across the desk and rubs my hand. "It's hard, but damn, it's time."

"So it would appear."

Taking a deep breath, she drills me with a look. "What do you need from me? You know my guest room is always ready for you."

"You're a love, but I'm...processing."

She gives me an eye roll that almost knocks her backward. We do that to each other. It's amazing neither of us has detached a retina.

"You process more than a Google server farm."

"I will neither confirm nor deny such rumors."

"Says the lawyer."

"Paralegal."

She points a purple fingernail at me. "We'll compromise with 'the one who does the actual work.' So, you're having a come-to-Jesus with Mr. Oblivious?"

"Tonight."

"Call me if you need me to come over. Or head to my place. I have wine. We'll sing. We'll cuss. We'll cry. Then I'll kick your butt into action."

"You do have my back." And she does. I count on her to wallow with me in the pity pool, then bust out the whip and chair. When it's her turn to don the tiara and chug the Moët & Chandon, I do the same.

Kase perches on the side of my desk, rolling her palm over my knuckles so I'll release my death grip on the pencil. Her skin is soft as she threads her fingers with mine in solidarity to keep me from breaking into sobs, letting me know she's got me.

"Last we talked, you were heading out to the thriving metropolis of Magnolia Bloom soon, yes?"

I'm grateful for the pivot. I can't lose it at work, but I know she knows, so she returns to the guest chair.

"Soon. Violet can't hang on much longer."

"Is it too late to ask her for a vial of the magic marriage dust? Your aunt loves you more than the sun, so surely you qualify for the family rate?"

I wish I could laugh, as she's expecting, but it's been all I can do lately to push aside my anguish over losing V so I can get through the workday.

"I wish it were so simple, but the myth is more...mythical. There's no fairy dust, no magic wand. Lore says if you marry in the famous chapel at Castle MacInnes, the whole until-death-do-us-part is literal. There's no shield against hard times, but you'll have a love strong enough to survive any storm. If it really were pixie powder, I'd find a vat and bathe in it, but alas..."

"Well, shoot. I was hoping."

"Me, too. Even if the myth and marketing get jumbled, it looks like I'll be the first MacInnes who wed there to switch 'Mrs.' to 'divorcée.'"

"'Magic buster' is a helluva résumé bullet."

I try for a smile, but my lips wobble. "I wanted the magic to be real. At a minimum, I didn't want to be the one to break it."

"You're borrowing trouble. You don't know that will happen, and even if you get divorced, it doesn't mean the fairy tale is over for good. For the castle, I mean."

"That's the thing. I don't tend to believe in the bibbidi-bobbidi-boo, but there's something special about Castle MacInnes, and I'd be flat lying if I didn't want to think, on some level, it's real."

"Then trust that what happens is meant to be, and if the castle can't survive one setback, it's too fragile to start with."

"That, Ms. Santiago, is blasphemy. I'll ask the jury to please disregard and redirect by asking if you're coming down for either day of the games. The castle's booked, but you'll stay with me, natch."

The MacInnes Highland Games have been my family's tradition

for more than eighty years. I've rarely missed one in my lifetime and know this year will be overshadowed by the sadness of losing V.

"Much as I'd love my annual turkey leg and kettle-corn binge, I can't. I don't see how I can finalize everything by then."

"If you can swing it, come. If you rub Penny's nose, you might have better luck with the merger."

"The fountain dragon is one of my favorite parts of the castle."

"Yours and everyone else's. I'll have to be careful, the way things are going. I don't think even Penny is big enough to fix what's wrong with me. I might rub her nose off."

The sounds of my officemates arriving filter through the door, saving me from more navel-gazing and becoming a maudlin mess. I suck it up and put on my game face, two things I'm exceptionally good at.

Kase checks her wrist and stands, smoothing the handkerchief hem of her couture top. "We'll talk more later. I'll go wait for Angelica, and you can work on your stress ulcer."

I stand, too, and pull her in, our hug tight, brief, but better than the coffee still waiting on my desk. I never turn down a good cup of false courage, but time with Kase gives a real recharge to my dwindling internal battery life.

"You got this, you know."

Her words are sincere, but a shiver races up my spine that has nothing to do with the AC kicking on for its first cycle against the early June heat. "I guess we'll find out."

She opens the door, looking at me over her shoulder, concern and support all rolled into one. "Love you."

"Love you more." I give her the get-out-of-here thumb.

The day is going to be hard, but I'll muddle through. Not because I have notes to type up before the team meeting at ten, or hours of case law to review, but because the day will eventually be over, and I'll have to go home.

There's no more avoiding. Time to deal with the real.

Easy to say. Hard to do.

Especially when it means the end of life as you know it.

CHAPTER TWO

VIOLET – 1967

JEFFERSON AIRPLANE IMPLORES us to want somebody to love from the speaker of the Daddy's fancy new transistor radio resting on the blanket. Having a gadget-obsessed father comes in handy sometimes.

"I'm not a nitwit, you know." I glare at Ephraim, ignoring Grace Slick's voice and the band's hard drums and guitars. The rest of the town calls him David, but I love Ephraim, both the name and the young man, who is either charming or entrancing, depending on his needs.

At the moment, his soul-dark eyes and the raven hair falling over his forehead keep distracting me from my attempt at badassery.

"I've never called you a nitwit. I've never even thought the word in connection with you." He grunts and stretches out on the blanket we've brought to the grove.

Graduation and summer are around the corner, but we're delighted the heat hasn't hit the usual oppressive levels. In the shade of the magnolia trees giving our home its name, the cool breeze carries the enchanting scent from the early blossoms nestled in their broad, deep-green leaves. It's a tease, we know, before the approaching East Texas inferno.

My mother thinks I'm at Tidy's, which is where I almost always am when I'm not home. We have homework to do, but we'll probably talk about boys. Then I'm babysitting Mina and Fina. The big shindig at the castle tonight has Mrs. Greene in a frenzy, "her" kitchen a vortex of preparation. I don't mind staying out of her way. I'd rather take the girls to play with the new puppies than be drafted into washing dishes. I'll herd them—Mina and Fina, not the border collies—to their house for an early bath and bedtime. That'll give Ephraim time to sneak over and sit with me on the patio.

I give a mental snort.

Sit... Yeah...

I don't care what he's told his parents. Tidy's my best friend and will keep my secrets. The twins won't know he's there. I don't know who keeps Ephraim's secrets. He hangs mostly with the jocks, and it's not like we have double dates with anyone. Ever.

He shifts his arm and creates a hollow for me. I snuggle my head onto his chest and breathe in the scent of Downy from his T-shirt and Irish Spring from his skin. The filtered sunlight plays across his shoulders and chin, capturing all my senses, muting Cat Stevens singing *Matthew & Son* into a background haze.

"Thank you for acknowledging my genius, but you still didn't take me to senior prom. I don't like hiding that we're dating."

His huff does not bode well for the direction of the conversation. "We've talked about this a thousand times."

"No." I angle away to look at him. "*You've* said it a thousand times. It's almost the '70s. We're different religions, not different species, and who cares? We're putting a man on the moon, for heaven's sake."

"True. We're landing a white, Christian man on the moon."

I play-punch him in the side.

He captures my hand and presses a kiss to my knuckles to distract me from getting miffed. More miffed. Additionally miffed. Exponentially miffed.

"Did you hear the news? The mess in New Jersey? There've been twelve race riots I know of. Our world is on fire."

"I'm not arguing that it doesn't seem like the country's imploding, but you're not listening to me. It's not the same with us."

Ephraim hikes onto his elbow and looks down at me, the too-long hair I love falling into his face. I can't stop myself from brushing it aside so I can look into eyes so dark they sometimes seem black when the light's dim. Eyes that see right through me.

Eyes that are so sad.

"In some ways, what's between us is more volatile. Magnolia Bloom's reputation doesn't include being socially forward, and you know it. I'm accepted because most of the kids in our class don't even consider me Jewish. I don't fit their mental stereotype on what being Jewish means."

I roll my eyes at his one-handed air quote around *being Jewish*.

He rolls his eyes in camaraderie and continues. "I play sports. Most kids can't reconcile a Jew who loves football and baseball and runs track. And I manage a decent game of pickup on the community courts."

"You're a regular Don Meredith, Carl Yastrzemski, and John Newcombe rolled into one."

"Newcombe plays tennis. I suck at tennis. But extra points for the sports references."

"Poor baby. Being valedictorian and an all-star athlete is such a burden for you to bear."

"Cut it out, and quit trying to sidetrack me. You have to understand that although my family isn't excessively religious, we are proudly Jewish. We don't keep kosher, so other than I don't eat lunch at school when they serve ham, no one notices. And knowing the words 'kosher' and 'Hanukkah' is the literal extent of Judaism for the fine folks of Magnolia Bloom. They wouldn't know Orthodox from Conservative from Reform if their lives depended on it. I'm expected to know your religion and denominations. That's normal."

I push up to mimic his pose. "You know I'm not the most observant Presbyterian, to use your benchmark, which adds validity to my argument, not yours. Still, the double standard isn't right."

"I'm not talking about what's right, or misunderstanding Judaism. Like it or not, East Texas is their world, and I and my family are allowed into it. Do you see? We have to maintain a place, a position. You don't."

"Are we having a theoretical discussion on religion and race in modern America? I can grab my notes from debate class if you want, but we might be here all day."

"Mmmm, might not be such a bad idea."

He leans over for a kiss. He tastes like Red Hots and Coca-Cola, and the spicy combo will spark my dreams until the day I die.

Then his expression sobers. "I would gladly walk with you on my arm, Violet MacInnes MacInnes, but it's not as simple as you and me."

I squint at him because he knows using my full name irks me. Some days I swear if I ever have a daughter, I'll break the tradition of all girls having MacInnes as a middle name so no one can take it from her when she marries. Other days, it's kinda cool.

Today isn't one of them.

Frustration rises in his voice. "You're not grasping how big the issue really is."

"But—"

"No buts! Do you honestly not see how careful a line my family and I have to walk? You're a MacInnes. Your family and your castle own more than half the town."

"And you're a Broder, and your Broder Factory owns the other half."

"Your family could survive the scandal of you dating a Jew. If I start dating a gentile, it's more than my mother going ballistic faster than a Saturn V rocket. It's what the rednecks might do."

"You're strong. We can handle it."

"Dammit, Violet!" He stops himself and takes a deep breath. "It's more than how *you'd* be treated. It also happens Clifford Saxon and his buddies might decide to teach the 'Jew boy' a lesson and burn our factory down. If we lived in San Francisco, or New York, or twenty other places, we would hardly be a blip, but we don't. We live in Magnolia Bloom, Texas. In 1967. Where it might as well be 1947."

He traces my lower lip with his fingertip. I stay silent. I know he's right, and I despise the Clifford Saxons of the world.

I'm sad and frustrated, and I want out of this one-track town.

"I do see your point. Really I do, but once we've graduated, we can leave. Start our own lives someplace where minds are broader than the one-lane bridge on Rain Creek Road."

Ephraim runs his knuckle down my face in a gesture so intimate tears fill my eyes. I push forward to kiss him and hope he tastes Doublemint gum and Barq's root beer and remembers me in his dreams.

I like kissing him. A lot. And it frustrates me that I want to do so much more and he won't give in to my wiles.

I chuckle inside. A seventeen-year-old girl's wiles...

Still, he's right. It's 1967. On a trip into Austin, Tidy and I were given permission to attend a lecture at Hogg Auditorium on campus. Instead of taking our seats and appreciating the beaux arts aesthetic of the beautiful facility, we hung out in her sister's dorm room in the shadow of the UT Tower. In a haze of pot and patchouli, Ginny gave us both condoms and a lecture on how to use them. Ginny is my idol as a second-wave feminist, wearing tie-dyed tunics and cutoff blue jeans. She keeps her long hair plaited in braids with a leather thong around her forehead.

And she's been disowned by her parents.

Ginny's marched for access to birth control for all women, not just married women. She's been arrested for being on her boyfriend's shoulders, topless, with a tempera-paint sign proclaiming Make Love Not War to protest the escalating conflict in Vietnam, now in its twelfth year. She is beautiful and fierce and proud.

But despite her bravura, I know the loss of family connection hurts her deeply. Yet she's more interested in keeping her sister, and me by extension, out of trouble. Pretty freakin' rad, any way you slice it. Of course, if Momma knew what I did, she'd have Daddy brick me into my room and not let me out until I'm twenty-five. Tidy's mom would do the same.

I may be a budding feminist, but I'm an underaged bud, and more important, I'm not dim, so I keep my hardly noteworthy rebellion on the QT.

"You know we can't."

Ephraim reins in my wandering thoughts. I have to think back on what we last said before my thoughts went off track.

"What I don't accept is you refusing to consider my arguments. There's a reason I'm the top debater in Mr. Chase's class, you know."

"You've mentioned it once or twice."

I do my practiced single-eyebrow raise. "We can go to college, start our family. Never come south of the Red River again."

The pain in his eyes is dark and molten, and I'm ashamed I spoke so blithely. I love my family. He loves his. We are both products of generations of heritage here in Magnolia Bloom.

"I got accepted to Wharton."

Those five words chill me. I've been accepted to the University of Texas, Baylor, and SMU. To my surprise, I also got into Rice. All excellent schools.

All right here in Texas.

"Pennsylvania." I can barely say the word out loud.

Wharton. One of the five schools sending acceptance letters to Ephraim, including UT and Rice. It goes without saying I've spun all my dreams around us going to college in Austin or Houston or Waco or Dallas, out from under prying eyes and nosy noses and small minds. Planning our classes. Late nights at the Union. Joining in marches.

Sleeping together. Marrying.

I hate my eyes tearing up and spilling over. Hate my emotions always being just under the surface, waiting to blindside me.

"I love you, V. I'll always love you, but we can't be together publicly."

My ability to be logical has sailed past its zenith. I surge to my feet, my breath quick and sharp.

"I have a thousand words for you, David Ephraim Broder, and until today, 'coward' wasn't one of them."

He reacts equally badly, standing and snatching the blanket and radio from the ground, stopping Jimi Hendrix cold with a sharp twist.

"Call me what you want, but someday you'll understand." He stomps from our alcove, then stomps back and hands me Daddy's radio.

"I can live with you being angry with me, Violet."

He pulls me to him and kisses me, a gesture of love and regret and frustration, and enough restrained passion to catapult all the others into the stratosphere. He rests his forehead against mine.

"I can't live with you being dead because of me."

I'm left alone in the alcove that's been our meeting place the whole school year. Whenever we can, we slip off for stolen kisses and long talks and barely contained youthful lust.

As silence envelops me, I hate him as much as I love him. I hate living in a world where people are killed because of the pigment in their skin or their choice of house of worship.

It's not supposed to work this way. Even if Ephraim's right and everything is on fire, I'm a MacInnes. Family lore claims love is magnified here. Love is more powerful here. Love born under our magnolias can overcome the biggest obstacles.

I hate the whole world for taking Ephraim from me.

And I hate myself because I let him walk away.

Most of all, I hate the castle for its magic not being real.

At least not for me.

CHAPTER THREE

PAIGE – NOW

MY DAYS HAVE BECOME SO rote, I'm home and in my post-work uniform of leggings and a tunic without a moment's thought. It's scary to realize I drove, changed, and am in the kitchen with the refrigerator doors open...and I can't remember any of the intervening steps.

It's my turn to fix dinner, so I default to the easiest thing in my repertoire. Besides, using the grill lets me enjoy the flickering light from the tiki torches illuminating the deck. I need a moment in nature, albeit classic cul-de-sac nature, after a long day indoors. I push with my toe to rock the wrought-iron patio chair, focusing my thoughts on the need to raise the canopy on the Chinese pistache tree standing sentinel on the edge of the wooden slats and how the flower bed needs weeding, the stones in the path need new filler sand, and four boards in the fence need replacing. It's enough to keep my attention from what's ahead until I plate the steaks, asparagus, and potatoes and head inside.

I know I'm dragging my feet, and it's not fair to let the food grow cold, but I don't call Zach to dinner until I'm seated. My arm rests on the folder I placed on the table earlier, but he barely glances at the file jacket covering the Petition for Divorce form I printed today at the office. No surprise. My husband is many things, but dumb isn't one of them. No one-liners fly from my mouth. I don't share today's sign at El Arroyo, although "Of course size matters. No one wants a small taco" is pretty funny.

Old-school Fleetwood Mac pours from the stereo. The tablecloth and runner are bright white, embroidered with pineapples and flamingos. An odd combination, I admit, but cute. The vase of gladioli and Gerber daisies on the half wall between the informal dining room and living room shouldn't work, either, but my favorite florist never fails to surprise me. I'm grateful for the bright spot in the room.

The folder reclaims my attention, and I can see the hidden pages in my mind. One of the benefits of being a paralegal for two decades is getting access to the firm's forms folder. Being the right hand of the senior partner includes permission to use it. Typing up a petition is no big deal. A mere recitation of facts. A cold retelling of names and dates.

In the District Court, State of Texas, County of Travis.

Petitioner: Paige Jeanette MacInnes

Respondent: Zachary Nathan Peters

Two children of the marriage, Aiden Nathan Peters and Ainsley MacInnes Wilson (née Peters), are emancipated, and neither is under the continuing jurisdiction of this or any court. Petitioner is not pregnant.

Insert manic laugh here. Your Honor, the necessary prerequisites for such an event have not been met.

Date of Separation...

There's the rub. Literally, we aren't. Separated, that is. We still live in the same house. Still share the same bed, some of the time. Still have intertwined finances.

Figuratively?

I can't escape my cautious nature. I've discussed with my boss using the firm when the time comes to divide the assets and debts of nearly three decades, but there's no need to spend the money on the original proceedings. A few hundred dollars in attorney's fees won't break us, but that's not the point.

I add salt and pepper to my potato, using my fork to mash in a second pat of butter. I refuse to worry about calories, because there are only so many ways I can divide my emotional pie. The slice for dieting has to wait.

Even as I have the thought, the bite of white-carb yumminess sticks in my throat. I manage a long swallow of tea to wash it down instead of choosing the wine I'd prefer.

Realizing I'm still stalling, I slide the file over to Zach. He opens it and looks down. He doesn't act surprised, but a hurt look sweeps over his face. The one I steeled myself against, more to stop from erupting like Vesuvius on steroids than owning the tar-sticky guilt I can never quite escape.

He won't meet my eyes.

There are good and bad aspects of being married to a man who has made aversion to conflict an Olympic sport. The good? Zach and I have never raised our voices to each other, cursed at each other, or called each other a hurtful name.

The bad? I can write a script for our "fight." He'll say, *I don't want to talk about this now* in three...two...one...

"I don't want to talk about this now."

Which is my cue. "Then when can we talk?"

Forty-seven seconds of silence commences.

His next line, *I don't want to get divorced*, in three...two...

"I don't want to get divorced."

I count to ten, taking long, deep breaths, proving therapists are liars. I'm not remotely calmer. I'm not more receptive. I can't form the perfect response to open an opportunity for dialogue ensuring vulnerability and healing.

"What else can I do? I've suggested counseling. I've given you brochures on seminars for *The Five Love Languages*. I've given you literature on a sexy couple's getaway in Tahiti, promising to reignite the passion in the most hopeless marriage."

"Tahiti? You've never been a beach girl. You sunburn."

In...two, three. Out...two, three.

"Tahiti isn't the point. When we go SCUBA diving, I manage to keep covered when we're topside. I can do the same on a beach. Tahiti's a placeholder."

I stop talking. He's doing it to me again. Deflecting to ease the tension. So, I wait.

The sound of a clock mocks me in my head. *Tick, tick, tick.*

I keep silent, forestalling the moment when I break down and beg him to talk to me. Worse, I'll start crying and reveal the emptiness threatening to turn me into a pitiful joke or a shrieking harpy.

I don't want to be either one. I want the old Zach, my Zach, the Zach who looked at me with hunger and passion. The Zach who showed off for me on the softball field or a set of skis—water or snow—always checking to be sure I was watching...and I was. The Zach who was sweetly enchanted when I put on my makeup. The Zach who told me I was the most beautiful woman in the world every single day.

Until he didn't anymore.

The man who loved me, and I him, with a depth that made oxygen seem quaint, something mere mortals need. Not us.

I snatch up the beautifully etched stemware holding a generous pour of my favorite merlot and toss down a bigger sip than is wise. The blackberry notes, soft tannins, and smooth finish barely stop my slide into a snide jumbotron. My jaw locks up so hard wine can't enter and words can't exit. My sole focus is keeping my bitch wings from flaring, flying across the room, and shaking him until he engages with me.

The ticking marches like a soldier toward an alarm bell. Another chance to talk is forfeited. History has already scripted the aftermath of this nonfight. He will not look, will not talk, will not suggest a future time to talk.

The kicker? Tomorrow, he'll act as though this conversation never happened.

I unlock my jaw and take another healthy slug, which infinitesimally dulls the hurt and stalls the tears trying to escape from under my manhole cover of tempered sarcasm.

"Can you at least acknowledge I've spoken?" I curse the break in my voice and the knot in my throat forcing the words to be whispered. "Even blow me off with an 'I'll think about it'?"

Before the alarm can turn into a bomb, I push from the table, wincing when the chair knocks into the china cabinet. I'd worry over scratches and repairs, but why? We'll sell it when we eventually create separate households, another casualty in a war where a shot was never fired.

Moving to the kitchen, I swipe my meal into the trash, rinse my plate, and put it in the dishwasher. I return through the dining room archway to top off my wine.

"There's a Waiver of Service of Process on the last page. Neither one of us wants you to have to be served by a constable." Reciting legal minutia lets me regain moderate control of my voice, but I have far less of a grip on the acidic swirl of sadness roiling in the cauldron of my stomach. "Sign it, and I'll take care of the rest."

Like everything else in our boring-ever-after lives.

I chide myself. I haven't always resented having to manage anything requiring an iota of follow-through. Now? Now the truth itches like a wet wool sweater. I've been in charge since before our marriage. I arranged for the blood work. Completed the paperwork for the license. Rented the tuxedoes for Zach and his three groomsmen. I even scheduled the rehearsal dinner. All things he or his parents should have done, in some alternate universe.

Every. Single. Detail.

I guarantee Zach has no idea where to find our birth certificates or Social Security cards. Or our wills. Or our home or auto folios. Forget him finding the twins' info. It's not like we need it much anymore, as they both have families of their own, but when we opened the new investment account and needed to complete the beneficiaries' portion?

It doesn't matter anymore. My give-a-damn is well and truly busted.

Zach doesn't speak. Doesn't look at me. Just sits there, cutting his steak into uniform bites and eating with methodical precision.

I take my wine to my bathroom and run the hottest tub I can stand. As I sink into the fragrant bubbles, I look around the extravagant space we designed. Far too big, but I didn't care then, and I don't care now. I love every square of mosaic tile. Love the jets in the tub, ranging from low to who-needs-a-man. Love the separate sinks with brushed-nickel faucets. Love the oversize, glass-doored stall with a raised showerhead for Zach and a lower one for me on the opposite wall.

I try not to envision the last time we steamed up the glass far more than we could blame on water vapor. It's been so long the memory is fading.

Strangely, it seems not so long ago that we saw Aiden's and Ainsley's pretend teenage horror when Zach would come into the kitchen and pat my butt or kiss my neck or engage in any other PDA. We reveled in torturing them, knowing the kids secretly delighted in having parents who are in love.

Were in love.

I was so arrogant. So sure Zach and I were special unicorns who beat the odds even finding each other, much less staying together. We were so young when we married, Aiden and Ainsley already the size of peach pits in my still-flat belly. "Too young," everyone said. Yet we were still holding hands when most of our friends and half our family members were divorced. Or multidivorced.

Pride goeth before...

I swipe vanilla sugar scrub onto my legs, maybe harder than I should, but I'm trying to distract myself. And failing. My heart is trying to chain-saw an exit route through my chest, and I'd give anything to have a mug of Zach's *nothing's wrong* sauce.

Hell, I'd take a tiny demitasse cup.

Inevitably, the bubbles fizzle, and the water cools. I glare at my innocent wineglass, drained of every dark drop. My shins are stinging, and there's nothing to do but drain the tub, dry off, and apply lotion.

I look at my bare left hand. My naked fingers. No need to take off my rings, like in the old days, to keep them from getting goopy. I haven't worn them in years—five to be exact—and tonight it slaps me, as if my fingers would leave metaphorical imprints on my own cheeks. Hard reality has sunk into my middle-aged, terrified-of-being-alone pre-frontal cortex. The long-running play I needed to believe was "Zach and me" is instead a soliloquy. A pitiful monologue.

I can usually suppress my sense of loss, but tonight the elephant in the room has become an enraged tiger, teeth bared, growl throaty and deep.

I focus on slipping on my gown. Not a granny gown. I refuse to be a stereotype. While my lingerie might not be from Victoria's Secret, it's pretty. Lacy.

And, once upon a time, so easy to remove.

I dry my hair, then slide under the covers. I run my hand over his side of the bed. I didn't expect him to be there, but the shock of the cool, empty place is sharp.

The old saw fills my head about it being better to have loved and lost than never to have loved before. But is it? My exhausted brain unearths memories of tangling up in these very sheets, sweating and laughing. Of lovemaking so deep and tender it brought me to tears. Of sex so raw and hard and glorious we were left in puddles of sweat with deliciously sore muscles.

When a stray thought runs through my mind about writing a memoir, this chapter would embarrass the kids to no end, but I'll never be a writer, so it's not like they'll ever know. They know their dad as their dad. The whip-smart programmer who can fix a car with as much confidence as a line of code. They don't know the slender, muscled young man who chased their mother around the house until she was happily caught. And caught again.

Then she chased him…

"God, I miss it." My words are lost in the still darkness.

I force my thoughts to an easy meditation to try to sleep. I can't call Kase because I know she's busy doing all the things that follow her home from work every day. I can't call Aunt Violet because she's busy dying.

Which leaves me vulnerable when the tiger leaps, and I'm defenseless against the unsheathed claws slicing up my soul. All I can do is let the tears escape into my cotton pillowcase.

CHAPTER FOUR

MINA – NOW

I TAKE my hand from V's door, offering a prayer for her to find peace. I want to beat on the solid walnut panels, but I wouldn't dream of disturbing her fitful sleep. I want to rail at God for being so blasted unfair. V's too young. We've got too much thrift-store shopping to do, quilting club meetings and sewing marathons to attend. I have two Vogue Patterns and one new Butterick we haven't cut out yet, and the pale blue gabardine I washed and folded is perfect for her.

She's got too much left to offer the world.

"Lord, I'm sorry." I rest my head against the cool wood. "I know you do things in your time, but I don't understand. If it's time for her to go, then free her or take her. Why does she have to hurt so bad?"

Neither God nor the door answers me, so I head down the long hall to the kitchen, knowing Fina is waiting for an update.

The overhead light in the smaller of the two castle kitchens seems harsh after sitting with V for so many hours with only the side lamps and her favorite candles lit. I step in, squinting, and address my sister's back.

"Not much longer now. The nurse gave her another dose of morphine, so she'll sleep awhile."

Fina concentrates on the soup cooking on the stove. She likes this stove better than the big one downstairs anyway. Homemade chicken noodle is all V can swallow, so this batch is enough to feed the Cowboys defensive line. When we say a Southern woman shows her love through food, it's the God's honest truth.

"I wish she'd let us call Paige. You know she'd be here faster than greased lightning." She gives the pot a hard rap with her spoon and sets it on a ceramic holder.

It's easier to pretend to be angry than give in to despair.

"Stubborn old goose." I sniff and move to the cupboard, pulling out freezer bowls and tops to portion the soup after it's cooled. "She's implacable, so I guess we need to talk about Paige. How are we going to reach our girl?"

Fina picks up her spoon again, stirring like she's trying to contact the Oracle of Delphi. Fina has always been Ms. Smarty-Pants, but I know who the Oracle is from my favorite historical romance, even if I don't have two degrees and teach online classes in medieval history.

"Our girl's as hardheaded as that one." Fina points toward V's bedroom. "We'll have our work cut out for us."

A laugh both sad and genuine surprises me. "We've had a lot of training in stubborn. Even Paige won't be able to withstand the both of us."

"True dat." She cuts off the gas and puts a lid on the pan. "Get your notebook and let's start making plans on how we stop our sweet Paige from making the worst mistake of her life. If she divorces, she'll break the magic."

"I know you don't mean that the way it sounds." My voice is sharp, and I don't try to soften it.

"Of course not. You know my first worry is Paige."

I'm bothered my normally ornery sister is so downcast. We're not the most demonstrative of twins, but I love her. Sometimes she forgets it. And my love isn't because she saved my life and, of course, my son's. We're forever knit together, and some things can't be understood by anyone who's not a twin.

"We're both stretched tighter than a timpani drum, but we'll fix it."

I want to add, *Like you fixed me,* but she gets riled up when I resurrect our past. Neither of us wants anything but the best for Paige, but it's more than her not learning from our lessons. Or about her being alone. A woman can be fulfilled and have a full, rich life without a husband, but Paige isn't me. Or Fina. Or Violet.

The fact remains if we lose Paige, we lose the castle. There are two separate and distinct castle doctrines in play. One is that a direct MacInnes female must be the chatelaine of this castle, and the other is that there's magic in the MacInnes chapel, and no couple married there has ever divorced. One principle is tradition, the other is statistically impossible, yet has proven true to this day.

To be clear, we've had lots of weddings on the grounds or in the ballroom, but those who take their vows in the special space built by Evajean and Alisdair MacInnes in 1885 are all a part of history. Or were until now.

"It's not fair, but our girl has a lot waiting for her when she gets here." I rearrange the bowls and lids from biggest to smallest, anything to give my hands something to do.

I end up with my thumbs tucked into the front pockets of my jeans, the ones V and I designed from a vintage Palmer/Pletsch pattern after a bolt of denim caught my eye. Of course, since V helped measure and calculate before my scissors cut the first piece, the end result was better fitting than any couture label.

Fina frowns, which isn't necessarily unusual, but there's a bitter turn to the corner of her mouth. "Sometimes I think the good Lord left 'fair' out of the mixing bowl for the bunch of us."

I shrug, trying to pretend I haven't had the same thought a time or two. "Maybe, but we've never been whiners."

"If we're being honest, it wasn't fair of V not to tell Paige the shape the finances are in."

My shoulders stiffen to defend V, but Fina beats me to it.

"She'd've gotten to it if she'd had time. It all happened so fast, but should'ves and would'ves don't matter. It's up to us now."

"I know." The weight of our responsibility is crushing. The cancer blindsided us all, and V the most.

I play with the edge of one of the bowls. "I've never spent much time thinking about how the manager of the castle comes from a direct female descendant born in Texas. It seems silly, but it only now occurred to me how it all works."

"I imagine we've never thought much about it because it wasn't ever an issue. Now we're staring down the fact that Paige is our only hope. Ainsley would be the next appointee, but she has those babies, so taking care of the castle falls to Paige."

"There's an error in your logic. The next appointee, as you put it, doesn't have to be Paige's child. Paige does have a sister. Moreover, Kiki was born in Austin. That's 100% Texan."

Fina uses a tea towel to polish a drip off the stove top, and I prepare myself for a lecture. "That's true. Ainsley may be officially next, but Kiki fulfills the requirements. Still, I can count the number of times she's come to Magnolia Bloom. She'd almost be worse than a stranger taking over."

I cock my head at my sister. "How in tarnation do you come to that conclusion?"

"A stranger would come because they want to be here. Kiki's hardly set foot on this continent, much less in this country, since she was old enough to say so."

My frown deepens. "She's in the Air Force. It's not like she gets to choose where she deploys."

Fina folds the towel and sets it on the counter with more care than the action requires and turns to talk directly to me. "The point is, Paige is our hope."

For the first time, anger jumps up and bites my behind that Violet set such a hard task in our laps. Ten years our senior, she was our babysitter when we were toddlers and our best friend as we grew into adulthood. We laughed together, cried together, worked together for decades. We are as tied to this castle, this family, this land as surely as she is, even if we aren't of actual MacInnes blood.

She's never once made a distinction.

But she's prickly as a pear cactus about handing off the castle duties. She's never been one to shirk responsibility, but somehow she can't face putting such a load in Paige's lap. She thought she'd have thirty more years to do the work, or surely twenty, as MacInnes women are usually long-lived. More, she thought Paige would've had a good, long time to decide on such a life-altering course.

"We have to sort this out." I wonder how we'll accomplish my statement of the obvious.

"I love tradition as much as anyone, but it's causing us a heap of headaches. Still, we have to play the cards we're dealt, so we'll come up with something. We have to."

CHAPTER FIVE

PAIGE – NOW

By SEVEN THIRTY WEDNESDAY MORNING, I'm on my second cup of coffee before my fellow paralegal and friend Grady strolls into the smaller of the two libraries the firm maintains. The room is sound-proofed by wall-to-wall law books, anachronisms in today's speed-of-light-driven law. I'd bet the current cache of students over on Dean Keeton Street haven't held an actual *South Western Reporter* in their hands, but for me, the musty smell doesn't stop it from being my go-to place.

I'm too tired and too sad to razz Grady for being late, which is our belabored joke. Besides, my work product has added nothing of value. The forensic accountant's opinion for our most pressing case might as well be in Cyrillic, and I can't tell him a single salient fact.

I've written *draft a Motion to Compel* on my legal pad, but I can't remember what I'm requesting to have compelled.

I wonder if Grady'll have to do an MTC for Zach in a few months, but why? He doesn't care enough to fight for me, so it isn't out of line to think he won't fight against me.

I pretend to sneeze to give myself an excuse to hide behind a tissue and pull myself together. If I don't, I might cost our client a chunk of the assets her state senator husband is trying to hide. I'm not particularly fond of her or consider her a scion of morality herself, but my feelings are as important to Mrs. Wounded Pride as they are to Zach.

"You look like hell." Grady puts his double-insulated mug with his initials outlined in crystals on the table. He plops into the chair next to mine, his perfectly pressed and monogrammed dress shirt tucked into his knife-creased slacks. Not a wrinkle or stray white cat hair in sight, and I know he has two Persians and one adorable rescue kitty of extremely questionable lineage.

"Good morning to you, too." I try to wipe the scowl from my face because it has nothing to do with him.

"I've got a great night cream, if you'd like me to order you a tube. Those bags under your eyes could haul groceries."

I cut him a glare. "Can we please leave my less-than-winsome looks off the docket and do some work?"

Grady gestures at the table. "The new batch of discovery docs?"

"Part of it. Can I mention I hate the esteemed senator's counsel?"

"Sure, you can." He pulls a stack of folders toward him and opens the top one. "Have they ponied up the info on the surprise Cayman account?"

I do a mental finger snap. Mystery solved on what I need to compel.

"Nope. The forensic accountant has to start again almost from scratch."

He shuts the folder and looks at me. "So, spill it. What's up?"

I scratch the edge of my list with a nail needing the undivided attention of a seasoned manicurist. "I gave Zach the petition last night."

He stops puttering, and the bantering tone leaves his voice. "I'm sorry, honey. You've gone around the track more times than an Indy car trying with him."

I shrug. Relationships have been the topic of many of our discussions over the last decade, but he knows only a slice of my story. He's a good friend and a reliable confidant, but I've never wanted him to think badly about Zach. I don't want anyone to think badly about Zach, because I'm self-aware enough to know I bear responsibility in this quagmire, too.

Grady's good people, and I hope the bookkeepers in heaven put extra jewels in his crown.

"What did he say?" He faces me directly, giving me his full attention. Bless his heart, he's the best listener in the world.

"The same thing he always says. Nothing."

"Men are jerks." His touch on my hand is short but has the power of a poem.

"Good news is, my file will be so small we won't even need an expandable. Nothing like this nonsense."

He gives a gusty sigh. "Well, this sucks. Zach's the best softball captain the firm's ever had. Could you wait until after the season? We could actually beat Winston and Sturgess this year."

"I'll take that under advisement."

He pats my knee. "You're a peach."

The door to the library opens, and my favorite of the executive assistants pokes her head in the room. "Paige, your aunt Mina's holding on 121."

And there it is. The moment I could never prepare for even though I've known it's been coming for months. Picking up the receiver, I take a deep breath and key in the code.

"Hey, Mina. How are you?"

It would be obtuse of me to be surprised to hear her tell me Aunt V has died in her sleep, but I can't stop the gut punch the words deliver. Peacefully and in her own bed, as she wanted. The viewing will be Saturday; the funeral is scheduled for Sunday.

Counting today, since it's barely started, I have four days to figure out how I can manage to be less of an embarrassment to the sea of Scottish family members I'll be dealing with for the next few months. Despite the heavy veer toward the Celtic in my genealogy, I somehow skipped the stoic queue when I was being knit together. Some of the more emotionally constipated in the family tree look at me with confusion, but benevolence. Others look at me with exasperation.

I wish I could count the times V said I had to be the reincarnation of my great-great-grandmother, a woman who refused to adhere to expectations and captured a handsome Scotsman who defied masculine stereotypes while being the very embodiment of the physical attributes. And each time, it confused the dickens out of me. I may share a birthday with our family matriarch, but I am the least adventurous and expectation-defying woman I know. As for Zach, while certainly handsome, he wouldn't know how to defy a stereotype if it came with written instructions and a YouTube video.

We talk for a few moments, exchanging the chitchat expected by Mina—my aunt by love, not by blood—until I finally sign off.

"All right, Mina, I'll be there as quickly as I can."

"Love you, girl."

"Love you more."

Grady waits through the exchange, and I hang up.

"If that's your aunt Mina, then Aunt V has passed."

"You're not the second-best forensic paralegal in the firm for nothing." I'm stunned my voice sounds quippy despite a mass of sadness the size of Mansfield Dam in my throat.

Grady stands and pulls me in for a hug. "You're clearly distraught for such a sentence to come out of your mouth." His expression turns concerned, all joking gone. "You've spent your whole life being everyone else's anchor, and no one sees you're drowning. When do you start taking care of you?"

My breath goes sharp and short, the panting barely giving me enough oxygen to stay conscious. I love him for his loyalty, but I... can't.

I pull away, gently so I don't insult him, and find my snark. "Clearly not today, but thank you, Dr. Brown."

"Hey, I love me some Brené, so you better beware, missy." He points to the exit like a policeman directing traffic. "Go. Send me a carrier pigeon from the hinterlands if you need me."

Knowing he's more than half serious about how backward he considers Magnolia Bloom doesn't hide the genuineness of his offer. Though not exactly BFFs, we're a lovely mix of truly caring for each other without being enmeshed. He knows how much I love Aunt V and spends a lot of time ribbing me over my East Texas roots, regardless of the fact I'm a native Austinite. Truth is, I'm far more Air Force brat than either Austinite or Magnolia Bloomian, but those are semantics.

"Sorry to leave you with a mess." I jerk a thumb toward the boxes.

"No sweat. Nick is done with the Stanton trial, so I'll ask him to step in."

My lip twitches. "Don't let me come home and find your butt hauled into HR."

I know Grady has a crush on the newest member of the paralegal team, and I'm almost certain the attraction is reciprocated. Other than offering my warning that office romances are rarely a good idea, I let Grady do his own adulting.

"My sabbatical has been in the pocket for a while. The partners have been lobbing me softballs for weeks, present nightmare case excepted. Sorry to state the obvious."

"I'll save my jokes about senility for when you get back."

"I can always count on you." I straighten his collar, although we both know it lies perfectly.

He stops me when I reach the door. "Hey, if you find any extra jars of pixie potion while you're there, send me one."

"What's with you and Kase and the magic fairy dust? I know I've explained myth and marketing a hundred times."

Grady shrugs. "Legends start somewhere, right? Can't hurt to look around."

I blow him a kiss and head to my boss's office to tell her the news, all of which has me headed home and cussing MoPac traffic well before noon. If I put myself in overdrive, with requisite stops, I can be in Magnolia Bloom by seven. It isn't the interstate travel that takes the extra time from Central Texas to the far east side of the state. It's the smaller highways turning into county roads that eat up the clock.

I make mental notes to call my siblings to give them the news. I'll probably connect with the boys, but will have to leave a voicemail for Kiki. They'll all send flowers. My brothers' kids will probably wonder who Aunt V is, but I'm not angry with them. They never had a relationship with V the depth of mine. After all, V was more mother to me than aunt, so it's impossible for my siblings to have the same kind of connection I've held close in my heart for over forty years. My mother told me V planted a flag in my affection within days of my birth, and ties so deep are intimidating to try to match. Impossible really. All of which means my nieces and nephews are even more distant from one of the most amazing women to be born in Texas.

And Texas women have no equal.

I know my father and mother will call later tonight. I do the mental math. There's a seven-hour time difference to Berlin, but they turn off their cell phones while they're sightseeing, and Dad hauls around an old-school SLR. Still, I'm sure Mina left a message at their hotel so they can make it home in time.

Not "home" as far as Dad is concerned, though. I assume he loved V, his twin sister, but I honestly can't swear to that. Moreover, none of us has ever discovered the secret explaining Dad's utter hatred of Magnolia Bloom. He enlisted in the Air Force before he graduated from UT, got married, and flew off into the wild blue yonder. He'll come back for important family weddings and funerals, but he and Mom never stay at the castle, never stays in the manor houses, never stays at a B&B in town. They reserve a hotel in Dallas and rent a car. Drive in. Shake hands. Give hugs. Leave.

Dad's unswerving avoidance of Magnolia Bloom influenced my entire nuclear family's weak connection with the castle and the town rooted in my soul. I didn't get the wanderlust gene and hated being a military brat as much as Dad hates East Texas. To this day, I have a hive-inducing aversion to moving.

The more unfortunate consequence of my father's view of his ancestral home, in my mind, is his influence on my brothers and, ergo, my nieces and nephews. They've never gotten to know the magic waiting here.

And now, because of me, they might never have the chance.

CHAPTER SIX

VIOLET – 1969

"Hold up a minute."

I heed Aunt Gavina's instruction as I slow my steps toward the skittish horse wide-eyeing me like I'm another two-legged intent on hurting her. She has no way of knowing she's won the lottery by being found by Aunt G.

I stop to give the terror in the luminous dark eyes a moment to calm. The pause gives me a chance to wonder why I once had a similar fear of Aunt G. For years, I quaked at the mention of her name. Now, having to go weeks without seeing her makes me resent college. She hates the phone, so our calls are rare and short, yet her not piling on about me coming home more often makes me double-down on guilt. I miss walking the castle's halls with her, especially the armory and other galleries. Stuff I previously thought boring, or not thought of at all, comes alive on those strolls.

"Hey, sweetie," I croon to the three-year-old tossing her head, warning me to stay away. "You're home now."

The softness in my voice clearly confuses the spooked animal. She gives an almost-human cock of her head, but decides she won't be tricked again. She runs as far as the paddock will let her, her hooves kicking up dirt, enveloping me in hot dust eagerly burrowing into my sweat and coating my nose.

The mare has clearly decided today's lesson is over, so I take off my hat and slap it against my thigh to knock off a bit of the grime. G straightens from her leaning posture against the fence, leaving her scuffed boot hitched on the lower rail and her arms crossed casually on the top. I slip through the slats and join her on her side of the enclosure.

"Buck up, girl. You did fine. Your goal today was to get within five feet of her. She's dancing on a fine line on whether we can ever get her back."

The young horse has seen and felt far too much in her short life and won't take her eyes off of us for an instant. "What do you do if we can't earn her trust?"

"It's not just people. She needs to tolerate her own kind, too, or she's going to have a long, lonely life in a separate pasture. I'll keep her protected, but I'm hoping to help her. It's a sad existence to be safe and utterly alone in a crowd."

I look at G and tilt my head in a way not far removed from the mare's. "Sounds like something out of a philosophy book."

She nails me with a look. "Read much philosophy in your vast education, have you?"

A blush hits me, but she's not being mean. She's being G. "No, but I took a class last year and heard a sermon or two."

She snorts. "Not sure how much philosophy you'll learn from a pulpit, but we'll let it lie for now. I'm proud of how good you're doing with the rescues. It's not easy on the body or a tender heart."

I lean my head the other way. "You think I'm tenderhearted? Gerome thinks I'm a bi—uh, a brat."

"Your brother may have shared a womb with you, but you might as well have been born on different planets." She holds up a stalling hand. "It's not that I don't love him. I do. He's handsome. Smart. Mostly good at taking extra-long showers and throwing a football.

Yippee. But I wanted more from him. I wanted all of you to have the MacInnes soul, not just the name."

The unspoken sentiment that I've met her expectations pushes up hot, happy tears.

G takes her foot from the rail, then pops me on the shoulder with her well-worn work gloves. "Before you go all cocky, we've got stalls to clean."

While I can state with certainty mucking a barn is my least favorite part of horse maintenance, as long as my afternoon includes Aunt G, I don't care.

An hour later, we're both dirty...or rather, I'm dirtier, and G looks barely mussed, a few strands of hay in her hair the only evidence she's worked harder than me. We move to the low-walled stall where Cotton is nudging her new brood with her nose, and G folds her almost-eighty-year-old self gracefully to the ground. My nineteen-year-old body doesn't seem nearly as supple. The collie eyes us warily as her pups abandon her for two new lap playgrounds.

Gavina smooths her hands over Cotton's face, and her tail thumps with returned affection. The girl on my lap decides my button is a treat, so I stop her fixated gnawing before she gets herself, and me, in trouble. She complies by deciding my knuckles are a better teething toy.

"You plan on telling me what's got you as moody as our friend in the paddock?" G switches out the duo battling for space in her lap for a new pair of black-and-white furballs.

"I'm not moody."

Her raised eyebrow would give Mr. Spock a run for his money. I've never been able to master it half as well, and believe me, I've tried. I toss a piece of straw for the pup to pounce on.

"I love UT. I love everything about Austin. It's all so new and big and busy. I love most of my classes. I'm making new friends."

"But..."

"But I miss Ephraim. My friends tell me to date around, and it makes me mad."

"Why? I seem to recall your young man doesn't seem too keen on y'all being exclusive."

"Exclusive, yes. Public, no."

For the first time in as long as I can remember, G's face turns angry.

At me.

"Listen here, Violet MacInnes. Do you want to end up like that mare? All alone and skittish to trust? You keep letting someone make you hide who you are, who you are to them, and you'll end up in your solitary paddock, hungry for a pack, but you've forgotten how to *be* you because you've been pretending for too long."

"But—"

"There's no buts. Hiding leads to pain. There's no other outcome."

I want to argue, but Brian Steele comes up to check on Cotton and the puppies, stopping short when he sees us on the ground.

"Beg pardon. I didn't mean to interrupt."

"Don't apologize, Brian. We're leaving." G empties her lap and rises with as much grace as when she sat down. She uses her toe to give a tiny nudge to the boy bravely attacking her boot. "You've done a beautiful job with Cotton and these new hooligans."

His tall, lanky frame straightens with pride. "Means a lot from you, Miss Gavina."

She pats his arm and heads out of the barn, leaving me to follow with my stinging pride. He gives me a shy smile, and I make myself smile back as I move past him to join G in the breezeway. Brian's a sweet guy. Kinda awkward, but cute.

G doesn't press for any more information or give any more advice as we go our separate ways, but I can't forget the shadow of pain in her eyes I know had nothing to do with me.

CHAPTER SEVEN

PAIGE – NOW

I MAKE the calls to my brothers, the kids, and Kase. I wish I could have talked with Kiki, but as I'd suspected, my call went to voicemail. My sister and I love each other, but our ten-year age difference and our wildly different lives mean we aren't especially close. I'm sure it's nostalgia from losing V, but I miss Kiki more fiercely than I ever have.

I press the button on my steering wheel one more time. "Call Zach."

"Calling Zach." The voice through the speakers is mechanical.

It takes a few rings before the call connects. "You're in the car early. Something up?"

We haven't spoken since last night...or what was me speaking and him not. When I left for downtown, his office door was shut. I made no attempt to slip out, but made no effort to engage, either. I soothed my conscience by reminding myself Zach moves into an otherworldly zone when he's coding. If he's working with one of his offshore techs, lightning could strike, and he wouldn't notice unless the internet quit.

Which left the silence in the house darker than the coffee in my mug.

"No…well, yes. V passed last night."

"I'm sorry. You knew it was coming."

I grind my molars and tell the devil on my left shoulder to zip it. In Zach's world, being forearmed with knowledge is comforting. Ergo, it's comforting to everyone. After all the decades together, I still have to remind myself he honestly believes he's helping.

The angel on my right shoulder tries to chime in with, *Good girl*, and I tell that side to shut it, too. Knowing Zach is well-intentioned doesn't mean his occasional inane comments don't drive me bonkers.

"I talked with her yesterday morning, but she was so weak we had to cut the video chat after a couple of minutes. Anyway, I'm almost there. My suitcases are packed, except for last-minute stuff. Just wanted to tell you."

"I'll check your tires and oil while you're changing."

"I appreciate it. See you in a few."

I make it home in far less than the hour-plus drive I usually endure and hurry to my office. I carved Aiden's bedroom into a space for me when he left home. White, lacy curtains, bookshelves stuffed within an inch of maximum mass, a chintz-covered chair of narcolepsy needing to be recovered. The pattern's dated and shows where I love to sit, one of V's quilts over my legs, a book from my teetering to-be-read pile on my lap.

Zach's office is on the other side of the double French doors added in the remodel, all dark wood and plaid themes. We never bother each other when we're working at home. The most I can explain about his job is he's the head of a group doing mission-critical work in global security and cyberwarfare. He calls himself a glorified code monkey, but I know his innate modesty is talking. Too many of his calls are from CEOs, CIOs, CTOs, and various other O's I can't define. A glorified code monkey doesn't fly off to distant parts of the globe on a moment's notice. And they don't bring home salaries allowing us to live a privileged lifestyle. It's not like we hobnob with the Dells, but we've given our kids great educations, and I'll be sad to leave the house. I could never afford it on my own, an equitable settlement notwithstanding. My salary isn't chicken feed, but let's leave it at I'm not the top breadwinner in this marriage.

The point being, I'm proud of him. I've always been proud of him. In some ways, his weeks of traveling likely made our marriage subsist for as long as it has. It's hard to fight when time spent together is precious. Or was.

I snag the noise-canceling headphones next to my speakers and notice the blue folder. My morning was so frenetic, I actually strung together several hours where I didn't dwell on it. On us.

I open the file, look at his signature, and pull off the sticky note reading, *I don't want this, but if you believe this is what you have to do, I've done as you asked.*

Thank you, Captain Passive-Aggressive.

Closing the folio, I move it to the holder on the side of my printer. It can wait until I return. What will a few weeks matter? It's not like anything will change while I'm gone.

I shut down everything electronic and make sure my magnolia-scented candle is cold. I can't help but give a last, sweeping look at the peach-painted walls with dark green accents, stopping to check that my "If Mama Says No, Ask Nana" cup is where it always stays, in my line of sight above the keyboard.

I focus on the left side of my shelf. The picture of me, delighted Mama and Nana, arm in arm with Ainsley, still my Mini-Me. She's prettier and has lighter hair, but she's unable to deny her maternal chromosomes. Perched on his daddy's knee, Callum proudly displays his trick-or-treating costume. Bella is asleep in her pram.

To the right is my favorite shot of Aiden and Chen from their wedding reception. Both so incredibly handsome in their tuxedos, beaming at each other with a love the photographer captured in an instant of perfection. In the next frame, Aiden holds Marceau after the adoption ceremony. Chen drapes one arm around Aiden's shoulders, and the other hand cups the baby's head.

All of which makes me swell with pride and so much love.

While the rest of my life is about to go sideways, these things won't.

I shut the door, force myself to straighten, and head for my bedroom to grab my suitcases. *God Blessed Texas* floats from my cell, and knowing who's calling eases the aching, empty space inside me.

"Hi, Aunt Fina. How're you?"

Of course, since she's Mina's twin, she also isn't my aunt by blood. Regardless, Fina and Mina might as well be leaves on my family tree. They'd gone from girls V had babysat to women who were her staunchest companions. The difference in their ages hadn't mattered any more than a lack of DNA.

"Girl, you're not driving and talking to me, are you?"

I can imagine Fina putting her fists on her bony hips, standing like an indignant ostrich.

"No, ma'am, I'm still at the house. I need to do a couple more things, then I'll be on the road."

"Well, you don't rush. The castle's quiet as a church on Monday."

"No bookings?"

"Only a family reunion, but the last few stragglers left yesterday. We've been keeping the calendar pretty sparse these last few months, but when V found out, she nearly did a culling, I tell you. We're sold wall-to-wall for the games, though, don't you worry. Anyway, no sense in hurrying."

"I won't."

"One more thing. Would you mind stopping by the airport and picking up the architect coming over from Ardgour? Violet arranged it all months ago, and we plumb forgot about it. His flight arrives at seven."

I'm stunned into silence. Mina and Fina are the epitome of provincial, but you don't "stop by" DFW International Airport. It's a small city in and of itself. And I'll be exhausted by then.

I don't need to know why an architect is coming over from Scotland. Over the decades, there've been numerous articles written on the castle, mostly photographic pieces, so the visit isn't unusual. The timing, however, leaves a lot to be desired.

"Paige?"

"Sorry, Fina. You caught me by surprise."

"I know it's a bother, but we told Leith he could use an estate truck while he's here, so there's no sense incurring the expense of renting a car."

"And it's our duty to save Mr. Architect From Ardgour rental charges why?"

"His name's Leith MacMaster, and he's your cousin Ian's best friend, so Leith is almost family."

"Of course, then. 'Almost family' makes all the difference." I tuck my tongue firmly in my cheek.

"Don't you be cute with me, young lady."

"Wouldn't dream of it."

Running an honest-to-goodness castle in East Texas requires a mind-boggling amount of manpower, and it's not unusual to toss a request to bring something from town onto a visitor's to-do list. No sense sending someone off-property if there's a body on the way. Grabbing a sack of feed while you're in town, however, isn't quite the same as picking up an international passenger at DFW.

"Of course, I'll do it. Text me the details. I'll be on the road soon and in Dallas in time to scout out where I need to be."

"You're a dear. Oh, and one more thing. Would you mind stopping by the hardware store to pick up pellets? They forgot on the last delivery, and I said we'd fetch them."

"I'd be happy to, but won't they be closed?"

"Noah said he's working late tonight. Inventory, I'm pretty sure."

"Okeydokey. Call me if you think of anything else."

"One more thing before I forget. You might pick up some milk while you're there. I used the last from the family kitchen for a smoothie for Violet."

I hear the catch in her voice and swallow against an identical one in mine. "Oh, sweetie, I'm so sorry. You've done so much, and I love you for it."

"I wish I could have done more." She sniffs back tears, and I can see her batting away my praise even without a video connection. "Enough of that. I just want to be sure you have what you need."

I immediately picture the smaller kitchen on the second floor playing host to many a midnight pantry raid. The second floor of the castle is divided into private quarters for the family and renovated rooms for guests. The big kitchen downstairs might have more room, but the family kitchen holds more memories.

"I'll take care of it, but I should get going." Before she one-more-things me again.

I followed the ping-pong of Fina's instructions after decades of practice and understand, as no city person could, the logic of being able to buy milk at a hardware store.

"All right. I love you fierce, girl."

"Love you more. I'll be there soon."

I planned on wearing my least-flattering, but most comfortable, yoga pants, topped by my favorite extra-long burnt-orange T-shirt, but I have to quickly rethink. My main concern isn't impressing Leith MacMaster from Ardgour, but that my comfort level of ratty when it's just me in a dark car doesn't extend to public consumption. I decide on comfy jeans and a tunic I bought at a Pecan Street Festival a few years back. The peacock colors in cotton knit might give the impression I have a sense of fashion, and in a last-ditch effort, I put on lightweight chandelier earrings to complete my Mediterranean theme.

With the clock now ticking more urgently than I'd hoped, I double-check my laptop is safely tucked into the padded compartment of my briefcase and begin hauling suitcases toward the garage.

The house is quiet. Silent. As if I'm already gone.

Zach is in his happy place. The garage is his sanctum sanctorum, like my study is mine, and I'm aware he isn't ignoring me. It's more that if he's busy, I can't try to talk to him. But as last night has proven, there isn't anything to talk about. I can't make him want me, and I can't make him want to heal our marriage. He's safely in the farthest recesses of his empty box.

I envy him his gold-medal-worthy ability to compartmentalize.

I immediately quash the guilt taking the express elevator up my throat. Zach isn't a bad man. Even his midlife crisis five years ago was kind, in the sense he didn't cheat on me. He just...went away while his body stayed firmly in his job and in the house we built.

He's still kind. Will turn himself inside out to help the kids. Loves the grandkids. In fact, he deserves a Grandpa of the Year Award.

But he doesn't need me. I'm no longer a lover, a companion. We aren't best friends anymore. We're barely roommates. I'm the ping to his divorce-is-not-an-option pong.

As if on cue, the hood of the car slams shut. I grab the travel mug Zach has left for me on the counter. Time to go.

He's wiping his hands on a shop towel when I step into his palace. A fan blasts air across the concrete. It mitigates the promise of a miserably hot afternoon coming through the open door of an impeccably clean and organized three-bay garage.

"You're good to go." He turns away to put the oil jug on its designated shelf. "Needed a top off, is all. I added a few pounds of air in one tire."

He opens the driver's door for me before heading into the house. He effortlessly hauls the suitcases to the trunk. I got red-faced manhandling them to the laundry room. He waits until I toss my purse onto the passenger side and slip into the seat before he hands me my computer bag. The engine's running, and the air conditioner's diligently pouring icy bliss from the vents.

I look at Zach after I put my cup in the holder. Still tall. Broad shoulders fill out his faded Cowboys T-shirt with the bleach stain on the sleeve. Still handsome. The perfect sprinkle of gray at the temples of an otherwise full head of dark, wavy hair always sexy-as-hell mussed because he's forever driving his fingers through it when he's coding. Still barely a thickening at his waist.

Damn him.

I force myself to concentrate on pulling and buckling the seat belt across a waist unable to make the same claim.

"How long do you think it'll take?" He pushes my door shut slowly until it latches, then bends so he's level with the open window.

You've told him five times, the devil on my left shoulder snarks, but my mouth says, "I don't know. My leave of absence is approved until September, but I'm not making any assumptions. Aunt V ran the castle like a well-oiled machine for so long, I'm worried. I know there's more than her asking me personally to take care of the contents of her apartment and keep the castle going until we get someone trained to take over, but I couldn't make her fess up. I guess I'll find out now."

I shut my eyes and take a breath. He doesn't need an in-depth explanation of my oddball family. "Sorry. But to the point, Ainsley wants me to help with Fourth of July here, so I'll probably come home after the games for a week or so. Her in-laws are coming, and she's panicking."

Zach's mouth purses. "You'd think after five years of marriage she'd stop letting them upset her."

Something gurgles in me. Not quite a boil, but definitely bubbling. "You'd think after five years of marriage, Richard would stand up for his wife."

The mouth-purse tightens, then, as expected, Zach retreats to the Land of Nothing's Wrong.

"I'll be there Friday. Early evening. I assume the viewing's Saturday?"

The petty, juvenile part of me wants to tell him not to bother. Luckily, the adult speaks first. "Yes, at seven."

"Text me when you stop for gas." He tap-taps the roof.

"Will do." I put the SUV into reverse but keep my foot on the brake.

Leaning in, he gives my cheek a light kiss. "Love you. Drive safely."

"Will do." I shut the window when his hands are clear and roll out smoothly. I'm long out of the neighborhood, almost at the light for I-35, before I realize I didn't look in the rearview mirror.

Did he wave?

Guilt barely has time to tune up an opening chorus when the Bluetooth chirps. I glance at the display on the dash, see Ainsley's picture, and dig deep for a hidden nugget of patience. I love my beautiful, vivacious, funny daughter. Deeply, but...

I hit the answer button. "Hi, Ains. What's up?"

"I was checking—"

"Hi, Nana. I got dink eye." At four, Callum doesn't trust the car's microphone, as evidenced by his volume.

"Pink eye." Ainsley's interjected correction is hardly necessary. I nursed both her and her brother through many bouts.

"Hi, baby." I can't be irritated at the bundle of energy with precisely two modes—light speed and dead stop. He's forty pounds and forty inches of pure mischief and love, and he's my delight.

"Are you on—"

"I love you, Nana. We're getting ice cream. Bella can't have any."

This is true. One usually doesn't give ice cream to a one-year-old.

"Love you more, sweetie."

"—your way?"

We've long since quit repeating the first parts of interrupted lines.

"About to hit 35."

"I wish Daddy'd go with you."

I swallow a wave of irritation. Does no one in my family believe me remotely competent on my own?

"This isn't the first time I've gone to Magnolia Bloom by myself, you know. I haven't needed to call Triple A or anything."

"Ha-ha. It's a long drive."

"Seven hours forward and two centuries back."

"True that. Call me when you stop."

"I will, but not every stop. Between you and Daddy, it'd take a week to get there."

"I wish I could come help you. I loved Aunt V."

"She would understand, although she never had in-laws."

"Gah, don't remind me. I'm already slamming Xanax like aspirin."

"Ainsley—"

"I'm kidding, Mom. You know the strongest thing I take is ibuprofen."

I do know, but it doesn't hurt to be reassured drug addiction is off the worry list. "Sweetie, I need to run. Austin traffic and all."

"All righty, then. I love you."

"Love you more."

"Come see me, Nana."

I hope he learns soon that every line doesn't have to be bellowed.

"I'll come soon, baby." I wonder if Ainsley has any idea how lucky she is Bella seems to lose her hearing when she's asleep.

I don't doubt for a second I'm blessed. One son, one daughter, two sons-in-law, three grand-loves. One who still coos, blows bubbles, and gums his perfect knuckles, or his toes when he can manage, instead of screaming at the top of his lungs.

Give him time…

I accelerate to merge onto the highway and try not to focus on the one major player missing from my love lineup.

In the silence, I have no distractions from the sense my tires have become giant spinning wheels, weaving gossamer threads of dread threatening to strangle me. Until now, I've been able to stuff my fears of what waits for me in Magnolia Bloom into the corners of my mind. Certainly not at Zach-level, but enough that I convinced myself I was merely flattered by V's trust in me. Now, I can no longer ignore the building terror threatening to turn my spleen inside out in anticipation of how the castle will react when I arrive.

Though not filed, the petition has been signed.

I've broken the magic.

CHAPTER EIGHT

MINA – NOW

THE AMBULANCE HAS TAKEN V's body away, the amazing hospice volunteers have cleared out their equipment, the linens are fresh, and the windows and French doors are open to clear out the scent of disinfectant. The afternoon sun is blazing hot over the lake, and it doesn't seem right the sky is brilliant blue and cloudless.

I run a hand over the corner of the quilt, smoothing a nonexistent wrinkle, and set off to find Fina. Despite the size of Castle MacInnes, the number of her hiding spots is limited. I know where my twin goes. I've always known.

I know she's not on the rear balcony, because I opened the doors to add more air flow to V's room. She could be in the turret, one floor up from V's office. My sister and V both made their spaces as unique as the women themselves. The bottom floor off the main ballroom is decorated for the guests because there's something about a turret that intrigues everyone.

If Fina needs fresh air and sky today, she'll be on the rampart around the North Turret. The third-story view comprises a front lawn needing more attention than our budget allows. If she strolls to the back, she can see over the front roof and down into the circular driveway guaranteed to enchant every guest who comes to Castle MacInnes. The drive under the raised portcullis is something out of a movie. Tooling around the fountain with the massive stone dragon lying under a geyser of water seals the deal.

Evajean MacInnes was a genius when she designed the castle and grounds. In the last hundred and fifty-plus years, things have certainly changed, but the enchantment of arrival at Castle MacInnes has not.

I know Fina heard the door open, but she remains stock-still, her arms wrapped around her slender waist. She has a light sweater in her hand, despite the fact it's already hot as blue blazes most days. Up here, though, the ever-present breeze can be cool during the day and downright chilly at night. My mind casts back to when we learned about the Society for Creative Anachronism and decided being connected to an honest-to-God castle had to be fate. We practically lived and breathed the SCA for a long time.

"Do you remember when we hosted the midsummer ball in '77?" I hope my question will hit her funny bone.

"We hosted a lot of events back in the day." Her tone indicates I've succeeded.

Fina was as fine a horsewoman as Violet and loved everything about the reenactors who shared her love of all things medieval. I was never fond of the giant beasts and made a place for myself in the sewing and dancing guilds. We spent many years attending events around the country, but there was no doubt the castle was a draw for those who loved to pretend to be in a romanticized version of the past.

"I wouldn't mind more SCA events." I drop my test of the waters casually.

"I would." Her reply is decisive, instantaneous.

My twin still blames herself for bringing Roylee into my life, although I've never put the responsibility on her. At the time, we were sixteen. It's not like she could have, or should have, vetted every man who attended the same events we did. We were teenagers having a great time. Being born fourteen minutes ahead of me didn't make her liable for my choices.

"You enjoyed yourself." I cast out another line.

"I got too caught up, too focused on myself."

She refuses to see it my way. Of course, it took a lot of years to deal with what Roylee did. In the end, I had my son as a gift out of a nightmare, and Trey often seems as much Fina's as mine. Still, she gave up something she truly loved. Someone she truly loved. No amount of finagling on my part in the intervening decades has returned her to the enchanted world she enjoyed.

"It was a special time." I plant my palms on the parapet and lean out to glance around. "You loved riding so much. If you hadn't been making out with that knight from the Steppes, his horse wouldn't have gotten loose and sent all the other knights tearing across the lawn after the equine escapee. It was practically out of a Monty Python movie."

She refuses to take the bait, instead turning away from her memories and the view to lean against the half wall.

"I'm having second thoughts. Should we set her up in the cottage?"

I hide a sigh and don't pretend to not know she's talking about Paige. "Here. If she stays in the cottage, she'll avoid the castle altogether. If she has to be here every day, maybe it'll help."

A long silence speaks of the difference between us, and I'm reminded I have only a birth certificate to prove we're twins. It's not her being all sinew and contemplation and me all fluff and impetuosity. It's more Fina takes every action as an indictment of her character. While it can take time, once I process something, I can usually let it go —file erased. Not my twin. She's a damn gigabyte of stubborn.

She lets her shoulders drop a twentieth of an inch. "Good idea. We don't have the luxury of time. If she bolts right back to Austin…"

"We have our marching orders, but this is so unfair. She's got her own problems without piling on saving the castle, too."

"Violet believes…believed in her. The magic is waiting for her to come home. To solve the mystery."

We certainly haven't been able to find Gavina's paintings in fifty years. Another case of a stubborn MacInnes waiting too long to take care of things. At least Violet left diaries waiting for Paige. Gavina didn't leave a note scribbled on the back of an envelope.

"Regardless, it's a lot to ask." The stone cuts into my palms, and the pain reminds me to relax my hands. I wish I had an equally handy reminder to ease the stranglehold of stress in the rest of my world.

"I agree, but we have to try. Keep her busy. Make her stay."

"Our Paige and Zachary aren't like the couple from Arkansas. We can't accidentally trap them in their room for a weekend and make things better."

I don't add, *Like you "accidentally" trapped me in the West Turret until you talked sense into me about Roylee. I was at my breaking point anyway, but still...*

A twitch plays at the corner of Fina's mouth. "Well, a little outside influence won't hurt."

"We don't interfere." I sniff in feigned insult.

"Strategic guidance, then."

To my surprise, I find I don't want to banter anymore. When I came searching for her, I thought I was doing well. Or, as well as could be expected for being heartsick and worried, all twisted together in a giant ball and taking residence below my ribs.

Turns out, the ball's a steamroller and runs me flat. I'm not near as good at putting the deep parts of me into neat boxes as my much older sister.

"I'm headed to the grocery store." I didn't plan a trip to town, but once the words are out of my mouth, I'm itching to go.

Fina's brow lifts. "Again? Didn't you go yesterday?"

"Day before, but I forgot half my list. I've been distracted."

The wind ripples around us, but not a hair moves in the sleek twist she manages without seeming effort. Just like her simple slacks and tunics, she always looks chic and put together. By comparison, I'm more like a stray barn cat and am forever trying to keep my hair out of my face with combs and barrettes. There's also a lot more gray in my brown than in her regal black, and we're not sixty until December.

I'm suddenly anxious to stop contemplating the ways we're different. Or how much I owe her. Or how much I love her even if she drives me to prayer.

She stops me as I head out. "Before you go, did Trey finish up those numbers?"

"He said he'd drop them by today or tomorrow."

My son, her nephew, is the attorney for the estate, and he's been working with us and the accountant on some money-saving suggestions. V was nothing short of a miracle worker for as long as we can remember, but she wasn't immune to insane tax hikes, soaring maintenance costs, and suffocating labor expenses.

But it'll take more than a few budget cuts to save Castle MacInnes, and we all know it.

CHAPTER NINE

PAIGE – NOW

THE SUMMER SUN is a blinding orange ball on the horizon when I hit the outskirts of the DFW metroplex, but I make no apologies for the calories in my third mocha latte. I used the coffee shop's Wi-Fi to search where I needed to pick up our international guest. I had his flight number, so it didn't take a genius to sleuth out which baggage carousel would be my most likely target. That left walking seven hundred miles through the complex even with the light rail, and finding a place to sit – which airports don't make easy these days.

This isn't a drive-up, get-in kind of gig, but in Fina's mind, it's a quick stop to meet Mr. Leith MacMaster, architect from Ardgour and best friend of Cousin Ian, who I'm delighted to know is coming to the games. I'm aware of the centuries-long connection between the MacInneses and the MacMasters as part of our lore. All the ins and outs? Not so much.

I texted Leith, telling him to meet me at the baggage carousel for his flight. I assume he has luggage, but even if he doesn't, it's easier to leave the instructions as simple as possible. So now I wait, reading a book on my phone, but I've rested a sheet of paper against my chest with MacMaster in black letters so he won't miss me.

I'm lost in Regency England when a shadow falls over me, and a masculine throat clears. "Ms. MacInnes? Forgive my intrusion."

The roll of my name makes my insides go liquid before I look up and stand. His accent isn't hard, not as harsh a brogue as Ian's, but enough to let me know he's a for-real-from-Scotland Scotsman.

And good God, he's gorgeous.

I'm not sure what I was expecting. Actually, I didn't expect anything, but I certainly didn't imagine six-foot-something of well-toned muscle and a head full of sexy, disheveled hair so honey blond I'm surprised he doesn't have a swarm of bees following him. And blue eyes so sharp they should be registered weapons.

"I'm sorry. Am I mistaken? Your sign says MacMaster."

I blush so hard it's a wonder I don't set the sheet of paper he's pointing to ablaze.

"It's me. I was startled. I'm Paige, and I'm here to transport you to the wilds of East Texas. Do you have more luggage?" He has a rather impressive backpack slung over his shoulder, but I don't want to assume.

"Nae, I travel light."

"Well, then, only a hundred miles to the parking garage and a thousand to the castle. We'll be there in no time."

A smile cracks a mouth with a full lower lip and a cupid's bow on the top that should be too feminine on a man. But it is oh so not...

What in the hell is wrong with me? For the love of Pete, did I roofie my own coffee?

"I know you can put eight Scotlands inside Texas, but you're bammin' me up."

"If you mean pulling your leg, yeah, I am." I manage to return to my regularly scheduled personality. "Truthfully, we do have a fair hike, and I bet you're tired."

"I'm a bit tuckered, but I'm good to go."

"Let's, then."

By the time we hit my SUV, we've established he's originally from Glenfinnan but has stayed the longest in Ardgour. He loves to travel and comes from a family of seven sisters, all dead set on finding him a wife. He cites their meddling as the prime reason he's out of the country most of the time.

I've managed not to interject a single word about my marital status. It wasn't intentional, not at first. I don't want my sadness, anger, and loss to intrude on a light getting-to-know-you conversation. Leith is a complete stranger. Him being a gorgeous stranger is beside the point. I'm not ready to discuss Zach with anyone right now besides Kase, and possibly Grady.

I pay to exit the parking lot, and we're on our way. As I roll the window up, Leith resumes where he left off.

"Now I know you're—what's the expression I looked up?— blowing smoke telling me you're a grandmother of three."

I laugh at the tone of his voice and imagine, in the dark interior of the car, he's arching one of those eyebrows at me.

"Hand to God. Callum's four, Bella's one, and Marceau's six months."

"I'm impressed. The best way to sell a con is in the details."

"Stop. You're sweet, but I assure you they're all mine, and I adore them. So, no girlfriend, eh?"

"Och, aye, no, though not for my sisters' lack of trying."

I shoot him a glance before returning my eyes to the road. "Isn't it a bit on the nose for a tall, handsome man with a wicked accent to be allergic to romantic attachment?"

"I'm willing. It hasnae happened yet."

"Be careful. Texas girls aren't shy. I know lots of hiding places in the castle, though, if you need any."

"I'll keep it top o' my mind."

We chat a bit more, and I tell him about the additional stop in town we'll have to make, but I can hear fatigue in his voice.

"Why don't you recline the seat and grab a nap? We've got a good forty-five more minutes."

"I wouldnae want to be rude."

"Seriously. Grab a catnap, and I'll wake you when we're close."

"Aye, then. I'm looking forward to meeting Violet, and I dinnae want to fall asleep shaking her hand."

A mew escapes despite my attempt to contain it. Clearly, the darkness isn't enough to hide my distress.

"Did I say something wrong?"

"I hate having to tell you, but Aunt V passed away this morning."

"Och, no. I'm so sorry. She was lovely to me each time we spoke."

"She was, indeed. I was racing to the castle from my home in Austin when I was tasked with picking you up."

"Then I've inconvenienced you. Another thing to be sorry for."

"Don't be. I'm happy to do it. I just wish we were meeting under other circumstances."

"You have no idea how much I do as well."

His long legs shift, and I can see the muscle in his left arm flex as he rolls his shoulders. In the muted light from the dash, it's an impressive distraction from the new wave of sadness threatening to roll over me.

I tap his armrest. "Honestly, shut your eyes for a mile or two. The control for the seat is on your right."

With the annoyingly sexist male thing of intuiting all matters mechanical, he's stretched out and instantly asleep.

Which leaves me alone with the night, the road noise, and guilt slicing through me. I should have made time to see her more often. Aunt V asked so little of me. Loved every greeting card. Called me as much as I called her. When I was growing up, she was the coolest, most modern woman I knew from a place remaining essentially stuck in a Southern time warp. Wicked smart, one of the best managers the castle's ever had, yet kind and funny and generous.

But I have no absolution. I hate admitting to myself, in the silence and the dark, how it hurt to see the worry in her eyes as my marriage failed. I was a coward, visiting less and less often as Zach and I grew further and further apart.

I shake the gloom away, or try to, and concentrate on the final leg of the trip into Magnolia Bloom. Oncoming headlights have gotten fewer and fewer, telling me as much as anything I'm close. When I'm fantasizing about falling asleep as easily as Leith, I see the welcome sign and turn left to head into what is euphemistically called downtown. A right leads onto Magnolia Drive and the final two miles to the castle grounds.

Magnolia Bloom has grown. Potholes have been filled in and some lanes repaved. There are new streetlamps, ironically done to look turn of the century. Giant urns have been set on the street corners, each already boasting mini American flags and red, white, and blue bunting I'd bet they put up for Memorial Day. The Fourth is just shy of a month away, the week after the games, so the merchant association's getting its bang for its decorating buck.

The angle parking for the venues surrounding the town square have wide enough stripes to accommodate pickup trucks and more than a few early-model land yachts. Most storefronts have wooden doors with leaded glass boasting fireworks and watermelon stickers on the panes. Only Palmer's Drugs has visible security bars.

I make it to the hardware store five minutes after nine and still have to circle the square twice to find a parking space. Clearly, the Chamber of Commerce is working on the Shop Magnolia Bloom campaign.

I turn off the engine and give Leith's arm a shake. "Wake up, sleepyhead. Last stop before you see a real bed."

He rubs his face, and I hear the sexy rasp of his palms against beard stubble. Then he runs his fingers through his blond waves, and an inappropriate, melty sensation blooms in my solar plexus.

I practically leap from the Highlander, and it hits me how ironic my car choice is. When I hurry through the double glass doors, I step into the past.

The smell of wood and feed and chemicals all rush at me on a blast of air conditioning intended to keep shoppers inside for the extra minutes that might invite impulse purchases. The floors are still the unpainted concrete I remember from childhood, the shelving mostly metal. The endcaps I can see range from American flags to stacked bags of deer corn, wood pellets to salt tablets.

"Can I help you, ma'am?"

A deep voice captures my attention, and I turn to the counter.

"I'm Paige—"

"MacInnes," the man finishes.

My pleasure is as warm as the thermometer outside. "Noah, it's good to see you. I'm glad I got here in time."

"Paige, it's good to see you, too. I'm sure sorry for your loss. We all loved her so much."

I refuse to let the hot tears springing to my eyes fall. "I appreciate that. It's going to be tough on us all for a while."

"If you need something, if there's anything I can do, you call me."

"Thank you. I will."

"Now, I told Miss Fina I'd bring the pellets after I got off, but she insisted I wait for you so I didn't waste a trip. I couldn't risk the rough side of her tongue by disobeying."

We exchange eye rolls. "I appreciate the dilemma."

Noah extends his hand across the counter, and I take it without hesitation. His brown eyes are as bright as I remember, except for the liberal addition of crow's feet from hours of fishing. Salt is winning the battle over pepper in his military-short hair, which is starting to give in to male-pattern baldness, but that doesn't damage the overall still-got-it picture.

Leith moves up beside me, and Noah gives me the *Who's he?* look.

"Noah, meet Leith MacMaster. He's an architect here to look at the castle and is a friend of the family from across the pond. Leith, Noah Dalton is a longtime family friend."

"Pleasure." Leith offers his hand.

"All mine. Now, let's load this order so y'all can get to where you're gettin'." Noah rounds the counter and joins us, directing his next question to me. "Are your Momma and Daddy gonna be able to make it? They're in Europe, right?"

"Germany, yes, and I hope they will. I haven't talked to them yet."

Gotta love small-town gossip. Moves faster than heat lightning.

My attention is pulled to the industrial refrigerator full of milk, eggs, cheese, and assorted groceries by the front door. I put up the one-second finger and grab a gallon, giving Noah a smile. "Put this on the bill, would you?"

"Of course."

Noah pauses and cuts me a grin. "I'm sure you've been told more'n once you're the spitting image of your aunt Violet. Only younger and prettier."

"I'm sure she would appreciate the sentiment."

I hide a laugh at his transparent flirtation, oddly and intensely aware of Leith on my other side. I shove down the voice scolding me I shouldn't find it so flattering. Noah stops by the pile of bagged pellets on the sidewalk.

"Is this what we've come for?" Before we can stop him, Leith bends —at the knees, not that I'm noticing—and grabs the top four.

Noah gives a wistful sigh. "Ah, to be young and fit again."

I have too many conflicting responses in my head, so I wrangle the milk to let me grab one bag, Noah another, and we follow the tall Scot. We've barely deposited our two when Leith returns with the final three.

Noah waves goodbye as we head off on the *final* final leg of the journey, the darkness becoming complete as we leave town. The Highlander in the Highlander seems awake now, and an urgency to fill the silence nearly overwhelms me.

"Noah is one of the men from V's church who took turns checking on her. The congregation is small but tightly knit, and their concern isn't for show."

"It's the charm of a small town. I know more villagers than city folk back home, so I understand."

As we round the last bend, I point to our right. "I wish there was a brighter moon, but if you squint, you can make out the turrets past those trees."

"I can't tell in the dark, but I'm guessing East Texas hardwood. Oak, pecan, hickory, black tupelo...and, of course, magnolias."

I cut him a glance but can't quite discern his expression. "I thought you were an architect, not an arborist."

"I might surprise you with what all I am."

The teasing in his voice about makes me throw us through the windshield as I hit the brakes in front of the warehouse. I pretend nothing is wrong and give the horn two quick taps. I step out and am immediately greeted by a happy woof, squatting so I can greet the border collie I adore.

"Missy, how are you, girl?" I scratch behind her black-and-white ears and run my hands through her ruff. She gives my wrist a lick but is too much the princess to be so gauche as to jump or try for my chin. She jerks to attention when Leith rounds the front of the SUV, and I can almost hear her trying to decide if he's friend or foe.

He stops and, to my distinct pleasure, speaks softly. "Hallo, beauty." He squats, too, and extends his hand, palm down. She takes her time, but eventually her tail wags, and she grants him the privilege of rubbing her silky head.

In the deep shadows caused by the headlights and the vapor lamps, I see Zach for a second, on one knee, petting Missy and being…Zach. Gentle and kind, ready to spout something funny or, more likely, a groan-worthy pun. Solid and dependable. All the things I love about him. Miss about him.

That's imprecise. He's still gentle and kind, and his jokes are still horrible, but the…space we shared is missing now. The connection having nothing to do with proximity.

Then the man stands, and Leith returns. And Zach is…gone.

The steel door to the warehouse opens on quiet hinges, and while neither Leith nor I can see anything except that the man exiting is tall and lanky, I'd know him anywhere.

"Miss Paige, good to have you home." He takes off his cap, the quintessential gesture of Southern politeness. "I'm awful sorry for the reason why."

"Thank you, Brian."

He opens his arms, and I don't hesitate to step into his hug. *Demon-*

strative isn't a word ever used to describe this particular man, but shared love and loss draws us together.

I've known him my whole life. And in all my years, he's never once called me or any MacInnes female anything but Miss or Mrs. I also know he's been in love with V since 1975. Somehow, he reconciled being caught in her orbit, and he's one of the few people V refused to talk about. Brian doesn't talk much in general, and he's a veritable vault when it comes to anything personal. But I saw looks pass between them, making me wonder.

I step away and nod toward Leith, who's been waiting in respectful silence. "We have the pellets from town, and this is Leith MacMaster, who I'm sure you've been told will be on-property for a month or so."

The two men shake hands, but I sense Brian is withholding judgment on our visitor until he has more data. He won't say anything, but he's always been careful about anyone new to the estate, considering himself an adjunct security guard on top of all his other duties at Castle MacInnes.

"Pop your trunk."

No need to clarify *SUV* versus *truck* versus *trunk*. It's like *pop* versus *soda*. Not worth debating.

I raise the hatch, and Brian throws a bag of pellets over each shoulder like he's forty rather than seventy. If the man has six percent body fat, it would be a stretch, but I'd give tall, lanky Brian odds over a bench-press cowboy any day.

He and Leith have the work done before I can offer to help, which is mere formality because it doesn't matter we're in the 2020s. Unlike Noah, who is a Southern gentleman through-and-through but of my generation, Brian Steele would have squint-eyed me if I picked up even one of the bags. He believes I'm fully capable, but as long as he's able, it's not an option.

My tired brain pokes at me again. Zach has a lot in common with Brian. I've never carried a SCUBA tank in my life, as Zach would be affronted if I didn't let him be my personal dive concierge. And it was pretty wonderful. One more thing to have to mourn and let go.

I look at Brian to corral my thoughts and wonder if V loved his old-style manners, or if they frustrated her.

Sadness pings through me that I'll never have a chance to ask.

When he finishes and returns to shut the hatch, Brian turns his clear, brown eyes on me. "You gonna take Miss V's place like she wanted?"

His blunt question stuns me. Not only am I not expecting it in general, but he's asked me in front of a stranger. Added on is I had no idea he's so familiar with V's wishes.

My pause makes him frown. "She waited on you too long. Don't make it worse by letting her down."

I'm not given a chance to respond. He tips his cap and is inside the warehouse, Missy following obediently, before I can form a retort ranging from *what I do is none of your business* to apologizing for failing V.

Leith, to his credit, doesn't ask about the strange interaction he's witnessed. Instead, he keeps his peace as I deliberately take the long way around to the front of the castle so he can appreciate the full view. I idle the engine and let him take in the beauty of Castle MacInnes.

"It's stunning. It reminds me of—"

"Inveraray Castle. Evajean's father is related somewhere in the family tree to the Argyll clan and parlayed their kinship to get her out of America during the Civil War. The design is part homage, especially the initial front view, but Castle MacInnes diverges radically, not the least of which being the portcullis we're about to drive under. You'll see shortly the interior is completely unique to Evajean's dream."

Each window on the third floor has a low-wattage lamp on the sill, giving a glow to the scene like it's a Thomas Kinkade painting. The breeze flaps the enormous Texas flag on its pole off to the left, and Leith points.

"That's not something you'd see on Loch Fyne."

"Not likely. We're proud of our heritage, but we're fiercely Texan."

"As is proper. Ian warned me about everything being bigger in Texas."

"A reputation not always deserved. I'm sure half the things you believe about the Lone Star State are wrong."

"Och, I'm for certain there's a fair bit about Scotland I'll have to correct as well."

"No doubt. We ought to add a game of Texas versus Scottish slang and see who can translate the most correctly."

"Sounds brilliant, but for tonight, I'm a wee bit puggled, much as a braw Scotsman's not supposed to admit."

My face heats with the dreaded blush I've never learned to tame. "I'm so sorry, Leith. I'm blathering."

"Haud your wheesht, woman." His brogue is obviously exaggerated and his tone teasing.

I bust out a laugh containing a hefty dose of gratitude for his kindness. "Did you tell me to shut up?"

"In the nicest of ways, of course."

"Of course." It looks like we're both about to fall into a fit of giggles, so I put the Highlander into gear and bathe in pride when I drive under the stone archway and raised metal gate. It earns an impressed whistle from Leith.

I take my time angling around the fountain I've loved since I first set eyes on it. "Her name is Penny."

"Pardon?"

"The dragon. She's Penny the Dragon." I pause expectantly. "Pendragon?"

He moans. "Och, no, that's terrible."

I laugh much harder than the moment warrants, but I'll blame it on being exhausted and pull around to the enormous front stairway. Fina texted me to leave my vehicle there for tonight, as there are no guests on-property. I'm happy to obey.

He's still shaking his head when he gets out and pulls his satchel from the rear seat to join me at the hatch. He grabs my two largest bags, each loaded to the hilt, like they're filled with pillows. I manage the smallest one and my computer bag and am ashamed my side aches when we make it to the top of the grand staircase.

Fina is exiting the front doors as I pause to catch my breath, and pulls me into a hard, bony hug. "There you two are. I was about to call the sheriff."

The joke is labored, and Leith frowns.

"She's bammin' you."

He raises one brow. "I'll make a Scot hen of you yet."

"It'll take more than a few slang words, so don't be hasty."

He puts out his hand to Fina as I make the obvious introductions.

"Ms. Fina, it's pure barry to meet you. And let me extend my condolences."

"It's delightful to meet you. I wish you could have met Violet. She would have loved to greet you herself, but it appears the good Lord had other plans." She takes my small bag and leads the way in. "Let's get you two to your beds, and we'll all visit in the morning."

It takes more than a quick minute to get the milk to the kitchen, escort Leith to his room, and finally walk me to V's suite. They're basically at opposite ends of the huge second floor, and I shoo Fina away after we roll my luggage inside. She needs to stop playing hostess.

If nothing, there are a lot of places to lay your head around here. The castle, the three manor houses, the duplexes and quads built over the many decades. The line of succession in terms of housing in the MacInnes family is as complicated as any royalty. And loyalty to the family business is equally entangled. But hospitality is given to all, and her duty to Leith done, Fina needs some rest.

I close the door behind me and step around my luggage. Fina or Mina left a lamp on for me on the side table, but the room is mostly in shadows. Still, I could probably find my way around the place with my eyes closed since I spent so much time here. The problem isn't the darkness, or the stillness, or the quiet.

It's that it's empty.

Brian's words ring in my memory, reminding me V wanted more

from me than finding a replacement as the manager of the castle and lands.

She wanted me to *be* her replacement, which is a whole level of complication I can't deal with right now.

All I can deal with, it seems, is texting Zach that I've made it safely and sinking into V's recliner. I know I should go to bed, but I can't face it yet. It's easier to be a coward and clutch the quilt she left draped over her chair around me so tightly I nearly strangle myself.

But it keeps me from falling apart.

CHAPTER TEN

VIOLET – 1971

Christmas at the castle was wonderful, and I'm sad the New Year's festivities are done. It's almost time to head for Austin to finish my senior year, and nostalgia has me roaming the family room and settling myself in the armory. Gavina finds me in the room that's seemingly misnamed. There are weapons here, of course, all antiques Alisdair collected to remind himself of his home and artfully displayed. It is by far the biggest of the three portrait galleries containing an array of notable artwork, and the one that makes me feel the most like a MacInnes.

I guess everyone thinks college will mysteriously change them. In some ways, it's absolutely true. In others, I find I'm still me. A little older. I hope a little wiser. Time will tell.

Gavina snags my attention from the open archway, joining me where I'm looking at the amazing painting of our founders. "What are you up to?"

"Wandering. Thinking."

"About anything in particular?"

"Remember in junior high when my teacher made me write a report on Evajean and Alisdair?" I nod toward the portrait.

"Like it was yesterday."

"I was such a child, thinking because I grew up here, I knew them."

"You were a kid, Violet. Don't beat on yourself."

I put an arm around her waist and hug her. "I was afraid *you* would beat me."

She pulls away enough to frown at me. She's all of five-two, so she's looking up a bit, but no one could doubt who has the superior power in the room.

"You thought I'd hit you?"

"Not literally. I was terrified of you back then."

"And now?"

I tug her in. "Now I'm sure you're the most awesome human on the planet."

She kisses me over my ear. "I'm glad we got that settled."

I turn to the artwork, instantly mesmerized by the beauty and skill. "This painting stuns me. It's as if any second now, they'll look right at me."

"Thank you."

I frown in her direction. "Pardon?"

She gestures to the artist's signature near the bottom edge. It's so tiny in ratio to the canvas, but I see a sweeping GMM. I bet I look like I'm at a tennis match as I volley between Gavina and the portrait.

"You painted this."

"Yes, in Paris."

"You're an artist."

"I'd like to think so."

Now that I know what to look for, I see there's an impressive number of GMM's on the walls around me.

"I've lived in and around every room, every floor, every nook and cranny of this castle since I was born. I'm twenty-one years old, and I've never known this about you. How is that remotely possible?"

"Wasn't important before now."

"Gavina, your work belongs in a museum. Okay, maybe not Evajean and Alisdair as this castle wouldn't be complete without them, but you're acting like you tapped some paint on a canvas. No big deal."

"Trust me, it took me a long time to hone my talent. You aren't seeing the first version by a long shot."

"We're putting the cart ahead of the pony. You're clearly a master, yet the only time I've seen you with paint on you is when we're white-washing the fences or redoing the barn."

She smiles, and it's both wistful and deeply sad. "I still dabble now and again. It was a part of my life a long time ago. I spent twenty years in Paris. I got to be in on the heyday of Dadaism, cubism, surrealism, and oh, it was fun. Not my style, mind you, but the freedom and the passion were...breathtaking."

"Like, wow, G. You're blowing my mind."

She shrugs, but I know the movement isn't dismissal but, rather, discomfort. G is a force of nature, but she's a behind-the-scenes mountain mover. She's never liked to be in the spotlight, and after seeing this, I wonder why even more. She should be doing tours to galleries around the world and holding court.

"It sounds like braggadocio, but while they were not my dearest friends, I knew Picasso and Valadon and Laurencin. I never could capture modern art, but the community was amazing, and there was no pissing match about style." She gives a laugh. "Oh, that's not true. There's always an asshole or two in any bunch, and artists can be a squirrelly bag of nuts. Still, it was magical. I learned from masters with a brush the world will never know, names you'd never recognize, but they taught me so much."

"You've got to tell me more. I'm gobsmacked I'm learning something so monumental about you."

"Piffle. It's not interesting to anyone but me, and it was a long time ago. I was a bit broken then, and I'm amazed I got away with my radical ideas."

I look up at the portrait yet again and see the two people there in a whole new light.

"It sounds ridiculous, but sometimes I forget they're your mom and dad."

"Indeed. It's because they're from a different era. Literally a different century. But they were real and alive and human. Ahead of their time in so many ways, and it helped I was a late-life surprise." Her smile is wry as she studies her mother. "I think Mum was tired by the time I came along and didn't have anything left to fight me."

Her voice clogs, and I rest my head on her shoulder.

"I loved them so much. I wish you could have known them. Da was larger than life. So strong. So fierce. So smart. Yet he was the gentlest man you could want to meet, but Nellie bar the door if you threatened one of his. And to see him with Mum was a sight to behold. I've never seen a love like it."

"I got a sense of that in my research, but this is a whole new ball of wax."

I scan the wall and find a smaller painting on the opposite side of the room that has always intrigued me. A beautiful woman is lounging on a chaise, her dress of the 1900s style, all white lace and, I assume, cotton. A large-brimmed hat rests on her lap, and her other hand supports her head. She's looking straight out from the painting, and it's so amazing it could be a photograph.

"Who is she?"

When I look, Gavina is fixated on the same portrait, and she's far away.

"She's the reason I went to Paris."

I almost miss her words, but there's no missing the longing, the love, the hurt in Gavina's bright green eyes.

And I have another astonishing piece of information about my great-aunt that I didn't know.

"You were in love with her." I realize I'm stating the obvious, but the words are out before I can stop them.

"To the bottom of my soul. But she was betrothed to a very wealthy man from New York. There was no place for us, then."

"But—"

Gavina shakes her head. "Don't think I didn't try every argument I could imagine. In the end, she had to be the woman society needed her to be."

"Do you ever see her?"

"No. It would hurt too much."

"Does she still live in New York?"

"As far as I know. I don't think about it…us…much. Time has lessened the pain to a dull ache. It flares when I poke at it, so I try not to. The truth is, I don't spend a lot of time lost in what could never be."

"But you got married."

"And divorced when it simply was not done."

"Did you marry in the castle?"

"Good Lord, no. I talked him into eloping because somewhere deep inside I knew we'd never stick. And I may talk a good game, but I couldn't bear thinking I'd break the magic when the end eventually came, on top of being a scandal. We had a few good years together, but I wouldn't live my life in a marriage with all the spark of a tepid bath. Everyone says he left me, but it's not true. I was happy for him to go on with his life, because I wasn't leaving Magnolia Bloom again. He was a wanderer, and I'd finished mine. As to other people's opinion of me, I learned long ago to not waste time worrying."

"G, you are now officially the coolest person I've ever known."

"While I'm flattered, my coolness has come at a price. But it's amusing to realize you, like most young people, think your generation invented dreams and desire and sex."

Her gaze is clearly on a photograph of a young woman in a flapper dress with the requisite beaded headband and a cigarette in a long, lacquered holder.

"That's you." Again, I state the obvious. Or what's now obvious. "My God, you were stunning. Not that you aren't—"

"Just stop. I know what you mean." She moves to the wall and levels the frame to ease my embarrassment. "My point, sweet Violet, is you live in an entirely different world than I did. I learned to keep secrets, but that had consequences. All choices do. As you continue your education, I urge you to resist living your life to others' expectations."

"I'm trying." I barely manage the words as a whisper, and she returns to hug me close.

"Never forget I'll always be here for you. I have faith you'll find the courage to manage your life your way."

Of course, my brain immediately summons Ephraim, and I'm afraid, very afraid, G isn't merely wise, but prescient.

As we continue to stand in silence, I shiver.

And it has nothing to do with the room's temperature.

CHAPTER ELEVEN

It takes only a few seconds to be proven wrong. The chair rocks underneath me, and V's scent overwhelms me as I bury my face in the perfectly stitched mariner's compass she won first place for at the county fair some years back. I start falling apart like a too-dry piecrust, memories and sadness bowling me over with twice the force of the wave nearly taking me out in Austin.

There'll never be another effusive greeting. No strong, wiry arms crushing me against a bony chest. No choking mixture of Aqua Net and White Diamonds. I gave Aunt V nice perfume every year. She'd use it a few times, but she'd always revert to her standard. It was one of her quirks. It wasn't about money.

Everyone outside of Magnolia Bloom seems to have an impression the MacInneses are real-life East Texas Ewings. The reality is, the castle is a working enterprise that has good years and bad, and while we don't have to drive horse and buggies, we also don't have a fleet of Maseratis hidden in a barn somewhere. But V could afford all the fancy labels she wanted.

She simply didn't want. She claimed she figured out she didn't care what anyone thought about her, and she was the only one who had a vote in her decisions. She bought what she liked, and that was that.

Which means V's apartment is an amazing juxtaposition of beautiful artwork and dime-store pillows. A cross-stitch of the Serenity Prayer is on the wall next to a small, honest-to-God Matisse that family lore claims he painted for Aunt Gavina while she was studying art in France. We have no way to prove it, but the fact remains it's real —and nestled between a magnolia blossom preserved in acrylic and a finger painting I did for Aunt V when I was six.

V's passion was books. In fact, she makes me look illiterate by comparison. The printed word was her one true weakness. She'd lend out her precious novels, but she kept a list of who had what, and it took an act of Congress for her to give one away. To my surprise, she embraced audiobooks as proof of God's benevolence. I know the shelf upon shelf before me is merely a portion of her collection of both printed and recorded works.

The other half is in the East Turret, the door to which would be visible on the other side of the room if enough lamps were on. The round room contains her office and second personal library, and I snuggled into one of the comfy chairs and read while she worked most of the hours I spent in Magnolia Bloom. I love the space more than any on the property. Now, I imagine the solid dark door with dread.

I clear my throat but don't bother to stem the tears rolling down my cheeks, one hot trail after another. The silence is broken by the metallic rattle of the air conditioner kicking on, and I snag a handful of tissues from the side table before giving in to the melancholy shredding me.

My sobs are ugly. Messy. Snotty.

They won't stop, even when my stomach cramps.

It doesn't matter V had a good life. It doesn't matter she's free of the pain from the cancer showing up out of nowhere, a merciless maelstrom of relentlessly advancing tumors.

I want her back.

Want her to whisper her comforting words.

Want her to tell me to pull on my big-girl panties, then fix us both a puts-hair-on-your-chest gin and tonic. Want the woman who loved me as if I were hers. Said she wished I were hers. More times than I can count.

Our wishes were identical.

I loved her. I still love her.

The fact there's no hot bowl of chicken 'n' dumplings waiting for me on her dining room table turns the waves of grief into a tsunami of despair.

It's too late, but I want V to sit me down and tell me, as I blow on spoonsful of flaky pastry, how to save my marriage. V would have answers to all my questions, although some would risk me spitting cream gravy while laughing. Some would make me cry. But all would make sense and help me figure out how to not ruin the magic of Castle MacInnes.

But V's not here anymore, and it's too big for me to absorb. Too heavy. Too much for my heart to accept and my head to figure out. I know I'm a grown woman. I know I've raised children of my own—and done a fine job of it. I know I'm logical and intelligent and methodical. I know I can slice and dice the data in a legal battle and bring home the winning swing-to-the-bleachers for our side.

And none of it makes one damned bit of difference right now.

I barely have the strength to climb out of her chair. The sum total of what I can do is walk on leaden feet to her room, lie down on top of her coverlet, and cry myself to sleep.

WHEN MORNING COMES, I'm half certain someone poured concrete into my eyes during my fitful dreams. Brilliant sunlight sneaks around the edges of the blackout curtains Zach installed years ago on one of the rare trips he joined me here. The blinding rays seem intent on stabbing me right in my pupils, which only adds to the fun of trying to release a crick in my neck the size of Enchanted Rock from sleeping catawampus all night.

Stretching my aching muscles, I run my hand over the stunning spiral Bargello pattern done in hues seeming impossible in simple cotton and stitched by V's own hand. I'd bet a good chunk of my retirement V hand-dyed most of the fabric in the purple she loved so much.

It's impossible to be here and not give in to wistful memories of when my brothers and I pretended to be asleep so we could stay in her bed instead of the guest room. We thought we were fabulous actors, and I can still hear Mom and V by the bed, Mom settling Kiki in her portable crib a few feet away.

"Look at those sweet babies," Aunt V would whisper. "I guess we can't disturb them now. Best leave them here."

I'd kick whichever brother giggled, praying Aunt V hadn't heard.

Of course, she had, and we all laughed as adults. V patted my arm and said, "Making memories is more important than spending one night in the guest room."

Truth is, V spent many nights in the guest room. Stunning how often I managed to be conked out in her bed in record time...every visit.

I plump the decorative pillows against the headboard and go to the master bath. As soon as I flip the switch, the light fixture and the sun's rays spearing through the high window show the depth of V's failing health. The major surfaces are clean, but the dusty corners reveal a lack of attention I've never seen before.

I don't have time to worry as I take a quick shower and dress. There will be a flood of people through the castle in the next few days, and although no one will be in V's private quarters but me, I won't put off my responsibilities...not in here, anyway.

Besides, I'll need all the tasks on my list to keep the anguish at bay.

Knowing Mina will arrive any moment, I scout out cleaning supplies and set to work on the bathroom. I force myself not to cry when I straighten the fourth can of Aqua Net under the sink and tuck the toothbrush and tube of Crest into the cabinet. I know I should throw them away. I will. Just not today.

Lemon-scented ammonia is swirling down the sparkling toilet when the front-door chime pings. The floor is shiny, the mirror streak-free, and a full roll of Charmin is on the holder.

Task one complete.

I open the door and smile at Fina's physical opposite. "Good morning, sunshine. How are you holding up?"

I buss a smooth cheek barely a decade older than mine. I forget sometimes, because it's not years making us seem so different. Logically, I understand Mina and Fina basically are in the middle, age-wise, between me and Violet, but they will always be more her contemporaries in my eyes.

The twins survived a lot, especially Mina, and she's come through life a little grayer but still vibrant and beautiful. I don't think she believes it, though.

"Oh, good as can be expected, I guess. From the looks of you, we both got precious little sleep last night."

"Gee, thanks."

"Pishposh, you know I'm teasin'. Where do you want me?" Mina sets down a laundry basket containing chemicals, brushes, and sponges.

"I've already done the front bathroom. Why don't you sweep and wet-mop the floors, and I'll tackle the icebox."

To my surprise, Mina doesn't engage in a bout of small talk, and I can see she's as stuck in her sadness as I am in mine. Instead of pressing her, I start mugs in the Breville Barista. V was mostly frugal, except when it came to coffee. Which made gifts a total no-brainer. I'd find the most interesting coffees and espresso beans the internet could provide, and both of us were ecstatic.

After delivering a fresh cup to Mina, I take a moment to open all the windows and the French doors, ignoring the siren call of the enormous balcony spanning from turret to turret.

I march over to the plain white refrigerator and pull up short as I scout the interior, stymied by the neat arrangement of margarine tubs I will bet top odds in Vegas contain anything but oleo.

A quick move of all the plastic cartons to the table proves me right. One, bacon grease. Two, I suspect King Ranch casserole. Three, a half can's worth of green beans with butter congealed on top. Four, a serving of peach cobbler. Five, a few tablespoons of the actual original contents. For a small refrigerator, it's filled with memories. I know V cooked a lot in her tiny space, often preferring it over the family kitchen down the hall and the bigger one on the ground floor.

I pop open a garbage bag and start the bittersweet job of throwing away these bits of Aunt V. Butter and mustard. Relish and pickled okra.

Verses in the song of V's life.

I crouch to reach the final shelf, and my legs give way. I push aside the cans of orange Fanta and cup my hand to scoop the vials of essential oils into the hem of my T-shirt.

The heaves come again, collecting in the well of my soul. I haven't checked yet, but I'm sure every room has a different atomizer I gave her over the years. I'd also bet a nickel she picked scents especially for an arriving guest.

But I'd bet a million dollars she uses "my" oils only in her room. The smell of Aqua Net, White Diamonds, and magnolia blossom will always be V's scent, etched into my mind like a thousand other memories waiting to be relived when I can find the strength.

I sink to the ground and clutch my stomach.

"How can I fall apart without you?" I keen, my voice high and despondent.

And what kind of monster does it make me that all I can think about is how I'm desperate to know how I'll manage without her voice of wisdom only a phone call away? Not for a thousand rubies would I wish her back, in pain and suffering, but I don't know how to navigate a world without her in it.

A knock jerks me out of my self-pity, but Mina answers as I get to my feet, wiping my face on a clean cloth.

"Good mornin', Leith. I hope you slept well." Mina welcomes him inside. "You had coffee?"

"Yes, ma'am." He hands her a canvas bag I assume has cleaning supplies in it. Which is strange because we have plenty. "Ms. Fina asked me to bring this by on my way out. I'm scouting the grounds today."

"Hello, Leith." He turns his attention to me, and I'm disconcerted to realize his smile is slightly crooked on the left, an adorable addition in the too-perfect-because-he's-not-perfect column.

Realizing I'm staring, I shift my gaze and fumble for something to say, lighting on the easiest and obvious. "Are you sure you wouldn't like a cup? Won't take but a second."

"I'm sure. I wouldnae want to be a bother."

"You're not, but I won't press." Not that a little pressing ever hurt anybody.

Oh, good God. I'm not above innuendo, but it wasn't even good innuendo.

The smile on my face might be dangerously close to frozen, because I can't figure out where the thought came from, and I'm not ready to explore it.

As if punishing me for my nonsensical thinking, my phone buzzes. I pull it out of my pocket and tell myself to stop acting like a ninny. It's coincidence my husband is texting me at the exact moment I've gone haywire over a complete stranger. A completely gorgeous and charming stranger.

Zach: You okay?

I want to respond, *No, I haven't been okay in far too long, and I'm not sure if I'll ever be okay again.*

Me: Fine. Busy cleaning.

Then I return the case to my jeans.

"I'll let you ladies return to what you're doing." Leith turns to the door, apparently oblivious to my discomfort. "If you need anything, text me. I'm happy to help."

I have to lure my mind away from the well-worn jeans so nicely molded to his slender hips and a derriere that either sees a lot of weightlifting, or has an awfully good trainer.

"Do you want me to take over mopping?" I force my focus on Mina.

"I'm almost done, and, sweetie, we need to talk for a quick minute."

My gut clenches in an *uh-oh*. I knew "a talk" was coming, but I assumed I'd be able to delay it until after the services. In retrospect, it's obviously silly, but I still feel wobbly as we take our cups to the table V kept pushed against the dining room wall to maximize her space.

"What's up?" I might as well get the conversation started.

"You know Violet wanted you to take her place, right?"

"As chatelaine?" I shake my head and stall with a sip of coffee. "Not until last night, and Brian Steele basically nailed me about it. Violet always spoke of me covering until things got settled, with her getting sick so fast."

"About that. She wasn't quite honest with you."

I push aside a growl, knowing Mina has far more insider information than I do. "V never lied to me."

"No, but she didn't give you the whole picture, either. You see, tradition says a female descendant from the oldest MacInnes child born in Texas is supposed to take care of the castle. Violet didn't have any children, so the rule followed to Gerome's children."

"Me and Kiki."

"Correct. You have a female child, but no one would think of asking this to fall on Ainsley's shoulders."

I close my eyes for a second, trying to do a mental family tree. "I see where this is going, but isn't this more tradition, not a rule?"

"Well…yes. Violet is the first MacInnes not to live a good long life. She thought she had twenty years or more, and by the time it was an issue, you'd be ready. You love this castle almost as much as Violet did, and Fina and I do. It all seemed perfectly logical."

"Until the cancer."

"Yes."

I take another drink and meet Mina's eyes. "It's not that I'm unwilling, or even that I don't want to, but I have a job, and my life is in Austin. I can absolutely see this as my second-stage career, after I've retired, but not yet."

Mina turns her cup in circles for a tense moment. "The thing is, we've had a few really tough years, and the estate is on a razor's edge right now. We can't hire a professional manager, and of course Fina and I are perfectly willing to keep running things, but the fact remains we're not family."

"Yes, you—"

"We're not blood, no matter how much we almost think we are. I know you don't like to talk about the...mystical side of all this, but the hard truth is, it's going to take a miracle to keep things running more than a few years hence."

I sit back, my lungs starving for air. "From a completely practical standpoint, the estate is a family trust. Surely we have talent we can draw from. Lord knows there's more than a few MacInneses around here."

"Again, yes. And V did have help besides me and Fina, but we need to circle back to the big question of how much you're willing to take on. I don't know the terms of the trust by heart, but once the line is broken and a manager comes in who's not, well, one of us, governing the castle may never be back in our hands again. I'm not sure what Castle MacInnes would be in that case. Maybe another tourist attraction instead of the heart and soul of the family? Or sold to some corporation? Who knows?"

I stall for time, fixing us both fresh mugs and staring long and hard out the French doors. "Mina, I understand what you're saying, but I can't give you an answer right now. I've taken off work for three months, and I bet I could stretch that a few more because I'm close to my boss. But I have a lot to think about."

"I know, sweetie. I'm so sorry to pile this all on you, today of all days."

I pat the hand she's put on my arm. "Waiting wouldn't fix anything. And while we're talking about broken magic and losing everything, or at least the heart and soul of this special place, you might want to second-guess me as the right choice."

I take a deep breath and let it out slowly.

"Mina, I'm filing for divorce when I get home, which means I'll break the magic of the chapel, maybe the whole castle. We also can't gloss over that I'm a MacInnes, which massively compounds the whole first-divorce thing. The double wallop of divorce and it being a MacInnes heir would tarnish our mystical guarantee. Not the best PR for the castle's magic."

Her smile is tight, but her grip returns, warm and firm. "Let's take one thing at a time, all right? Let's get through the services, give you a chance to dig into the files and see if something jumps out at you that we've missed, and then we'll make a plan." A thin laugh escapes her. "Maybe you'll even solve the mystery of Gavina's missing paintings. No sense borrowing Monday from Sunday."

"Thanks for the added pressure. I hadn't given a second's thought to the lost artwork."

"I should've kept my mouth shut about that, but Fina and I were talking about it, so it's on my mind. I'm sorry."

I lean in and press my forehead to hers. "You're precious, Mina. I'm so glad I have you, because I think my to-do list is about to be so long it rolls out the door."

She pats my cheek and sits back, seeming strangely relieved even though we haven't really solved anything. "That's all we need for today. We're in a fine kettle of fish, but the estate has seen hard times before. We got through them. We'll get through this."

I put on a bright smile, not sure where I managed to conjure it from, and nod. "Okay, then. One thing at time. If I have you and Fina, I'll be okay."

"You always have us, sweetie." She stands and takes her cup to the sink. "Now, you finish up in here, and I'll do the back rooms. It won't take long."

Once I'm alone, I sit for a long moment, then wander over to click on an atomizer on the entryway table, adding the magnolia blossom oil I kept stocked for V. And for myself.

I go to V's tiny craft corner, smashed between the two bedrooms and originally a walk-in closet, and sit before her beloved Singer. Tracing the stitching on the precisely folded quilt top on the sewing table, I refuse to dissolve into memories again. If I do, I'll never finish the chores, and I won't let V down.

It's a good time to remind myself, somewhat forcefully, I've helped win multimillion-dollar lawsuits. I can help save Castle MacInnes.

Next week.

CHAPTER TWELVE

MINA – NOW

I ENJOYED HELPING Paige clean for a couple of hours, but I sure did hate having to serve her a giant dish of to-dos when she's barely had time to unpack. She was the sweetheart I've always known her to be, but when she shooed me out well before noon, needing time alone, I didn't argue.

I felt restless so I headed into town. I stopped by the bakery, and now I'm at the market. I don't know why grocery shopping calms me down. Maybe it's quiet time with a purpose. Maybe it's because the produce inspires me to suggest recipes to Momma, still cooking part-time for the castle at eighty-eight. She swears it's what keeps her young, and I don't doubt it. She misses being able to do all the work for the big events, especially the weddings, but Fina and I put our respective feet down a few years ago and made her stop. But we can't take the kitchen away from her entirely.

I finish texting Momma to send me anything she might've forgotten on her shopping list, then toss my phone toward my open purse. I shush the doctor's voice in my head scolding me to use a smaller bag so I don't keep injuring my shoulder. Men don't understand.

Maybe it's time Magnolia Bloom hired a woman doctor.

Joy Baker, who's usually at the cash register if Bethanie isn't there, calls to me as I pass the display of polished eggplants she's arranging.

"Hey, Mina. Here to see your boyfriend?"

I jerk around, confused and inexplicably irritated. "Boyfriend? What the bald-faced heck are you talking about?"

"Mr. Nelson, a'course. He never comes out of his office unless he sees your car on the video monitor." Joy shoots me one of her are-you-serious glares. "Do you honestly believe the store owner bags everyone's groceries?"

I stare at her, clenching my jaw so it won't drop. Of course I noticed Mr. Nelson around the store. The Magnolia Market is his.

"Stuff and nonsense, Joy."

I can't keep the skepticism from my voice, especially since she has been teasing me since junior high, and age hasn't broken her of the tendency. While she's never mean, the last thing I need is to make a display of myself for her amusement. She can't honestly expect me to buy that Chester Nelson, who grew from a scrawny boy with an unfortunate overbite into a handsome, successful businessman, is somehow interested in me.

"I see you don't believe me." Joy adds another purple globe to the pile.

"It's not that."

"It's that you don't believe me."

Oh, boy, I'm not getting out of this one. "More like you're reaching."

She waggles the stem end of her eggplant at me. "Don't you think it's time to get out of your own way?"

I blink at her, unable to form a response.

"Fifty-nine's not dead, you know. At least I'm not." She tosses her long, glossy hair no one believes is a natural shade of amber, no matter how many years she's denied going to Dallas to have her roots done.

The truth doesn't sting, but it sure prickles. We're the same age, but Joy seems to take life by both hands and wring everything she can out of it. Every weekend, she's at Tidy's honkey-tonk in tight jeans and tighter shirts, drawing men to the dance floor like a proverbial candle flame. I've always envied her confidence, even as a teenager.

Maybe I envy her the dancing most. We both made some bad choices when we were young, but she didn't let them break her. And she didn't ruin her sister's life.

"You're smart and beautiful and funny, Mina. It's time you allowed another passenger into your car. Tool down the road with the top down. You've waited too long and let the specter of Roylee haunt your rearview. Look ahead, woman."

Again, I blink. Joy and I are hardly BFFs, so I'm not prepared for the tortured metaphor or her level of personal observation. I do the only thing I can.

"I need to hurry home."

With the social acumen of Forrest Gump, I whirl away and push my buggy down to the milk and eggs as fast as I can before I'm offered any more unsolicited advice. I mean, honestly.

Still, it's been more years than I can count that anyone has been in my car besides my sister or my son. Certainly never a stranger. Well, Mr. Nelson's not exactly a stranger, and I may have noticed him a time or two passing through the aisles.

I no more finish my thought and queue into the checkout line when I see him at the bagging end of the conveyor. My heart flutters like the kaleidoscope of monarch butterflies migrating through last month, and goose bumps spread beneath my new Butterick blouse. I finished the hem and pressed it yesterday, and until now, I hadn't given a second thought to the fact I dress far nicer than might be required for the Magnolia Market. My eyes are drawn to my patent pumps. I don't try to deny I have an obsession for finding my shoes at resale shops and flea markets, but there's no denying wearing Ferragamos to grocery shop may be something I need to be honest about.

With myself, anyway. I'm not about to give Fina another snowball to lob at me when she teases me about my sewing and footwear.

I want to leave my cart and walk out, but just as I mean to look away from his deep green apron and his still-thick, neatly styled white hair, Mr. Nelson's gaze shifts.

To mine.

He gives me a head tip, the common courtesy the bedrock of his always-a-kind-word personality. The corners of his mouth curl up, and I see it then. It's been so long, but the fervent flash in his gaze, so quick I may have dreamed it, resonates in me as...appreciation.

Lord, give me strength.

I can't walk away now, so I wait through Deidre Engelson's fishing expedition for every single nonexpired coupon in a plastic sandwich bag that's seen better days. I can only inspect so many overhead lights and store windows for smudges. Which I guess is why I notice for the first time how hard he's worked to modernize the store, with bright lighting and by replacing large sections of the old linoleum with wood flooring, yet maintained a small-town vibe.

I shift my focus to the small display of magazines and candy, adding a roll of wintergreen Life Savers and the latest issue of *Southern Living* to my cart. I smile at Bethanie, Mr. Nelson's youngest daughter, who sidled into town a couple of months ago. She looks away, avoiding me and giving a deep sigh to express her disapproval of Deidre's dithering.

If Magnolia Bloom had a bookie, the over-under would be pretty hefty on how long Bethanie'll stay this time.

"Good afternoon, Mina. It's lovely to see you today." Mr. Nelson's all charm when it's my turn, and he bags my choices.

All I hear is *lovely*, and my cheeks heat. With my blinders removed, I have to admit Joy wasn't lying. Women are often described as lovely, but when I meet his Paul Newman blue eyes, I realize I have encountered my first lovely man.

"Mr. Nelson. Beautiful day."

Beautiful man. I immediately swat away the thought, wondering if I've suffered a small stroke.

"When will you start calling me CT?" He adds a smile as he puts the package of angel hair pasta into the bag.

CT is certainly better than Chester.

"CT, then. The T stands for…"

"Tennyson." His smile becomes a delightful self-deprecating quirk, and I notice his teeth are well-cared-for white. "I like my middle name. Never cared for my first."

Sons of the South aren't often named for British poet laureates, but I find I want to grin back at him. Instead, I concentrate on my own coupons, the difference being mine are in order of my list and all expiration dates were checked before I left the castle.

My buggy wasn't full, yet I seem to have racked up quite a list of CT Nelson discoveries in a short time. Like how he has long, tanned fingers, which seems incongruous with someone who works in an office all day. The tanned part, not the long part. The long part makes a vision of him playing a piano spring into my head, and I have no clue if CT Nelson plays the piano. Or the banjo. Or is first-chair kazoo in a traveling band.

Bethanie rips my receipt off the machine, and the curl of paper she hands me cuts through my musings.

"Have a nice day."

I confess she does not sound sincere, but I have no space to worry about Bethanie. I'm too preoccupied with getting out and getting home and getting far away from the silver-fox allure of CT.

"I'd love to take these out for you." CT indicates my cart of bagged groceries.

I do a double take and nearly stumble as I hear, *I'd love to take you out.*

I recover, but I know I've probably blinded the man with the whites of my panicked eyes. "I've got it. You have a good day."

My attempt at a sunny delivery is more partly cloudy, but I need out. Blessedly, the only thing following me is CT's, "Drive safe. Have a good week."

My imagination whirls over the exchange the entire drive home, a mental carousel of the times I've seen CT Nelson and the reactions I convinced myself were mere polite courtesy.

The intimacy of those subtle moments echo through me, ripe and fresh. I've not always been a good judge of desire, but I do recall the early years when I discovered not all boys threw rocks...or fists. I remember the moment I looked at Ken Carmichael, both of us twelve years old and standing beside each other at recess while the captains were picking sides for dodgeball. My stomach filled with bubbles I couldn't blame on Dr Pepper.

Which describes my insides perfectly right now.

I drive to the castle on autopilot, reminding myself my teenaged only-in-my-mind infatuation with Ken Carmichael as we grew into our teens ended when his dad got a new job in Tulsa. Still innocent and clueless, the vacuum in my new-to-boys soul let me be blindsided by too much attention from Roylee Baxter. Now would be a good time to do a deep dive into my personal history to remind myself what my naiveté got me.

No matter how nice the Ken Carmichaels and CT Nelsons of the world might seem, I am an appallingly bad judge of character where men are concerned, and I have to purge this craziness from my system. I park by the kitchen door, vowing to cast aside my schoolgirl silliness.

Fina joins me at the trunk and grabs two bags. "Trey called. Said he tried to call you, but you didn't answer."

I search my pockets for my phone and find them empty. Now I have to figure out where I've left it on top of everything else swirling between my ears. I'm not only mad at myself, but out of sorts with my son. He's canceled dinner with me three times now, and I assume he's calling to do so again. He can't see his new girlfriend is a grown woman and doesn't need him running and fetching for her every minute of the day.

My frustration with my too-kind son has to wait.

"Did Paige come out while I was gone?"

"Not yet. She brought milk, though. It's upstairs."

"Good. I bought enough cereal to stock the family kitchen for her and Leith so they don't have to come down if they don't want to, but maybe I should go after more bagels and English muffins."

"There's plenty of food. No one will starve."

"I don't want either of them to have to bother."

"They're grown adults, you know. Besides, if she and Leith run into each other during a midnight refrigerator raid, might not be a bad thing."

"Fina! We shouldn't be thinking such things. Or interfering."

A mischievous twinkle sparks in my twin's eye. "V's already meddling, and she's barely passed through the pearly gates."

I squint at my sister. "You attribute divine intervention to everything. God's got bigger things to worry about than micromanaging relationships."

She shrugs. "Leith's arrival yesterday is the kind of thing V would have planned."

"She made these arrangements with him months ago. You don't just hop a plane from Scotland on a whim." I recall the itinerary on the corner of my desk upstairs and how excited V was for the friend of the family to come research the castle for an article in an architecture digest.

Then I remember my interaction at the Magnolia Market and my sudden regression to a boy-crazy teenager, and I have to nod.

"On second thought, I wouldn't put it past her." As if I'm holding it, I can see the picture attached to the itinerary. "He's a right handsome man. What if it backfires on us?"

"Paige is a grown woman, and we both know she hasn't been happy in a long time. I'm not trying to set anything up crossing a moral line, but I'm also not upset if she has a chance to see there's life out there if she decides she's done with the one she's living."

"I thought we were trying to make her and Zach wake up and see what they're losing."

"Paige is too young to settle for good enough. I don't know where it will lead, but I want Paige to have choices."

"But what if those choices break the magic? What if we lose the castle?"

The stubborn set I'm quite used to seeing on my twin's face turns hard as concrete. "Then the magic deserves to be broken."

"Serafina Greene! When did you do a one-eighty?"

She hides her face in her hands and stands there for a long

moment before those bony shoulders go rigid and the old Fina returns, yet I can still see sadness in her eyes.

"I've had a hard day today. Missing V. Pursuing should-haves and would-haves and might-have-beens. I got riled up."

"We're both off-center, but don't worry. I had a nice talk with Paige this morning. We can't protect her, but maybe we can put a detour sign in her path."

I just hope we haven't sent the train careening off the tracks instead of onto a new course.

CHAPTER THIRTEEN

PAIGE – NOW

I FINISHED CLEANING, unpacked my suitcase, and have everything tucked away. Without any more distractions, I set myself up in the wrought-iron rocker on the balcony, frowning at the brilliant blue sky and fierce afternoon sunshine. I understand it's been only a skosh over twenty-four hours since my world shifted in so many ways, but the sky should be gray. There should be low, dark clouds and a roiling skyline shot with lightning so the weather matches my mood.

When the doorbell forces me vertical, I *oof* at the crick in my back, feeling every one of my almost forty-seven years.

Instead of Mina or Fina, I find myself facing my handsome passenger from yesterday.

"Hello, Leith." I give him the come-in sweep of my hand.

"I'm here to take you to lunch."

"Did we make a date last night and I forgot?"

He gives me the slightly crooked smile I've already noticed and bookmarked in my mind. "No, Ms. Fina told me to ask you for a tour of the castle, then pay for it with lunch. I'm happy to do as I'm told."

He steps in so I can stop the rapid escape of the air-conditioned coolness into the cavernous interior of the family floor. "Why am I sure that's a load of bull hockey?"

"You giving me a tour in exchange for lunch?"

"No, you being happy to do as you're told. Your trust-me-I'm-innocent face needs some work. But your acting skills aside, for as long as I can remember neither Fina nor Mina grasp that I can feed myself."

"Their generation equates food with love. Same at home for me."

I toss him my own, not-crooked smile. "You know Mina and Fina are only fifteenish years older than me, right? But to a young'un like you, it probably seems like eons."

"I didnae know, but I'm guessing you and I aren't more than a few years apart. You sound like I'm a wee lad."

I shrug. "Maybe because you're still single, footloose and fancy-free, despite traveling the world. My color-where-you've-been map would be almost blank."

I lead the way through the apartment to the tiny kitchen as much to distract myself as him. Before he arrived, I was looking around the suite, finding myself wandering the rooms as if I'm missing something. The problem is, I don't know what I'm searching for and can't pinpoint where the looming sense something's off-kilter is coming from…other than the glaringly obvious, of course. It's more than V being gone and me seesawing between being furious with Zach and missing him with an ache that's going to take a long time to ease.

I get it. I acknowledge I'm still waffling, but shouldn't I be? Shouldn't there be some part of me that doesn't want to destroy a union of almost thirty years?

Maybe it's the double punch of losing V and the final death knell of my marriage happening literally within hours of each other. Maybe I'm not used to young, virile men seeking me out, even if only for lunch. Maybe I'm tired and have turned into a bad Victorian heroine in need of a fainting couch.

I cut myself some slack. I've never been a whiner, and I'm not whining now. I'm sad and hurt and lost, and it's not out of the realm of reasonable I'm not firing on all cylinders.

"Would you like something to drink?"

"No, I'm good. Had a liter of water downstairs."

"All right, then, let me get a pen and paper, and I'll draw you a quick sketch, and then we'll do the nickel tour. I know there are drawings and blueprints in V's office, but I haven't even gone in there yet. I'll get them to you, though."

"I appreciate it."

It doesn't take but a moment to settle at V's small table, where I was with Mina not long before. I make some quick swipes with the pen and start.

"Be kind, because I'm no architect, but if you think of the perimeter of the castle as the outer walls, then the area where you saw Penny last night is the inner bailey. That open area is the front third of the rectangle. The rooms along the sides of that inner bailey are all event rooms and our prized chapel. You'll hear Mina and Fina call the front event spaces the salons. I don't know why, because they're all different sizes, but the name stuck from somewhere in time."

He nods as I make little tick marks on my drawing.

"If you imagine when we came in last night, facing the portcullis, the front turret to your left is called the West Turret, and the South Turret is to your right. On the ground floor, South has a very popular bar, both with event guests and the locals. West has a coffee shop and bistro. North has the gift shop. East is a room most often booked by the hosts of events happening in the ballroom, as it's closest to that space."

"Got it."

"You walked up the grand staircase yesterday and saw the entry."

"And it's pure barry. We were all tired, but it's breathtaking."

"No argument from me, of course. We used the elevator installed in the '40s, but there's nothing like taking the actual stairs."

"I did so this morning. Poked around a bit. I know you proceed back to the ballroom. That's simplified, but I see the ground floor is your public space."

"Exactly. It's super rough to put it this way, but the front third is the inner bailey, the next third is the entry and formal salon, and the last is the giant ballroom. From the back of the ballroom, there's the portico, then the stairway to the lawn, then finally the acreage all the way to the lake. The rooms on both sides are a mixture of smaller meeting rooms, the kitchen, storage, and myriad other things. We even have a few rooms we can turn into guest quarters in a pinch."

"You're confirming my impression."

"Good. The second floor comprises guest rooms and the family suites. There are times we'll rent the family space, the giant living room area, but never the back apartment. There are two—this one, which is Fam One, and the second, not surprisingly, is Fam Two. These flank the hallway that leads out onto the balcony. Other rooms on this floor are used for storage, the small laundry and kitchen—"

"Which aren't small at all. Not by European standards."

"True, but names are sometime incongruous with reality around here. But the point is, the second floor is called the family floor, even though it's mixed-use. That turret," I gesture to my right, "is the East Turret, and that's V's office. Above it is Fina's office."

"Who's in Fam Two?"

"No one right now. The last person living there was a cousin who was the family historian. She passed away, and V told me some months back that the next person in our very complicated system of who gets to claim the space hasn't decided if they want to or not. With V getting sick, we haven't invested a lot of hours figuring that out."

"I've studied many a castle, some public, some private, some a mix, and can tell you this is all right on par with what I've seen all over the world."

"I have a bucket list of castles I want to see when I retire and have the time to travel. The thing is, it takes some of the mystique away when you know how complicated running an estate like this is."

Which I'm expected to take over.

"To wrap up, the third floor is mostly more guest rooms and storage. All the turret rooms I haven't mentioned before are our most-booked spaces. It's stunning, really, how much money people will pay to stay in them."

"Not surprising to me. It's quite romantic."

And romance is not a subject I want to discuss right now.

"So there you go. In a nutshell, the first floor is the drive-around starring Penny the Dragon, the breathtaking entry and front hall, the ballroom, and out the back to the lake. The second floor has guest rooms and family space, including the galleries and library, and the third floor is mostly guest rooms. That's quite oversimplified, but a decent snapshot."

"I'm itching to explore it all."

"Come look at the balcony, then. The view is amazing."

I'm gratified at his low whistle of appreciation as he eyes the expanse from turret to turret, his expression delighted as he leans over the balustrade to take in the view from here all the way to the water.

"I think I'd rather pitch a camp bed and stay here all night."

"I've fallen asleep in the swing many times." I wave to the wrought-iron furniture and the comfortable, colorful cushions.

The high-noon sun bathes him as he turns and does the hips-against-the-railing, hands-in-pockets posture so masculine and attractive it makes me swallow.

Hard.

He's so comfortable with himself, so casual, and it's all said without a word. I met the man some eighteen hours ago, and yet it's like we chat on this balcony every day.

It's ridiculous, and I have zero answers for why my common sense seems to have completely abandoned my usual modus operandi.

Realizing I've left him in silence during my mental gyrations, I try to find a pleasant expression. "If you'd like, I'll walk you around so you can see what I drew so poorly."

"I'd like that. Then I'd like to take you to eat, as promised. Fina suggested a place called Vivann's On the Square."

"Best sandwiches and soup anywhere."

"It's a go, then."

I decide to give in gracefully. "Let me grab my shoes, and we'll head out."

"My pleasure."

I hurry to the bedroom and shut the door, adding a spritz of perfume after I tie my sneakers and put on a dash of mascara. I'm not exactly ready for a cotillion, but I won't frighten small children.

I know it's just a tour of the castle I love so much that I could do it blindfolded, followed by a meal in town.

The problem is, it feels like I'm taking the top off my own personal Pandora's box.

CHAPTER FOURTEEN

VIOLET – 1971

I LOVE ALMOST everything about the University of Texas. Austin is about as far from Magnolia Bloom as you can get, philosophically speaking. To this day, Momma's stunned I picked UT over Rice, but Daddy's proud as punch. He still wears his class ring engraved with a longhorn on one side and the tower on the other and has already ordered the ladies' version for me.

Right now, my passion for all things burnt orange isn't what's got me so preoccupied I nearly rear-end a Beetle turning right on 21st Street. It's the second time I've circled the drag looking for a parking place, and I hit the horn.

The driver ahead of me seems lost, which is a little on the nose as an analogy to my impatience. His problem's fixable. He needs to crank the steering wheel, press the gas pedal, and turn. My solution's not so simple. Spending spring break in a South Padre dive hotel with my secret boyfriend, followed by two weeks of frantically counting days, is a type of trouble I don't know how to handle.

I wish I could talk to Tidy, but I can't risk it. She's my best friend, but she's also as firmly rooted in Magnolia Bloom as I am. I need someone who will probably never set foot in town again.

A slew of muttered curses later, I park and run across Guadalupe, headed toward Ginny's dorm. Tidy's sister is almost a sister to me and the one person who might help.

To my shock, I nearly collide with Ginny as I round the fountain.

"Hey, Violet, where's the fire?"

Tidy and Ginny have never been super close, but Ginny models what I hope to become. Maybe not literally, since she's in graduate school and I haven't put that on my list yet, but in every other way. She's been a source of information, inspiration, and a solid shoulder to lean on in my upended worlds. She understands, like few others can, how I'm neither an Austin hippy-feminist nor a Magnolia Bloomian lady of breeding and obligation. Or rather, I'm both, pulled apart by the competing forces.

Right now, I'm about to vibrate into individual atoms and explode like a supernova.

"Hey, sorry." I'm breathless, but not from my run. Seeing Ginny has knocked the air from my lungs. They're for real now, the questions I'm poised to ask, the things I need to know. That realness is sharp, slivering through my insides and drawing my stomach tighter with every cut. The rest of my life might be on the line. Whatever the outcome, I'll never be the same.

Ginny frowns and cocks her head. "What's up? You're nervous as a long-tailed cat in a room full of rocking chairs."

My laugh cracks. "You have a second?"

She leads the way to the quad, and we take chairs under a majestic oak. "Is it Tidy?"

I shake my head. I look down at my clenched hands, then straight at Ginny. If I'm grown up enough to have sex with my boyfriend, I can look the person I've come to for help in the eye. "It's me."

She rummages in her satchel and pulls out matches and a pack of Virginia Slims. She offers me one, but I decline.

Tidy fell in love with both cigarettes and marijuana, and as her stalwart friend, I've tried them. I want to like pot and definitely want to be one of the cool kids, but it makes me hungry and sleepy. Truth is, I prefer vodka, and I'd give my entire month's allowance to have a bottle right now.

"You gonna talk, or we gonna stare at each other all morning?" Ginny adds a smile to take any sting out of her words.

"I, uh…" I pull my backpack onto my lap and clutch it against me, unsure where to start. Everything's such a mess. "I spent spring break with my boyfriend in Padre."

"Not surprising, but you sure are pale after a week at the beach."

A month ago, I would have blushed. "We didn't splash in the water much."

"Good for you." She waits for a moment, her expression slipping to concerned. "I hope."

I haul my bag in tighter. "You know the condoms you make sure Tidy and I keep with us?"

All humor is gone from her eyes. "Yes."

"Well, one broke."

"Jesus, Mary, and Joseph." She stabs at the ashtray on the table.

"Yeah, well, this conception wasn't immaculate."

She takes her time lighting a fresh cigarette. "You're sure?"

"All I know is I'm late. I haven't had a test done or anything. I don't have a clue where to go for one."

"It could be stress. My period stopped for two months before finals last year."

"I doubt it's stress."

"Me, too, but I'm stalling."

I'm not sure how, but as I sink into the chair, the tension threaded through me loosens. Giving air to my dilemma grounds me, and the fact Ginny's not berating me frees the rest of my reluctance. "I didn't know who else to talk to. I can't tell Tidy."

"Hell, no. She'd call our mother so fast she'd make Ma Bell dizzy." She holds up a placating hand. "Not to tattle, but because Tidy would do anything for you."

"I know, but she'd panic, and I'm nearly hysterical enough for both of us."

She takes a shaky drag on the cigarette. "What do you want to do?"

"That would be the ten-thousand-dollar question, and I don't have an answer."

I pride myself on making sound decisions. We used protection. We were careful. We had the best week of our lives. I love Ephraim in a way I've loved no one else. My heart numbs at the crossroads I stand before, either direction a choice I never thought I'd have to make.

"What does Mystery Boy say?" Her tone tells me she knows. "If it broke, it's not like it's a secret."

I dig madly in the front pocket of my bag for a tissue. I grab one and close my eyes, mopping up the drops before they can stream down my face. "He said to let him know, and he'd give me the money for a…procedure."

Like he'd spilled a drink on my shirt and offered to pay for the dry cleaner.

"That's mighty white of him."

I can't argue with her. Ginny's never liked Ephraim. I've never told her his name, so she's called him Mystery Boy from our first conversation, when I revealed the depth of my relationship with him and our inability to give each other up.

"Is that the route you want to take?"

Blood rushes to my face, and I know without needing a mirror I look like a boiled lobster. The words stick in my throat, and Ginny takes pity on me.

"Stay here." She rummages in her pocket and stalks over to the soda machine.

I stare until the table blurs. I'm about to graduate from college. Everything is supposed to be about beginnings and bright futures, but it looks like all my open roads are blocked. Even if I'm not pregnant and the roads reopen, I'm different already, and all the paths before me seem less glittery.

Ginny returns with a Coke for each of us.

I take a sip, hoping the soda will calm my stomach and nerves.

"I wanted him to ask me to marry him. I didn't plan this. I wasn't tricking him. But it happened, and I thought…"

"Men are pricks." She grabs for her smoke. "It's clear from what you just said he assumes you'll get an abortion."

I wince at the word. The world, or certainly women in the United States, are waiting for the courts to decide *Roe v. Wade*. If I do this, my only choice is illegally.

I take another sip, and everything dulls. I've been numb since I told Ephraim, like my body and mind don't know what to do with his quick-fix solution.

"He didn't mention marriage." The ten-minute conversation I'll remember forever tightens my throat. "He kept talking about how we're about to set off on our professional lives and how we're too young."

She rolls her eyes and takes a swig from her bottle. "You ain't the first girl to get pregnant accidentally, and you ain't gonna be the last. Do you have a plan?"

"I don't even have a rough draft. It's all I can do to act normal. I've done nothing but think. I haven't eaten, I haven't slept. And he hasn't called me."

I bite my lips at the worst part, the thing strangling my insides.

Her eyes narrow and harden. "I hate gutless pricks."

"He's not—"

"Don't you dare make excuses for him."

She's right. God, she's right, and I appreciate her stark truth and indignation. Up to now, I've been flailing, trying to keep my head above the dark water, and Ginny's offering me a life preserver.

"I've been waiting to come talk to you until after I missed my cycle. Now I have, and I'm—" A mess? Numb? Frantic? I'm a cocktail of all those adjectives.

Ginny leans across the table, her hand outstretched, and I grip it like I wanted Ephraim to hold mine.

"I'll help you if you need to find a doctor, but I'm not sure it's what you want."

I don't know what I want. Why don't I know what I want?

"Talking to you, telling someone, has helped."

And opening this first floodgate has given me the strength to go talk to the only other person who can help, the person I've been so afraid to tell. The person I'm terrified of disappointing.

"I need to go home. Right now. Talk to Aunt Gavina."

"Can you trust her?"

"Aunt Gavina's a vault. She'll help me think things through." I give Ginny's hand a last squeeze. "Thank you."

"What for? I didn't do anything."

Oh, but she has. She unclamped the vise I felt trapped in and freed a beat of hope.

"You listened to me and said you'd help me no matter what. You're pretty damned rad."

"If you say so. But you can't wait long."

I'm not waiting. I'm not packing a bag. I'm not wasting another minute getting to Magnolia Bloom.

"I'll make a decision by Sunday. I know I can't put this off long, if I need a doctor."

"I'll be here, no matter what you choose. Call me or come get me."

Ginny stands and snags her backpack from the ground, giving me a tight, understanding smile. She tosses back a, "Peace out," as she rounds the corner and disappears.

I practically run to the car, shut myself inside, and take my first full breath of the day. I turn the key, and my Vega chugs to life as I make my way off campus.

The ramp for I-35 sits just beyond the traffic light, and my spark of hope ignites as I head toward the only other person on the planet who will support and not judge me.

The only person who loves me completely. One hundred percent. Full stop.

The only person who can keep me from losing my mind.

CHAPTER FIFTEEN

PAIGE – NOW

THIRTY MINUTES LATER, Leith has driven us to town in the estate truck Brian has clearly assigned to him. Vivann herself, after offering me kind and heartfelt condolences, sits us at a quaint table on the glassed-in front deck. The location is perfect, having glorious air conditioning to mitigate the summer swelter, and the view is fabulous. The fabulousness sitting to my right, stirring things in me long stilled, is in blue jeans and a black T-shirt fitting in all the right places. The picture is enhanced by, but not limited to, the impressive biceps stretching the bands of his sleeves.

I have to make a decision, and quickly, about the giant ball of awareness and anxiety playing table tennis in my gut. Whether I want to deal with it isn't in question. I have to figure out exactly what permission I'm giving myself in regard to my behavior with Leith, and I can't avoid it for long.

I'm miffed about it, to be honest. Facing what my life will look like post-divorce is an obvious hurdle, but I didn't expect to contemplate it quite so quickly. Nothing is *happening* with Leith, I remind myself forcefully. A friendship hardly as old as the reduced-price bread in the bakery doesn't deserve that kind of pressure.

I look at the menu, a brilliant mix of artery-clogging favorites, as well as healthy alternatives Vivann created to tempt a few hard-liners away from the edge. Half the men in the room look like they need to keep portable defibrillators in their trucks. I decide on fried chicken salad and tomato bisque. My stomach wants comfort food, and I'm not arguing.

After we both take sips from the tall, ice-filled glasses Vivann's daughter brings, Leith smiles.

"You ken iced tea simply isn't a thing in Europe, aye?"

"How sad for you." I grab his wrist, making as pained an expression as I can manage. "Your lives really aren't worth living, are they?"

He chuckles. "Clearly, nae." He takes another sip, looks at the glass as though it's a divining rod, then shakes his head. "Thank you again for the tour and information. You're right, of course. There's so much more to see. The armory is amazing by itself, and yet it's just the start."

"I try to tell people it's like going to the Smithsonian. Or maybe the Metropolitan Museum of Art. I know that's not exactly apples-to-apples, but the point being there's too much to see in a day. A week, even. I've had the honor of having a lifetime to explore, and even I still find new things."

"Violet was a genius for insisting I stay at least a month. And considering I get a Highland games included in it all? It's perfect."

I take a deep breath, appreciating the scent of the teetering pile of onion rings being delivered one table over. "I love the games so much. Doing one in your country is on the same list as castle-hopping."

I butter a piece of baguette and let him take in the surroundings I've long taken for granted.

"Let's do the getting-to-know-you stuff. What brought you here, specifically? Is it just because you're friends with my cousin?"

"I'm an architect by trade, as you know, but I do architectural photography by hobby. Ian's told me for years about his daft American cousins and the castle in Texas. I asked him if he was wrecked, but he promised he hadnae so much as a dram of Glenfiddich. After showing me his full bottle of twelve-year, he told me Evajean MacInnes designed the castle in an age when such was unthinkable. How could I resist seeing for myself?"

"I'm not trying to be a party pooper, but Castle MacInnes has been in a few magazines, so you aren't the only one curious about the bonkers Americans."

"After my own daft clan, Americans are my favorite."

I have to laugh. It's impossible not to. "Good to know."

"So, tell me more about Austin. You said you live there?"

I nod. "Born there, actually, and ended up there for college after being dragged around by my father's Air Force career. He skipped both the stay-put and the Magnolia Bloom genes, leaving town twelve seconds after he and Mom said I do. I, on the other hand, am molecularly connected with the Magnolia Bloom."

"You've perfectly described my love of Glenfinnan, once the tourist rage passed. I dinnae live there anymore, but some places always remain more than lines in the address book of our lives."

"What a lovely way to say that. I think there's a poet hiding in you, Leith MacMaster."

"Only a bad one."

"I disagree, but to digress, why do I suspect you are not on the Harry Potter fan train?" I love the scenes in the movies where the Hogwarts Express transverses the Glenfinnan Viaduct, but I can see where the locals aren't so enamored.

He shrugs. "No spells or robes for me, and only a few ijits nearly lost their daft heads on the viaduct. The places I love were mostly spared being trampled by people with fake wands wanting to redo the final battle like some kind of SCA reenactors."

"Y'all have the SCA? Pretend lords and ladies and barons and baronesses?"

He hitches an eyebrow. "All our baronies are real, but aye. We have some of the pretenders, though not as many as here."

"You'll have to rib Mina and Fina about that. They were members of the SCA for years, and we still host big feasts and such every now and again. To tell you the truth, it's fun seeing everyone in their garb and watching all the dancing and such, but the accents are terrible. You could probably make a pretty penny as a dialect coach."

He shoots me a look of horror. "Och, no. I'll stick to architecture."

"Understood. I'm quite sure Magnolia Bloom and our lake are no Glenfinnan and a loch, but I understand how things can get spoiled by the best of intentions."

"Perceptive and beautiful. A powerful combination."

I have to shift my gaze. The interest in his eyes makes my stomach go clenchy. The still-healthy part of me would be lying if I said seeing light in a handsome man's face didn't cause a fizzy-bubbly sensation. I'm not looking for it, but the lovely warmth in my center that I haven't felt in a long time makes my unresolved dilemma about acceptable flirtation levels rear its head.

I pray none of this shows on my face.

"So, tell me about your wains. In the car, you mentioned Aiden and Ainsley, right? And grandchildren, which I still don't believe."

I can't keep surprise from my voice. "Excellent recall from a short conversation."

"My memory's dead brilliant for things sparking my interest."

I swallow and try to pretend nonchalance. "Both are married. Ainsley has two children, and Aiden has one. I adore both their partners. The whole kit and caboodle are the light of my life."

"Said like a true nana. And neatly packaged by a legal eagle."

"Paralegal, not attorney, but I'm done with the law. I have been for a while. Annnnd I'm bored. Tell me more about you."

"That short story isn't exactly riveting. I loved uni, love what I do. I've lived in six countries. Love traveling, which is why my accent is kind of all over the place."

I shake my head. "Like there's any one accent in any country. There's no 'American accent.' People from Boston are as American as anyone from Atlanta, and they might as well be from different planets linguistically. Right here in the great state of Texas, outsiders think we all talk like hicks, but I suppose stereotypes exist for a reason. So, I will proclaim your accent authentically Scottish."

He gives me a bow worthy of a lord at court. "Thank you, Madam.

However, my sisters love to give me shite about sounding Irish half the time because I lived in Dublin for nine years, but point being, a Glaswegian sounds quite different from an Aberdonian and many points in between."

Our lunch arrives, and I realize I'm hungrier than I thought. My crisp greens and perfectly browned chicken are exactly what I need, and clearly the chef did Leith's burger just right, because he digs in with relish.

I put my fork down before I embarrass myself and inhale every morsel.

"I have a standard American mutt accent because my Dad was in the Air Force, and I never lived anywhere longer than two years growing up. It not only informed my speech patterns, it made me allergic to traveling, except on vacation. For most of my adult years, I didn't care if I went farther from Austin than Magnolia Bloom. Now…"

I trail off, knowing the truth. My previous contentment to stay right where I am has been displaced by a searing desperation to run. Flee. Escape. And then I turn right back around, seeking what's familiar, what's comfortable, what I've spent a lifetime building.

Thankfully, Leith is not privy to, yet again, one of my whipsaws between what I want and what I think I'm supposed to want. It would be so easy if Zach were a giant jerk who did horrible things to hurt me. Instead, I remember the man who grew up with me, was my best friend, my confidant, my lover, and I think he's hurt himself the most of all. In a way, I'm the collateral damage.

Even if I spend a lot of time playing myself in an exhausting game of emotional tennis, the one thing I'm sure of is, things can't stay the same. I don't *want* a divorce. I don't *want* to lose him and the golden years I dreamed of sharing together. But I can't stay where I am.

For much longer, anyway.

Leith's voice draws me back from the abyss. "I wanted to see the world before I was forty. I didn't quite make it, but I'm done cuttin' about. Time to go home, stay a wee bit."

So just turned forty, eh? Older than I thought. Still, six or so years isn't too bad a spread—

What the hell is wrong with me?

"So that's why there's no one special waiting at home? Too much gallivanting?"

"Good a reason as any, aye?"

I barely have time to swallow a fresh bite when a female voice speaks right behind me.

"Paige? I'm glad to run into you."

I jump, bumping my spoon and sending bisque onto the pristine white tablecloth.

"Oh, my, I'm so sorry. I didn't mean to startle you."

I look at the thin woman whose face is as brittle as her hair. "Excuse me?"

"You don't remember me. I'm Madison, Pastor Crowder's wife. We're so sorry for your loss." Her sugarcoated tone indicates she's considering graciously forgiving me for not recognizing the honor of her presence.

I offer my hand out of an inbred courtesy I find hard to defy. Our handshake lasts less time than sorbet melting on August pavement. Her grip is the limp-fish style I despise.

"Aunt V did love the church." It's all I can manage without losing my forced smile.

"Is your husband here? It's Zachary, right?" She looks around the restaurant as if she expects him to be behind the server passing by.

"No." I offer nothing further, rearranging my plates in an obvious hint the conversation is over.

Leith looks at me and picks up a French fry from his platter, but he doesn't express the question in his eyes.

"And your children? A boy and a girl. Twins, right? Are they with you?"

An itch tickles at the base of my skull. Tidbits of scathing comments from Aunt V about the pastor's wife surface. I've given Madison exactly zero seconds of thought, but V's distaste clearly flavors the memories, and I've always trusted her impressions.

"No." My face is a rictus of politeness. I'm not about to give her any details about my family.

"What a shame. I know Miss Violet would have loved for them to be here when we send her off to the Lord's house."

I have the distinct impression Madison is certain she's in control of V's ingress into heaven, and the acid in my stomach churns. I refuse to affirm her assumption, and my tight smile offers no additional information.

Silence is my weapon of choice against nosy Rosies, and I unsheathe a saber. I'm not disappointed when Madison moves her gaze into the diner, and I don't miss the displeasure tightening her thin lips.

"It was so nice to see you, Paige. I'll see you Saturday at the viewing. I'll tell Harville to come visit you. He's a wonderful comforter and counselor."

"That's quite all right. I'll give him a call later to discuss the service, but there's no need for him to interrupt his day to come over."

"Oh, no, he—"

"It's quite all right." My tone is so firm even Clueless here can't miss it.

"Well..." Madison clears her throat. "Well, I see my lunch guest has arrived. You have a nice day, y'hear?"

She escapes before I have a chance to insert an introduction to Leith, who mumbles something I didn't catch.

"Sorry?" I lift an eyebrow.

"I cannae repeat it in front of a lady, but that wench is a bit much."

"I love understatement, but I don't want to talk about Mrs. Pastor Crowder, whose husband is a nice man, by the way."

"I can't imagine Ms. Violet liking someone who isn't." He picks up his glass and tips the rim at me. "Now, where were we?"

I catch a drop of sweat slowly gliding down my tea glass on my fingertip. I use the time to rub the cool bead between my fingers and recall our conversation and the side trails my thoughts seem to find with too much ease.

"We were talking about you being a world-traveling lothario who steals women's hearts, then races off to the nearest airport or dock."

He barks a laugh, and his face lights up, the smile curving those too-sexy lips and tipping eyes such an incredible shade of blue that Pantone is surely begging him to let them license it. The color card would say *Perfect Blue*. Maybe *Sexy Blue*. Or maybe *blue guaranteed to make a grown woman act dazed and confused*.

"That's what we were saying, is it? I'll take your word, but my memory must be mince, which is why I don't remember anything about you being married."

"I told you about kids and grandkids and—"

"Which don't require marriage."

I wobble my head in a yes-no. "True. I wasn't hiding it. Intentionally, anyway. I guess I'm avoiding the subject. My husband, Zach, and I...I'm filing for divorce."

"I'm sorry. Truly. It's hard, even if it's the right thing." He takes a bite of burger to stall. "I don't mean to be a neb."

"You're not prying." I'm pleased my Scottish-slang-to-English is kicking in. "It's a logical curiosity, and truth is, things have been coming to an end for a long time. I didn't pull the trigger, so to speak, until very recently. We are...were...coming around the bend on thirty years."

"History isn't always enough."

His voice tells me he understands, and I appreciate the sympathy.

"I know. The hard part is, Zach's a great guy. We've had a lot of good years. He's a great father and grandfather."

"Well, damn me, then." Leith adds a twitch to one side of his mouth.

"Pardon?"

"I wanted you to say he's a right scunner so I could hate him and offer you my shoulder for comfort."

His smile is open, teasing. Something behind his eyes, though, tells me his flirtation is more than casual but not improper.

Yet.

I push the thought away, refusing to believe whatever has my imagination in overdrive.

"You, Leith MacMaster, are a flirt."

"Och, aye, I cannae deny it."

I honk a laugh and clap a hand over my mouth, embarrassed at the looks I earn from around the room.

"But Mum would be proud I made you smile when you're so sad."

I touch his arm for the briefest second. "You're very sweet."

He covers my hand with his and gives my fingers a squeeze. "I'm happy to be your knight in shining armor any time."

We return to our respective lunches, but I'm rattled by what's occurred. I know I can't speak for him, because every word of our conversation, every glance between us, is completely proper for the rest of our meal, yet they leave me a few degrees further off kilter.

By the time we've finished our excellent meal, I've regained my equilibrium. Leith gallantly refuses to let me pay and, with old-world manners, escorts me to the door. He holds it while I lead the way out, but the sound of feminine voices forces him to remain doorman to none other than Madison and her lunch companion. Everyone stops around me on the sidewalk.

"Paige, this is my friend Bonnie, who's moved here from Dallas. You and she have so much in common. She has a daughter a bit younger than your Ainsley. I was hoping to introduce you two, and I'd love to be introduced to this handsome young man."

Leith offers only silence, and even I'm uncomfortable.

Madison has the grace to look chagrined, but she plunges on. "Are you here for the services for Miss Violet?"

"Partly."

For some reason, I take pity on Madison and smile at Bonnie from Dallas only to realize she's all but devouring Leith with her eyes. My blood pressure rises more than my ire at Madison. Quick as a flash, Bonnie turns her full attention to me.

"I love the castle." Her breathless exuberance is grating, irritating me almost as much as her grabbing my hand even though I didn't offer it. "I'm so jealous you live there."

I cough a laugh. "Well, I don't, but it's pretty amazing."

"I would love to come see it sometime."

I'm a bit disconcerted and reclaim my hand with a tug. "Call the office. There are public tours most weeks when we don't have fully booked events."

"Oh, I don't mean the ballroom. I want to see the private stuff and the servants' quarters and all. I'm a huge *Downton Abbey* fan." She smiles at me like I should understand.

I'm afraid I'm in for tooth damage if I spend much more time in the company of Madison and Bonnie. I relax my jaw so I can put an end to the awkward moment. "We haven't had servants in many, many decades, and the family suites are family-only. Give the office a call, and they'll be happy to help."

I look at Leith, hoping he knows the hardness settling over my expression is in no way directed at him. "We have to go."

I do an about-face and head in the opposite direction of the truck Leith's using. It's ridiculous, I know, but I'm not stepping around Madison's blockade on the sidewalk. If she thinks I'll play power escalation with her, she's got another think coming. Kase would be disappointed I didn't take a stripe off the busybodies, but some people are not worth my energy.

Leith, bless him, follows me without missing a beat and comes up beside me as we take the long way around the building.

He opens the passenger door and lets me settle in. "I'm sorry about all that."

"Why? You didnae do anything wrong."

"I don't know why I'm reacting so horribly to Madison. Maybe it's from things Violet said in passing these last few years, but regardless, I'm sorry you've gotten a bad first impression of Magnolia Bloom."

"My first impression is a bonnie lass, and I like her fine."

My breath whooshes out of me. I'm afraid I'm in danger of an emotional concussion. I've also had about as much as I can deal with for one day, and it's barely afternoon.

"Let's get you home."

Leith pulls out smoothly, and it's mere moments before I'm waving from the path by the kitchen as he drives away. I wait until he's out of my line of sight to press my hand against my forehead to check for a fever. I didn't ask him what his plans are for the afternoon, and now he's gone. I'm both disappointed I don't know and astounded I care.

I've hardly taken five steps down the path when my phone buzzes.

Zach: Problem with the rollout. May be late Friday.

Oh, thank God.

Me: No problem. Stay in Austin if you need to.

A pause, then another ping.

Zach: No, I can still make it.

Dammit...

Despite my forehead feeling cool, it's clear I'm coming down with something. It's the only explanation for the bizarre leaps I've been making. I haven't had time to consider life post-divorce. Honestly, I haven't looked at another man with thoughts of anything more complicated than friendship in thirty years, so at the least I'm inexperienced. At the most, my fireplace is swept clean.

Which might be the crux of what's wrong with me. There's an ember hanging on inside my ain't-dead-yet lady parts, a hope for a better future.

And Leith's standing offstage with a bottle of lighter fluid.

CHAPTER SIXTEEN

MINA – NOW

"Momma? You up here?"

I hear Trey's voice and hurry out of the portrait gallery into the long hall, a duster in one hand and a can of Pledge in the other.

"Here, baby."

He whips around toward my voice. We meet in the open family room, and he wraps me in a hug guaranteed to feed my soul.

"Good God, Momma, weren't you dusting the last time I was here? And the time before?"

My scowl is more of a smile. "I could have worse obsessions, you know. And it's cheaper than therapy, so you hush and let me be. Truth is, I was talking with Miss Evajean, and you interrupted me."

Trey's eyes twinkle, a trait I've always loved about him. "How is the castle matriarch today?"

"She's in a mood, if you must know. Mostly about people interrupting her while she's got things to do."

"Far be it from me to keep you two from your conversation. I swear, someday I'm gonna come up here and die of fright to find her stepped down from her picture and chatting with you like it's Sunday brunch."

I force myself not to smile. "What makes you so sure she doesn't?"

Trey bends to kiss my forehead. The one thing he got from the useless waste of oxygen named Roylee was height, so I guess I have to count that under silver linings.

"I won't keep you from your gossiping, then." He teases so I'll sputter.

Which I do. I pretend to spray him with lemon-scented polish, and he holds up his hands in surrender.

"I'm here to drop off the spreadsheets you wanted."

"You could've emailed them."

"And then I wouldn't have gotten a hug, so it's an excellent investment of time and gas."

I look at the man who isn't especially muscular but is especially kind. And especially handsome, in my eyes. I will go to my grave grateful Trey takes after my daddy in every important trait.

Intelligence. Kindness. Generosity.

A man who'd die before he'd cause a bruise on a woman, inside or out.

Oh, I know he's not perfect. I'm his momma, but I'm not blind. Still, Trey's the opposite of the man who provided half his DNA. He might not keep girlfriends for too long, but I've never heard a harsh word through the gossip mill from any of them.

I shake the Yahtzee cup of my thoughts to put them in a different order.

He follows me down the hall to my office, and I put the cleaning supplies on my desk. I'm sure I could have claimed turret space like Violet and Fina, but I'm just fine with my little niche in spitting distance of the family kitchen. Makes it convenient when an event's in full swing, keeping me closer to the action.

Trey hands me the papers and a thumb drive, and I add them to my in-box.

"You hungry? I can make you a sandwich."

"I'm good. I came by to check on you, is all. You can't blame me for worrying. I loved Miss Violet, but nothing like you and Neenie."

I smile at his nickname for his aunt. She about melted the first time *Fina* came out *Neenie*. If memory serves, he was just three, but it stuck.

"We're both making do, just sad. To be expected." I cock my head when a memory strikes. "So how's Angelina? Busted her ankle, Fina said?"

"She's...fine."

There's something in his voice I can't place. It's almost like he's peeved, but I'm not convinced I've got it right. I want to ask, but I stop myself from interfering.

"I have to pick up a prescription for some pain pills from Doc, then ice cream from the market."

The mere mention of the market brings CT's smile to my mind and trips up my heart. I turn away for a second to hide my reaction.

The good thing is, sons don't tend to be particularly tuned in to their mother's blushes. His obliviousness also allows me to hide the frown compressing my mouth. Trey has had girlfriends I've liked, but Angelina is grating on my last nerve. I've always admired my son for his kind nature, despite the trauma we never talk about, but sometimes I worry he's too nice. I've seen him mad, but I've never seen him act on it. He tends to stay on the agreeable end of the spectrum at all costs.

Fina's arrival makes us both turn. "Well, hello, Trey. What're you doing here? I thought you were burning the midnight oil these days as Magnolia Bloom's most-sought-after attorney."

He kisses her cheek. "Hi, Neenie. I don't need to remind you I'm Magnolia Bloom's only lawyer, but I'm not here to discuss my caseload. I'm too busy interrupting Momma's conversation with Miss Evajean."

Hmmm. He skips right over the work question, and my internal mother's radar goes off.

Without batting an eyelash, Fina turns to me. "Did she have any interesting insights today?"

"Nothing special. We talked about having nosy siblings and being abandoned by our young."

I watch two of my favorite people carry on in a way usually guaranteed to lighten my spirit, but my intuition says Trey's about to sink knee-deep into trouble. It's hard to force myself not to pry. He's plenty old enough to ask me if he needs my help, but try telling my maternal genes.

Fina tips her head in my direction but speaks to Trey. "Do you happen to know where your mother left her phone? She was so busy flirting with our neighborhood grocer, she's gone and lost it. Again."

Trey raises both eyebrows at me. "Momma? Flirting? Now that's two words I'd a never thought to hear together."

To my shock, I hear myself get sassy instead of denying it. "Well, goes to show you might not be as smart as all those diplomas on your wall indicate."

"I'll accept being taken down a peg or two any day if it's by news this good."

I stop with my one attempt at being funny. I've never given a second of thought about how Trey would feel about me dating, as I don't date and don't intend to start. Still, it's awfully sweet to know I have his approval.

Trey chats with Fina for a moment longer, and if they include me in any more teasing, I don't notice. It all leads to hugs and goodbyes, and just like that, I'm alone again with my rag and my Pledge.

Something nags at me, and I can't place it. It's not Trey's girlfriend issues, although I'll need to keep half an eye on this new one. It's not Fina, either. She loves Trey like her own, and he's gotten two moms for the price of one. I don't normally dwell on the past, but the fact I'm the reason Fina never had children of her own is a bitter pill I still swallow. She's never blamed me, and she's certainly never blamed Trey, but she gave up the young man who loved her but wasn't willing to settle in Magnolia Bloom. Fina wouldn't leave me—unmarried, pregnant, bruised, and scared.

My dangerous situation went from bad to worse for years. Until Trey nearly paid the ultimate price for my cowardice. Still, Fina stayed, keeping all the secrets with a tight-lipped ferocity I will always love her for. But the nagging I can't figure out isn't about my sister. Or my son.

No, it's about me, and I blame Joy Baker and her meddling at the market for addling my senses. I tell myself I'm too busy to dig into nonsense and head for the gallery and my unfinished duties.

CHAPTER SEVENTEEN

PAIGE – NOW

THE REST of the day yesterday passed in a blur, and I have to think for a minute to register it's Friday. I've had another full day of grieving, but I've managed not to cry as often while I fill boxes with V's clothes to get them ready for the different charities in town. It's kept me busy, along with remembering dinner last night with Mina, Fina, and Leith, where I didn't do a thing but laugh at his anecdotes about my Scottish cousins, meaning all I've thought about today is visiting Scotland.

Going to my ancestral land has always been on my list. I want to go to France, as well, as that's Evajean's heritage, but Scotland has always called me with a strong thrum. I told Leith about wanting to visit castles and lochs and meet any of the hundreds of kin I can claim. He's offered to escort me any time, which had me staying up half the night putting together sample itineraries in my TripIt app. I'd need a year and all of my savings to complete a portion of the folders I created, but that's the thing about the internet. You can dream all you want, and it doesn't cost a dime.

Zach teased me about my apps and my hard copies, about how detailed our dive excursions or other vacations were, but I defended myself by reminding him I was always willing to diverge from my spreadsheet if we ever felt so inclined.

Those unexpected choices were the parts of the trips I loved most. What I called having an adventure. It didn't matter where we were or what we were doing. It mattered only that I was with him.

I force my mind away from such dangerous thoughts. I can't let myself fall into the temptation of canonizing the past. Those memories are wonderful and can never be taken from me, but I can't let myself dwell on them. None of it changes the fact my present doesn't include the laughing, smiling, playful man of those special times. I'd give a lot to have him back, but it's clear I don't get to make that call.

After checking the time, I get cleaned up and make it down to the front salon for my duty of greeting guests for the informal gathering tonight. This event space is one of the more popular because Penny keeps sentry over everyone entering or leaving through the oversize glass door. It's more intimate than the main ballroom, and of course, the drive around Penny's fountain for drop-off is half the experience.

Every time I imagine the sound of tires on the gravel, the bottom drops out of my stomach. I've checked my phone a hundred times, hoping to see a text from Zach saying he can't make it after all so I can graciously reply I forgive him. Not in those words, of course, merely a carefully crafted absolution.

I love being magnanimous.

I've barely started my chores when I hear one of the interior doors creak.

"Paige? You in here?" That's the thing about doors in a castle. Even the well-tended ones can't help but shift, swelling and contracting with the seasons and the humidity, so Castle MacInnes probably accounts for a sizable portion of WD-40's profit margin all by itself.

I smile and twist my head around. "Over here, Mina. Taking care of the tablecloths."

We have no idea how many will stop by, so I've covered two long rectangular tables for serving and have four of the large rounds for sitting ready to go. We won't have anyone over after the viewing tomorrow, then Sunday we'll meet at the fellowship hall after the official funeral. Tonight is for those who want to visit the castle and chat. No agendas, no schedules.

I follow the sound of her pointed-toe shoes clipping over the hardwood floor. A glance at her newest Ferragamos makes me jealous. I suppose they could be Prada or Jimmy Choos, but it's unlikely.

It's a detail I love about Mina. She's the absolute salt of the earth and unfussy in every way, except for her love of Italian leather. She's worn Ferragamos for as long as I can remember and has every color of ballet flat. I doubt Mina's ever worn a bow in her hair in her life, but the same can't be said for her shoes.

"Why do they call it a viewing when the deceased is cremated?" I mumble around the hairclip between my teeth.

I'm scraping my hair back with my fingers and hoping the look I achieve is a casual I-woke-up-like-this and not good-God-woman-get-to-a-salon.

She shakes her head. "Lord, I don't know. It's gettin' now to where no one gets buried in a coffin anymore."

"That's a trend I can get behind. I'm considering being a tree. Or part of the manmade coral reef off of Florida."

"I like the tree idea. No, thank you on the other."

"Let's hope it's a long, long time before you have to worry about it."

She catches the end of the tablecloth I flip at her, and we make quick work of the remaining tables.

"That's that, then. Let's get the food out."

We join arms and head to the big kitchen. As if she arranged it, the brakes of an approaching vehicle squeak, and the quick toot of a horn sounds. To my stomach's delight, I walk outside, and it's not Zach's Tesla greeting me, but what I now think of as Leith's truck. He climbs out, and it's like my blood's turned to champagne. I'm bubbly. Not a civilized flute, but more a giant stein's worth.

"Hallo."

An absurd giggle nearly escapes, but I strangle it down. A giggle? What am I, twelve?

"Hello, yourself. What are you doing here?"

Leith tips his head toward his truck. "Ms. Fina accepted my offer to help and asked me to bring the food. She's at the church and said she'll be over in a thrice."

"It's a good thing the castle has several refrigerators."

"Indeed. I might live several thousand miles away, but whether it's a Scottish kirk or a Texas church, the ladies go into overdrive for weddings and funerals."

I move toward the truck. "For sure. Can I help?"

"Absolutely." He opens the door of the crew cab and hands me a box. I count three more, and since I can barely see over the side of the truck, there's no telling what might be in the bed.

Mina and I make several trips, with Leith's help, and the salon quickly starts to smell of all things Southern. In other words, Eau de Love. Casseroles. Side dishes. Deviled eggs. Gallons of tea—sweet, of course. Three-liter bottles of soda. Cups. Cutlery. Plates. Napkins.

It's a dragon's hoard of home-cooked heaven with the exception of one bowl filled with a mysterious mound so green the food coloring must be chlorophyll. The Jell-O salads are shaky and neon, but I was raised on Knox Blox, and I survived. The crowd will, too.

I quiet my internal Judgy MacJudgerson. Caring is cooked into every single calorie, and I am grateful for the kindness, if not the stress on my waistband.

"The pastor said he'd be here around seven," Leith says. "His beloved notwithstanding, he seems to be a nice man."

Leith gives me the yes-please head bob when I offer him a pecan brownie from the plate I uncovered.

"I'm glad he has your endorsement. Coffee?"

I head for the fifty-cup chafer urn releasing the smell of Southern pecan roast into the room.

"Aye, please. Black."

I make us each a cup and return as Mina is bustling between the tables, setting out napkin holders and condiment carriers. Hopefully, everyone will come hungry.

The opening of the front door causes all our heads to turn, and I move to welcome the first guest of the evening.

"Kase! I thought you couldn't come."

"The other side needed to push the meeting to Monday, so here I am."

"And I'm so happy I'm beside myself. Come on in."

I let the door go so the hydraulic and spring hinge can shut out the heat. I know these terms because I've heard V mutter about repair costs and labor hours.

It's one of the many bits of castle minutiae crossing my mind lately.

"You plan on introducing me?" Kase shifts a shoulder toward Leith, who's stood. I give an internal sigh as I see the blinded look in his eyes.

I make quick work of the Kase-Leith, Leith-Kase and refuse to fall prey to pissiness at his star-struck expression. I'm used to invisibility with men when Kase walks into a room. Hell, I'm transparent to women, too.

To his credit, Leith regains his equanimity and returns to his normal, affable self. I can't quite explain why it matters, and I don't want to dissect my moment of pique.

The arrival of Pastor Crowder saves me, and as I invite him inside, I'm certain my memory and Leith are both right. He insists I call him Harville, and he is indeed a nice man. I've barely gotten him a cup of coffee before he asks if we might speak alone for a moment. Surprised and fighting a sense of trepidation, I follow him outside, and he waits until I've taken a seat on the stone wall protecting Penny before he settles to my right. The fountain tosses water high into the air, but we're far enough away to escape a dousing.

"Is there anything I can do for you before the viewing tomorrow?"

An innocuous enough lead-in. "It's kind of you to want to meet with me, but I know you have V's final wishes."

"I do, and they'll be honored. I want you to know if you need peace, at the church, please come to my office."

"The offer is sweet, but I'll be strengthened knowing how loved V was."

"She was indeed. I'll miss her fiercely, and now I don't know where I'll find decent chicken 'n' dumplings."

I chuckle as he expects. "I can give you the recipe, if you'd like."

A shadow passes over his face so quickly I almost miss it before a bright smile claims his mouth. "Fantastic! I always thought Miss Violet would take it with her through the pearly gates."

"She left her prized recipe box with instructions. She said since she isn't around to see anyone mess them up, I can hand them out to anyone who asks."

"That's our Miss Violet."

I look at the man married to Madison Crowder and find the image incongruent. My memories of our brief hellos were nearly derailed by my unfortunate encounter with Madison, and I'm glad to see Pastor Crowder is both exactly what I expected to find in a small-town preacher, and yet nothing like the box I constructed for him. He is tall, slim, carefully dressed, and confident, but softly spoken. Unexpected is the intense kindness he radiates, and I truly believe he's concerned for me. Maybe it's completely unfair, but I guess I was expecting a fixed smile and barely hidden impatience to get a job done.

I can see now, though, why V shared delightful tales about the new pastor and how much he's revitalized the dwindling congregation. They've had to hire a separate youth minister to handle the growing younger crowd.

I glance at my watch, not wanting to be *that person* doing the oh-my-look-at-the-time act, but I need to tend to the growing crowd. "You've been quite gracious."

"It's my pleasure, and I hope you know you can call on me any time. To talk. Anything."

There's an easing in my stomach. Nothing huge. More a hint of comfort knowing he'll make tomorrow lighter with his kind presence.

"Before I go, though, I need to complete one of V's final orders."

I stop midrise and resettle, curiosity overwhelming me. He stands and moves to his car, which I now notice is in the driveway. He returns with a clear plastic storage tub. It looks to be filled with books.

"These are your aunt's journals." He notes surprise on my face and clarifies. "These are the early years of her journals. The rest of them are in her office in the East Turret. She said I was the only person she trusted to bring these to you. Unread."

Images of hours spent with V in the turret flood me. I loved the space she created more than any other place on the estate. The round room became half office, half private library and an island of patterned rugs and overstuffed furniture. It was my Aladdin's cave of seclusion, my escape. And I know exactly where V would have put the rest of her writings.

"These are different." He pauses, weighing his words. "She said you're not to read them until after the funeral, and she hoped you'll not think badly of her for things she did in the past."

"Now I'm really curious. Weren't you?"

"Strangely, no. Oh, a little, since I must be honest, but not nearly enough to make me want to, one, disobey her request, and two, risk changing my opinion of a truly amazing woman. I want to believe nothing I read could do that, but I am human."

"And so was V. We tend to canonize the dead pretty quickly, but as much as I love her, I know she wasn't perfect and have never expected her to be."

"Which is a good thing."

For a moment, I'm completely sure he's thinking about something else, but his face clears, and his genuine smile returns. "If it's all right, I'll take them to her...your suite."

"I'll do it. It's quite a hike there and back."

He gives me a typical, Southern gentleman frown. "Absolutely not. I'll put it inside the door, if it's open."

"It is. And thank you."

"Keep some coffee warm for me." The box looks heavy, but he lifts it with ease, and I have one more surprise bit of information about the kind pastor.

"Will do."

He heads up the main staircase, clearly familiar with the layout of the castle. I put my curiosity aside, and before I can do more than check on Kase's merger, the arrivals begin. In no time, I'm pulled into the stream of conversations happening around the room.

Less than ten minutes later, Harville slips back into the salon and is pulled into a different eddy before making a gracious exit. I realize I have to eat a pretty big piece of humble pie. I previously judged the man based on my dissonance with organized religion, and I was grossly unfair.

I put aside my worries about the pastor and make more rounds. I remember a few of Violet's close friends, but most of the ladies and all of the gentlemen are strangers. To them, I'm Violet's Paige. Ergo, they've known me all of my life, too. They ask about Aiden and Ainsley, Chen, Richard, Marceau, Callum, and Belle. And Zach, usually as an afterthought, but often enough to make a guilt I don't consider fair ride herd on me the entire evening.

I look around the now full room. The dense fog of sadness cloaking me gains a hurricane's worth of rain. These people all love me because V loved me. Oh, not in the same way, but I definitely benefited from reflected kindness.

I've barely convinced myself I'm a mere half hour from a glass of wine with Kase and an early bedtime when the door swings wide once again. I'm slack-jawed when my sister walks into the room, rumpled, still in her BDUs. Her rich black hair is pulled in a tight bun, and she has her cap in her hand.

"You got here."

She laughs and hugs me tight. "Nothing escapes your steel-trap mind."

"I'm cursed with yet another comedian. I thought you couldn't make it."

"The military in a nutshell. No is no until it's yes."

I've only been a dependent, but even I know that's the sad truth. "I'm not complaining. Did you talk to Mom and Dad?"

"They should be on the ground in Dallas about now. They're probably close to their hotel as we speak."

"You didn't want to stay with them and come in tomorrow?"

She looks at me like I've lost my mind. "Seriously? I have a chance to spend an extra few hours with my favorite sister, and I'd stay in a hotel room?"

"I'm your only sister," I remind her dryly.

"Yeah, but I need the wisdom provided by your advanced age."

Kase moves beside me in time to hear my sister's jibe. "Don't be mean to the elderly, Kiki."

"Sorry. My bad." My exuberant sister hugs Kase as if she's her best friend and not mine, then turns her tired eyes on me. "Got room for a weary protector of the free world?"

"Let me think." I pretend to concentrate fiercely, tapping my chin. "There are no events at the moment, we have twenty guest rooms in the castle proper, and Fam Two and Manor One are empty." I give my head a sad shake. "Can't squeeze you in. Sorry."

She gives Kase a help-me look.

I give my sister a nudge. "I'm in Fam One, of course. Come in and say hi before we head up. Kase and I were just about to jet."

She glances past me at the reduced but still robust crowd. Her pinched expression causes a rumble of concern.

"Something wrong?"

"I'm not ready to be sociable. I left my duffel outside, so I'll grab it and head for the apartment. Take a shower while you finish up."

"Go. Transmogrify. Kase and I'll meet you on the balcony with a bottle of wine."

Her smile goes strained, then brightens. "Do you have any mineral water?"

"Sure. There's a case in the pantry. You know V loved it."

"Perfect. I'll see you in a few."

The crowd thins naturally over the next half hour, and Kase helps me urge the lollygaggers to go. I'm surprised but delighted when Leith stays and takes charge of the clean-up duties, then wishes me and my bestie good night.

We move side by side into the grand foyer, pausing at the bottom of the imperial staircase, where Kase gives an awed headshake.

"You know, I've been here a dozen times, probably more, and this never fails to wow me."

"I've been here a million, lived here, and it never gets old."

Our heels click on the marble of the steps, and we stop on the half landing to look up at the French chandelier Evajean's stepmother gifted the couple after the castle was complete. I know from V's research Evajean and her father's second wife were never close, but they repaired their strained relationship over time, and the priceless crystals above us are certainly a nice indication they mended fences.

We continue onto the carpet runners on the second floor to my new digs. I pick up the box Harville left, as he'd said he would, and grunt.

"Do you need help?"

"I got it. It's V's diaries, delivered CIA-like by Harville." I strain and move the box out of the way.

"Oooh! Mystery."

"I've been given orders not to read them until after the funeral, so I'm both intrigued and scared, but I'll honor her wishes."

We kick off our shoes and sink into opposite ends of the sofa.

I flex and extend my toes with a groan. "Does it make me horrible to say I'm glad that's over?"

Kase runs her hand over the simple log cabin quilt I haven't moved from the couch. Simple in design, perfect in execution.

"Of course it does. You're a horrible, evil person and earned yourself several more lifetimes of servitude and drudgery."

"Good to know. I was worried I'd misjudged."

"Misjudged what?" Kiki asks from the hall archway.

"How horrible a human being your sister is." Kase deadpans her pronouncement.

Kiki shrugs. "This is news?"

I give both of them a dirty look and change the subject. "You don't look like the same person."

It's not a toss-off statement. Her fatigues make Kiki look badass, but her gray sleep pants and oversize purple T-shirt with *Adult-ish* emblazoned on the front show a woman who's exhausted and… defeated. Her midnight hair is damp, many shades darker than my brown, but her defiant strands are trying to pull up into her natural wave. A wave she curses and one I had to pay a salon hundreds of dollars to achieve back in the day when I was willing to endure perm rods and hours of chemical stench.

Kiki is like Kase. A natural, easy beauty who doesn't realize how put together she is with such little effort. I missed out on those genes, but it's useless to mention it. She'll focus on me and miss the point.

"Come on, you two. Outside on the balcony for a quick update, then bedtime."

I'm hoping playing hostess for a few more minutes will distract me from the increasing *Jumanji* call from the box in the entry hall.

CHAPTER EIGHTEEN

VIOLET – 1971

I'M MORE tired than I expected when I hit Magnolia Bloom. Other than two stops at Dairy Queens for root beer and bathroom breaks, I've been defying the speed limit and praying I wouldn't get pulled over.

Maybe God is feeling guilty about the shit hand I'm holding, but whatever the reason, I make it home without a ticket. Which is a good thing, because Daddy says he's not paying any more of them.

As I pull through the front property gates, the castle is lit up like a beacon, impressive in the early evening, but a breathtaking sight once the sky is dark. I have to stop because I'm smiling and crying at the same time. There's enough breeze to flutter the Texas flag off to the left, and with the spotlight below, it makes me proud for the thousandth time. I suppose it will for a million more.

The full light-up's a signal a big shindig is in store, and I regret having to skip a drive under the portcullis and a spin around Penny's fountain. Stopping by to touch Penny's nose is as much a ritual as stopping in the kitchen to grab a bite of whatever amazing thing Mrs. Greene's making. From when I was a kid, I'd talk to Penny, and while she never responds, sitting on the gray stones surrounding the fountain, the sun refracting through the spray cascading over her has occupied a lot of my time. Penny's a constant, her curled body, flared wings, head resting on her front leg always the same. She's dependability. Strength. Protection.

I put the car in gear and curve left until I see the door to the kitchen, one of the last locked at night. I'm glad Mrs. Greene isn't in the brightly lit room when I breeze through and all I have to do is fake a smile at a girl who looks a few years younger than me chopping celery at the large sideboard.

As I hurry to Gavina's rooms in Fam One, I'm a mixed bag of nearly vibrating out of my skin and wondering if my legs are filled with lead. The suite, and its twin Fam Two, are part myth and part practicality. I've stayed with Gavina so many times over the last few years, the mystery is gone and it's her home now. Both suites are reserved for the eldest direct descendants of Evajean and Alisdair's firstborn, and the three manor houses are given to family members who stay on the estate. It's a chart as complicated as any royal hierarchy, and I'm glad I'm not the one who has to monitor it.

I stop outside the door, staring at the doorbell nestled inside the scrollwork frame. My eyes sting, and my throat's tight, but I stuff down the overwhelming urge to cry. What if I'm wrong? What if she isn't as cool as I've believed for so long? What if she tells me to go lie in the bed I've made?

My fingers shake so hard I miss the button the first time, then I jab it with determination. I can't endure any more. If she sends me away, so be it. Better to know now.

I hear the four-note chime, muffled by the heavy door, but the notes are clear enough to make my stomach churn harder. For a moment, I consider racing to the nearest bathroom and hurling up my root beer.

Before I can jet, the door opens. Gavina takes one look at my face, drops the book she's holding to the floor, and pulls me to her with both hands.

She shifts enough so I can come in and kick the door closed, shutting the world out. In the safety of her embrace, my sobs come as heaves, starting at the bottom of my soul and pulling from every atom of my being.

She lets me get it out. No shushing. No *now, nows.* Her hand smooths my hair, then goes to my back, as though she's making sure my heart doesn't try to escape.

I have no idea how long we stand there, but eventually she leads me to her living area and hands me tissues. She moves to her bathroom to wet a washrag, returning to offer me the cool cloth to clean my face and soothe my fevered skin.

She waits for the hiccoughing to slow and it appears I might have some voice. "You ready to talk, or do you want me to fix some tea?"

I manage a warbled laugh. "Both?"

"All right, then, come on."

I follow her into the tiny kitchen with enough counter space and a two-burner stove she can fix her meals when she chooses not to go to the family dining room. The kettle's on the burner, and cups are already on the small counter before I take a seat on one of the tall stools on the other side of the breakfast bar.

Gavina reaches out, and I relinquish the washrag, which she rinses and returns so I can press it against my puffy eyes.

The tears are more slow rain than torrential downpour now.

No sense hemming and hawing. "I'm pregnant."

"I figured it had to be something pretty big."

I drop my head. "I'm so sorry. I'm such a screw-up."

Moving around to my side, she takes my shoulders. "You stop, you hear me? You aren't the first woman to face an unintended pregnancy, and you won't be the last."

"Ginny said the exact same thing." Something eases in my chest the tiniest bit, knowing two women I admire share the same sentiment.

"Ginny Tilson? Tidy's sister?"

I forgot she has no way or need to know all the players in my life, despite the endless hours I talk to her. "She's at UT, finishing graduate school. She's been awesome."

"I don't remember much about her. I know Tidy more, of course, because of y'all's friendship." She fishes in her compact refrigerator for milk. She takes lemon and sugar in her tea. I prefer cream and sugar. Right now, I'd drink vinegar if it means being with Gavina.

"Want to give me the details?" She putters with the sugar dish, slices a lemon, opens the drawer for spoons.

"The short version is I was with Ephraim in South Padre over spring break, and we had a birth control failure."

"So you know exactly when it happened."

I don't have to spell it out for her. "I'm three weeks, almost to the day."

The kettle whistles. Gavina turns and efficiently makes us perfect cups of tea. We're in the living room before she asks anything more, me with my sneakers off and feet tucked underneath me. She's in her favorite overstuffed armchair, a pile of books on the table beside her.

"Do you know what you want to do?" She takes a sip from her china cup. "And what does your young man say?"

My *young man*. Her words for him are so impersonal, but like with Ginny, I don't dare challenge her opinion. She's never liked Ephraim, and her disdain is entirely based on her perceptions of his treatment of me. And I have no evidence to refute her anymore.

I put my saucer on the coffee table and wind my fingers together, burying my fists between my knees.

"I don't have a young man anymore. His only suggestion was to get rid of it. He offered me money." My voice cracks with sadness, and I suck down the urge to cry again.

Gavina winces, then shakes her head. "Is that what you want?"

I wish I knew. I've asked and asked myself and tried to sort through my options. My thoughts go to static, and I have no rabbit ears to adjust to correct the blurred screen in my mind.

"I don't know anything yet. It's all so new and scary. Some minutes, it's so real I'm crushed under the weight of it all. The next, it's surreal and a nightmare I'm going to wake up from."

"I'm guessing you haven't told your mom and dad yet."

The blood drains from my face so fast I'm lightheaded. "I can't. They'll hate me."

"They'll never hate you. They love you."

I shake my head, the movement frantic. "Daddy will be devastated. He'll never love me again."

Gavina pushes out of her chair and joins me on the couch, angling herself so one arm is behind me. With the other hand, she pushes the hair off my face and tucks it behind my ear.

"I wish I could tell you he won't be disappointed, but it's not the same as not loving you anymore. You don't have to make a decision today, but whatever you want to do, it has to be soon."

"Do you think I should have an…get an…terminate?" I don't care if it's 1971 and I'm a woman of the second feminist wave. The A word in the abstract is fine, something I believe all women have the right to.

Except when the woman is me.

"Love, I can't decide for you. If it's what you want, we'll figure it out, but it's not your sole option."

When Gavina cups my face in her palm, I press my cheek into the warmth and believe, for a moment, everything might be okay.

Someday.

She releases me and takes my hand in hers. "Let's talk about logistics. If you want to terminate, we have to see a doctor quickly."

"Ginny knows some people. She said she could help me."

"Good. I also know a few other resources, so option one is covered. Option two is you keep the baby. We go talk to your folks and figure out how."

Terror strikes deep in my gut, and I shake my head vehemently. "No, I can't do that to a child." I squeeze her hand, hoping she'll understand. "I can't make a child grow up with a bastard stigma on his, or her, head."

Gavina looks at me, her eyes hard, but I know the expression isn't about me. And I know she has personal experience with being on the wrong side of the socially acceptable line.

"I take it marriage is out of the question."

It wasn't for me. Marriage was my preferred option, one I didn't question. Turns out, Ephraim has other ideas about the culmination of our relationship the whole time we were seeing each other.

"It was never an option for him."

A fierce anger sweeps across her face, but she covers it and keeps her expression grave. "Then choice three is adoption."

"Here? Where everyone will know, and I'll forever wear a scarlet A?"

We share a short, sharp, sad laugh. Of all the people I could talk to about public judgment, G would be the one to know.

"We could go to France. Tell everyone it's a gap year for you. I still have friends there. You'll be three months along at your commencement, so you shouldn't be showing yet. Or minimally, and you can hide it with those peasant blouses all the hippies are wearing these days."

My thoughts whirl so fast I forget to rib her for the hippie comment. In all my musings, I didn't include a European solution. It didn't enter my mind.

"You'd go away with me for a year?" My fingers tighten around hers.

She shakes her head in disbelief. "Of course I would, sweetie."

"But...Paris." The memory of our conversation in the gallery sweeps over me, and the pain in her eyes is palpable. Deep and aching, nuanced and fleshed out as only a wound decades old can be. "You have...memories."

"Too many to count, but it's been a long time. Moreover, we wouldn't be staying on artists' row. We'd be in the countryside, in a chateau."

"Sounds fancy."

She wrinkles her nose at me. "It's a lovely house with a quintessential vineyard and everything bucolic, not Versailles."

"Your friends won't mind us descending on them?"

"It's friend, singular. Someone I've kept correspondence with who lost her husband a few years ago and has been begging me to come stay."

Worry returns with a slap. "The invitation is for you. Not you and your irresponsible, pregnant niece."

"I'm confident the offer extends to my brilliant, maybe-not-perfect, pregnant niece."

I launch myself at her and end up half splayed on the couch with my head in her lap as she gently strokes my hair off my forehead. The snowy static in my mind gradually clears, and for the first time since Ephraim and I looked at each other in horror at the broken condom in his hands, I take a full breath.

I fight my eyelids determinedly slipping shut, as if they weigh a thousand pounds each.

"Rest. We've got time."

When I open my eyes again, wobbling as I sit up, the room is in deep shadow. The near darkness is barely relieved by the sunset visible through the French doors leading onto the balcony. Fam One shares the idyllic space with Fam Two, but it's empty at the moment, so the huge area is silent and private.

"Would you like to go outside? The evening is beautiful." Gavina gives my hair another stroke.

I meet the steady stare of her green eyes, and her warmth and love and constancy pour over me. As I hoped, Aunt G turns herself into my rock, my steady, safe place.

"Did you sit here all this time while I rudely passed out?"

She cocks her head as if I've asked the silliest thing. "And where would I have gone? Grab a quilt. The wind's still cold."

We each claim a rocking chair of wrought iron and watch, wrapped in our blankets, the spring sunset's final moments. The sky's darkest indigo chases royal blue to brilliant pink until the tiny arc of yellow sinks into the horizon.

Sunsets over the river are amazing. Tonight, I can't take my eyes off the display and stay quiet until the stars pop out, freed from the sun and uninhibited by light pollution. The music from the ballroom below drifts up along with muted voices, but I'm cocooned, protected by Castle MacInnes's immense stone walls and Gavina's limitless compassion.

Night has fully released her darkness when I know the answer, filing a bit off the rough edges of my shattered nerves.

"If you mean it, I want to go to France after graduation. Your plan is brilliant."

The lulling clip of Gavina's rocking stops. "You have to be sure, honey. You only have a few weeks to make a different decision."

"Abortion's a philosophical discussion until you're staring it in the face." If I claim to be an adult, I need to say the word and discuss it calmly.

"Adoption isn't a panacea. It's not a simple answer, merely different."

"I know, but pretending won't fix anything."

Gavina's laugh comes to me from the darkness, light and gently teasing. "You always were the practical one."

She probably can't see me, but I shrug anyway. "I had to be. Gerome's cornered the market on irresponsible. Someone has to be dependable."

I don't hide my bitterness. 1971 or not, my twin's antics are dismissed with a typical gender bias my Women and Feminism professor could use for an entire year's syllabi. Momma and Daddy freaked out like the world was ending the first time they heard I'd gotten drunk at a frat party, but they never gave Gerome's antics a second thought.

They'd never recover from my pregnancy.

We sit in the velvet darkness for so long, the party underneath winds down and the chill wins out. We head into Gavina's suite, and I fold my quilt as I go, holding it against me.

"To bed with you, now. No one's been in the guest room since the last time you were here."

"I should call home. You know nothing stays secret around here, so if I don't show up, they won't let it go. Luckily, it's Thursday, so I'll say I have studying to do for finals and came home early. They don't question when I stay with you, and I bet they won't give it a thought."

"You're probably right. You check in, and I'll go turn down the covers."

As predicted, Momma doesn't question me, spending more time

asking me about Gerome and what he's up to. As if I know what my twin's doing any more than they do.

G puts out a guest toothbrush and brings me one of her nightgowns. She takes my clothes and tells me not to worry. She'll wash them so I'll have clean things tomorrow. To no one's surprise, the need to sleep is overwhelming, so I can't argue with her, knowing she'll do the laundry I should do myself.

It's almost a cliché how much I need to escape, and my gratitude bubble expands even more as Gavina sends me off to my room.

For tonight, I'm safe, but I know sorrow is waiting in the wings.

CHAPTER NINETEEN

PAIGE – NOW

SATURDAY IS A WHIRLWIND OF ACTIVITY, and before I can accept it, six o'clock has rolled around and I'm at the church making sure everything is set up. Kase and Kiki both, bless them, understand I need time alone and promise to follow in a half hour.

I'm still hoping I won't be struck by lightning because I released a pent-up breath when I got Zach's text letting me know he can't make it after all. In fact, he's on a plane to San Diego to meet with whichever O he's mentioned but I can't keep straight. I know the situation is dire for him to stay away. He would be here if he could, despite how much he hates funerals. There's too many upset people, and he can't fix it, so he'd rather have a root canal without anesthetic. Weddings aren't so bad. Everyone's high and happy, and even better, there's dancing. Memorials are his nightmare.

I suppose I'm half forgiven for being glad he's not here since it spares him half a bottle of antacid.

The sanctuary is empty when I walk down the aisle toward the small but beautifully crafted box that doesn't seem big enough to contain my V. Organ music drifts from the speakers, but the church is cold and mostly quiet. An explosion of flowers fills every inch of available space. Standing wreaths are staggered so everyone can see a bit of each one. Three cross sprays are staged left, right, and center behind the table in the center of the transept. There are flower bouquets in a profusion of colors, and baskets bursting with deep-green ivy.

I recognize a few of the names on the cards, but so many are unknown. I'm surprised to see a gorgeous standing arrangement of orange roses, myrtle, yellow gerbera daisies, and more I can't name from Broder Vanity. It's a reminder of one of the good things about a small town. The MacInneses and the Broders kept Magnolia Bloom alive during many dark years of depression and war, buffeted by times of plenty filled with bountiful harvests, healthy herds, and fleets of tourists.

I shake away the thought and keep cataloging. A beautiful live-plant basket from Zach. Gorgeous arrangements from my brothers.

Roses. Orchids. Carnations. Chrysanthemums. Hydrangea. Larkspur.

The arrangement I ordered to be placed around V's urn is over the top, and I refuse to apologize. It's a field of magnolia blossoms as big as saucers, and V is resting right in the center. Good money in Vegas would win on Violet being darn sure she passed while they were in bloom. The florist blended the perfect mix of white lilies and greenery to create a stunning piece. I take a picture with my phone to text to Zach and thank him for his plant. I send another to the kids and my siblings.

Immediate pings come in.

Aiden: WOW.

Ainsley: OMG.

Zach: Beautiful.

I put my phone away and rest my hand on the box's shiny pecan surface to let myself cry. I need to release some of the anguish, or I'll never be able to speak.

I hear slow footsteps behind me and still have my head bowed when a hand swipes over my shoulder blades. I can make out it's

Uncle Thomas. He's actually V's uncle, so my great-uncle, but he's a wonderful man with a giant heart who's seen his own share of bigotry and sadness, but joy, too. After his retirement from the military, he and his partner, Monroe, have lived the past two decades in peace here on the estate.

I turn and let him enfold me in his long arms, still strong despite his eighty years. I press my forehead against him and try to keep from soaking his jacket. Tears shudder through him, and we don't try to pretend we're trying to stop.

Eventually, the moment passes, and we both straighten, wiping our faces with tissues from the many boxes staged around the room. Monroe moves closer, and I gather him in for a long hug.

"Thank you." It's the first of a thousand times. He nods shyly and steps away, leaving me and Uncle T.

"Have you eaten? Might be in for a rough evening."

With the inescapable profusion of perfume from the flowers, I'm glad I chose to wait. "I will later. I can't yet."

A hummingbird stroke on my elbow makes me turn. Monroe is holding out a cold bottle of water. He's dried the condensation with his handkerchief, and I accept his sweet gesture even though I'm not thirsty, because I'd rather be buried in red ants than hurt him.

In my entire life, I've maybe heard Monroe say twenty sentences. It's not that he can't speak, but he becomes desperately uncomfortable if people pull him into the edges of the limelight. I accepted his discomfort long ago and honor his wishes.

We all turn as the doors open, and Monroe disappears into the corner of the room as Mina and Fina join us in the aisle. Hugs are given all around. We're all grateful for a moment together as family.

Our moment is over quickly. In minutes, the door never has time to close. Mina's son, Trey, escorts Mrs. Greene, leading a clutch of women we call the Grannies of the Grove. All matriarchs of their respective families, all still feisty and prone to causing trouble.

There are three modes of communication in the groves of Magnolia Bloom: telegraph, telephone, and Tell-A-Grannie. Lines may go down, service may be interrupted, but the gossip mill of the

Grannies is a force of nature God himself hasn't figured out how to disrupt.

I appreciate the humor buoying me as my eyes take in the crowd. Church friends. Estate friends. Family. People from town and the factory. Madison Crowder makes sure everyone sees her hug me, but I let it pass. Noah and his daughter Sarah pay their respects. So many from last night are here, and three times as many are new.

I'm introduced to so many people it becomes a blur. Tidy comes in, and although I haven't spoken with her but a dozen or more times over the decades I've been coming to visit V, she's still feisty and funny. I'm glad to see her.

Vivann tells me not to worry about a thing. Vivann's On the Square will take care of all of the drinks, paper ware, and cutlery for the gathering in the fellowship hall tomorrow. I know without asking the amount of food the church members will bring will make the food stuffing the refrigerators at the castle look like paupers' fare. I express my gratitude and move on to the next person waiting for me.

It's Traycee Everson, the owner of the new boutique in town, simply named the Magnolia Bloom Emporium. I've been assured it's a treasure. I assure the lovely young woman I'll be by as soon as I can to see the shop. Traycee's sister Tanisha is there, too, and their Gran, who's sitting with the Grannies.

Brian Steele, of course, comes in and offers me a warm, solid hug and a kiss to my forehead. I don't think he can talk, though, as his jaw works hard when he sees V's urn. I don't try to make him, simply offering my thanks as he moves away to stand in the back of the room next to Leith.

Afterward, I stop trying to keep names and faces in my memory. I wonder if my cheek is a veritable palette of lipstick samples, but I don't mind. I can see a matching profusion on Kiki's cheek and a few on Kase's. Every kiss, every handshake, every hug are reminders of how much V was loved and how much I'll miss her.

Harville comes in, and the crowd gravitates to him, but I'm grateful. My hand's a bit sore.

When the group thins, I notice a man at the rear of the sanctuary, not far from Monroe but clearly not standing with him. I can't explain why I'm drawn to him. Maybe it's because I remember him stopping by the front earlier, placing a veined hand on the side of the urn for a moment longer than most.

He's an older man, his suit fashionable yet somber, his hair gray, his glasses rimless on his handsome face. Maybe his expression is so sad and drawn it's as if I'm looking at a mirror of my own turmoil.

Then it hits me. He's Grandad's boss, David Broder. Violet's father, my grandad, died when I was young, but I remember visiting the factory with him and attending many Broder Vanity picnics. V never went, and for some reason the memory pokes its head up, but I can't imagine why, so I move down the aisle and offer him my hand.

"Mr. Broder. How nice to see you again. It's been a very long time."

His handshake is warm and firm. He holds on to my fingers and covers them with his other hand. "Too long. Please forgive me if I'm intruding."

"Good heavens, no intrusion. I'm a bit surprised, but it's no bother."

"I felt I had to be here. My family...I..." His eyes stray to the front of the church. "We and the MacInneses are...always have been close."

That was the most awkward we'll-miss-V speech I've heard tonight. "Of course. Thank you for coming."

I'm saved from a strained silence when two women step up and hold out their hands, calling him Mr. Broder, so I assume they're factory employees. I step out of the way so they can talk and wend my way through the remaining crowd.

Kiki catches my frequent looks at the doors and moves to my side to slide a warm arm around my waist.

"I guess Mom and Dad aren't coming." She adds a squeeze.

"Apparently." It takes everything I have not to let my anger show. There's no need to bite at Kiki. She's as well aware of our childhood years of benign neglect as I am. Maybe more so as the baby of the family. Still, I'm equal amounts disappointed and furious.

I finish the final goodbyes to the many visitors. Uncle Thomas and

Monroe leave after a last, warm hug. Trey takes his grandmother home, and Mina and Fina try to stay. I make them go with threats of driving them myself if they don't skedaddle. I send Kase and Kiki right behind them. By ones and twos, the sanctuary empties, and then it's me and Harville. And V.

"How are you holding up?" His hand on my arm is warm, soft. Comforting. Yet there's a firmness in his touch saying, *I'm here. I'm strong. Lean on me.*

"I'm fine. I can't thank—"

"Stop, please. This is my calling and my joy. Is there anything you need?"

"To sleep for two days, but that has to wait." I squeeze his hand and step away. "I'll see you tomorrow."

A movement captures my eye, and Madison steps out the side door by the choir loft, prim in her chiffon dress of mint green, with sleeves, of course, and properly long enough to cover her knees.

I give a chin thrust in her direction. "Take your wife home, Harville. I appreciate all you've done."

He looks over his shoulder and gives a small start. I'm curious but can't be rude and ask why he's surprised. Instead, I drive away, leaving the Crowders to their privacy.

CHAPTER TWENTY

MINA – NOW

THE CHURCH PARKING lot is half empty when Fina and I walk out. The
viewing was lovely, and Momma and the Grannies were on their best
behavior. Still, it pains me to see Paige keeping herself together when
I know she's exhausted. She hasn't stopped since she got here
Wednesday, and adrenaline and caffeine will keep her engine running
for only so long.

I stop by the passenger door of the car, looking at the clapboard
church. It's now the center of a hodgepodge of smaller buildings and
rooms attached to the original brick chapel Evajean and Alisdair had
built in 1880. We still use the chapel for smaller services and baptisms
and such, but the "big" church now barely holds our growing congregation. Growing and happy thanks to Harville's determined shep-
herding.

"Maybe we should go back in." I half turn to put movement behind
my suggestion, but Fina stops me.

"Let her be. Harville will shoo her out of there in a minute."

I'm not an overly devoted member, but the congregation is mostly honest, kind, and compassionate. The few outliers don't count, and I know Fina is right, especially about Harville.

"Mina!"

The voice comes from behind the last line of cars, and I turn to see CT Nelson hurrying across the lot. Of course, I saw him during the evening, but I managed to stay out of range. Now I'm trapped, and Fina aims her laser gaze at me.

I put a smile on my face as he moves close, looking dapper in his pearl-gray suit and deep-maroon tie. He's removed his Italian fedora, acknowledging Fina, but his smile is for me.

"Good evening, CT." I'm grateful for the shadows hiding my consternation, and I run a nervous hand down the navy pencil skirt I made for the services.

"I've been meaning to get this to you. You dropped it in the store, and it slid under a display. I'm sorry it took so long."

He offers me my missing phone, and our fingers brush. I snatch my phone away like I've been shocked, which in a way is exactly true. I'd almost swear Brian Steele's fired up his welder and struck an arc between our fingers.

"How very sweet of you. I'm sorry for the inconvenience."

"No bother at all." He moves so he can see me better in the vapor light. "I was hoping to talk to you earlier, but we kept missing each other."

I swat at a pretend mosquito to avoid meeting his eyes. "There was quite a crowd. Violet was part of the glue in this town. Everyone's tired."

Please take the hint and make a pleasant exit.

"I won't keep you, then."

I reach for my door handle, but look up when he doesn't move. CT glances between Fina and me, and when he stands tall, my uh-oh meter fires.

"I was hoping to take you to lunch next week. I know tomorrow there'll be more food here than an army can eat, but maybe on Tuesday?"

I haven't been asked out many times in my life, so I'm hardly one to judge, but for it to happen in a dark parking lot, after a viewing, with my sister two feet away strikes me as funny. Ridiculous, even. I can't help it. I laugh.

His face falls, and now I'm a monster, wondering how I got both my feet in my mouth at the same time. "CT, forgive me. I'm tired, and I haven't been asked out in more years than God has little green apples. You caught me off guard. I'm sorry for being horrible."

His smile is forgiving and holds a bit of mischief. "I'll let you make it up to me by saying yes, then."

I know I'm trapped, so I strive to be gracious. "Of course. I'd love to."

I'm not sure where lying outside of the Lord's house versus inside ranks on the sin chart, and I'm afraid to find out.

"Good. I'll see you tomorrow, and we can make plans, but for now, I'll let you ladies be on your way. Drive safe, you hear?"

He puts his fedora on at a perfect, jaunty angle and walks away. Or should I say *struts*? No, too arrogant. What's the word for walking like your feet are a little lighter and you're not tired at all?

And how have I not noticed how handsome he is?

"Your phone's got a camera. Take a picture. It'd last longer."

I glare at Fina over the roof of the car. "You should take your act on the road. You're hilarious."

She smirks as we climb in, and she heads for the exit, the delay with CT meaning we're one of the last cars to leave. She barely has to pause before she makes a right turn, and we're on our way home.

I put my face in my hands. "I'm a fool."

"Took you long enough to figure it out."

I lift my head to glare at her. "You're not helping."

"Am I supposed to be?"

"Yes! What should I do now?"

"I don't know. Go to lunch with a handsome, successful man? I mean, the horror and all, but maybe you'll survive."

"I don't date!"

"And whose fault is that?"

"Look who's talking."

We both stay miffed, me crossing my arms over my chest and Fina paying excruciating attention to the road.

The good thing is, it doesn't take a heck of a long time to travel from the castle to anywhere in town, and our duplex is another quarter mile on the other side. Which means we don't have to hold our tongues for more than fifteen minutes before we're both out of the car and stomping off to our respective doors.

I slam mine. She slams hers.

And I'm wondering which of us is more upset.

And why...

CHAPTER TWENTY-ONE

PAIGE – NOW

THE TWO K's and I stayed up way too late, again, but I can't complain. My sister's career moves her all over the world, and the consequence makes our visits rare. Since her being here is a precious surprise, I take full advantage of the time. I know there's something different about her, but she steers all conversations away from herself no matter how brilliantly I try to find out what's going on.

She's avoided me the entire day, but we've had too much to do for me to nail her down. Now, ever the diplomat, she's headed for the front of the chapel, where the Sunday sunshine is filling the space with light. My parents are making their entrance with an entire five minutes to spare before the service.

I'm saved from having to do more than offer my mother an air kiss and my father a tepid hug before we need to take our seats. Then Harville, bless his heart, begins the service and gives me a reason to chill out my resting bitch face and pay attention to his kind and generous words.

Harville makes me laugh and cry, surrounded by the sweet perfume of magnolias lingering in the church. It's a true eulogy, full of tender words and witty anecdotes. The sanctuary is packed, and I'm touched Traycee from the Emporium came in advance and draped one of V's quilts over every pew. Each treasure brings V's energy to the room in such a single, sweet note, I'm all choked up. Again.

Kiki squeezes my right hand, Kase my left, reminding me it's time to share my words. I entreat whatever benevolent spirits might be present to let me finish without breaking down.

Miraculously, I'm almost all the way through before my throat closes up. A long drink from the bottle of water Harville left for me on the pulpit and a kind blink from him when I glance his way are probably the only things letting me finish.

"I know you're not supposed to admit you have a favorite relative, but any of you who know me know I'd be a liar and might risk the building falling on your heads if I denied Aunt V was my favorite person in the world. She was a surrogate mom and best friend. She was a trustworthy ear and a quick kick in the pants. I have an idea Saint Peter is standing on a golden street somewhere, looking around, bemused and wondering how he's been displaced as heaven's master organizer."

A round of laughter, accompanied by nodding heads, circles the sanctuary.

"She was a woman ahead of her time. A champion. A social justice warrior before there was such a term. And before I go on too long, I know she wasn't perfect."

I gather enough strength to finish.

"But she...was to me." I grab my tissues and bolt from the dais.

I sit, and Kase and Kiki pull me into a group hug. The rest of the testimonials are a blur. With the miracles of modern technology, I take over livestreaming the service to my private social media account to keep me distracted. Both the kids and my brothers have expressed their gratitude, since they aren't here except in spirit, and I'm glad I can bring them in.

The service ends, and we all head to the fellowship hall, where I record for posterity the mounds of fried chicken and platters of brisket, the Pyrex dishes galore of mac and cheese and hash brown casserole, and the entire conference table of coconut cream and apple pies, dump cakes, and chocolate sheet cakes, and vats of banana pudding and peach cobbler. And, of course, endless jugs of sweet tea and urns of coffee waiting to wash it all down.

As promised, Vivann has brought enough plates and cutlery to serve an entire army regiment, and I suppose with half the town attending, she's not far off.

"Pope on a pogo stick. I see enough to feed half of Edinburgh."

Obviously, I don't have to turn to know who's behind me. "Probably. I appreciate you coming to the service."

"It was lovely. You were lucky to have had your aunt for so long, and she was lucky to have been so loved."

"I couldn't agree more." I wave toward the waiting bounty. "What would you like to try first?"

"Dessert, of course. I see coconut sprinkled over a mountain of meringue, and it's calling my name. I'd better be careful, or I'll be splitting my dungarees by the end of the day."

Through sheer force of will, I keep my eyes away from his slim-fit slacks. He winks and heads for the dessert table as Kase comes over.

Her eyes are glued over my shoulder. "Mmmm, that's one yummy Scotsman."

I bark a laugh but try to keep the volume muted. "Kase, you are incorrigible."

"No argument." She pulls her gaze to me. "I'm sorry I have to go."

I shake my head. "No sorries. I'm glad you came. You didn't have to."

"Of course I had to, you nut. I hate bailing on you."

"I'm fine." She gives me a look, but I hold firm. "Kiki is staying for two more days, and I'm excited to catch up. Still, I'm ready for this to be over and to have some time alone."

"Processing time."

"Yep, processing time." I glance at the clock. "You'd better go, or you'll miss your flight. And don't speed."

"Yes, Mom."

To my consternation, Madison takes the vacated space as soon as Kase leaves.

"My, she is lovely." She indicates Kase's retreating figure.

I swear I can hear some offensive version of *for a woman of color* left unsaid. I scold myself and hope I'm not putting silent, racist words in Madison's mouth, but if she says them, I'm going to go honey badger on her right in the middle of the family hall of St. Andrew's.

"She is indeed. Inside and out."

"Did y'all meet at the university?"

"Nope."

Madison's expression goes sharp, but she doesn't back down. "I know I've seen her somewhere, but I can't place it."

I dig deep for some of V's Christian charity. "If you've ever bought Balm de Beauté Cosmetics, then—"

"Of course! I knew it."

Of course she did...

"Excuse me, Madison, I need to speak to my parents."

I've managed to avoid their table, finding a way to duck to another person or into the prep kitchen if it looked like either one of them was trying to snare my attention. If I'm being honest, I know they haven't tried at all.

I can't hide any longer, though, and move to where they sit with Uncle T and the choir director's wife. Mom is dressed in understated simplicity, the fitted A-line dress enhancing her tall figure. Her make-up's flawless, and not a strand of the same midnight hair she shares with Kiki has dared to escape her sleek chignon.

"There you are. The service was lovely."

"It was. Glad y'all could make it." I try—oh, how I try—to keep censure from my voice.

Mom, to no surprise, reads the statement as a vocalization of the obvious, because it wouldn't occur to her I'm upset. Or, more precisely, upset with them.

"It's been a hurried couple of days. We missed one flight and had a layover that nearly did me in."

"Horrors."

I look over at my father, who bears little in common with his twin. I know twins aren't required to resemble each other, especially fraternal twins, but other than sharing V's dark hair, which has gone to the rich silver women pay huge sums to replicate, they might as well have been from entirely different families.

Uncle T sees me on Mom's other side and leans around so he can speak to me. "You hanging in there, kiddo?"

"Hanging in. Hi, Dad."

"Hello, Paige. You did a fine job."

I didn't do much. V arranged everything, to no one's surprise, but I find myself irritated he doesn't know that, and my gut volcano turns on a slow simmer.

"I'm glad you think so."

Kiki joins us and puts her arm on my chair. "Hi, Mom. Dad."

"I thought you couldn't make it." Dad's voice carries no rise at the end, making it not only not a question, but also sprinkled with accusation.

"I had to pull about twelve strings, but luckily it worked out."

Dad gives his head a shake. "Violet would've understood. You should've saved your leave."

Kiki frowns. "I'm not here for Aunt V, Dad. I'm here for Paige."

A taut silence reigns until Mom jumps in. "That's exceptionally nice of you, Dominique." She casts me a look. "I hope you appreciate all the trouble she went through."

What the actual hell? I literally cannot. I can't form more than a perfunctory response. "Of course I appreciate it. Why in the world wouldn't I?"

Mom puts on her not-in-public-Paige face. "No need to be snippy. I'm simply making an observation. But listen, why don't you girls pop over and have brunch with your father and me before we leave tomorrow?"

I glance at Kiki and then stare at my mother in disbelief. A Vesuvius level of lava climbs up my esophagus and threatens to scorch my vocal cords into a pile of ash. *Pop over* to Dallas and have brunch? Drive over an hour each way to have brunch because my father can't abide being in the confines of Magnolia Bloom?

Kiki senses my tension, as she seems to have since she was born. She was hardwired to keep the peace, hiding her distress when Mom and Dad gallivanted off to whatever officer's event they were hosting or attending. Kiki couldn't stand for the few minutes we had as a family to be taut, so she would calm the waters by redirecting any way she could, usually by being cute and delightfully charming. I can tell she's reverted to habit because her arm around me goes stock-still before she rubs her hand across my shoulder blade. I'm not sure she realizes she's doing it.

"We're going to hang out with Uncle T tomorrow." Kiki's voice is too bright, too happy. "Why don't y'all stay here tonight? It's not like we lack beds. We can catch up."

Mom frowns. "Don't be silly, Dominique. We don't have our things, and besides, your father is tired. We should be going as it is."

My father doesn't look the least bit tired. I glance at the fierce sunshine, guessing it's barely four o'clock. Hardly the witching hour. God forbid Dad get caught in Magnolia Bloom after sundown. I wonder what would happen. Would he turn into a gremlin?

No, wait. Too late.

I want to snap a retort, but I bite my tongue. And it hurts. But it keeps me from wasting my breath.

Dad pushes his chair out, one of the legs screeching on the tile. I wince and hope the whole room isn't looking. Mom, of course, jumps to her feet, too.

He gives me an awkward pat on the shoulder and pulls Kiki in for a hug. "Hope we see you before Christmas. Proud of you, girl."

No surprise. She followed in his footsteps and has become an accomplished officer and career serviceperson.

He cuts a glance in my direction, and I stuff the urge to snap to attention and salute.

"Safe travels, Paige. Hope to see you soon."

When have you ever wanted to see me? And what about your grandkids? Do you even remember they exist?

Kiki walks them out of the room, leaving me in stunned silence. Uncle T, being Uncle T, slides over next to me.

"Hey, kiddo. I'm sorry."

"Nothing for you to be sorry about, for heaven's sake." I look at the now-empty doorway. "I wonder if he'd know my birthday."

"September seventeenth, like Evajean's."

It's reminder seven hundred and fifty-four why he is one of my favorite people on the planet. "Of course you know, Uncle T."

He does a quick count of the remaining crowd. "Ready to blow this pop stand? I need to take Monroe home, and the cleanup committee is on the job."

"Sounds like a good idea. Hug Monroe for me."

"Happy to."

Kiki returns in time to hear his assurance that he'll see us in the morning for breakfast at the castle. Mina and Fina are doing mimosas and migas for anyone who wants to head over. All in all, it ends up being less than an hour before Kiki and I are at V's in blessed, air-conditioned silence.

I almost scream when my phone pings.

Zach: So sorry I couldn't be there. How'd it go?

I don't dare admit how grateful I am he didn't come, so I tell mostly the truth.

Me: Everything went beautifully. I'm in a carb coma from the social, so I'm talking a nap.

Zach: I love you. Sleep tight, then.

Me: Will do.

I turn my phone off, and Kiki and I head for our respective rooms. I strip and toss on my coolest nightgown and climb under the covers, not caring that I'll pay for it later when I'm wide awake at three o'clock. I'm anxious to crack the spine on V's first journal, but for now, I need to sleep.

For about a year.

CHAPTER TWENTY-TWO

VIOLET – 1971

I DRIVE HOME by myself from Austin the last day of the semester. My last day as a college student. The weeks since I talked with Ginny and Gavina have flown by, yet also crawled like an ice-bound freighter. Gavina and I have everything mapped out, and I'm counting the hours until commencement, because as soon as humanly possible afterward, G and I will be on a plane headed for France.

My foot taps the brake too hard when I see Ephraim's car behind Daddy's Lincoln Mark III. I park in the space next to the land yacht, turn off the engine, and inhale long and deep to calm my shaking hands. The last conversation we had ended in a fight, with me shrieking he doesn't love me like some Shakespearean heroine. I didn't mean it, and he knows it, but I get so hurt that he won't talk about anything deeper than studying for finals.

I know I'm a simpleton for believing, in spite of my planning with G, he'll change his mind about marriage. I'm not about to alter the plans G has made, but I need to believe he merely needs some time to wrap his head around how different our lives will be. After all, plane tickets can be canceled, and while it hurts he's barely called me since spring break, I've been giving it my all to be patient.

But seeing his car makes my electrical system go haywire. The only conclusion I can make is he's here to surprise me and tell me he's ready. He shouldn't be home yet from Pennsylvania, so there's no other reason for him to be at my house, waiting for me.

I check my hair in the rearview mirror and dig in my purse for my lipstick. I wish I had time to fix my hair, but I'll have to settle for running a comb through it and sliding on my favorite headband, always in my bag. Until this very second, I hadn't acknowledged the depth of my willingness to forgive him for his cold reaction to this pregnancy. It isn't like the hurt is gone, but getting married and making everything right goes a long way to healing.

The second I open the door and step into the kitchen, Momma gives me a brilliant smile. "Welcome home, Violet. Daddy'll start unloading your car. And look who's here."

Momma's tone is about two shades too perky and conflicts with the red in her eyes, telling me she's been crying. I'm not super close to my mother, but I can see something is off. Like, big-time off.

My father comes in and gives me a hug, then announces he and David will talk shop and we should join them when we're ready. Translation: The men will talk business while the women fix food and drinks.

My instant reaction is to balk, but something in Momma's expression stops me. I force a smile for Daddy, even though I want to snap at him for being a sexist jerk. I try to catch Ephraim's attention, but his back is to me, and he's already laughing at one of Daddy's lame jokes. Daddy's probably saying something about the seventeen-inch solid-state Admiral TV Momma bought with S&H Green Stamps. It's a wonder Momma didn't glue her lips together licking enough stamps to fill a hundred and fifty books.

Momma's clutching the sink by the time the door shuts, and I turn to her. She's hardly asked me a thing about myself in months, but I fear she knows my secret despite every word out of her mouth being

Gerome this and *Gerome that*. I've taken advantage of the distraction and stayed invisible.

"Momma, what's going on?"

It takes a full minute before she can look at me. "Gerome called. He's enlisted in the Air Force and isn't coming home before he leaves for basic training."

I sit down on one of the padded kitchen chairs with a thump, grateful I manage to avoid an ignominious crash to the floor onto my butt. The Vietnam War is a taboo subject around here. Daddy is hard-headed about supporting President Nixon, and I about lose it any time I bring up the senseless deaths and the insanely long conflict we should never have gotten into in the first place. Momma plays Switzerland, trying to be neutral, insisting I respect my father, yet failing to demand he acknowledge my opinions.

It doesn't happen, so we do what all good American families do. We don't talk about it. We've all held our collective breaths for the four years Uncle T has been in-country, but then he went and signed up for another tour because, well, that's Uncle T. But Gerome?

"Oh, God, Momma. I'm sorry."

Irritation bubbles as I think of my brother. The military is the perfect place for a wild child, and Gerome's antics have no doubt caused more than a few gray hairs and bouts of heartburn. Once again, he's taken up all the oxygen in the room with Momma and Daddy spending every minute worrying about what he's up to. For once, I'm glad he's yet again made the world all about him. It keeps Momma's attention off me.

"There's more."

Momma's voice jerks me out of my reverie. "More?"

"He's marrying Christina. They've been planning it for months and he never said a word." She looks at me, her eyes wide and her hands shaking. "Not a word!"

I admit it's selfish, but I panic. Mother will expect me to be at Gerome's wedding. We've told everyone about the trip to France, saying Gavina wants one last hoopla in Europe, adding the gap-year angle for me.

"When?" I ask so casually she has to see what a fraud I am.

She doesn't.

"The week of graduation. Y'all's commencement is on Saturday, and the wedding is on the Wednesday following."

Oh, thank God. V and I aren't leaving until Friday...if we even leave now that it appears Ephraim has come to his senses.

Momma puts her back to the countertop and wraps an arm around her waist. "Well, we'll deal with what we have to. The important thing today is your father needs to be sure David remembers how close our families are."

I frown, completely confused. "Pardon me?"

Fear cuts across me, and again, I wonder if she knows. Austin's a small town, but not Magnolia Bloom small. I've never seen the clinic's doctor or nurses before, and I saw no one there who could have reported Violet MacInnes came walking out of the Red River Women's Center with reddened eyes and a swollen nose.

Momma straightens and wipes her hands down the front of her dress to smooth it. "They're doing a big layoff at the factory right now, and your father is five years from retiring. We can't take any chances, so you be nice to David."

If Momma only knew...

"I'm always nice to David."

"Yes, well, his people have been good to the town, and your father loves his job."

His people?

I somehow manage to keep my eyes from squinting and my mouth from broadcasting that *his people* will soon be *my people*. I can't imagine how she'll react when I convert for the baby's sake.

In terms of our relationship with the Broders, Daddy's the senior operations manager at the factory, making him a solid member of both sides of the Magnolia Bloom divide. Daddy's been a solid bridge my whole life, now that I think about it. Maybe I've worried about the religious complexities for nothing.

"Get the silver tray from the dining room cupboard." Another Green Stamp score of Momma's.

The silver? For pimento cheese sandwiches, potato salad, and baby gherkins? I shake my head and obey, and we have all the food and sweet tea ready to take outside before Daddy and Ephraim have any quality man talk.

She looks at me. "We can't take any chances. David will basically be your father's boss in a month, but we have to smile and show it's fine." Her mouth goes taut. "Better to have a boss who's young enough to be your son than no boss at all. Do you understand?"

I don't, but I nod anyway.

He'll be her son-in-law soon. Surprise baby or not, Ephraim and I love each other. We have our moments, especially with trying to navigate our college decisions, but I know him. Family means everything to Ephraim. He loves me, and he'll love our baby. Him showing up today proves it. He's finally accepted what we have to do.

"I didn't want to mention it, but you're old enough now to know these things. Everyone's on edge after David's cousin was attacked last month when he was closing up the factory."

"What?" My hand automatically goes to my stomach. I quickly add the other so I appear to be holding myself, not cradling the life inside me.

"Violet! Lower your voice. It's all calming down, but it's one more thing your father has to be careful about right now."

Ephraim's warning about the danger his family has always endured is suddenly real, not theory. I always blew it off, not wanting to believe it. I shove aside the thought. I'm about to blow a gasket, needing Ephraim alone so we can talk, when he comes into the kitchen.

"Can I help you, Mrs. MacInnes?"

My gaze goes right to his face. This is the first time he's seen me since the eventful week, and I wonder if he'll notice my breasts are fuller and there's the tiniest rounding of my belly that I can still pass off as water weight.

"Oh, aren't you the sweetest?" My mother gushing makes me wince. "You stay right here and catch up with Violet while I set up outside."

She takes her tray and hip-bumps the screen, exiting before either of us can move.

I meet his eyes. "Hi."

"Hi." He returns my greeting with a flicker of heat in his gaze. It's a far cry from the fire usually melting me in an instant.

I walk toward him, and since we're aware of the thin veil of the screen, our hug is awkward. Ironically, it's a good thing. It affirms my mother's belief we're staying in our respective Magnolia Bloom lanes. They'll learn soon enough about our merger.

"Momma told me about your cousin. Why haven't you mentioned it? Is your family all right?"

He looks away, his cheeks reddening. "I didn't want to get into it with you. It's proof of what I've said all along, and I didn't want to risk another argument."

I think about our happily ever after, but I'm sidetracked by the strain on his face.

"Have they caught anyone?"

"Really?" He looks down his nose like I should know better. "Good ol' Sheriff Woolsey is going to assign a lot of man-hours to the case?"

The screen door's hinge creaks.

"Look at you two," Momma coos, coming into the kitchen. "Still such good friends after so long. Y'all come on out now."

We share a look but hide it from her. It takes everything I have not to pull him aside, but I can't come up with an excuse to steal him away for any length of time.

"We'll be right there, Momma."

I move so we're not in their direct line of sight. "I'm so glad you're here."

"I knew you were headed home. I called, and Tidy told me, so I stopped by to check on you. Make sure you're healing. To be sure everything…went well. I didn't want to talk about it over the phone."

"Make sure I'm heal—"

It strikes me he's barely looking at me. No lingering hot gazes into each other's eyes, no illicit touches.

"I talked to some of the guys about it, and a couple have been through it with their girlfriends. They said you'll be sore, but since it's been over six weeks, we can be together without any issues."

I stare at him, speechless. I open my mouth, try to speak, but nothing comes out, so I close it again.

He tries to touch me, but I rear back in horror. He misunderstands, because he tries again, capturing my hand before I can stop him. I dare not jerk away and alert Momma.

"Is it true? Are you sore?"

I look around for movie props, certain I'm in some kind of science-fiction film, or maybe someone's going to jump out and yell, "Surprise! You're on *Candid Camera,*" even though that's utterly macabre to imagine, considering the subject at hand. Before my eyes, time contracts and expands as I try to process all the data thrown at me.

He believes I've already done it. Done as he asked, though he never once asked what I wanted. It's too early in my pregnancy, but something in my belly flutters.

And my world upends.

It's the two of us now. Me and the tiny life inside me high-fiving my tummy are headed to France. There'll be no hasty vows and counting little fingers and toes.

I'll have to deal with it all without him.

"The reason you're here is to make sure I've had the abortion and to find out if I can have sex yet?"

His voice and eyes are both defensive. "Well, no. I'm here to check on you. I might shouldn't have brought anything else up. Honestly, Violet, I'm here to be sure—"

"To be sure you're off the hook. To make sure your world has been put to rights, and there's nothing inconvenient in your way."

"Now wait a minute. It wasn't inconvenient only for me. Both of us would have lost our entire futures."

"Just. Stop."

On the inside, I'm an ice sculpture on two legs. From my headband to my high-tops, I know two things. One, I have to survive the next fifteen minutes before I can make a reasonable excuse to head to my room. Two, I have to get away from David Ephraim Broder before I say something I'll regret forever. Words that might be just, but could never be unsaid.

"Hey, you two," Momma trills from the patio. "Come on out here."

"Don't worry, Ephraim. I've taken care of everything. Your future is fine." Amazingly, my voice is mechanical but functioning.

I pivot around him, pasting an I-don't-have-a-worry-in-the-world smile on my face as I lead the way to the patio.

Now all I have to do is find a way to swallow Momma's blue-ribbon pimento cheese.

CHAPTER TWENTY-THREE

PAIGE – NOW

IT TURNS out I was wrong. My *nap* turned into twelve straight hours of sleep, and now I'm in the kitchen, the five a.m. darkness outside a blanket of peace. I'm puttering, trying not to disturb Kiki, but it seems my efforts are wasted. She's sneaking into the kitchen in shorts, tank top, and trainers, clearly unaware I'm present.

"Good morning."

"Jesus, Mary, and Joseph." She slaps a hand over her chest. "Don't do that."

"Do what? I was here first."

She gives me a stink eye and turns to the counter. "The scent of fresh coffee should have told me you were up. Clearly, I'm not meant to be a detective." She pours herself a cup from the pot, grimacing as a precious drop hits the hot plate.

"What are you doing up so early?" I hold up a hand. "Never mind. No Sherlock here, either. I revise my inquiry to, when did you take up jogging?"

Her long pause seems incongruent with my question. She takes her cup to the table set before the spotless window on the other side of the room.

"Do you have a minute?" she asks.

"Sounds like a trick question."

"More like a stalling one."

I sit down and open my hand halfway across the table, palm up. She takes it, and for a moment we're transported in time. The decade difference in our ages is both a blessing and a sadness. We're close, but we never got to do the my-best-friend-who-does-everything-with-me thing.

Lacing my fingers with hers, I confess, "Sometimes it still takes me aback when we're together and I see this amazing, beautiful woman. I can't help but wonder, where's my baby sister?"

"She's been around the world and made some incredibly poor choices. She's certainly not a girl anymore."

I look into her eyes, holding them when I can tell she wants to break contact. "What's up, honey?"

She starts French-braiding her hair to keep her hands busy, a habit she formed as soon as she had the manual dexterity.

"I'm an alcoholic, Paige."

I cough a laugh. "Come on, quit joking. I know you've got something important on your mind and—"

"Paige, stop. I'm not distracting you. I'm not deflecting. I'm telling you I'm an alcoholic. Talking to family members you can trust not to hurt you is part of recovery."

I shake my head. "But I've never seen you—"

"Hammered? Black-out drunk? So high I can't stand, much less walk?" Her laugh isn't meant to convey humor. "I don't mean to be a shit, but how often have we seen each other over the past two decades? Two times a year? Three? Addicts are amazing at putting on the face they know people want to see."

"I'm sorry. It wasn't my intention to be dismissive. I'm...stunned. You have to give me a minute to process."

"I know, and I shouldn't jump straight to defensive. It's a big part of my step work."

"If anything, I'm angry with myself that I never saw, that I wasn't there for you."

Her smile is sad, but she continues. "Well, big sis, this isn't about you. It's about me, and I've been a pretty amazing actress for a long time now."

She's close enough for me to brush back a strand of hair escaping her braid. "You've been pretty amazing at everything you've ever done."

"Yeah...about that. It's a huge piece of my puzzle. I'm so afraid not to be perfect I set myself up for a nasty fall."

I head for the coffeepot. "Have another?"

"I won't refuse a top off."

I look into her half-full mug of unrelieved black. "I don't know a single serviceperson who puts cream or sugar in their coffee."

"Takes too much time. You learn to drink it straight."

"I'm not there yet." I take my favorite oat milk creamer out of the fridge and turn my serving a heavenly tan.

She takes a sip, giving the universal coffee lover's sigh. "Delicious. Not remotely close to my usual can-stand-a-spoon-in-it mess hall poison." She wraps her hands around her cup and looks at me. "Sis, I've spent my entire life trying to make other people comfortable. I hid me behind a smile and, for the last two decades, in a bottle."

"What changed?"

She can't look me in the eye as shame blankets her whole body, dropping her head and rounding her shoulders.

I want to touch her, reassure her, but I sense she's not ready. "Tell me, Kiki. It's all right."

"Oh, it's far from all right. I was involved with someone in my chain of command, and it blew up when I got a DUI with him in the car. He's got enough clout to cover it up, but I had to voluntarily separate or be court-martialed."

"Court-martialed!"

"Conduct unbecoming, but the powers that be who know don't want any press, because my commander is well-connected politically. Luckily, it saves me from disgracing myself and losing everything."

I straighten in my chair, stunned and unable to form a coherent thought. "But the Air Force is everything to you."

"Not anymore. Not now."

I shake my head to clear it. "Wait a minute. You lose your career, and he loses...nothing?"

"Pretty much. The DUI was a career killer by itself, but our relationship going public would have been monstrous for him."

"That's not right."

"Doesn't matter. All of this is the result of my choices, so it's wasted energy to talk about him."

I take a minute to organize my thoughts and haul in a deep breath. "Do you...do you love him?"

"What we had wasn't love. A lot of lust. Mostly convenient, for both of us. But no, I didn't love him."

I sit back and carefully fold the tea towel I threw over my shoulder. "I'm not sure if that's a good thing or not."

"It's definitely a good thing. Messy, but good."

A deep breath ends with me puffing my cheeks and letting out a low hiss. "All right, I'm in shock, but for now, what do you need me to do?"

She smiles at me, the expression so wistful it makes my heart twist. "Do you know you're one of the things I talk about most at meetings?"

"Me? Good heavens, why?"

"You're my big sis. You're the one who never judges me. You're the rock of all four of us kids, even if Adam and Eric don't say it. You're pretty much perfect."

My tears fall despite an effort to stop them. "You couldn't be more wrong, sweetie. List all the words opposite of 'perfect,' and you've got my profile."

Grabbing napkins from the holder, she offers me one and keeps one for herself.

"I'm sorry. I should've chosen a better way to say it, because what you learn in recovery is no one's perfect, and trying to be gets us all in trouble." She gives me a head waggle. "You are the perfect sis, though. Being fallible only makes you more so."

"I'll take it. So tell me more."

She gives me the short version of years of using alcohol and various drugs, both legal and illegal, until her life became a mess. Guilt chokes me again because I told the truth. I never noticed. What I discounted as simple fatigue from travel and a hard job were actually the ravages of her habits and hiding a lot of hangovers.

"So, now I know. You don't have to hide anymore. Which brings us back to my question. What can I do to help you?"

She stands and takes my hand, pulling me to my feet. We hug and aren't ashamed that it's a long time before we let go so she can put her cup in the sink.

"You help me by being you." She says it so matter-of-factly, so sincerely, the ache in my chest eases.

I blow her a kiss. She snatches it out of the air and presses it against her cheek.

"What I need is to go running and do some moving meditation. Then I'd like to spend the day with you. Talking. Puttering. Doing whatever you need done. It's easier to do this in spurts, rather than try to process it all in one fell swoop."

"Deal. I gave up running for Lent forty years ago and have maintained my resolution. You go be healthy. We have plenty of time before brunch." I pause, concern slapping away my complacency. "Wait, there'll be mimosas downstairs. Do you want to skip it?"

"You're sweet, but I'm not super fragile. Not as much, anyway. I can be around alcohol, as long as it's not a bar. Or a football game. That would probably trigger me."

"If you're sure, great, but I'm happy to stay up here with you."

"I'm good. I promise."

"Okay, then. See you in a bit."

She turns to me as she exits. "I love you, sis."

"Love you more." The screen is barely shut before I jerk open the refrigerator to begin an inventory of what's available so I can create an amazing breakfast for my baby sister when she returns.

I have to pause as a tidal wave of emotions nearly drown me. My breath is short, my skin flushed and clammy, despite the air conditioner doing its level best.

I sit down and look out the picture window into the middle distance, letting my attention soften to give me what I need. Then it hits me what a mess my family is. I can't handle this right now. My world is imploding from all angles, but Kiki couldn't have known her bombshell makes the final straw, like a ten-ton tank's fallen out of the sky and landed square between my shoulder blades.

My only option is to do what I've always done. I grab my phone and open my notes app. It doesn't matter if I don't have the strength. I'll have to fake it, because right now my sister needs me, and before that, she needs breakfast.

One thing at a time.

CHAPTER TWENTY-FOUR

VIOLET – 1971

I SWEAR by everything that is holy, if this wedding doesn't commence in the next five minutes, I'll strangle the bride-to-be before she can become Mrs. First Lieutenant Gerome MacInnes.

"Get a grip, Christina." The maid of honor gives her friend's shoulder a shake before she can hyperventilate again.

"God, what am I doing?" She stands in front of the cheval mirror, and I can't tell if it's practiced hysteria or the real thing.

I edge away, one of five attendants scattered around the room and the one least wanting to step into her impending breakdown. I'm in the wedding party only because she felt she had to include me—at the last minute and causing quite a scramble, no matter how many times I tried to convince her it wasn't necessary.

At the moment, I want to toss her the same question. If she's so racked with uncertainty, maybe she and my brother shouldn't get hitched today. I hope Christina's success in winning my brother over to have the ceremony at the castle is because of her commitment to the MacInnes lore, not because she wants pretty pictures.

So now we stand around the small conference room we turned

into the bridal lounge. It's the closest to the chapel with enough room to hold us all, and for the moment, we're all in a holding pattern, trying not to wrinkle our Gunne Sax dresses or dislodge our sheer organza floppy hats. I've never been more grateful for the current fashion trend being the opposite of fitted and formal. The gathered tiers are perfect for someone trying to hide she's pregnant and unmarried while the people around her are unpregnant and getting married.

The maid of honor repowders Christina's nose and shoos her mother from the room. With one parent out of the way, bridesmaid number three peeks around the door to wave the proud papa inside.

"How's my girls?" he booms.

Boom is the only volume Mr. Barnesdale knows.

"Oh, Daddy!" Christina launches herself into her father's massive arms, and I have a moment of fear her wail might be heard in the chapel—and the next county over.

"Don't muss your dress, honey." Mr. Barnesdale gives the wedding planner a do-something look as he awkwardly *there-there's* Christina's back.

The harried coordinator steps in, pulls Christina away, and gives her a touch-up of Petal Blossom lipstick. The look she gives Mr. Barnesdale is clear as day, even to me on the other side of the room. It all but screams, *Get her out here now!*

I couldn't agree more.

"Let's go, Christina." He speaks with enough authority to line up the five of us in teal satin and haul Christina into place to go last. We make it all the way down the aisle with no trips or falls, and I can start counting the seconds before the nightmare—for me, anyway—is over.

I don't hear a word of the vows. For my survival, I train my eyes on the beautiful tapestries turning the stone walls from a wash of gray into an embrace of history and lore and promise. I've dreamed of standing where Christina now holds hands with my brother. In my fantasies since I was a girl, I'd be in my ivory gown with its extended train, my gauzy veil gently obscuring my vision as I wait for my intended to lift it, drape it over my head, and kiss me. I'd sense the castle itself smiling, welcoming me and my new husband to a long line of forever love.

I keep my eyes averted as Gerome and Christina kiss. Of course, my blasted eyes seek out Ephraim, sitting with his family and the girl he brought. Rumor is she'll be Mrs. David Ephraim Broder within the year. She's the daughter of Mr. Broder's partner. Her family is super conservative and members of Temple Emanu-El of Dallas. She knows all the right people and all the right rules. She's pretty. Smart. Known to be kind. She's perfect for him.

I hate her.

He looks straight at me, and I'm grateful the audience will believe the distress I'm not hiding is restrained joy for my brother's happiness.

No one will guess I'm crying from part humiliation, part despair. No one will know Ephraim sliced me open and removed my heart without anesthetic when it finally penetrated my thick skull his only concern has been ensuring I don't throw a rock into the placid pond of his life.

I believed for years that what kept us from being a public couple was logical and reasonable and acceptable. It was humiliating to absorb that what he wanted was someone to worship him and sleep with him and otherwise stay silent in the background.

My ego is a pile of bloody pulp under Ephraim's self-centered cleats.

Thanks to Professor Easterly and three semesters of psychology, I know I'm reacting from my lizard brain, not my wizard brain. I'm so mad I could punch him in the nose, but I'm so sad I have to lock my knees to keep from crumbling into a sobbing mess.

I loved him with every clichéd fiber of my being. I held on to the belief, despite all the clear evidence to the contrary, things would work out. It took an emotional brick upside my stubborn head to accept he loved sleeping with me, but he never loved me.

It was always a veil I threw over our relationship so I could keep the illusion hazy and pretty and comfortable.

I suck in a breath and search out Aunt G. *You've got this* pours from her beautiful green eyes, and I find the strength to straighten my spine.

No one but G knows I'm dying inside, drop by salty drop.

I couldn't have planned a better cover for my broken heart if I'd tried.

CHAPTER TWENTY-FIVE

PAIGE – NOW

MINA AND FINA didn't allow me to do one thing for the brunch. Kiki turns on her natural charm and vivacity, and I find myself hanging back in the same conference-hall-turned-party-room we were in last night. I watch her too closely, knowing it's because I'm anxious, circling like a mother hen so one of the pretty flutes of orange juice and champagne doesn't sneak into her hand.

I have no right to sheepdog her behavior. Except for the occasional holiday, I haven't been a part of her life since she enlisted. It's beyond presumptuous of me to monitor her drinking because she shared such personal information with me a few short hours ago.

It's clear, though, or it appears clear, she's genuinely having a good time. Her hands are busy with a strong cup of coffee, and she's talking with Uncle T. I'm delighted they're reconnecting. They have the military in common, on top of family. I hope she's building with him what I had with V.

There's a roll call of family and locals seated around the tables. Noah and his daughter. Tidy. Mrs. Greene and the GGs, the Grove Grannies. Traycee, her sister, and their Gram. CT Nelson from the grocery store. So many more. All needing a little more time to process our shared loss.

My butt hits the security bar on one of the four French doors opening onto the long patio serving all the party rooms on the east side of the castle. The entire length feeds onto yet another beautiful staircase leading down to the east lawn. I slip out quietly, refusing to acknowledge the hurt knocking like a door-to-door salesman on my heart that literally no one noticed.

I wind and wend my way around to the family graveyard, a place I've always loved to visit when I need to clear my head. It's almost pathetic how carefully I avoid the area where the earth has been turned and V now rests. For a woman who prides herself on intelligence, I'm proving myself much the opposite with how deftly I'm playing ostrich.

I head for the center of the area bordered by the antique iron fence. An enormous magnolia shades the pink granite headstone for Evajean and Alisdair. *MacInnes* is carved underneath a spear thistle, each letter still tidy. Generations have tended the massive marker, repairing it as needed. It has survived a century of wind and weather due to the care of generations of family who have kept a legend alive.

Behind the headstone is a giant dragon, her wings spread out as if daring anyone to touch her monument. I've always pretended this is Penny's mother.

God, I love Evajean. No weeping angels for her and Alisdair.

Evajean Campbell Whitson. Born September 17, 1850. Died September 18, 1950. She lived until the day after Violet was born. V had always been sad she hadn't known Evajean, the woman who set the benchmark for the usually long-lived MacInnes line.

Alisdair Callum MacInnes, born October 15, 1840, preceded her by some twenty years, defying the average male lifespan of the time to depart this mortal coil on November 2, 1930.

I'm not remotely a historian, but Violet had a special affinity for these two, and not because they're the reason we're all here. She told me about having to do a school report on them as a teenager and hating it at first. Being a typical kid, she'd resented having to learn about her ancestors and thought she knew these amazing people.

At the time, she was terrified of Aunt Gavina, but the report had turned Gavina to Violet what Violet became to me. Mentor. Friend. Stalwart supporter. I should know more about these amazing women, all of them trailblazers in each of their lifetimes. I'm ashamed at my lack of blazing anything.

I drag my eyes away from the headstone, forming an apology to Evajean for failing her. For failing all of the line she began, turning a history of carrying a pennant of fortitude and perseverance into a present of waving the white flag of defeat.

Folding myself to the ground, I bend my knees and rest my arms on them, burying my face and trying to relax my shoulders. I'm not making excuses for myself, but this is the first major event in my life I've had to do alone. I've been a bit blithe with Kase, thinking I'm done and have let Zach go. The truth is, for all his faults, he's the definition of stalwart. And from the day we met, he's been my rock.

I guess that's what V meant about me being like Evajean and Zach being like Alisdair. We didn't spawn a dynasty, but he and I had had the kind of love and devotion V had attributed to the ancestors before me.

I've never thought of it that way until this very moment.

I know she can't hear me, but I say it aloud anyway. "The difference, my sweet V, is they got through their hard times. I'm not made of the same stuff after all."

I try to take long, slow breaths, hoping I won't dissolve completely from the bone-deep ache of realizing, for the first time in my life, I'm completely and utterly alone.

I'm more than hurt. It's deeper than sad.

I'm afraid.

The fear swirls and strengthens until I'm trembling in terror. I met Zach so young. We married so young. I never lived in a dorm or a tiny one-bedroom apartment. Never learned how to be autonomous.

I was a kid when we met, eighteen when we married, and a mother of twins not all that long after. I don't regret a minute of it, but the consequence of all those decisions have distilled into this moment where, if I'm a typical MacInnes female and, barring a disease cutting my life short like V's, I'm sitting square in midlife. I've got an additional fifty or so years ahead of me, and I have no idea how to navigate them as a single woman.

I'm no Victorian heroine, wrist-to-forehead afraid my life is over without a man, but the truth is I don't know how to negotiate the world without being the other half of a partnership. I console myself, telling panicked me I'll learn. I'm nothing if not resourceful, and I'm sure my bookshelf will be filled in short order with tomes about embracing singlehood and I'll be researching travel groups for women.

Today, those details are so barely on my radar they might as well not exist. Today, I'm lost. Today, I'm petrified. Today, I'm not simply alone. Alone isn't necessarily bad. Alone, by itself, is manageable.

I'm lonely.

I'm desperately sad to be letting go of what was once an essential part of my identity. Regardless of all the whys and hows, of who's to blame, there was a long, long period of my life where Zach was the center of my world. It's tearing me apart to grieve the loss of a breathtaking closeness, the fracturing of the fusion that was once the fuel of my existence.

When the tears come, it's not to mourn my beloved relative. It's to bury a piece of me I once thought I'd die without.

As they always do, the tears subside, but I shudder for long moments more. I'm worried the meltdown won't stop, when I hear footsteps in the heat-stressed grass behind me. I don't turn, longing for Uncle T's gentle touch on the top of my head.

Instead, I hear an accent already natural to my ear.

"It boggles the mind. All the changes they saw."

I scrabble for the packet of tissues in my pocket and spare myself the embarrassment of looking like a snot-slicked toddler after a tantrum. My face somewhat clean, I lift my head to glance over my shoulder. "Indeed it does. The turn of the century. World wars. The Depression."

"Jazz. Airplanes. Rock 'n' roll."

He joins me on the ground, sitting beside me and draping his long arms over his similarly bent legs, hands clasped loosely in front of his knees.

"Your list's more upbeat."

He keeps his eyes locked on the gravestone. "Are you all right?"

I have a thousand-year argument in my head in the ensuing ten seconds. "No."

"I didnae think so."

I wipe the last tear from my face. It's nice to sit in the shade, the morning breeze playing with my hair and tugging at his crisp, white cotton shirt.

"When you left a moment ago, you looked...lonely."

If I'd been standing, I'd've been knocked down. Even seated, it's like I've been kicked in my stomach by one of the horses about to be let out to graze.

"Please don't." My voice cracks. Breaks.

"Don't what?" He cants his head at me, clearly confused.

"Don't be...understanding."

He pulls his hands apart and then, as if he's wondering why, clasps them together.

"Paige, I'm flummoxed. If you want me to go away, I will."

"No, it's more I don't know how to react. How to do—" I gesture between us. "This."

"I'm not the quickest man on the planet, but I'm guessing *this* has to do with your husband."

I snort. "Yeah, you could say so. And you could say I married as a teenager and I have zero idea how to talk to a man who I can no longer deny is sending me signals I had forgotten existed. If I'm even reading them correctly." I close my eyes, then fix them on the magnolia. "And adding the fact we've know each other a mere few days."

"My gran would say some souls have known each other for lifetimes and recognize each other in an instant."

"I'd agree with your gran, but she's not here to help me figure out how to flirt, since I never knew how to in the first place. When you meet at sixteen, wed at eighteen, and start having babies before the ink is dry on the marriage license, it doesn't give a woman many notches on her belt." I snuffle at my own bad analogy. "Who am I kidding? I never got to buy the belt in the first place."

"I promise you I'm nae the—what did you call me in the car? A world-traveling lothario? My sisters would keel over."

He laughs at himself, and it makes me like him even more.

Dammit.

Better to spell it all out.

"Leith, I've felt invisible for a long time. I look at all these people," I wave toward the castle, "and it's like I can touch the love V created in her chosen family. I know some of these folks are real DNA relations, but I mean, she never married and had kids, so she created this."

He frowns at me. "I don't follow."

"For years, I had an idyllic marriage. My husband's a great guy, and we were so connected, it was kinda scary. Our friends called us icky and gooey. Honest to God, I felt like Cinderella after the ball, and he was my Prince Charming."

I rub my arms even though the climbing temperature is conquering the morning coolness.

"And then, when we broke, five-ish years ago, it went away. I lost half of who I am. I don't know how to be alone, how to start over, no matter how long it's been coming. To be honest, all I am is terrified."

I rub my lips together, but my balm is gone, and my skin is dry. How appropriate.

From the corner of my eye, I see his shoulders drop.

"I never meant to be improper, Paige. I took, from what you shared with me, while not official as far as the courts are concerned, you'd moved on. I never intended to push anything, but every time I see you, it's like I'm a compass needle and you're a magnetic pole."

"Thank you for not saying true north. A line from a bad rom-com would've made me slug you."

His soft laugh moves something inside me infinitesimally toward I'm not a freak after all.

"Despite my sisters' teasing, I have shite for pickup. It's the real reason I've had few girlfriends, and none for long, and I've never felt any of them was the one."

"You'll know. Your gran's right."

"She definitely is."

I rub at the raging headache building in my temples. I'm not good at this. I don't know how to do this. I don't know that I want to do this.

I don't know that I *don't* want to do this.

I pluck at the grass by my toes, the blades brittle from the already brutal June heatwave.

I feel you, grass. I feel you.

"I've held on for years now. Hoping. Praying he'd come back. It didn't have to be perfect, but I'd have settled for a semblance of what we had." I toss down the now-shredded stems. "I finally had to let go."

"I'm truly sorry. It's tragic you've had to give up something so amazing. I can only imagine."

Great. One of the cutest guys I've ever met, who's been flirting with me for days, thinks I'm tragic. Lovely.

"Let's get you something to eat."

The cherry on my grouchy float is his fluid grace when he stands and offers his hand to help me up. Why does he have to be handsome and sexy and strong? All the boxes, checked, on what I like in a man.

I'm caught off guard when he leans toward me, his face nearing mine until his lips touch the skin in front of my ear. When he pulls away, he looks deep into my eyes, the blue of his so crisp they're almost too bright to hold.

"*Tha thu bòidheach*, Paige."

I'm frozen, immobilized by the deep rasp of his voice, the kindness and yearning in his eyes. The hands hovering, waiting for a signal from me.

It takes all my strength to take a barely discernible step back.

I clear my throat, pretending everything is normal, even if it's the least-applicable word in the dictionary right now. If I don't insulate myself with all those people having brunch, I'll launch myself at him and make a clown of myself on a level from which I'll never recover.

"I don't know that expression." I deflect to his beautiful words.

Brilliant, Paige. Simply stellar dialogue.

"It's the entirety of what I know in Gaelic. It means 'you're beautiful.'"

Pure, unadulterated panic replaces every drop of blood in each vein and artery, from my toenails to my hairline. I look around, probably resembling a robot gone haywire, as if the headstones surrounding me will give me something, anything, to say.

"You learned the phrase to impress a girl you wanted to date in your Gaelic class." I offer a quick thanks to whichever ancestor gave me the quip to try to put the conversation on track.

He takes the hint and puts a hand to his chest, pretending to stumble. "Och, you wound me, woman."

I flap at the magnolia, hoping my gesture doesn't look as desperate as I imagine it to be. "Did you know this magnolia is on the registry as the fourth largest in the United States? The last measurement was seventy-nine feet tall, and the canopy is over forty feet across."

Leith's smile is small and sweet and understanding as he tucks a strand of my hair behind my ear. "It's magnificent."

Unfortunately, his words aren't directed to the tree.

I imagine my face turns every shade of red in the Pantone book. Scarlet? Carmine? Candy apple? All the above and more as the blood rushes back after abandoning me seconds before. I whirl and start toward the salon, managing to keep my pace a hair under an all-out run.

"It's a testament to Evajean and Alisdair." I narrate, as if I'm a tour guide. "It's been here over a hundred years, which is long-lived for a magnolia, but the arborist said it's still healthy."

I fill the walk with every factoid I can remember about the cemetery and the planting details of each tree. Considering the very reason he's here is to learn about the Texas MacInneses, my sudden dive into being the castle tour guide is completely logical.

Even I have to roll my eyes at myself, but talking's my best option right now. It stops me from thinking.

We rejoin the brunch crowd, no one the wiser other than a raised where've-you-been eyebrow from Kiki.

Leith pivots to leave, and I put a hand on his arm.

His impressively muscled upper arm...

"I appreciate what you said. Everything." Luckily, I'm speaking at my normal register.

He takes my hand and raises it to his lips, kissing my knuckles. "Any time. I mean it." He lets my fingers go, and the moment is broken. "Before I head off, I've been meaning to ask if you have the castle blueprints you mentioned the other day. I'd like to grab them. I haven't wanted to bother."

"No bother. I haven't been in Violet's office yet, but I'll look soon."

"Good, then."

The second he's gone, Kiki's beside me, looking between us with bright curiosity.

"Wanna tell me what that's about?"

"It's no big deal." But it could be, and I know it.

"Looked big dealish to me."

"It was a...moment. It's over."

She wraps an arm around my waist and pulls me toward the buffet line and the silver serving chafers waiting with fluffy eggs, tortilla strips, and the perfect amount of jalapeños. "I'm here to listen when you're ready."

I take a plate from Mina, ignoring the equally curious question in her eyes.

They'll both have to stay frustrated. It'll take some time to process what happened.

And right now, my body, mind, and soul are wiped, numb, and dazed.

CHAPTER TWENTY-SIX

MINA – NOW

CT, bless his heart, has agreed to take me to Atlanta for our lunch. He offered to go all the way into Dallas, but I said our neighboring town was fine. I don't get over there much, and although it's not impossible, we're far less likely to run into anyone there I know. Which is exactly the point. I've agreed to this date, and I abide by my word, but I'm not ready to parade around downtown with him yet.

Or ever.

He seems content to drive a notch above the speed limit. I want to tease him about being Mario Andretti, but it'd be too much like flirting.

I don't know how to flirt. I'm too dadgum old to flirt.

I hear Joy Baker's voice in my head and can practically picture her pointing an eggplant at me. *We ain't dead yet. At least I ain't.*

The air conditioner vent blows CT's cologne my way, and I spend a good minute trying to figure it out. I like perfume, so it's a game I play, like I do with fabric, wondering if I can see what other people miss. The easy notes are lavender and vanilla. Then there's bergamot. I have some bergamot lotion, and it's one of my favorites. The spicy comes from cinnamon and orange blossom. A little sandalwood. And... Dang it, I almost have it...

Cedarwood. That's it.

I may not have all that right, but the scent is darn sure the short side of irresistible. He's taken a light hand with the atomizer, and it makes me want to take deep breaths, not hang my head out the window before I choke to death.

Roylee bathed in Stetson. I swear, if the tiniest whiff of the stuff hits me even now, I have to fight losing my lunch.

I chastise myself for letting a terrible man invade my precious time with CT, but Roylee stole so much from me, leaving me a ransacked house with nothing of value in the mess and muck left behind.

"I...your cologne. It's nice."

"My Annabelle, gave it to me for Christmas. It's in a bottle shaped like a man's body. She thought she was so funny, but I like it."

An awkward silliness fizzes in me like shaken Dr Pepper, but I have to be honest. "I do, too."

He moves his eyes off the road long enough to glance at me.

Lord, but he's got the sweetest smile. It's soft and light, and his joy climbs all the way to the corners of his eyes where the crinkles squinch.

Like my stomach and my spleen are squinchin' right under my breastbone.

What in the name of jumpin' Jehoshaphat am I doing here? I need to tell him to turn around, take me home. I—

"I'm excited you've joined me today." CT turns down the already low volume on the radio.

I've been so caught up in my head I didn't realize there's a Charlie Pride station playing until my eyes light on the stereo display. I'm frantic for something to keep him talking and me listening.

The answer is literally in front of me. I can talk about cars.

"This is a pretty Cadillac. Fina had one when she was traveling to Dallas for her classes. She's moved entirely online now, but for a while, she was sure burnin' up miles on the highway. Didn't get the greatest gas mileage, but she said it was a good tradeoff for all the hours on the road."

Brilliant, Willamina Greene. You're a conversational savant.

"I'm not trying to be rude, because I like your sister very much. Fina's a fine woman, but I don't want to talk about her."

"Oh," I manage, my voice small. "What…what would you like to talk about?"

"How about you tell me about yourself."

"CT Nelson, you have been in this town as long as I have. You know I've worked in the castle since Moses was put in a basket."

"Maybe not quite so long." His deep voice is definitely teasing. "And you know my family's owned the market since God's dog was a puppy. So tell me something about you I don't know. What do you like to do in your spare time?"

"Sew?"

He frowns. "'Sew,' like with a needle and thread, or 'so' as in 'so what'?"

I close my eyes and curl my nails into the leather seats. I take a deep breath and beg the good Lord to let me not sound like a child.

"Needle and thread," I clarify. "Violet taught me how a long time ago when I needed to do something to let me pretend I'm…smart. She also taught me to quilt, but I love making clothes. It makes my frugal Momma so happy to see me wearin' something from her magazines, but she knows I made it ten times better and twenty times cheaper."

He does the cut-his-eyes-to-me-and-to-the-road thing. "Did you make your dress?"

I look down at my lap as if I need verification that I'm still wearing the Bellville Sassoon dress with a bateau neckline from the fall Vogue look book. I like the cap sleeves, and I chose the blue gabardine I never got to make for V, not only to honor her, but because the fabric avoids wrinkles.

I need to speak, not reminisce, but so he'll keep his eyes on the road instead of on me. "This fabric was the last thing Violet and I bought together at the shop."

"It's pretty. The color is perfect with your eyes."

Oh, my. Oh, no. Oh, Jesus.

I relax my hands before I claw chunks out of his comfy seats. "Now you tell me about you." My voice borders on desperate. "What do you do when you're not at the store?"

"Mostly, I enjoy taking the kids and grandkids out on the boat in the summertime. My grandson's six, and the stinker can out-ski and out-wakeboard his daddy and me."

"I forgot you have grandchildren." Did I know he had grand-children?

"All of them are Annabelle's."

Of course. His other daughter, Bethanie, the semidependable cashier, has never procreated. I'm the last person who can throw stones from my glass house, but that girl's career seems to be making bad choices.

He proceeds to list names and ages and school levels, all the infor-mation infused with pride, and we're parking in the crowded lot of Finnian's Fine Dining before I have time to get nervous again. In fact, CT keeps up such a stream of anecdotes about his family, we've given our menus to the waiter and are waiting for our orders before he runs out of steam.

"I've talked your ear off."

I shake my head. "I don't mind at all. Like, I didn't know you have a cabin on the lake. I bet you can see the castle's dock from yours."

"I can. We've spent many an evening in the lawn chairs, jaw jacking and listening to the music from some event or another drifting down the shoreline."

It's a lovely picture. Something I can imagine but have never expe-rienced. After Roylee threw me into the lake, I've been too afraid to—

It strikes me then, as I lift my water glass, that I was wrong. My mess of a house isn't empty. There's plenty left inside. Plenty of fear covering the furniture of my life like a layer of dust no microfiber cloth or can of Pledge can clean up.

Fear is the legacy of Roylee and all the choices made in the wake of disaster.

I try to hide it, but I run scared a lot, and a lot like my morning coffee, it quietly fuels my days.

I stumble into words so that I don't hightail it out of the restaurant. "I love when we light the big fire pit. We haul out the hangers and go through about twenty bags of marshmallows."

The warmest chuckle comes across the table. "Nothing beats s'mores around a fire."

"Not much, but have you ever had 'em Irish-style? With those Andes mints?"

"My, no. Sounds amazing."

"It's a good thing I can't find those suckers everywhere, or I'd weigh seven hundred pounds."

"Your scale is safe, and you'd still be as pretty."

By the grace of God and his angels, the drinks arrive, and I'm saved from spontaneously combusting in the middle of Atlanta, Texas.

I cast around my mind for yet another subject. "Are you prepared for the games? Every room's booked between here and Dallas, and I'm not sure there's a campsite left for the taking."

"Goodness, yes. The Eighty-Fifth MacInnes Highland Games will be quite grand. My grandson Donnell will be doing the caber toss for the first time."

"Lord, those young'uns tossin' those itty-bitty cabers are so adorable, it about ruins me."

"Donnell's little outfit is the cutest thing you ever did see."

I have no idea where I summon the nerve to look at him a bit sideways. "Will his granddaddy be wearing the tartan?"

"Of course." He side-eyes me back. "Willamina Greene, do I need to be careful about my kilt getting tossed up?"

I think—no, I'm sure. I am going to die.

Every atom in the dining room turns. Morphs. Flips inside out. My instincts scream, *Danger!* I've gone too far. My blood rushes to my feet. My skin turns to ice.

"I didn't—I'm sorry. CT, I swear I didn't mean—"

He grabs my hand and strokes it like he's touching a rose. I yank it away. He doesn't understand. I look around wildly, trying to find the damned door.

"Mina." He speaks urgently, his hand sliding across the table, but stopping short of mine this time. "It's all right. I was joking."

I grab my glass, water sloshing over the rim before I'm able to drink like I've been in the desert for a month.

CT sits there, his face a canvas of mortification and guilt. A millennia later, or maybe a few seconds, I put the glass down with a steadier hand.

"Mina, please forgive me. I didn't mean to be crude."

Where a laugh comes from, I will not know until Gabriel blows his horn. "You weren't crude. You were sweet and trying to be funny, and I've made a monumental mistake. I never should have said yes to this luncheon. I'm an idiot."

This time, he does touch my hand, or rather, the back of my clenched fist, on the table. It's barely more than two fingers against my clammy skin, but the gesture is sweet and kind.

"Please don't ever use that word about yourself. Ever. I was pleased as punch you agreed, as I've been wanting to take you out for a long time. I'm not the best at courtin'. My momma used to say words were my eighth-best skill."

Courtin'. Now there's a concept as foreign to me as dancing is to a duck. The only courtin' I've ever done is to go to the courthouse. Twice. Once for getting married to my worst mistake, and the other to sign the paperwork certifying the bastard's death.

What I do know is CT's a kind man, and I won't put him through any more of my funny business.

"It wasn't you, it was me. You've lived in Magnolia Bloom long enough to know I've got more baggage than American Tourister. I should never have put you through my silliness, and I won't subject you to it again. I'll stay home, like I'm supposed to. Stay in my lane, like they say these days."

He takes a deep breath and seems to make a decision. "While I'd normally never tell a lady to ignore her intuition, you're wrong. No woman as lovely and funny and talented as you should stay home.

There's nothing frivolous about you. My day brightens on the too rare occasions I see you."

I should hear kindness, but the old me hears false promises. Small flirts meant to draw me out so he can cage me.

Maybe it's the exhaustion from the crash of my adrenaline rush. It's been so long since I've felt this tidal wave—and had to hold on to survive until the water receded—I've tricked myself into believing I'd never go through it again. Although none of it's CT's fault, I'm done in.

I find some scrap of calm when I meet his eyes.

His kind, lovely, inviting eyes.

"You've been sweet, but I'd like you to take me home. I'm sorry you've gone to so much trouble."

"If you want to go home, I'm honored to take you. I wish you wouldn't need me to, but I'll not try to dissuade you."

In the history of my life, has a man—*poof*—agreed to anything I've ever said or wanted?

I'm so not prepared. I sit against the padding of my seat with a thump. "Well, all right, then."

He pays the waiter for the meal we haven't eaten and escorts me to the car. The whole way home, he regales me with stories about the customers at his store, a big saga about his last boat purchase, and so many other things, I'm waving goodbye from the porch of my side of the duplex before it seems possible. I promised him that someday we'll try again, but we left it so open-ended, I'm choosing to believe he was being polite.

I'm many things, but foolish is generally not one of them. Not anymore. I'll never be ridiculous enough to try a date, lunch or otherwise, ever again.

I go into my home, flip the never-used deadbolt, and head for my sewing machine.

CHAPTER TWENTY-SEVEN

PAIGE – NOW

I'M A COWARD. A wimp. A total chicken.

I spend a solid week hiding. I stay curled up on the overstuffed couch in V's turret, reading through the meticulously organized folders she's left for me. Kiki's gone to Alaska to finish the details for her separation from the Air Force. After the tenth time I insisted she come here when she's free, she told me to shut up, but I hope she returns soon. The bond I have with my sister has taken a fragile, but promising, turn. There's a kinship here I've missed, a surprise well inside me I need filled. I have a best friend, but there's a space for my sister waiting to bloom and grow if I tend it.

I find I want to know the woman my sister is now. We didn't have many quiet moments together, but I cherish the few, easy conversations over coffee and most especially her candor. Kiki's cold, hard truth about her alcoholism and path to recovery speaks to me. She shared her deepest secret, and I find I want to share mine, as I now believe she, better than anyone, might understand my plight with Zach.

Later. For now, she gets to go first. Be first. She doesn't need me piling onto the burden weighting her shoulders.

The whines of the riding lawnmowers rattle my attention to the task of packing up fifty years of V's life. I step away from the line of boxes and listen to the furious clamor of untold bodies readying the castle for the masses.

Mina and Fina are twin cyclones preparing for the games. The kitchens are all-hands-on-deck for making and freezing food for the feast. Housekeeping's washing and folding a mountain of towels and bedding. Gardeners are gathering every last tomato, carrot, potato, and leek of the summer harvest. Grounds keepers are building corrals for the sheep-herding demonstrations and lining off the different fields for the games. One thing I know for sure? Every single bullet point will be checked off on Mina's clipboard before the first banner's hung or a shield's planted at a tent face.

The mighty Greene duo appreciates my offer, I know, but I have been firmly told—and with a brook-no-argument finality—that my job is to stay out of the way. Other than making a late-night trip to the grocery store to stock V's small refrigerator and ensure a full cabinet of coffee beans, I'm alone in the midst of a tornado.

I go to the window and catch sight of the cabers being unloaded from an oversize trailer. It takes two workers, sometimes three, to haul the logs off the flatbed, so it's no wonder the one-man event elicits the most cheers during the contests. My favorite events, though, are for the wee ones. I can already see my Callum in a couple of years joining the ranks of the juniors tossing their miniature pikes.

I'm super excited to learn Cousin Ian is bringing over three of his six girls. I squint, trying to remember the ancestry. Ian is the however-many-greats grandson of Alyssa, Alisdair's sister. The stories of Alisdair's love for his sister are almost as famous as those about his love for Evajean. Alyssa moved to Scotland after marrying Niall MacMillan, and a life-long, but love-filled, rivalry ensued between Alyssa and her new clan and her brother and his brood on the far shore...not the least of which was how many children they'd each add to the gene pool.

All amusing mental wanderings aside, I'm worried about Mina. She's withdrawn, quiet. And when she does talk, it's to bark orders. Barking is to Mina what being a jerk was to Mr. Rogers. The impossibility of her drill sergeant mood nags at me. Something's wrong. We're all out of sorts, but Mina's curt replies aren't caused by sorrow. There hasn't been time to reach the anger stage of grief yet.

I answer texts from Zach and the kids, talk to Kase every other day. She's in the weeds with business negotiations while still running a thriving business, so I'm giving her space. I'm surprisingly content in the cocoon of my thoughts and commitment to cleaning out V's suite since I can't help with the setup. I have stacks of boxes and rolls of tape, and since I'm in no hurry, I work slowly through the lifetime of household goods one collects from staying in the same place for decades.

Which means I'm slapped in the face when I remember I'll soon be doing this in my own house. Panic rises and overflows, sending my nerves into overdrive. I put a hand on the window frame, my chest tearing apart like I've been prepped for open-heart surgery. I want to yell into the void the question I've ignored and see if an answer echoes back.

I keep waiting for my gut to give me a thumbs-up, for the absolute certainty to kick in that I'm doing the right thing. I want a sign from the universe, an everything-will-be-okay, stay-the-course message. In the confines of these stone walls, I'll admit I'm a secret mess, a tangle of wanting, not wanting, and numbness. Isn't it supposed to be clear, this choice I have to make? Do I have to wait until Zach gets here to see if the castle boots us out the door?

Married or Divorced. I sure as hell have stared at those two doors long enough. The petition's ready. I've turned the knob. So why, after so many years of heartache, am I hesitating to walk through and shut the damned thing?

My psychic BFF's ringtone comes from my phone. I walk to V's chair and sit, swiping the icon of the video camera to bring Kase's beautiful face to my screen.

"Scary." Not an unusual greeting between us, for sure.

"My bat signal went off. What up, buttercup?"

Guilt rides herd on my need to offload my sorrows. "Nothing worth interrupting your schedule. I know you're busy being a beauty mogul, hon."

Her snort is indelicate. "Hon? You haven't been in the backwoods long enough to trip and fall into the darlin's and bless-your-hearts. Here I thought I should worry for your dust and ragweed allergies."

I drop my chin and give her puppy-dog eyes. "Can I have a pass because my defenses are low?"

"Twenty-four hours. No extensions."

Her chair squeaks, and although it's out of screen range, I'm sure she folds one of those ridiculously long legs underneath her. She leans her head on the chair's headrest, and I can see fatigue marring her forehead.

I shake my finger at her. "You've not been sleeping, young lady."

"I know, Mommy, but I promise it'll be over soon, and I'll give you every boring detail. I'd kick the winning financial field goal, if the other side would stop moving the goalpost. It's not worth talking about yet. Which is a brilliant segue, if I do say so myself, into you telling me what's going on."

"Nothing of consequence. The growing stack of boxes you can see behind me made me think about the house, so I've been reminiscing. Everyone warned us building a custom home was divorce fodder, but Zach and I loved it."

"You two were unicorns."

I'm lost in memories and know Kase understands. "I love every single square inch, but giving up my objectively ridiculous closet will be the hardest to leave behind. Even if I take the house in the property settlement, it makes no sense for me to keep so much space for myself."

"Probably not the wisest thing to hang out with the ghosts of a once-wonderful marriage slowly fading out of existence."

"Poetically put, and absolutely true."

"See? I'm not always mean to Zach."

No, but she's unswervingly loyal to me. "Did saying it give you heartburn?"

She reaches onto her desk, then shakes a bottle of antacids at the camera. "I'm prepared." Putting it down pops her out of view for a second. "Are the kids leaving you alone? The office?"

"The kids check in once in a while. Grady has been an angel about only calling if it's important. Mostly, I've been going through the motions of sorting through V's life and reading her journals."

"The reading police will issue you a ticket if you keep up that page-a-day speed."

I lift a volume and show her the binding of my current edition. "It's all the time I have left with her, so I'm not on a cannonball run. Anyway, remember the man at the viewing I pointed out? Turns out, he's her old boyfriend David, but she calls him Ephraim."

"Whoa. Interesting."

"Yeah, I'm as guilty as any person of not seeing their elders were young once, but I'm doubly guilty of being sure I knew V more than most people. Looks like I might be wrong."

Kase leans in for a close-up. "She's a real-life Dexter, isn't she? Or she was cooking up something in the kitchen other than grits."

Leave it to Kase and her obsession with TV crime drama. "Not that kind of secret life. I'm at the point in the journal where she's in college and planning her whole life around this person I know she didn't end up with."

"What kept them apart?"

"He's Jewish."

"And?"

"And apparently he couldn't see past it. She wanted to make it work, but he kept putting up barriers." Maybe I've found the problem. The unknown parallels between me and the aunt I believed to be near perfect. "They clearly didn't end up together, so I'm curious about why. I'm also learning a lot about her friend Tidy. Listen to this. They sunbathed on the dock, slathering on baby oil with iodine mixed in."

"Get out! SPF zero?"

"Negative SPF would be more accurate."

"I have the perfect fix for crispy skin forty years too late. It wobbles the mind they'd bake themselves with baby oil."

"And iodine, but it was the '70s. It seems Tidy was in an abusive relationship, but instead of listening to V's advice, she turned on V and gave her crap about how Ephraim treated her."

"Harsh."

"Yep, but maybe V needed to hear the hard truth. They got over it, because I know she and V stayed friends. Tidy owns the dance hall downtown."

"Sounds like a real-life *Dallas* or *Dynasty*."

"There's no JR, and no one's been shot yet. It's fascinating, though."

"Which is an easy segue into asking if there've been any convos with Mr. Everything's Fine?"

"He's sent a few texts, left a few messages."

"Sorry, sweetie."

"I'm out of sorries. Not yours, of course. I know you mean it in the kindest way. The word doesn't mean anything anymore."

"It sure as hell doesn't fix anything."

I sigh. "I don't mean to be snarly. It sucks we don't have a better way of expressing concern and regret. But enough of my maudlin crapola."

"So is there's any movement from Mr. I Shouldn't with the sexy brogue?"

I'm glad my phone isn't super high-tech so my blush doesn't flash-fry the camera. "No, and I'm not seeking any moves." Or looks. Or anything.

She raises an eyebrow. "Really?"

"Yes, and leave it alone."

She gives me the Kase-eye. "For now, but—" A tone pings from her computer, and she looks away. "Gotta go. We'll circle back, and I want juicy details. Love you."

"Love you more."

We click off, and I put my phone away, making a mental note to go to Tidy's bar soon. I've had only a second to exchange the briefest hellos and condolences with her, and now that I know more, I need to see how her life turned out. And I bet she can give some details about the mysterious Ephraim.

For now, curiosity about the noise leaching through the French doors stirs my curiosity and my need for some exercise. I brush my hair back into a simple ponytail and change into jeans, a tank top, and sneakers. Not exactly my best haute couture, but I give myself a crisp reminder there's no one I need to impress.

The day is glorious, but hot, so I hug the tree line as I walk the grounds, staying out of the way of the anthill of activity. Shouts come from all corners, and the whirr and whine of power tools fill the air. I pass a tent where a sign is being mounted for the kettle corn booth and recognize those legs on the ladder. And the Wrangler logo.

I mean, everyone recognizes the pocket W. It's the firm specimen beneath the logo that stops me short and stirs several internal organs. I have to stop this insanity. I've never been afraid of desire, of passion, but those all bloomed inside the proper boundaries of my marriage. Now, one look at Leith and I want him, and I don't want him. I long for my old life and then long for something new. Something I'll treat better, but only if my effort is matched in return.

I let my tumbleweed of indecision and regret roll by. How am I not supposed to notice the denim straining over a mighty fine derriere that's either seen a ton of gym time or hiked every Highland hill?

As if he can hear my salacious thoughts all the way across the lawn, he turns, waving as he sees me. He gives me the universal one-finger *wait a minute* and hurries down the ladder. I should be flattered at his haste. Instead, my pulse is racing with uncertainty and indecision. Give a quick wave and head inside, or wait?

My indecision gives him time to jog over.

"Mornin'."

"Good morning. You've been drafted into helping, it appears."

"Aye, but I don't mind. I booked the trip because of the games as much as wanting to explore the castle, so I'm happy to lend a hand."

"Ian and crew should be here tomorrow."

His face brightens and his eyes crinkle. "It's wild it's been two years, and when I see my best mate again, it's in America."

I give a nod toward his jeans and Luccheses. "Careful. Ian may not recognize you in all your Western flash."

"Like 'em?" He lifts one foot to show me the doggin' heel on the tan calfskins he's breaking in. "I was hoping you'd come with me to buy a cowboy hat, as I couldnae make up my mind, but these beauties wouldnae stay on the shelf."

My stomach tries to shake hands with my backbone at the thought. He's already too much for my system, but add a hand-creased 10X Stetson silverbelly? I might go round-heeled right in the store aisle.

I deflect, of course, returning to footwear. "Thank the country gods you didn't buy ropers. I'd've sent you to Scotland on the first plane outta Dallas."

He balances effortlessly on one foot and dusts off the pointed end of his new purchase. "Glad to know. The sales lass did mention people around here are in one camp or the other on the proper toe."

"There's only one right camp, and I'm glad you chose wisely."

"Me, too. I wouldnae want to leave yet."

A flush heats up my chest and races up my neck. I'm searching for a pithy way to hide my epic ridiculousness when I hear Callum's rallying cry. "Nana! Nana! I'm here!"

I turn and squat in time to catch the four-foot asteroid as he launches himself at me. "Hi, baby. I'm so happy to see you."

And startled. And...I wouldn't say annoyed, but I've had enough surprises, both good and bad for the year, much less the last month. I wasn't expecting them for another four, maybe five, days, and I need control over *something* in my life. Irritation rises up my throat, a string of long-buried words about respect and my schedule, but now's not the time to tame a monster I helped create, and certainly not in front of a stranger to my family.

I close my eyes as Callum's hands slip around my neck, and his legs wrap around my waist. Something eases in me. My ball of all-boy energy could slather me in cheese dust and East Texas clay, and I wouldn't trade his sticky-fingered love for anything. The clench of Callum's arms is like being wrapped in angel's wings.

"We drove *so* long, and Bella cried all the time, and I got a treat at the store because I was good, and I won the quiet game. Wanna see?"

He holds out a stuffed animal with oversize eyes and a not insignificant number of orange fingerprints all over the cotton print with silver scales.

"It's a dragon, not a dinosaur. He has wings." He wiggles the fabric flap to be sure I understand. "And dinosaurs don't have wings. Well, some do, but this one doesn't."

"He's very handsome." I press a kiss to his already sweaty temple. I see Ainsley moving at a much slower pace, so I take the pause to make introductions to the openly curious Leith.

"Leith, this fireball is my grandson Callum. Callum, can you say hello to Mr. Leith? He lives in Scotland."

Callum is instantly captured. "Hi, I'm Callum, and I'm four. And you have dragons! You have the Lick Next Monster, but she's not a monster. And she might not be a dragon, because she doesn't have wings, but she's pretty, and I think she is a dragon who got stuck in the lake. Have you seen her? Is she nice?"

To his credit, Leith nods kindly during the summation of one of the biggest and most debated legends of his homeland. Dammit. I already know he loves puppies. Why does he have to be nice to kids, too?

Throw me a bone here, Leith. I need some reason to not like you so much.

"Hallo, Callum, it's pure barry to meet you. And no, sadly I cannae say I've ever met Nessie, but I bet you're right and she's a friendly lass."

I catch Leith's amused eyes. "Callum, as you may suspect, is captivated by all things dragon and dinosaur."

"You cannae fault the lad for that."

Ainsley moves up beside me, Bella against her shoulder underneath a light blanket.

"Hi, sweetie. I'd like you to meet Leith MacMaster. He's a friend of Cousin Ian's, here for the games and to do a story on the castle. Leith, my daughter, Ainsley."

He offers his hand and adds a proper nod to make any Texan or Scot proud. "Delighted."

"Welcome to Texas." Ainsley adjusts Bella and accepts his handshake. "Is Ian coming?"

"Aye, with three of his bairns."

Leith answers for both of us, and I look at my beautiful Mini-Me, except Ainsley has highlighted her brown hair to lighter golden blond and scraped it into a mom bun. Unlike me, she's CrossFitted her way into the jeans she wore in high school.

"Hi, Mom. We decided to come early. Richard's parents couldn't make the trip to Austin after all, so we made a family decision to join you."

"Not that I'm not glad, but did you think the cell towers are down out here?"

I love my children, but sometimes I swear they're barely more capable than babies, bawling at the drop of a hat and expecting me to kiss their boo-boo or supply their tenth juice box.

Guilt assails me at the urge to scream. I love being a mother, and I'll always be a mother. But being a coworker, a wife, a parent, and a friend have shoved Paige the woman to the rear of a long line. I don't want to be front and center all the time, but I need my turn. Just every now and then. Once in a blue moon, I need Paige to be the shiniest star in my family's sky.

Ainsley frowns. "I thought...we thought we'd surprise you. Aiden and Chen were fine with us piling into Fam Two. Daddy's on his way. Mina said the room's ready."

Ah. She did say *family* decision.

Callum takes my face in his hands. "Nana, Bella frew up, and it was stinky. But she does that sometimes, so you can't be mad at her."

I kiss his candy-coated cheek without wincing. "I'm glad you are so sweet to your baby sister. Everybody throws up. We can't help it."

His eyes grow wide. "You frew up? Are you sick?"

"No, I'm not." I forgot how literal four-year-olds tend to be. I forget a lot of things sometimes, especially when it comes to putting myself first. "We should get the kids out of the sun." I let my grandson wriggle down, keeping hold of his hand. There are too many saws and ladders and distracted workers who might not see a little boy until it was too late.

Ainsley gives the cotton blanket a fluff to move the air around Bella. "Mina had some guys take my bags up to the apartment. And yes, let's get out of the heat."

I turn to Leith. "Don't work too hard, you hear?"

"Wouldnae dream of it."

Ainsley gives him the smile responsible for many a broken teenage heart before Richard won the day. I'll check where he is when we're alone, but for now, she's 2013's Miss Barton Springs again.

"Mr. MacMaster, it's certainly a pleasure."

Leith pretends he's been shot. "Mister? Och, lass, if you don't call me Leith, you might send me to my grave."

"We can't allow such a tragedy, can we, Leith? I look forward to seeing you at the games."

I wave goodbye and lead the way, letting Callum's detailed explanation of the latest episode of *Dinosaur Train* fill the walk. It's much better than letting my eyes stray to the man who tempts me more than warm, sweet kettle corn.

Or drowning in the dread that Zach is on his way.

CHAPTER TWENTY-EIGHT

VIOLET – 1971

FRANCE, it turns out, is fifty times more beautiful than any travel brochure.

We spent the first two months acclimating, visiting all the tourist spots on our list, then settling in to hillsides and seasides, towns and smaller villages, cheese shops and wine shops and tea shops. G and I are usually content to leave each other alone with our thoughts. I know she's reliving memories of a lost relationship and years with some of the most famous artists in history. I'm lost in absorbing the kicks of the beings inside me who love the early hours best for jumping jacks.

For the past two months, Chateau Desjardin has been a piece of heaven outside of Arbois. I've fallen in love with the Comté cheese, but for all we're living in France, I haven't had much to drink. Seems my little ones don't care for alcohol, so I've been quite the teetotaler in one of the world's most amazing wine regions. I hope to try the Desjardin *vin jaune* before we go home. I've never had yellow wine, and it's renowned here.

The October temperatures are cool in the evenings. Avril and her grandson, René, are holding out for another week before harvesting, but their excitement's almost palpable. *Desjardin* might be on the nose, but doesn't detract from the beauty of Avril's gardens and her commitment to the family vineyard.

And Avril is the worst cook I've ever met.

We'd all had a big laugh, Avril poking the most fun at herself. I assured her it wouldn't have been fair if, on top of having a home out of a movie set on a bucolic vineyard, she were a gourmet chef.

It did turn out, to my feminist surprise, her grandson loves the kitchen, and Avril and René's wife, Sophie, are the ones who come in sweaty from tending the vines to find him standing at the stove with a towel thrown over his shoulder. René's older than I am, maybe thirty, and Sophie is super sweet. We can't communicate because my French is as horrible as her English, so we nod a lot when we see each other.

G finds me on the porch as a perfect sunset is fading on the horizon, backlighting the vines. The wind wafts the smell of dirt and growing things I've been around all my life. The scent of rain adds a top note I now know as well as the magnolia blossoms back home.

"How're you doing?" She takes the chair beside me after giving my shoulder a quick squeeze.

I rub my big belly, which Dr. Marseilles assures me isn't unusual at seven months, especially for twins. When he said he heard two heartbeats, I felt terrified, but I'd already known. Like I know they're girls. Gavina didn't make fun of me when I told her. She put her hand on my stomach, saying, *Sometimes we know things. Doesn't matter if other people claim we can't.* So I have zero doubt I'm right, and not because of the MacInnes propensity for twins. I can sense the girls are already each other's best playmates. God knows they play tag enough to prove it.

I take their tendency to use my bladder as a bouncy castle as a sign they're healthy. As for me, I'm worried about my mind.

It's like I've built a wall between us. Or maybe a better analogy is I'm in one house, and they're next door. I'm willing to share a cup of sugar or help with some errand, but I won't let myself know them. I don't talk to them. Or sing to them. I feed them the cheese they seem to like and get up nine hundred times to pee for all of us.

I haven't told them I love them. I've said those words in my mind, but I can't out loud. I thought it was agony to sort through the tangled threads of emotions I have for Ephraim, but I'm smart enough to know what's coming will make that pale in comparison. So, I keep the words inside, not because I don't have them, but because if I let them out, I might never be okay again.

"I'm good." I smile the smile I've perfected. "Avril and René were hilarious at dinner. They're so sweet to switch between English and French so both Sophie and I can be included. And it didn't take you a full week to get your accent back."

G studies me in the way I don't like, letting me know she's on to my *things aren't fine*. "I didn't catch it all. Something about the heat-wave when we arrived burning off any mildew from the wet spring. They're hoping for a stellar vintage."

"I'm excited to watch, and help where they'll let me."

It won't be long now. Halloween's almost upon us, then Thanks-giving. Well, our Thanksgiving. Then it's a matter of counting the days to see if I spend Christmas pacing the floor and waiting, or if I'm in a bed recovering.

I've accepted I'll head home with my tummy deflated and my arms empty. No, not accepted, but acknowledged. I try not to dwell on it. It doesn't make my decision an easy one. At a minimum, I won't be, can't be, the same person I used to be. What the future holds? I have no way to know.

I hope my heart will merely be bruised, but my gut has steeled itself for broken.

As is our way in these four months, G lets me stay lost in my thoughts, but tonight she clearly has something on her mind.

"Is something wrong?" I shift in my seat so I can face her better.

Her shrug is a bare lift of her bony shoulder. "The cold is seeping into my bones a bit." She rests her elbows on her knees and folds her hands, the stance she reserves for our serious talks. "What do you think of René and Sophie?"

"They're so loving with each other." Loving like I wanted with Ephraim.

She straightens the placket of her sweater, but I know this isn't about being neat. "I didn't want to mention anything until you'd been here awhile. They don't know you're looking for a couple to take the babies. Neither Avril nor I wanted to get their hopes up."

My breath escapes in a long sigh.

One of my guests kicks hard, and I automatically stroke the hard knot pressing against my hand like a casual wave to a neighbor.

"It's getting close."

G keeps her eyes on the sun, a bare arc now above the horizon. "Time and tide."

They may wait for no man, but no man is waiting for me. Over the months, as I've walked these breathtaking hills, I've let Ephraim go. Or more truthfully, I've moved him out of my constant thoughts, which is harder to do when our creations never cease letting me know they're here.

As if I can forget, even in the rare moments they're asleep.

Divorcing myself from my dream has been a slow process. Some days I sneak into maybe land. Maybe if he knew I'm having twins, he'd want me. Maybe he's realized he misses me. My common sense slaps me into reality and reminds me *maybe* is a terrible foundation for the rest of my life and a future I won't give my girls. Ephraim knows exactly where I am. I haven't run away in the literal sense, and my family certainly knows where to find me. To them, I'm on a grand gap-year tour with Gavina as my tour guide while she travels down memory lane. The point being, if he had the slightest interest in contacting me, all it would take is an overseas phone call.

The sharp dagger to my soul is I haven't even ranked the bit of extra postage required for airmail. I'm certainly not risking my children's futures on a man who deems me not worth a dollar for an international stamp.

"You've known Avril for decades. Sophie and René are kind, loving, educated, and family-oriented. If you believe they're the right couple, I'm fine with it." A kick lands solidly on some unsuspecting internal organ, but I will not budge. A judgment-free home with two loving parents is the ideal option for my babies, and I'm unshakable in my vow to give them the best life I can, even though it will be without me.

Sophie and René seem perfect, actually. I've caught the way they look at each other when they think no one can see. The passion between them is deep and real and palpable. They'll shower the girls with undying love, and as a mother, I have no greater concern.

"I'll talk to Avril tomorrow, and we'll go talk to their attorney."

My hand goes to my belly automatically, and I'm sure of the kicks I'm feeling now. One is harder. The other faster.

"Good." I wish I could say *great*, but at least I'm past *okay*. I stand, pulling my heavy sweater around me. "I'm taking a walk, if you don't mind."

"Of course not. Take a flashlight if you'll be out long."

Typical G. No admonitions it's too chilly, too dark. She trusts me to be an adult.

I grab the light stationed on the end of the railing and walk into the dusky twilight. The path leads to a stone building a few yards away where I know the barn cat has had kittens.

Addressing the insistent and persistent fluttering on my left side, I rub and wait for the kicks, wondering if my babies will ever tire of chasing each other around my womb. "I hope you'll trust me to be an adult, too. I'm trying to do the right thing and be the best momma I can be. I hope you'll forgive me."

The tiny foot distending my taut skin takes my breath, but doesn't give me a yes or a no...

CHAPTER TWENTY-NINE

PAIGE – NOW

I LEAD the way to the suite next to V's. I knew the kids would stay in Fam Two with their respective children, but I held on to hope I'd have a few more days' respite.

Ainsley heads straight for the television and, with practiced clicks, has Callum's favorite show on at a reasonable volume.

"Mommy needs to talk to Nana, okay?"

The fact he's already wiggled out of my grasp and is on the way to the carpet in front of the big screen is all the answer we need.

Ainsley has taken the blanket off Bella, and her deep-black hair is sweat-plastered to her beautiful little head. I understand why. Our family skin type does not tolerate long exposure to the Texas sun, especially for the babies, but it still breaks my heart.

I move the lever on the ceiling fan to increase the output, and Ainsley sighs her appreciation. She settles into the rocker while I fix our tea.

"Why isn't Richard with you?" I hand her a glass and take the matching leather recliner.

I keep my tone neutral. These last weeks have been nice, in a hermit-slash-depressed sort of way. I have never been afraid of silence, and the truth is, most days I put on neither television nor radio. Sometimes, the busyness in my head doesn't need a soundtrack.

"He said he's coming tomorrow, but I kinda hope he doesn't. I need some space, or I might kill him."

I make a squinchy face. "I'm trusting that's hyperbole, but do you want to give me some detail?"

Tears pool in her eyes, brown like her Daddy's and holding a lake of misery. She takes a long drink of her tea. "I'm tired, Mom. He doesn't try."

My heart twists. I know her pregnancy with Bella was hard and she was bedridden the entire final month. While both she and my beauty came through the delivery fine, postpartum baby blues hit her with a vengeance. Still, by the time we had Bella's first birthday party, Ainsley assured me she was normal, mom-of-two tired.

"Try how?"

"It's like we aren't married anymore." She stops and rubs Bella's back. "I don't mean it literally, of course, more like we move around each other, doing the things we need to do, and fall into bed exhausted every night."

"You do realize you had a baby thirteen months ago and have a child who has more energy than, oh, two yellow dwarf stars."

Ainsley frowns, but her expression is full of humor. "I remember."

"I hope you see Richard's world has been shaken off its axis, too. Some couples therapy might be something to consider."

"I have considered it." Her shoulders go rigid with indignation. "I asked him to go. He said we don't need therapy. Everything's fine."

"Ains—"

"Mom, I appreciate the advice, I do, but you can't understand what I'm going through. We don't have a perfect marriage like you and Daddy."

I go cold, from the top of my head to my toes digging into the front of my shoes. Sweat breaks out on my neck, and I shiver, but Ainsley is shifting Bella and doesn't notice. Maybe I've been wrong to never speak of any tension between Zach and me to either of our kids. Or maybe the signs were obvious only in my mind.

"Your dad and I..." My voice is strained to my own ears. "We don't have...we aren't—"

"You'll say you guys are like everybody else, blah, blah, blah. You're not. You never fight, and Daddy is always there when you need him."

Like crystal thrown against a wall, my heart shatters. I can't tell her you have to actually care enough to fight, and sure, Zach is there if the refrigerator conks out or I need air in my tires. The other kind of need...not so much. Not anymore.

I form my words carefully. "It's never a good idea to judge your relationship by another person's. Like I don't, and shouldn't, see the everyday minutiae of your relationship with Richard, the same is true of your daddy and me. We're human, and—"

"I know. But he won't listen. I mean, really hear me. Since Bella was born, I'm...lonely."

I fume at her interruption, but truthfully? What possible words of wisdom can I offer besides platitudes, which I despise?

And truth be told, and as selfish as it feels, I'm not sure my well has anything left I can pull up. Mom guilt washes over me, but to my surprise, instead of doubling down on myself as I once might, a wave of anger comes in on the next surge. I love my daughter with all my heart. No one would dare suggest any hint to the contrary. But honestly, if I can't manage to complete one sentence, it doesn't bode well that I'll have a real turn in the minds of any of my family.

When am I allowed say my shoulders can't hold any more?

Ainsley is staring out at the lake, so she misses any mental musings dancing over my face. I flop my hands toward her in the gimme motion. "Let me take Bella, and you go soak in a long, hot bath. How's that sound?"

Her face lights up. "Ohmygod, Mom, you are the best ever."

We transfer the sleeping angel without waking her, other than the winky-eye-hey-whattaya-doin' moment before she snuggles into me and returns to dreamland.

The next thirty minutes are pure baby bliss. Bella might not travel well, but once she wakes up from her nap, she and I have a grand time playing peekaboo and *Nana's gonna eat your toes*, which sends her into paroxysms of laughter. Ainsley still isn't out when I glance at Callum, who is singularly uninterested in being interrupted. By the time I clean up my angel's attempts to feed herself a jar of pureed green beans, Aiden and Chen arrive.

Then it's hugs and baby-swapping Bella for Marceau, more Nana kisses and trips in and out of the apartment. Ainsley enters, refreshed and dressed in tan capris and a navy tank top, her hair still wet but combed, and the boys help put the portable cribs together. They pretend to argue over who gets which room and lay Bella down for a tummy-full nap. Marceau has achieved the eyes-closed-end-of-bottle bliss and will soon be joining his cousin, leaving the adults to chatter incessantly and tease nonstop.

I barely have a chance to check the freezer and start a meal list when the door opens again, and Zach arrives. Ainsley and Aiden both told me he was coming, but it still takes me by surprise because I simply didn't want to accept it. I'm stunned into immobility as the kids and Callum descend on him like he's the messiah returned.

He and Ainsley hug, followed by Aiden, then Chen last in the bro-hug-back-slap thing. He swings Callum, screaming with delight, overhead. It's such an amazing picture. Utter, genuine love flows around the room.

My eyes flood, and I race into the bathroom, locking the door behind me, clutching the sink to stay upright. I take deep breaths to get a hold of myself. I've seen the scene a hundred times. More likely a thousand. I've never been reduced to near hyperventilation before.

Then again, I've never looked at the man who has owned my soul since I was a teenager and known this might be the last time I'll be part of such a perfect, idyllic scene. Somehow I doubt divorce lends itself to such tight family moments.

We haven't spoken since I left Austin. Our texts have been few and perfunctory. The frame holding together what I thought was a damned near perfect family is coming apart at the corners.

I jerk the tap open to run cool water and wet a facecloth. Then, as if God is having a grand time tossing wait-there's-more confetti at me, it hits me my fear has come true. My chickens have come home to roost. The fat's in the fire. There's no more time to prevent a show-down with Castle MacInnes and the magic I fear I've broken.

We've broken.

Zach and I are in the castle. At the same time. In the same room. The annual games are a major tradition Zach enjoys. He's always the most welcome member of both the setup and tear-down committees, but he has no idea what his appearance has set into motion.

I look at myself in the mirror and try to believe that at least, one way or the other, the castle will make its determination, but the grimace I see staring at me would scare Bella to tears.

Quashing my ridiculous mental wandering, I dry my face and hands and head out of the bathroom to find Zach in the kitchen, putting sodas and beer in the fridge from his cooler. I stop myself from shaking my head. It's not like I drink soda, and I'm marginally fond of beer, but of course he's putting them in this suite and not mine, because heaven forbid if the kids want something that's not right at hand.

In the Zach category, the needle hasn't moved a fraction of an inch in the past weeks, now seeming like months. He's still tall and fit and so handsome I realize he will have to become a monk or beat women off with a stick when he returns to the market. Truthfully, he's a beautiful man. But appreciating his physical attributes aren't the issue.

"They're cold. Want something?"

Got any morphine on ya? "No, I'm good."

He stands and moves to me, leaning down to kiss me as if it's a normal day.

I can't.

I just can't.

In a split second, I turn my head enough so his lips graze my cheek, and he has the gall to look hurt.

Like this isn't verse 8,947 of the song of our marriage where we're so far apart the Palo Duro Canyon looks like a dry puddle, but he's pretending everything's all right?

I do an about-face and head for the door, suddenly desperate to go to the grocery store. I pause as I hit the living room to see if anyone has any requests, and my assembled progeny erupt into laughter. I realize no one saw me walk through, much less notices I'm leaving.

I exit without a sound, my steps harsh on the carpet as I grab my keys and purse.

I'm almost all the way to the market before I realize I've left my phone. I never leave my phone. Never let the battery go dead. Never let it stray far from my sight.

And for the first time in my memory, I don't care that I have no idea where my electronic leash might be.

CHAPTER THIRTY

MINA – NOW

I'M BARELY inside the kitchen when Fina starts in. I'm hot and itchy from my last trip around the grounds to see how things are progressing, but I'm pleased at how much has been accomplished this morning.

"I'm worried about the pastor."

"Can I have a glass of water before I take on another dilemma? It's not yet noon." I sweep a tea towel along my face and arms. I don't mind the heat so much, most days. It's nigh onto needing gills winding me up.

Without pretending to hide it, she heaves a sigh and fixes me a tall glass and adds one for herself. By the time she joins me at the table, I'm lifting my hair to let the air conditioner kiss my hot neck with some blessed relief.

"I assume you mean Harville." It's not a question.

She gives me her signature one-brow lift. "Do you know any other pastors around here?"

I enjoy the stream of cool air on my fevered skin and hope the angels are taking good care of whoever created air conditioning, because at this moment, the holy trinity is Trane, Lennox, and Carrier.

"There's Father McKinley."

"Priest, not pastor."

"They can be both." I add a squeeze of lemon to my glass, the sharp, citrus scent one of my favorites. It smells fresh and clean, especially on a day like today when I'm anything but.

"Are you trying to be testy with me?"

"Seems to be working." And entirely due to my insides being in a tizzy. Truthfully, it's more like a storm has rolled in with a high-pressure system lying on top and keeping it rotating in one spot. My disastrous lunch with CT is my personal funnel cloud, holding stationary and wreaking havoc with my intestines.

And my heart.

Fina's lips are tight. I wait, not filling the silence as I usually do. She takes a breath and starts again. "Lately, Pastor Harville's been sad, distracted like I've never seen him."

I've noticed, and the burden he carries in his eyes seems weightier than merely mourning our sweet Violet. He's a good man, but I'm grumpier than a hungry barn cat with no mouse, and my claws are unsheathed for a good swipe.

I turn my coaster in a slow circle. "Why are you worrying about him right now? We've got more than we can handle on our own plate."

I can't tell what she's weaving into with this fraying thread of a conversation, but the fabric of it has nothing to do with the pastor.

"I've been thinking." Fina sips her water, crunching a piece of ice and eyeing me over the rim of the glass. "It's time Castle MacInnes got back in the love business. I enjoy the events, but we've lost our way when it comes to the magic this place holds. We haven't done a good, old-fashioned matchmaking in a long time." She purses her lips. "Paige seems good and stuck, although that's understandable, but I believe we have other more ripe fruit to pluck."

Lord, help me. I want to say my sister's lost her mind, but Fina's the one blessed with all the smarts. My fear is the point we're heading to looks an awful lot like a cliff.

"I'm not sure why this particular bee chose your bonnet today. We're fuller than a hound tick for the games this year, and I have yet to bend my mind around your sudden concern for the pastor. I don't see the connection."

"They're two different subjects, and I mushed them together. Sorry. Let's stick with the castle. While nobody loves the games more than me, we make more from weddings than we do from these large shindigs."

I take a breath and relax a bit. This is a subject we can agree on. "There's certainly less preparation and cleanup, and the grounds suffer less stress. It's unfortunate the magic doesn't extend to upkeep."

"Amen. This place needs a makeover, and the chapel needs a nonstop conveyor belt of couples in love." She gives me an arch look. "I'm having to do double duty on the planning around here since someone spends so much time at the grocery store."

I narrow my eyes at her. "That's the second not-so-subtle jab you've taken at me. You want to tell me what's up?"

She stands, picks up her glass, and takes her sweet time at the tap refilling it. Her eyes close in a protracted blink and open on her target—me.

"You've been lobbing heads like you're a guillotine, and it's not like you. What happened with CT that's got you so wrecked?"

"Nothing. He's a perfect gentleman." I thought I was doing a great job of hiding the fact my insides feel like they've been pulled outside. I have to suck in several long breaths to stem the tears that have been locked and loaded. I want to tell my sister everything. I want her to give me the rough side of her tongue and tell me what's what. I want her to tell me what to do.

I need to know how to still the pounding of my heart when CT's near.

But I can't ask her. Not anymore. Not about relationships. We've done a dance since Trey was twelve years old in which we talk about any subject on God's green earth except the men in our lives. Or, more truthfully, there haven't been any men in our lives. Thing is, I can't fib to her. There's a difference between keeping your mouth shut and flat-out lying.

"The drive over was real nice. I got all flustered and made a pigeon out of myself at lunch and had him bring me home. I'm so embarrassed, it's a wonder you haven't had a pile of ashes to clean up when I stand still for more than five minutes."

She doesn't touch me, but she does reach across the table. "Tell me what happened."

Her voice is so quiet. So kind. It's her sister voice. The real sister voice, not the teasing one or the miffed one.

I relay the kilt exchange, and she gets a big grin on her face that fades into deep sadness.

"Oh, honey."

She retracts her fingers when it's clear I'm keeping mine in my lap. Then her expression morphs into the battle mask made for firstborns.

She'll never let me forget she has fourteen minutes on me.

"When will you banish Roylee's ghost? Hasn't that bastard been a squatter in your head long enough?"

"Like you can talk about staying locked in ice. I haven't seen a name on your dance card all these years, either." I clap my hand over my mouth, ashamed at myself before I've stopped talking. "Fina—"

She raises her hand. "We can pull taffy over my situation another day. I want to know if you plan on letting one wretched waste of a human stop you from exploring what might be with the nicest man in Magnolia Bloom." She palms the table with a slap. "I'm asking you to have dinner with the man, not tackle him and drag him to the chapel."

My throat goes so dry I can't swallow, so I choke out, "I'm broken."

Fina pushes to her feet, the chair skidding back. "Then it's time to get to the repair shop. While you're at it, ask for a lube and oil change."

I stare, openmouthed, as she flounces across the room and out the door.

"She's one to talk…"

Guilt overwhelms me. I've made a storm of my whole life, not only wrecking me, but tearing down my sister's dreams, too. She picked me up out of the rubble of my own making, dusted me off, nursed me to rights, and stayed. Stayed when she shoulda gone.

I add my glass to the sink and search for my clipboard. She might be my sister and have the right to say more to me than most, but I can't handle her tough love right now. I thought it was what I wanted, but turns out I was wrong.

I don't have time to worry about it. Fact is, I need to let her know she can worry all she wants, but she'd be wasting her time.

I'm not going to lunch or dinner or the moon with CT Nelson. It was a momentary dream, and it's time to let go of the nonsense.

And if she's got a coupon to some kind of personal Pep Boys? She should use it on herself.

CHAPTER THIRTY-ONE

PAIGE – NOW

IT'S NOT a long drive to town from the castle to the grocery store, but I find I don't want to go back yet. My high dudgeon is enough to make me wish it was early enough for a glass of wine. Which makes my thoughts veer to Kiki, and I start worrying about her and wonder if I might mellow on merlot a little too often myself.

As I near the church, I remember Harville's text to come by any time for something of V's he forgot to give me. A glance at the dash tells me it's not yet five. I'm not sure what office hours he keeps, but now seems as good a time as any.

There are only two cars in the parking lot when I pull in. I have to do mental math on an imaginary calendar to figure out it's Wednesday, so it is a workday, and we're darn near done with June. Makes sense. By the end of today, the castle will see the first campers setting up and checking in. By tomorrow night, we'll almost be at capacity. Friday will be utterly insane up to the opening ceremonies and feast, then it's a full weekend of wall-to-wall, nonstop Scottish.

I love every minute of it. In my lifetime, I've missed exactly three years, and I remember the disappointment like broken bones aching when the weather gets bad. For today, the temperature is still oppressive when I open my car door, glad my flip-flops protect my feet from the heat radiating from the asphalt.

This building is much newer, relative to the other buildings making up St. Andrew's. The sun glints off the aluminum framing the glass, and I've barely made the first step when the door slams open. Madison comes barreling out, forcing me to step aside to miss being bowled over, but the woman who prides herself on sickly sweet courtesy barely glances in my direction.

I catch the door before the pneumatic hinge shuts it, wondering if I should turn around and go to the store, but something pushes me to go inside the quiet building. The lights are dimmed in the reception area, the church secretary obviously gone for the day. There's a glow illuminating the hall, so I head toward the private offices.

Harville's chair is turned so he's facing the window, so I give a quiet rap on the doorframe to let him know I'm here. To my surprise, he jerks like he's been caught doing something wrong. His shoulders stiffen, he sucks in a deep breath, and he grabs at a box of tissues on his credenza.

When he turns to me, it doesn't take great skill to deduce he's been crying. He's wiped his cheeks, and the face he presents is the same warm, welcoming one I've seen every time we've been in the same room, but there's tension in the corners, and his eyes are rimmed in red.

"Paige, how nice to see you. Come in."

"I'm so sorry. I should have called, but I left my phone at the castle, and you said drop by any time. I'll come back later."

Great job, Paige. Nothing says *hey, how are you?* like awkward rambling.

His indrawn breath is deep and slow, but he shakes his head and stands. "No need. I'm glad you stopped by."

I can't see how that's honest. The man's clearly upset, but if I wasn't looking at his puffy eyes, I wouldn't know a thing was wrong.

Hmmm. I never knew pastors were such great actors.

I advance into the room, moving until only the distance of the desk separates us. "Harville, I don't mean to pry, but you look far more than upset. More like distraught. And I'll be honest and tell you Madison barreled past me as I was walking in. I know I'm not one of your congregants, but would you like to talk? Or maybe because I'm not one of your congregants."

The shake of his head seems automatic rather than true, but he stops himself, as if he's having some kind of mental argument with himself. After a moment, he gestures to one of the guest chairs.

I sit and maintain eye contact without expectation. I do this a lot at the office when I interview clients or witnesses. I have to persuade people to tell me things they don't want to, or fess up to what they've lied about, or spill the second part of half-truths. So it's not horribly uncomfortable for me to wait, hoping my energy is giving off my sincere desire to help him, if I can.

"I apologize for not making sure my door was shut. You shouldn't have seen that."

"There's no need. I'm sure you thought, at this time of day, the building would be empty. I'm the one who should be sorry for barging in here."

"Not at all. I did tell you to come by."

I put my purse on the chair next to me and lean in. "It's none of my business, but if you need an ear, I'm happy to stay."

He looks at me, the tension leaching the barest bit from his shoulders, his Mr. Rogers smile returning. "You know you're the spitting image of Violet, don't you? Not just in terms of appearance, but in spirit."

My smile comes from the one happy spot currently clinging to my soul. "I'm not sure you could pay me a bigger compliment."

"She took it upon herself to be the pastor to the pastor." His eyes go wide, and he holds out a hand. "I tried to resist, but she insisted."

"Violet could get God to go to confession, so I know exactly what you mean."

His laugh is rusty, a little watery, but I'm glad I pull that much out of him.

"True statement. I pity the entire holy trinity right now."

"Let's leave the heavenly hosts under V's tender ministrations and circle back to you, since you're deflecting."

"Yep, just like her."

"So let me have it. Let me return your kindness to me."

"It's a short story, but a harsh one. Madison left me. Not as in 'exited the building,' but 'left.' For Amarillo."

I cock my head, raising an eyebrow. "Is there something significant about Amarillo?"

"Only that the man she's been having an online affair with for two years lives there."

I have to release the breath I caught in surprise. "Oh."

His expression is stricken, and my heart breaks that he's trying so hard to appear calm.

"He owns a car dealership and apparently is quite wealthy. Equally apparently, Madison didn't quite understand I've never wanted to pursue a giant congregation and the resulting donation box. It appears she also didn't grasp what my taking this position meant in terms of downsizing from our already frugal life in El Paso."

"I see."

"She said she won't live like a beggar any longer in this, as she put it, Goodwill and Walmart hell." He adjusts the papers on his desk and aligns his fountain pen and matching mechanical pencil parallel to the edge of his blotter.

I relax and put my hands loosely in my lap. I may not have perfect radar, but I know there's more to this than Madison's disappointment in their financials.

"I see how Madison dresses, so I'll label that pure hokum. She might not be a regular at Saks, but I'll bet she never actually shops secondhand." I shift my head the other way. "But the truth is, we have an exec admin at my office who dresses like she's Jackie Kennedy reincarnated, and she won't buy a thing if it's not from Savers or the Salvation Army. It's her zen to find diamonds in the dross, so I'm gonna call BS on Madison."

"Fair enough. And my truth is, I could probably get over it if her parting shot wasn't to tell me she'd gotten pregnant last fall, after years of us trying, and she got rid of our baby so she wouldn't be trapped."

My breath leaves my lungs in a whoosh. The pain etching deep lines on his face is clearly drawn from the depth of his sweet soul. "Oh, Harville, I'm so sorry."

Tears pool in his eyes, but he doesn't let them fall. "Why didn't she think she could leave the baby with me if she decided to go? I wouldn't have made her stay, no matter my commitment to the vows we took. Why did she—"

He cuts himself off, jerking his chin up like he's tossing the tears back into their ducts.

"Anyway, I apologize for dropping my burdens into your lap. I shouldn't have."

"I'm honored you did, and I'm begging you not to apologize again. It's a huge bombshell to absorb."

"If she'd given me a chance, I'd have tried to meet her halfway. Tried to find a way for us to fix what was broken."

I'm quite certain Harville Crowder isn't a perfect man, and I'm the last person who expects a preacher to be a paragon of virtue. But what I know about him from V and my own experience makes me want to chase down Madison and jerk her sideways for being so vicious and cruel.

I strive to keep my tone clear of my desire for a little street justice against a woman who so callously tried to destroy a man she vowed to love and honor. I can't fathom her need for such vengeance.

"No matter what happened between you and Madison, and even if she has the right to control her body, she had no right to eviscerate you this way. She wanted to annihilate you, and that I can't forgive."

Everything about his posture screams reluctance, an automatic desire to refuse the comfort I'm offering. Somehow, he thinks he's allowed to offer succor, but not receive it.

"When she told me... I've never seen pure malice before, not on anyone."

"It's going to take a long time for you to come to terms with what she did and how she's treated you so cruelly. You might want to consider some counseling."

He let out a long breath, as if he's been holding it this entire time. "Thank you, Paige. I mean it. You've been kind to listen. Again—"

"If you dare apologize again, I swear I'll spend all day at the dunk tank on Saturday and drop you until you're half-drowned."

Every year, the church elders from around town take turns in a dunking booth to the delight of kids barely old enough to throw a ball, to high school athletes trying to impress their dates. We always have a small midway of games to keep the youngsters occupied, and "baptizing the preacher" is a perennial favorite.

"I don't dare risk such humiliation." He stands and walks around the edge of his desk, offering me his hand. I take it and rise, and add a warm hug to our handshake.

"I truly am sorry. I'm sorry you're hurting, and I'm sorry for what Madison is putting you through. I'd like to reiterate I'd be honored to lend you an ear any time."

"And the street goes both ways. If you'd like to talk about anything, I'm here."

My gut immediately seizes, and of one thing I'm certain. I'm not ready to talk about my own list of sins, both committed and merely considered. Harville would be a safe confessional, but the man needs some time alone.

"If I'm ever brave enough, I promise I'll choose your wise counsel."

"I'll hold you to it."

I pick up my purse and head for the door. "For today, be gentle with you. You have a lot to process."

"We pastors have pastors, so I'll touch base with mine later. For now, I need to put my sermon notes in order." His smile, albeit a sad one, reaches all the way to his eyes. "Want to know the definition of coincidence?"

"Sure."

"My sermon is on how to help a friend through tough times."

My wince is intended to show camaraderie, and I hope he sees it. "Yikes."

"I'll have to credit you with a nice paragraph on putting intention into action."

"Aww, I'm glad." I hitch my strap to my shoulder. "Now, I'll let you get to preacher-ing and me to grocery-ing."

"I heard your brood has descended. I look forward to this weekend and seeing them all."

"I'll be delighted to perform the introductions, but if you want to have coffee or share a breakfast burrito between now and then, you have my number."

"Indeed I do."

I walk out, turning at the last minute to add, "You're a good man, you know?"

"I hope so. But like Thomas, I have my doubts."

"I'm afraid I'm not good at Bible references, but I am good at reading people. And you're good people. Don't ever doubt it."

His face flushes, and he makes a shooing motion with his hands. "Go on."

I make my way to my car only to hear my name called as I open the door. Harville hurries toward me, a small box in his hands.

"Nearly left this, and it's why you came today. Violet brought it after she dropped off the journals, said she forgot to include it."

I open the lid and see a Scottish cairngorm citrine, the smoky yellow and translucent quartz left in its rough-cut natural beauty. The tear-shaped gemstone, hand-wrapped in gold wire, is attached to a fine chain. It's clearly a unique piece, done by an artist and not mass produced. I lift the necklace and look under the velvet display, but there's no accompanying note.

A frown makes me squint. "I have all of V's jewelry at the apartment, and while beautiful, cairngorm isn't particularly expensive. Why would she keep this one separate?"

His shrug says he's equally curious. "I don't know. It's not like she feared her valuables being taken."

"Another mystery. I'm up to her senior year at UT in her journals, and I know something big is coming up. Maybe it's related."

"Maybe. If it's something you consider proper to share with me, I'd love to hear about it."

"I promise I'll let you know. Now, I really am leaving this time."

He waits until I've pulled out of the parking slot before heading back to his duties. As I drive to the Magnolia Market, I offer a rare prayer for him to let go quickly and find peace. Everyone's trauma heals differently, and we can't please the people around us who wish we'd hurry up.

Goodness knows I know what it's like to hang on too long.

I park the car and open the box again, my curiosity in overdrive. "What is going on, Violet?"

No one answers my inquiry, so I put the necklace away and head inside, trying to recall the mile-long grocery list I left behind in my notes app. For a moment, worry rises, but anger zooms in and burns it to ash.

If I forget something, one of them can dang well get it themselves. I'm not the magic grocery fairy.

Or, rather, as of today, I'm breaking the wand over my knee and throwing it away.

CHAPTER THIRTY-TWO

VIOLET – 1971

I HEAR Sophie and René talking in the hallway, their voices low. I wait for them to knock, politely of course, as they're outwardly patient but inwardly eager to come in and see the girls. It's wonderful, on one hand, to have help. One of the other four adults is always available to hold Juliette while I'm nursing Noelle, or vice versa. They all are almost as enraptured with these two amazing creatures as I am.

But this morning, I pretend I don't hear. However they interpret my silence, their footsteps fade, leaving me alone with my angels.

I slip a tiny sock barely bigger than my finger on Noelle, and she kicks at me, even in sleep.

"You'll always be the prickly one, won't you, my little Christmas girl?"

I keep my voice low. I don't want to give myself away in case anyone's in the hallway.

I shift to attend Juliette, but of course the girls are right beside each other in the bassinette. They won't sleep if they aren't head-to-head, so I don't try. She pushes her tiny toes at me as if she's seeking more contact.

"You're my old soul. Your sister's going to need you." I touch the barest tip of my finger against her tiny, puffy, perfect hand. She gives one of those humming sighs I usually hear at the end of a feeding, the vibration racing from my nipple straight to my heart, where I'm storing these memories that will have to last a lifetime.

I wrap Noelle like a burrito, except for her arms. I don't care what the nurse says, Noelle is fine with her body being swaddled, but if her arms are trapped, she will wriggle and jiggle until she gets them loose. Juliette frets, so although I should let her squirm awhile, I pick her up and settle in the rocker, arranging the blanket so I can see her relax as I set the rocker in motion.

It doesn't take but a minute, and she's content again. She'll tolerate being in the bassinette if Noelle is right beside her, but her favorite place is the crook of my arm, tucked against my breast. I have to remember to tell René to tell Sophie that. Juliette likes to be snuggled close, with as much contact as possible. Noelle wants to be left alone, except when she's hungry or needs a fresh diaper. Then you'd better be there lickety-split, or your ears will pay.

Juliette grabs on to my finger in her sleep, so her hand follows as I stroke her fat cheek. The doctor confirms they're perfect, already gaining at a good clip. Low birth weight is common in twins, but they're making up for lost time.

Time. The one thing I don't have. That I can't give them.

My body's recovering from the realities of childbirth. Like every other new mother, I thought I was ready. I read books detailing the physical process, talked to the midwife, but on the page, the pain and exhaustion and contractions and pushing are all theoretical.

I steadfastly keep my eyes away from the suitcases waiting by the door. I can't waste one single, precious second doing anything except memorizing the faces of these two lives I would die for. For these few weeks, I've held them and touched them and fed them.

Noelle wiggles and makes her shudder-breath.

"I'll give her to you in a second, impatient one." I keep rocking my contented Juliette. "Just a few more minutes."

My last few minutes, but she doesn't know. Won't ever know.

It's almost feeding time, and I'm both anxious and dreading this one final time I can sustain them, give them what immunity I can before I leave.

Hold them against my shattering heart.

As if she hears me, Juliette opens her eyes, slowly and sleepily. The midwife would tell me the movement of her lips is gas, but I swear it's a smile. She's too young to really smile, but I don't agree. I shift my gown off my shoulder and release my nursing bra. I'm already quite adept at rearranging her and positioning her to nurse.

I still gasp when they latch on. My nipples are so sore, but I grit my teeth through it, and we settle into the best part of my days. Each draw on my breast makes my heart squeeze, and the matching uterine contractions are lightening. Nature is healing my body, every cell of which is connected to these two incredible beings, but I'm sure I'll die when I let them go. So I guess these contractions are good, because they keep my blood pulsing through my veins for a while longer.

As if she's aware her sister is getting attention, Noelle wakes. Before she can grab a lungful of air and voice her indignation, I stroke her cheek. "Hey, greedy guts. Your turn's coming. Give your sister a minute?"

She turns her face toward my voice and locks eyes on me. We talk while Juliette finishes, who, unlike her sister, is perfectly happy with being burped and put down so Noelle can have her chance.

Despite my best efforts, my eyes are drawn to those damned, damned, damned suitcases. Noelle kneads my breast with her tiny fist, and I have to stuff down the desperate need to scream, rage, pray, demand God give me a way for my girls to stay with me without either being ashamed every single day of who they are or fighting to refuse to be so. That outcome doesn't exist in this world. Maybe in 2071, but not 1971. So I push away the final shreds, the last wisps, of wishing things could be different.

There's another knock at the door, but Gavina doesn't wait for permission. She comes in, quietly but determinedly, and sits on the bed beside the rocker. She meets my eyes and gives me a sad smile before stroking Noelle's arm.

"We've got to go. We'll miss the flight if we don't leave soon."

We haven't talked that much because I don't have words. She's said we can stay longer. It's only plane tickets.

Though my heart is screaming at me, tearing through my chest to demand one more day, I know I have to go. Now.

Because I love prickly, demanding Noelle and soft, patient Juliette too much to take away this chance for them to live full, happy, blessed lives, and one more day would never be enough. Ten thousand one-more-days wouldn't be.

Gavina changes Juliette while I burp and take care of Noelle. We're quite a team, and it's been amazing to have her with me.

"Will you tell René to put my bags in the car?"

She gives me one of her signature long, deep looks.

Then I'm alone with my babies. They're both full, dry, and happy, doing their jerky newborn exercises, side by side in the crib.

I hurry and dress, then race back, using one hand for each of them to stroke the dark peach fuzz on their heads. I lean down to kiss one, then the other, wiping off the tears landing on each smooth forehead.

"Take care of each other. And please, somewhere in your tiny, perfect hearts, remember me."

Sophie hovers in the doorway, and somehow, God only knows how, I give her a smile. She rushes over and pulls me into a hug, crushing my sore breasts.

"Merci, merci, merci beaucoup."

I push away because if I don't go, I'll collapse, and it wouldn't be fair to expect René, strong as he is, to pick up my broken body and haul it away. He comes in, as if called by my thoughts, and takes me in his arms, his hug less effusive than Sophie's, and presses a long kiss against the top of my head.

He moves to put his arm around his wife, and each put a hand on the bassinette.

"We will write you."

I know my headshake is desperate, but I can't endure much more. "No. I mean, God forbid if there's some tragedy, yes, but otherwise you need to go on with your lives, the girls' lives, without the specter of me in the background. Noelle and Juliette deserve to grow up completely wrapped in your love with no ghost haunting them."

Avril is waiting in the car. She gives the horn a toot, and I know she's not being mean, just letting me know it's now or never. She's taking Gavina and me to the airport so Sophie and René can have their first day all alone with my two miracles, and she's already told me a hundred times she'll remember me, pray for me every day.

I want to tell her not to bother. God doesn't hear prayers from me or for me. Save them for Noelle and Juliette. But I don't.

Gavina takes my hand in the hall, the same hand she held for eighteen hours while I brought two pieces of perfection into the world. She wiped my sweaty forehead. Let me swear a blue streak. Made me take one more breath and bear down one more time when I was too spent to hold myself up.

She doesn't let go on the long drive to the airport. Doesn't let go as we wait in the terminal. Doesn't let go as she sits beside me on the plane. As we taxi down the runway, I release her hand, wrapping my arms around my stomach as I curl in on myself, a tight ball with my head against the cold, cold window.

I arrive in Magnolia Bloom wearing a pair of pants one size larger than when I left, but the same peasant top. I won't wear anything fitted until my breasts have dried up and there's no sign left of what I've done. The extra weight can be blamed on too many charcuterie boards and glasses of wine. My lack of conversation on jet lag.

Gavina's last words on the plane, before she let me sink into the dark, quiet place that'll be my home for a long time, were about an interview she arranged for me at Saks in New York City with my cousin Laurie. I could pretend I'm above using family connections for a job, but I'm so not. Like she has for this entire year, Gavina has taken care of me, and now she's given me a way to escape. She knows without me telling her that I want to leave this town with a fervor bordering on pathological. She knows more than most anyone can and helps me hold it together so I can keep playing my part.

Then I'm moving fifteen hundred miles away and never looking back.

CHAPTER THIRTY-THREE

PAIGE – NOW

I WONDER what the Guinness entry is for the longest trip to the grocery store. I might try and add it to the MacInnes twin record. Just as the no-divorce record for couples married in the chapel is statistically impossible, the number of twins running in this family should be, too.

But there you go...

Strangely enough, walking the aisles calms me after a few minutes. This isn't my home store, and I don't know the layout by heart, so it makes me pay attention, and I appreciate the diversion and the time sink. Unfortunately, I eventually have to drive back to the castle.

"Hey, Mom. Let me help."

Whether Aiden was waiting for me or it's coincidence, I don't argue while he strings bags up his arms and holds two more against his chest. I'm left with the handle of the extra bottle of detergent, as God knows there's going to be piles of laundry, and we climb the steps to the family kitchen next to our suites.

"Where's Chen?" My heart pumps harder with every stair, and I witness firsthand what my son's dedication to free weights and jogging has earned him.

"Chen's with Ainsley wrangling the little people, and Dad's off helping with construction. If there's an idle power tool and a task, you know he can't resist."

Truth. I remember when being irresistible applied to me, too.

He puts up everything other than the breakfast-for-dinner ingredients, the easiest thing I can put together since I was descended upon by surprise. I set a pan of eggs on the stove to boil and crack a dozen into a bowl with vanilla, cinnamon, nutmeg, and some sugar. I whisk in cream and open the bag of Texas toast, wishing I'd been able to find brioche.

"Thanks for getting all this food, Mom. I'd've gone with you if I'd known you were going."

I bite my tongue so I don't say, one, everyone shouldn't have assumed I'd go to the store, and two, I shouldn't have to blast an air horn and demand help to get it. But I don't want to waste this moment being bitchy, as I rarely have alone time with my son.

"You're welcome, but you handle the next, inevitable trip."

"Deal."

I put Aiden to work hulling strawberries with a straw and slicing a fresh pineapple while I haul out the griddle big enough to handle a crowd.

"Marceau is so perfect. How is it possible he's grown so much? And you'd better give Chen a big ol' kiss from me for being such a great guy."

I kiss Aiden's forehead and sneak a piece of sweet yellow fruit, wiping the juice from my chin. I retrieve an apron and tie it on before it's too late.

"That's an easy order to obey. I'm a lucky man."

I wag my fork at him. "And don't you forget it."

"Not likely, I promise."

"So, how many teeth are in?"

"Two bottom. One on top's trying to erupt. Good God, I didn't know a baby could produce so much spit. Did you know about this?"

I raise my eyebrows in innocence. "Do tell. Babies drool?"

"I may never have a dry shirt again."

"You get them back eventually. It's all worth it."

I lift the lid on the pan to see if the water's boiling, then set a timer.

"Deviled eggs?" Aiden asks hopefully.

I give him a stink eye. "If I'd had notice, I would have done them yesterday, so no. It's egg salad for you."

"The humanity." He moans, throwing his head back.

"Go on, you nut. I can handle the rest of this."

"Nope, I'm on penitence duty. Chen has Marceau, and I've been informed if I come to the room before I've helped you check off any less than four things on your list, I will be sleeping on the swing tonight."

"I'm impressed. And grateful. Kiss your man twice for me."

"Yes, ma'am, as soon as I help you." He glances over at the paper pinned to the refrigerator with a magnet. "Cut up cucumbers, halve the cherry tomatoes, and drain the corn."

I point to vegetables waiting to be washed and the cans needing their tops cleaned with soap and hot water. "Help yourself."

We work together, our chitchat companionable, and it lightens my heart. I have good kids. I've never felt otherwise, even if they're spoiled sometimes.

I look at the man who's efficiently slicing and dicing, and for reasons I wish weren't obvious, a cloud passes over my heart. In Austin, it's not a thing...him and Chen. No one looks twice, or if they do, it's to coo over Marceau and tell them how lucky they are.

But this is Magnolia Bloom, a town I truly love, but it resides deep in the heart of East Texas. And it's not known for being a progressive hotspot.

"Sweetie?"

"Yeah?"

"You might be careful this weekend."

He looks up, his brow furrowed. "Huh?"

"Magnolia Bloom isn't Austin."

His frown turns into a grin. "You mean I shouldn't wear my pole-dancing unicorn shirt with the glitter on it?"

"I'm being serious here." I aim my death stare, hoping it still works.

"Mom, this isn't my first round of the games. If you recall, I placed sixth in the caber toss two years ago." He stops chopping and does the man-flex of his not unimpressive bicep, then gives me his full attention. "If these good people can't handle a white man married to a first-generation Chinese-American, with a son who's Puerto Rican and Jamaican, that's their problem, not mine. Chen and I have dealt with this since the day we met, so stop worrying."

"It's just…I don't want to have to pull out my community center jujitsu moves if someone dares say, much less do, anything to you."

"Keep the gi in the suitcase, karate kid. We got this."

"I'm—"

"Nana! Nana!" Callum barrels into the room and into my thighs.

I'm grateful I have a nanosecond to turn and put myself between him and the stove. "Careful, baby. This cooktop's hot. Go over by Uncle Aiden, and I'll make you some dinner."

"I want cereal for beckfirst."

"No cereal. Too much sugar. How about eggs in a basket?"

"Yes, please. Hi, Uncle Aiden. Where's 'Ceau? What are you doing?"

"He's with Uncle Chen right now, getting dressed, and I'm helping Nana make breakfast for dinner, then corn salad for the party on Friday." He keeps his knife well out of reach as Callum's half on top of the table. Aiden leans and whispers sotto voce, "Do you think if I ask Nana real nice she'll make me eggs in a basket, too?"

Callum nods solemnly and answers, nowhere near sotto voce, "She's really nice, and if you say please, she makes you two."

"Good to know." He raises his head and winks at me. "Nana, may I please have two eggs in a basket?"

"How can I refuse such good manners?"

I've already hollowed out circles in the center of a stack of buttered bread so I can switch between the easiest breakfast known to man and French toast. Between the two, I can feed an army without breaking a sweat. I have six slices starting to brown, crack an egg into each waiting hole, and my spatula is ready to flip by the time Ainsley comes in with Bella on her shoulder. Zach's right behind her, and before they can say, *What's for dinner?* I have a dozen eggs in a basket warm and ready and a pile of French toast.

I bustle around as they take places at the table, helping themselves to plates, dipping spoons of sliced strawberries and pineapple into the waiting ramekins and dolloping on fresh cream. Chen pours juice or milk as requested, and conversation flows across the polished pecan table as easily as the warmed maple syrup being passed.

"Mom." Chen calls to me over the hustle and bustle. "Sit down and eat."

"In a minute. I've got to cool these eggs, or the yolks will go green."

"I can do it. Sit."

"It's okay."

"Sit. Now."

I raise my eyebrows. Chen is always polite and rarely—okay, never—this forceful. I've hidden my worry his genial nature will be to his detriment with my sometimes bullheaded son, so I'm glad to see the gumption.

Aiden cuts in. "I'll do it. I'm finished."

I find myself with Bella on my lap, her blue eyes locked on me with her I'm-an-old-soul stare. Secure in the middle of the table, Marceau activates his baby bouncer by diligently trying to stuff his big toe in his mouth. I stroke my thumb over his precious chubby cheeks, take a swipe with a cloth at the impressive amount of drool poised to fall on his bib, laugh out loud at his no longer toothless grin. Between these two, my heart might burst.

I manage to get a slice of toast and some fruit down without interruption before Zach moves into the chair next to mine. He smiles at me, and I smile back because there's no reason not to. I'm not mad. I'm not playing the silent game, because I hate it. Besides, when we're not not-fighting, I like talking to him.

"Did you have enough to eat? Can I get you anything else?"

"That's sweet, but I had plenty."

He wiggles Bella's foot so she shifts her attention to her granddaddy, studying him as if she's deciphering the secrets of the universe. "How's it going?"

"It's coming along. I knew it would be a big job, but I'm muddling through. I thought I had a handle on what it takes to run a place like this, but wow, was I naïve. Still, Violet was a miracle worker, and as long as I don't massively screw up, we've got time to sort out all the bits and pieces. I hope."

He shifts his finger rather suavely to my arm and traces a line from my wrist to my elbow.

"I've missed you."

"I—thank you."

"I'm sorry I didn't make the service."

"Honestly, I understand."

"You always do." He takes his finger off my arm and bounces Marceau for a moment. "Give Bella to Chen, and let's go for a walk. The kids should clean up anyway."

Go for a walk? Not completely unusual, but Zach's a more let's-go-dancing kind of guy since the nature of the activity keeps conversation to a minimum. So if he wants to go walking, does he want to talk?

Damn my imagination. Damn him for making me go to mush with one look.

We've said four sentences to each other, and now I'm forgetting all my vows to myself? Then again, it's always hardest for me in the daytime, when he's being sweet and charming.

He starts again when I don't answer. "I'd like to—"

"Daddy, can you come help me?" Ainsley's distressed cry comes from the doorway. "I can't make my laptop connect to the Wi-Fi."

"Sure, honey, one second."

"Can you hurry? I'm late for a vid call with Richard."

He gives me his smile and stands, moving off to follow our daughter. And as quickly as my pulse started racing, it flatlines.

I'm Charlie Brown, lining up to kick the football Lucy holds. I fall for it. Every. Single. Time. I didn't used to be, but now I'm a distant third in the race of Zach's life, and I'll forever trail the kids and any other human who needs his help.

For the next hour, Aiden and Chen tag-team cleaning and preparation. Egg salad and corn salad are in the refrigerator. Chen slices bolillos for sandwiches and gets all the condiments, deli meats, and cheeses lined up. He arranges sodas and beer, chips and cookies. All we'll have to do on Friday is pile the food into coolers and haul them to the parade ground.

Babies are fed. Callum's engrossed in his show. Ainsley's got her cell phone locked against her shoulder. I hear softness in her voice but no distinct words. This is call number two with Richard, and I'm hopeful. Chen and Aiden hold hands and take Marceau in his stroller for a walk in the rising moonlight before everyone's off to bed.

A fear I didn't know I kept wrapped around my heart releases like a sore muscle under the hands of a master masseuse.

My kids will be all right.

It's what every mother prays for, and my gratitude is boundless.

I wish Zach were here with me, but after he finished with Ainsley's emergency, someone called and asked if he'd help with some lighting conundrum before they quit for the evening. Instead of holding hands with my husband as we fondly congratulate ourselves for being phenomenal parents, I'm walking alone to Violet's turret.

Might as well do something useful and find those blueprints for Leith.

CHAPTER THIRTY-FOUR

MINA – NOW

I HOPED, coming to the store first thing Friday morning, I'd avoid CT.

Nope. There's his Cadillac in his reserved spot.

Unless I want to drive all the way out to the Walmart on our side of Atlanta, which I vehemently hate to do because shopping local is my religion, I have to suck it up and go inside.

How in blue blazes does an institution as big as the castle run out of salt on opening day of the games? I've got to get in and get out, pronto. I have ten million details left to deal with before the opening parade tomorrow morning.

"Good morning, Mina."

I put on my best smile and turn, waiting as he hurries toward me from the front of the store. "Good morning to you. You're here awfully early."

"Can't not be with the town bursting at the seams."

"I know. We've got a bumper crop this year. We're estimating five thousand all total."

"The chamber's certainly happy, and the business league. We need it, with the economy and all."

I cut him a smile. "You know, I've been attending Chamber of Commerce meetings for a decade, and you'd swear we haven't had a robust economy in a hundred years."

His cheeks color the sweetest pink. "It's the nature of us crotchety old men to see gloom waiting around every corner."

Have I ever seen a man blush? I'm pretty sure I haven't. I try to remember when I still had schoolgirl crushes and schoolgirl dreams and hopeful guesses about the nature of romance. But have I ever known a soft man?

I've known funny men. Or boys, really. Even Roylee started out making my insides sweet and warm, like a cup of hot chocolate.

And then he changed.

Or rather, he always was Roylee, and I was blind for not seeing the script of my coming nightmare sooner.

I force a smile and banish the dark memory to where I store them. "It's time for some female blood on the board, then, don't you think?"

"If you're volunteering—"

"Lord, no. It's a job for some youngster who has the energy."

He chuckles, but shakes his head. "I think you have more energy than any ten who might take the job, but we'll agree to disagree for now."

I move toward the aisles, but instead of taking the hint and ending our conversation, he moves in step with me.

"What do you need today? I'm surprised you could peel away from the preparations."

"It appears, although it boggles the mind how, we need salt, and you don't put on a feast for two hundred without salt and pepper on the tables."

He frowns. "I can imagine a hundred things you might be in here for, but I'd never guess salt."

"I know."

"Let me grab you some commercial bags I keep stocked for Vivann's and the other restaurants. A box of Morton won't do you. Wait here."

He hurries away, and I'll be stir-fried on a Sunday if I don't stare. He's tall, but not overly, not overly muscular, not overly...anything. He has a softness around the beltline that doesn't bother me at all, because it gives me hope he's not the obsessive type. Too many folks our age are joining those gyms and tossing tractor tires and running five thousand miles a week.

Now, I like a fit man. The field events tomorrow are my favorites. But it's one thing to watch a man heft a telephone pole to toss it end over end, and another to live with someone who wants to. And with CT, I'm feeling a lightness I've never imagined experiencing, and certainly have never felt before. It appears there just might be a gentleman or two who defies my long-held belief about the males of our species. I haven't been around CT long enough to confirm my hypothesis.

Right smack in aisle twelve, an idea strikes me like I'm the lightning rod on top of the castle.

I told my stubborn sister I have no business dating, and I aim to prove I'm right. I'm not seeing anyone, casual or serious, ever again. I may not have my sister's book smarts, but I have several degrees from the school of hard knocks, and sometimes they count for more. My PhD says, given the opportunity, CT will rip my heart out, veins and valves and all. I'm slap out of trust.

A laugh escapes at my brutal pun, but when things get beaten out of you, you know when they're all gone.

I don't believe for a moment CT would hurt me physically. I wouldn't insult him in such a way even in the silence of my mind. But all the same, he'll eventually prove me right. And I need to show Fina I'm the smart twin every now and again.

Movement to my right grabs my attention. I smile at CT's daughter, who's turned on the cash register and is tying on her green apron.

"Good morning, Bethanie. Are you coming to the games this weekend?"

"No." She opens the register drawer and starts putting her cash in the slots.

She's clearly unhappy to be functioning at this early hour. I wasn't particularly happy when I was her age, so I'd be a hypocrite to tear into her about her attitude.

CT returns with two bags of salt, putting them on the conveyor belt. Bethanie flips the mechanism, and they slowly roll toward her as I stand with her father, scared and off-center, but mulish about following through with my thunderclap idea, even if I'm sweating like stripper in a church.

"Listen, this weekend will be busier than a kicked-over ant pile, but would you like to have dinner with me next weekend?"

His surprise is so palpable it'd be funny if my guts weren't tied tight enough to hold a bucking bronco.

"I'd love to."

"Sunday next at four o'clock? My duplex?"

"Sounds marvelous. In the meantime, you call me if you need anything."

"I will. See you around the games."

He smiles and turns away. Stops. Turns back.

Smiles again.

Then moves to his office, whistling.

I get my feet moving, taking one step forward as I dig in my purse for my wallet. I can't find it, so I pop it on the edge of the checkout, and that's when I see the display case. There, between the Butterfingers and the PayDays, is a box of...Andes mints.

My heart gives a kick, does a do-si-do. I've shopped in this store for forty years. The older Mr. Nelson, and now CT, never carried Andes mints before.

My mention of s'mores made with the chocolate mints was hardly more than a casual reference, a bit of flustered conversation. I don't want to believe he brought in those candies on account of me. I sparked an idea in a smart businessman is all. Doesn't mean a thing.

I take five from the box and put them on the conveyor and move up to a bored Bethanie. I give her my payment and hoist my bags of salt into my arms.

I'm right about this one, Fina.
I am.
And I will prove it.

CHAPTER THIRTY-FIVE

PAIGE – NOW

THE SUN STREAMING in through the turret windows cuts me right in the eyes, and I push up, groggy and achy, from the couch. Around midnight, Zach came in, telling me to not stay up too late. He kissed my forehead and went into the suite to take a much-needed shower, and I continued my mission to find the blueprints. I had success sometime around one, much too late to take them down to Leith's room, so I kept sorting papers on the desk and searching through files. I have a stunning amount to learn if I want to make even a reasonably informed decision, or be any help at all.

The clock on the wall shows it's after six. Zach always rises early, so I'm safe heading into the apartment, as I have no doubts he's already down on the grounds, hammering or sawing or mowing or whatever-ing.

I jerk to a halt in the doorway. He's sprawled out on the bed in his customary stomach-starfish pose. The sheet is half on and half off, his tan amusingly demarcating his narrow waist and one bright-white cheek of his still-perfect butt.

The sight, many years more than two decades later, still makes my thoughts veer toward the X-rated.

He's snoring. The muted light shines on the broad forehead, not-quite-straight nose, high cheekbones, and slightly parted lips I've woken up next to somewhere in the neighborhood of ten thousand mornings...give or take his business trips and an increasing number of recent nights spent in separate bedrooms.

I can see a prescription bottle on the nightstand and know why he's still tangled in the covers after the sun has creased the horizon. His allergy medicine knocks him out, and I'm stunned he used it. It normally takes a bipartisan act of Congress for him to take a pill of any kind, so he must have been pretty miserable. Whatever the reason, I'm grateful it saves me from having to explain why I didn't come to bed.

Like I'm starring in an episode of *Mission: Impossible*, I use stealth and cunning to snag fresh clothes and sneak out to shower in the guest bath to make myself reasonably presentable. A peek confirms he's still in antihistamine dreams before I head to the family kitchen.

I do the squeak-stop thing in the entryway and wonder if I have a string on my back, because it sure seems like someone keeps yanking on the little plastic circle. Leith is at the table, a bowl of cereal in front of him, reading a book propped against the milk carton.

"Good morning." I keep my voice perky as I regain a modicum of equilibrium.

"And to you. You look chipper."

"Wish I felt it. Listen, I found the blueprints last night. You can stop by V's office in the turret. Your name's on the folder on the desk. Or I can go get it for you."

"No, I'm happy to fetch them this afternoon sometime. There's something itching at my brain, something not right, so I'm on a mission, and the paperwork will help."

"Nothing worse than an itchy brain, so if there's something else I can do, tell me. I added a recent topological survey, but I'm not sure what else might suit."

"That's braw."

I open the freezer and pull out bags of diced potatoes and precut onions. It's mostly automatic, requiring a minimum of attention to detail. Leith looks at the growing pile of breakfast-taco items and waves a hand.

"Are you making brekkie for a regiment?"

"Yes, otherwise known as the horde masquerading as my family. My criteria are volume and quick when we're all together, but it's so rare these days, I don't mind. I love having the kids and grands around, so I keep the menu simple."

"Your daughter is lovely. She looks like you, but I'm sure you've heard that once or twice. Now I'd like to meet your son and the other wee wains."

"I'm sure Marceau would be delighted to show you his new teeth coming in, but with five thousand people descending on this town and the grounds, who knows?"

He rises and puts his book away, pressing a proper bookmark between the pages. I can't not notice and think, *Another check in the yummy column.*

He picks up the milk, and I wave a hand at him.

"You can leave that. I'll do it."

He pauses, holding the milk in one hand and the box of cereal in the other. "Can you dinnae no' do that?"

"I'm sorry, what?"

"Can you not take on every single task as your duty?"

"I don't."

"You do. Mina and Fina had to come up with some malarkey about being too busy to show you what needed doing, or some such, for you to stop taking on twenty jobs getting ready for the weekend. They said you've already got a mountain of work waiting for you in your office. Violet's, I mean. I don't know what, exactly, but they said it's a lot."

I pop the potatoes into the oven, pausing in my search for the giant skillet for the onions I need to brown to frown at him. "The entire reason I'm here is to help."

"Help, aye, but you're trying to take on everyone's job and yours, too. Next thing is you'll be using the rivet gun to finish the grandstand, or herding the sheep yourself."

I stiffen, trying to summon a reasonably polite way to tell him to mind his own business, which isn't fair since he's right. It doesn't mean I like that he's known me for a matter of days and already sees right through me. It's usually Kase's job to call me on my tried-and-true distraction tactics. Seems she has a backup quarterback on the field. It's one thing for my best friend to call an audible. It's another for a man who's already got my backfield in motion.

I can't say any of that. "I might."

"And it wouldnae surprise me."

I set the timer on the oven and snap the tea towel off the counter to wipe my hands.

"Why are you busting my chops this morning? Did I do something wrong?"

He stops and drops his fists from his hips. "Nay, you havenae. I dinnae know what's got me off-kilter, so excuse me, all right? I look forward to seeing you around the festivities."

He's gone, and I don't have time to dissect what just happened, because although breakfast tacos are simple, they do require a bit of attention. Then, of course, the teeming mass descends, and the usual family chaos ensues.

As I expect, Zach takes a taco and heads straight out to involve himself in the last bits of construction. Richard arrives, to everyone's surprise—and, I hope, to reconcile with Ainsley. She squeals in delight. Callum screams, "Daddy!" Bella starts crying. Which sets Marceau off.

I throw my hands up, yell in the general direction of the vortex for them to clean the kitchen, and escape to the turret.

I haven't read a word in V's journals for the last two days because I've lost my idyllic quiet and my...space. Not my physical space, naturally, but the place I set aside just for Violet and the journey I'm taking through her past. After my conversation with Harville, I'm itching to catch up. While there's plenty of activity both inside and outside, these next hours are basically the calm before the storms of the Friday evening ceremonies.

As I step into the coolness, the thick stone walls wrap around me like a hug from a patient friend. I stand for a long minute, the tension melting away as if the sanctuary is denying entrance to my stress. My shoulders let down from their defensive-lineman position. My stomach unclenches, telling me I'm dangerously close to joining Kase in a roll-a-day antacid habit. My arms and thighs release like I'm relaxing from a forty-hour plank.

When I sit in V's chair, I stroke the carved wooden arms, proudly realizing I'm the next in a long line of MacInnes women who've sat here and handled the business of the castle, even if my tenure's temporary. This chair starred in a lot of V's stories while I was growing up, one of the more amusing being the collective gasp when she moved it and the desk from the library. As the chatelaine at the time, she had the authority to do so, but no one before had dreamed of exercising the right.

Like V, I hid under Evajean's desk as a kid when I needed to escape any of the events happening across the hall in the enormous family living room. There are hundreds of places to hide in a castle, but the turret is special. I'm as strongly drawn as an adult to the security of this desk as I was as a child, so I understand why Violet moved it here. Both levels of the library are magnificent, but this small, round room is a place of sanctuary. Protection. A womb of cool and quiet where you can escape, for a few minutes, the hectic pace of the world.

I flip on the desk lamps, the glow of the LEDs catching the cairngorm. Like the journals, the piece of jewelry has never left my mind, but was shunted into a corner with all the busyness raging around me. The beautiful, smoky quartz swallows the light deep into the long point, illuminating it from within. The pendant's ghostly streaks of yellow and brown call me with the same *Jumanji* drum as the diaries.

Holding the necklace in one hand and a journal in the other, I settle in and start reading. Within moments, time ceases to have meaning as I instantly break the rule I made to dole out the pages. I read as if the world will end if I don't finish, barely able to absorb the version of V's life I didn't have a single clue about. I'm terrified for her and horrified at the choices she felt compelled to make. Then I'm so angry at Ephraim Broder I want to yank my jeans on and drive across town to punch him, and I'm nigh onto a certified pacifist.

And then I'm in France. I slow down because I know what's coming. I can't stop, but I know.

When I reach it, I put the journal down to sob into my hands.

My mother's heart rips open for V. I cannot fathom how she found the courage to do what she did. I was about her age when I had Ainsley and Aiden, but with monumental differences. I was married, and sure, we were young and poor, but I had a loving spouse and the safety net of family support.

She had none and no one. Only Aunt Gavina.

I remember holding my babies. I remember being terrified, not having a clue what to do despite all the books I'd read and all the advice I'd received. I remember asking the heavens who had been foolish enough to trust these two innocent lives into my keeping.

Absolutely nothing prepares you for what happens when you touch those tiny hands, and count those tiny toes, and place those perfect pink lips against your breast and feel them suckle for the first time.

And Violet felt she had to give them away.

Take care of each other. And please, somewhere in your tiny, perfect hearts, remember me.

"Oh, V."

To have such love that she would choose her babies' future over her own needs, her own happiness. What courage it took to give those girls lives filled with love and free from scorn. I don't know that I could have been so brave. And I get it. Adoption isn't a perfect answer. As Aunt Gavina said, it's not a panacea. But that doesn't negate the ache I'm feeling for Violet.

Now I understand why she never liked Christmas.

I'm not sure how long I stare out the turret window, wondering about Noelle and Juliette. What they look like now. I see a vineyard in France and imagine a childhood in the slower pace of a tiny village.

My childhood was filled with packing and unpacking in crowded military base housing, never lighting in one place long enough for real friendships to form. My summers right here in Magnolia Bloom, though amazing, were still transient, each day tainted with knowing fall would come, and I'd be yanked away again.

My watch chirps, startling me, warning me it's time to get busy. I tap the screen and silence the alarm so rudely bringing my attention to the room.

A knock at the doorframe turns my head. I'm ready to tell whichever child is there to leave me alone, but it's Leith.

"I'm sorry to disturb you. I came for those blueprints."

I stand and pull the folder I left for him from a wire rack.

He walks around to my side of the desk to stand close as he accepts the papers. "I also came to apologize. I was out of line this morning."

I shake my head. "It's fine. I probably deserved it."

"If so, it wasnae my place."

"Let it go. It's not worth stressing over."

"Maybe, but I find myself worrying for you. Today, more than ever, you seem like you're drowning, and *that's* stressing me out."

"I have to own I've built an expectation in my family that I'll drop everything in my world the second they step into a room. Everyone gets a piece of the guilty pie here, but it's mostly my own fault. As to this particular moment, if you're reading my energy as agitated, it's because V's diaries have really shaken me. I need to process, is all."

"Now I'm going to sound like one of those books you said—a rom-com?—although there's nothing funny here. It's tearing me up to see you so sad. You're too beautiful, too smart, to have such shadows in your eyes."

My gut is a Vitamix of exasperated and pleased. Every time we talk, or so it seems, he remembers some obscure thing I've mentioned, and he's known me an amount of time that can still be counted in short weeks. Would my own family know I like romantic comedies on occasion?

"What am I supposed to say, Leith? I've enjoyed your company very much, but my world is upside down. And to tell you the truth, I'm exhausted. I'm lost and I'm sad and I'm scared and I—"

I can't take a breath before he tosses the folder on the desk, and then his hands are on each side of my face, holding me as he leans in. Oh so perfectly, his lips cover mine.

I should pull back.

I should push his hands down.

I should step away.

Walk away.

I should.

But I don't. I suck in a breath with a hint of a whimper.

His lips are soft, gentle yet determined, asking yet taking. He uses those long fingers to tilt my face to give him better access, and I still don't stop him. Still don't say no.

Another gasp parts my lips, and his tongue seeks mine, and God help me, but I give in. I give back. I give up any pretense I don't want this moment, whatever it is, however wrong it is.

Time suspends, and there is nothing but the exquisite sensation of his fingers combing into my hair, his breath on my cheek, and his kiss telling me exactly how much his pulse, his need, his desire match mine.

I reach up to touch his face in return, to let him know—

A screech from the lawn permeates the window, wrenching us apart.

I leap like my feet have springs. I want to move forward. I want to move back. I want to know why the universe has put this kind, handsome man in my complicated path. Though it wouldn't be complicated if I would Make. A. Decision.

Leith starts to move toward me, but I put my hand out between us.

"Don't, please." If he takes another step closer, I will, too. And I can't promise I'll stop at a kiss.

"Paige, I—"

"I can't. Leith, I can't do this." But I want to. I so want a man who wants me, and I want him, too. They say the heart wants what it wants, but mine's split. Part of it, if not dead then in a coma, fights the part still needing to dance. "You're ten kinds of sexy, but I'm not divorced yet."

For the first time, it's there. The microscopic spark of hope that if Zach and I are over, I won't end up alone. That I still have something another man may find attractive.

"Isnae that formality at this point?"

I almost cave, but formality is my story, and I'm sticking to it.

"Maybe, but it's not something I can override. Maybe I've worked in law too long, but there are lines, and this is one I won't cross."

"I dinnae mean to—"

Oh, God. Don't. Don't say you're sorry. Don't take it back.

"Please. Don't apologize. That was...amazing and a balm to my rather serrated ego."

"I'm not sorry for the kiss, but I dinnae mean to add to all you've got chasing around your pretty head."

I need you to not be so intuitive. I need you to not be so ridiculously handsome. I need you to not be so kind. I need you to fly away on your next grand adventure and forget I exist.

I need to not wallow in gallows-worthy guilt.

"I should be mad at you for shaking up my world like a paint can at Lowe's, but I'm not sorry, either. Confused, yes. Sorry, no." I summon an Oscar-deserving smile and pretend he didn't rock my foundation farther off-center ninety seconds ago. "For now, I need to dress and head down for the picnic and fireworks. Will I see you there?"

"Aye. I've already made some mates on the building crew, and we've claimed a spot to lift a brew or two."

"Wonderful. I'll see you downstairs, then."

As far as dismissals go, I hope he takes no offense, but I really—like, *really* really—need him to go away.

He picks up the folder he tossed aside and uses the edge to salute me. "See you there."

I fall into the chair, unsure how I got to this place, and uncertain if I want to leave. I press my lips together, the tingle of fire still there. Dragging my fingers into my hair and clutching my scalp, I squeeze, knowing I'm in trouble. I don't have to wonder if he truly likes me anymore. He's shown me. And I've shown him.

And my decision looms before me like the ghosts of MacInneses past.

What did Ginny, Tidy's sister, say in an earlier journal of Violet's? *Jesus, Mary, and Joseph...*

I'm not sure even they can help me.

CHAPTER THIRTY-SIX

VIOLET – 1974

THE FRENCH DOOR behind me opens, and the ambrosia scent of coffee wafts on the chilly morning air. Gavina joins me on the balcony, puts a mug for me on the table, and sits, content to watch the first rays of the sun playing peekaboo with the horizon. It's March, so the wind is still cold, but not bitter. All the same, with the quilt wrapped around my shoulders, I take a sip of the elixir of the gods. It's natural to sigh.

"This is fabulous." I glance over and add a grateful smile to my honest compliment. I haven't smiled much these past weeks, everything I see making me remember my girls, but the tears have slowed.

"There is no substitute for a French press." She takes her own sip, gaze glued to the skyline.

"Did you know Momma gave me the perfect excuse for staying with you and being so moody?"

"Do tell."

"She asked if I was mooning over some boy I fell in love with overseas. I ran with it and said I needed some quiet time here to heal from my infatuation. Daddy's acting like I'm gonna have a fit of the vapors."

I can feel Gavina roll her eyes from where I sit. "Your father may be my nephew, but he doesn't have the sense God gave a goose. In this case, let it work for you."

"Daddy's not a bad man."

"No, but like your brother, he's oblivious to half the population that doesn't wag around a penis."

I spit out the sip I took. "Gavina!"

"Oh, please. The world won't stop turning if we call body parts by their real names." She holds up a hand. "I didn't come out here to talk about your parents, your brother, or any relevant body part except your heart."

She lets the gently brightening sky engross us for a long, restful minute before continuing. "I have something for you, now that there's enough light for you to see."

A box slides across the table, and I open it, my breath catching as the sunlight strikes a smoky topaz wrapped in gold wire. "It's beautiful, but I don't understand."

"That's a Scottish cairngorm my aunt Alyssa gave to me before she passed. You have to remember I was a late-life surprise. She was older than Da, and never as close to me as I am to you, but she was a wonderful woman. She loved Scotland, and I visited her many times where we had a lot of debates on mysticism and religion."

Yikes. Those had to have been some heated conversations. Gavina is the epitome of a straight shooter and doesn't cotton to mystical woo-woo or the hard and fast rules of religion. I long for her confidence.

"I would've liked to have been a fly on the wall for those arguments."

Gavina shrugs a shoulder, and her face takes on the soft look of reminiscing. "Alyssa had a spine of steel, but she was always willing to accept other people's beliefs. As to the mystical, she believed with all her heart her mother's stone has magical properties to heal a broken heart. Somehow, the quartz was supposed to balance my energy and help me make peace with my decisions." She nudges the corner of the box. "I'm not sure about all that, but I will confess I've spent more than one afternoon lost in my head and holding on to that amulet."

I don't want to disappoint the woman responsible for patching up my soul, but if she thinks giving me a necklace will fix me, she's wrong. My heart broke in two, and I left both parts behind in France. It will never heal.

I can't risk hurting her, so I play along. "If I remember correctly, Alyssa had a wonderful life, despite marrying late for her time in history."

"She did, but her mother didn't. Da never talked of his father, but in her later years, Alyssa told me the man was an abusive alcoholic and her mother had nine children to keep alive. She didn't have it in her to defy the man to protect the bastard son her husband had with another woman, but Alyssa wouldn't let her half-brother starve or freeze."

A year ago, I would have hated Alyssa's mother with a vengeance. I'd've acted as judge, jury, and executioner on her character. Life has already taught me a bitter lesson in tempering my judgment. This wiser Violet has a kinship with Alyssa and, surprisingly, is slightly more forgiving of a mother who made decisions that seem harsh by today's standards. In her time? The woman was literally saving her children's lives the only way she knew how.

"I would've liked Alyssa."

"You would have loved her. But the short version of the long story is Alyssa believed the stone gave her mother the strength to endure a marriage I wouldn't wish on my worst enemy. She never openly helped Da, but she slipped Alyssa food for him. He signed on as a cabin boy at ten years old. Can you imagine? And he survived to grow into a fine man."

"I remember those details from the report I wrote a thousand years ago in high school."

G's smile twitches. "I'd forgotten."

"I haven't. It's what started my time with you. I need to make a note to send my teacher flowers for insisting I write about my family history."

It strikes me how the smallest things in life can evolve into the greatest things. How an English paper, an assignment I loathed, brought me my Gavina. The woman I love most in this cruel world.

"Alyssa would say it was your ancestors reaching from the heavens to ensure you learned of them. The only way the gods die is for the people to forget them, and the truth's the same for a family legacy. Which takes us full circle to the necklace. Your great-great-aunt Alyssa is responsible for bringing magic to the castle. Even more, the cairngorm finds its way to a MacInnes woman who battles heartbreak and loss. You might not be inclined to kindness toward your great-grandfather's mother, but she actually kept all nine of those kids alive, in a time when no one managed such an impossible feat. So Alyssa found a way to forgive her for being a hard woman, because she was a determined one."

"And Alyssa gave you the stone because you had to give up your love." I keep my voice soft because it wants to break on the tears jammed in my throat.

"Indeed, and you've given up yours." She points to the gem I'm clutching. "I don't know if magic is real, or if we convince ourselves by making the evidence fit our vision. But I do know Alyssa MacInnes MacMillan saved a boy who came to America and fell in love with a headstrong girl from Galveston, and the two of them launched a dynasty. Alyssa and Niall were the first couple married here. And the lace altar cloth kept in the sealed glass case? She made it by hand."

"I've looked at that piece a million times. I had no idea."

"It's so much more than pieces of string."

"I always thought that. Anyone setting eyes on it can see it took hundreds of hours of painstaking precision. What I didn't see—I guess, in my defense, couldn't see—was the magic she infused in every knot."

"I don't know lace or fabric. That's your expertise, but I do know it's called needle lace, and she made it on a trip to Scotland because it was something she could do during the long weeks at sea. Since that first blessing, every bride in the chapel has worn a piece of Alyssa's lace on her wedding day, although now the ribbons are woven by her granddaughters. Still, the chain has been unbroken for all these years."

She sets her coffee aside on a small table and shifts her chair to face me, her arms resting on her thighs. "Right now, you're fractured, but in time, you'll heal. I want you to have the stone so the strength of the women before you might mend you."

I know Gavina sees me through a lens of love, a filter I hope she never takes off. On the whole mending thing, though, she's wrong. Maybe I can glue myself together, eventually, but I'll never be more than holding on.

She gives me her signature silent look as if she read my mind. "There's a Japanese pottery technique where they take a broken bowl and infuses gold into the cracks. They highlight the broken place, the flaws people see. They call it the art of precious scars."

Of course G finds a way to weave in craftsmanship, but the organ keeping me alive is too damaged. There's not enough gold in California for me, or an artist skilled enough to make my fractures beautiful.

I cut her a side-glance. "Are you veering into the magical mystical stuff here, G?"

"Nothing magical at all. It's literally down to earth. To pottery. To torture my analogy, Alyssa found her vein of gold, her great love, late in life. She told me I would, too, but she was wrong."

"I'm so sorry. I wish—"

"If wishes were horses, beggars would ride." She rocks in her chair, squinting against the fully risen sun. "I made my choices. I had a second chance at love, and I was too closed down, too obstinate, to try again."

I'm speechless, stunned to learn a piece of G's history she's never shared in any of our deep conversations.

"You never told me that."

"Because the time wasn't right. You need to accept you can never truly know another person, even a person you love. I don't believe we're supposed to, but I do believe the magic happens when you take the chance. I didn't. My reasons are many, and today's not the day to recount them."

She stops. Stares. Her eyes glisten with regret, and my already tattered heart tears wider.

"Don't follow my path, Violet. Let the crystal help you heal. Choose to be happy, wherever you might live, and in time, trust your heart to the right person."

I put my cup down and clutch the quilt around me. "I've been thinking, these last months. It's all I seem to do, but I may have a way to climb out of my misery."

"Are you going to New York?"

"No. I've decided I won't let anyone take Magnolia Bloom away from me. I thought for a while I wanted out, to leave and never look back. I may be young, but I've never been a coward. I ran once. I'm not doing it again."

"Good for you." G's voice is so quiet I almost don't hear her.

"You're stuck with me." I try to tease, but tears rise fast.

"Not stuck. Blessed. And on that note, I'm heading inside before these old bones freeze solid. You come in when you're ready."

I study the amulet worn by the women who've shared a lifeline with me, an ancestry of endurance. The magic of the castle says you won't be exempt from heartache, but you will have the strength to persevere. As the light refracts around the cuts and curves of the stone, I hope the magic isn't saved only for weddings.

My heart lifts, believing for the first time I might not be a harbinger of doom for Castle MacInnes. I might not get the white gown and veil, but I'll be all right.

I hold the crystal to my heart.

And breathe.

CHAPTER THIRTY-SEVEN

PAIGE – NOW

I SPENT the entire evening last night trying to screw my head on straight. Luckily, Cousin Ian and his brood, not to mention all the other family members wanting to chat, made it easier to ignore my jumping pulse every time Leith came into view.

While it was a fun night filled with food, dancing, and fireworks, nothing compares to this joyful madness created by our clan lining up for the parade. We sewed MacInnes tartan bunting for Bella's and Marceau's strollers, and my, oh, my, the men look amazing in their kilts. We had one made for Chen as an anniversary present, and he's been game-on to wear it ever since.

Even though the Scot comes from my side of the family, Zach and Aiden look like they could be brandishing claymores and taking down English invaders. They're both so handsome my heart squeezes like the oranges I juiced for breakfast. Zach's sporran was Granddaddy Alisdair's, I wonder for half a second if I'll have to fight him for it.

I shake my head to make the thoughts go away. Now is not the time to dwell on Zach or Leith. Or endings or beginnings. Or possibilities. It's time for bagpipes and drums and dancing and caber tosses and herding demonstrations.

The entire length of the grand hallway is a sea of kilts and tartan skirts, clan sashes and Jacobite shirts, hose and ghillie brogues.

"*Tha thu bòidheach*, Cousin."

I step into Ian's big hug. This is the second time in my life I've heard that phrase, the second time in as many weeks, but my cousin's deep brogue doesn't make my heart beat, my breath go shaky.

"You look braw yourself."

"Aye, that's true." He puffs his chest, but I know he's being his goofy self.

I haven't been in the same room with Ian more than a few times over the years, but from the moment we reconnected last night, I know as well as I know my name the redheaded joker loves his family and his clan with a passion to make any Scot proud.

He'd make a damn fine Texan.

"I'll be rooting for you in the caber toss."

"That's grand." He throws an arm around Leith, who's walked up. "Now if we could get this scrawny bawbag in line, he wouldn't have to compete with Callum and the other wee wains."

"Ian!" His wife's voice, not quite a shriek, interrupts whatever retort Leith might be loading.

Ian sighs. "The chief calls. I must attend."

I shake my head in mock despair as he hurries away, his size alone cutting a swath in the assembled mass. It appears there's an imminent disaster with his eldest's velvet vest. Her hair ribbons match her purple plaid kilt, and I see the tears from here.

I turn from the family scene and angle to the man I have several names for, but *scrawny* is nowhere on the list.

"*Tha thu—*"

"Yeah, yeah." I interrupt the deep voice which *had* caused my respiratory system to go into overdrive. "Ian already told me."

"The bampot stole my thunder."

I attempt my best Texan Highland accent. "Haud yer wheesht."

He throws his head back and laughs. "You're learnin', lass."

"I may not be a native, but I am Scottish, you know."

Something flares in his eyes. "Och, aye, I know."

I look around, a bit frenetically, trying to find Zach. Not out of guilt, although there may be a twinge running amok in my gut, but for introductions. My plan is foiled, to no surprise, because he's walking next to Ainsley, his determined stride telling me he's attending to her latest emergency. Uncle T and Monroe wave, putting a smile on my face.

I don't have time to worry over Zach. If he doesn't return on time to walk with me, he'll be along when he's finished. I adjust Violet's sash on my shoulder, wanting it to be perfect, and the tears I thought I'd burned through last night threaten to reappear. There are cousins galore in the crowd behind me, but with V gone, my father is the next direct descendant from Evajean and Alisdair's firstborn. He should be here, but he's never, not once, walked out with the family as an adult. My brothers have the most minor interest in our heritage, and Kiki is thousands of miles way. That leaves me to be the only one to bear the standard.

Except...I'm not.

There are two women just a bit older than me in France who have the right to be ahead of me, if they wished it. If they knew—

"Are you all right?"

Leith's tone is concerned. Deep. Stroking right across my heart. And I need him to stop doing that. Stop looking at me with care and worry etched on his face.

I pull in a full suck-it-up-buttercup breath, straighten my shoulders, and smooth my shirt into my waistband. "Yes and no. It hit me like a sledgehammer the job's mine now. To lead the family out. And I miss Violet badly."

I check my brooch, not because I need to, but to give my hands something to do. And I move the subject off of me.

"You look pretty spiffy yourself. That kilt must have taken up half your backpack."

He certainly does the MacMaster tartan justice…

He gives a snort at my poor attempt at a joke. "Ian carried it over for me. I wouldnae have gotten my *sgian dubh* through customs."

I can't help but look at his knife properly tucked into the top of his kilt hose straining around an impressive calf. "True. Airport security couldn't care less where you wear it or why."

"I havenae found them overly understanding. They've a distinct lack of sense of humor."

Fina rings a small handbell to command all our attention. Leith gives me a wink and melts away to where he'll walk with Ian, and my family forms behind me.

Right as Fina moves to signal the doormen, Zach races up and stands beside me, giving me his sorry-I'm-here-now smile. It strikes me, as I looked around for him earlier, I felt more wistful disappointment than anxious need. I wouldn't have held up the procession, and that is yet another change in me I don't have time to explore.

The doors open, and Fina waits until I'm by her side to hand me the shepherd's crook Violet had carried, as had every MacInnes before her. She and Mina walk with us, as they always have, but Fina will peel away to be first on the grandstand. She takes great pride in calling the roll of the families in attendance, and in many ways, the MacInnes Highland Games are as much Mina and Fina's baby as ours.

The drum major calls his orders, the pipes and drums strike their notes, and the trio of color guards bearing the flags of the United States, Scotland, and Texas lead the procession. A sea of tents shades the crowd, and a wave of cheers greets and follows us around the grounds. It's over too quickly for me, but I take the microphone and ask Harville to do the invocation before the combined Girl Scout and Boy Scout troops sing the national anthem. The pipers play *Flower of Scotland*, which causes a lot of sniffles, and the Eighty-Fifth MacInnes Highland Games begin.

Mina has my morning rigidly scheduled, but I don't mind judging the dancing, the piping, the drums, or the herding. My vote is entirely ceremonial anyway, but it's part of the expectation. I clap and gasp as hard as anyone at the impressive displays of strength in the caber toss, stone put, and hammer swings. The area is a smorgasbord of smells, ranging from kettle corn to turkey legs to, of course, barbecue, and there's never a moment of silence between the band stages, the dance exhibitions, and the drums and pipes playing somewhere.

By the afternoon, my feet hurt, I'm sweaty and sticky, and I'm in sensory overload. There's no doubt I'm an extrovert, but days like today test even my sociability, so when I realize I can slip away to the grove for a moment, I don't think twice.

The last person I expect to find on the far side of the not-quite-perfect ring of magnolias is Leith MacMaster, standing like the image in my head of Alisdair—feet slightly apart, hands on his hips. He's watching the lake visible through a break in the trees.

"Well, hello." The sounds of the activities are muted in this space, making my voice too loud in the solitude.

"What brings you here?" His voice is light. Friendly. Tossed over his shoulder like an invitation to have a cocktail.

"Apparently, stalking you."

I meant the words to be playful, but heat washes over me as he turns to face me, his smile slow, one eyebrow inching up.

"That sounds promising."

"Stop it." The heat turns into a second-degree blush. "You're a flirt, you know that?"

"I'm a Scotsman alone with a beautiful woman. What else would I be?"

"I don't know, but you're about to behave."

"If I must." He sighs resignedly and gestures around us. "Fina told me this is *the* grove."

"It's smaller than you expected, isn't it?"

"Aye, but the magnolias are pure barry. Still, the word 'grove' gives a different mental picture."

"To me, it's perfect. Big enough for four or five picnic blankets, but not enough for a crowd."

"That it is." He gestures toward the lake. "Walk with me?"

I look in the direction of the grounds, then to the lure of the water. "Sure. For a few minutes."

We stroll toward the deserted benches by the cove. The sounds from the revelry are a dull rise and fall of applause and shouts. Boats, in full water-sport frenzy on the lake, create an endless rhythm of waves lapping and retreating against the slanted bank. The scents of magnolia and jasmine waft on the wind barely making the heat tolerable, but I pull my hair up anyway, twisting the not-quite-dry strands into a knot and securing it with the band I put on my wrist hours ago so I wouldn't forget.

"You have a lovely neck." His voice is low. Soft.

I'm caught off guard, again, and try for nonchalance. "It's a sweaty one needing the breeze to kick up, which was why I was taking a break, in addition to being peopled out."

"Is that the reason? The heat and people, I mean. Is that really why you're walking alone, your shoulders round, your eyes sad?"

"Leith, don't." I turn my face away. "I appreciate your kindness, I do—"

"I suppose this is where I should confess I'm not in the grove by accident. Fina did point it out, but I saw you walking this way, and I took the chance you were coming here."

"See, that's another thing you shouldn't say. It's—"

I cry out in pain as my foot mismanages a rock. My ankle rolls. My knee gives. I go down in an instant, breaking my fall with my hands.

"Paige!"

"I'm all right." The lie is a hiss as I try to stand, my palms imprinted in the dirt, my knee definitely promising to bleed. I want to slap away his offered hand, but being ridiculous on top of my current level embarrassment would accomplish nothing.

He helps me, but the instant I put weight on my ankle, I come dangerously close to renewing my sprawl on the ground.

"I've got you." His steady, strong arms confirm his claim.

Before I can do more than squeak in protest, I'm hoisted against his chest. I put my arms around his neck automatically, yet illogically, I lean away.

"Leith, set me down. I'm much too heavy."

"And that's absurd. You have two choices. Tent or castle?"

He's already walking, but I wiggle anyway. "I mean it. Put me down."

"No. Pick your destination."

A quick glance over my shoulder gives me my answer. "The tent's closer."

"Fine. Now, be still."

I nearly die as heads turn toward us as he wends his way through the canopies and chairs toward the tent draped in the MacInnes colors and placed for maximum viewing of the event field.

Everyone seems to see me at once. Zach takes in the picture and frowns, but starts walking forward. Ainsley cries out, "Mom!" Aiden and Chen are up and moving. My sweet Callum starts crying. Richard hangs back.

Leith releases my legs, making sure my good one is solidly planted, but doesn't remove his arm from around my waist. Zach moves within catcher's space, and the two men look at each other, the tension in the tent palpably weird.

I try to break it with introductions. "Zach, this is Leith MacMaster. He's an architect from Scotland doing a piece on the castle and a longtime friend of my cousin Ian. Leith, Zach Peters."

Leith offers his hand. There's an infinitesimal hesitation before Zach takes it, but it's enough to make me blink in surprise. Zach is, to the point of ridiculous, never rude.

"I'm surprised my wife hasn't mentioned you."

My wife?

My head rears back, my eyes glue to him. When, in twenty-seven years, has he ever interjected a *my wife* into a conversation?

They finish their handshake, do the male-chin-thrust thing, and I don't have time to decipher anything else as Callum attaches to my bad leg, threatening my precarious balance.

"I'm all right, baby. Nana fell and got a boo-boo. Would you find me a napkin?"

He takes off for the picnic basket, and I make quick introductions to Aiden and Chen. Leith releases me, and my son instantly offers his support. To be fair, Zach did, too, but I picked Aiden.

I nod to Leith. "Thank you for your help."

"It was my pleasure. If you need anything, please call me, but I can see you're well taken care of here."

"I am. Enjoy the rest of the games."

"I will."

Leith waves a general goodbye to my family and walks away. I rigidly do not watch. I'm too busy stuffing down the slow boil of anger in my stomach at *my husband* as I inch over to a lawn chair. Again, the flurry of attention is centered on me, and it makes me more upset than the fall did. Zach checks my knee, Ainsley puts ice in a plastic bag once home to a sandwich, Chen brings over another chair to prop my foot on, and Aiden searches for the first aid kit he knows good and well I've packed in the wagon.

Everyone assures Callum that Nana is fine, but he hovers as Zach gives my knee a quick cleaning with the alcohol wipes. It earns a hiss from me, and I have to turn it into a sucked-in breath of *ha-ha, it doesn't hurt* for my little man's sake. We allow him the honor of putting on the adhesive bandage, which mollifies him enough to let Ainsley pull him off the front lines.

"Well, that was embarrassing."

Thankfully, the festivities are drawing to a close for the day, and the crowd will be thinner when I make my graceless retreat to the castle.

"What happened?" Ainsley's sitting crisscross-applesauce on the blanket, holding Bella. Callum immediately claims his daddy's lap.

"I was chatting with Leith, and we were walking. I stumbled on a rock and went tail over teakettle, and now I'll self-destruct from embarrassment."

"Oh, Mom." Ainsley rolls her eyes. "You aren't the first person to fall down."

"Mama's right, Nana. I falled down before and hurt my knee, too."

"Nana's fine, baby. I promise."

"Should I take you to the emergency room?" Zach asks. "The kids can take the stuff back."

I work to keep frustration out of my voice, mostly because I'm still seething at his Tarzan routine, and I can't say anything until we're alone. "I. Am. Fine. I'm sure it's a sprain."

Zach sits down and offers me a beer before opening one for himself. I take it gladly, hoping it will calm me, but by the time the kids have gotten all our bits and pieces packed up, the ache in my foot pales to the snarl of my insides. I'm more than ready to head in.

I signal to Aiden. "Honey, help me hobble in. Between you and Daddy, we'll look like we're competing in a five-legged race, but it'll get the job done."

"I'll carry you." Zach stands and bends toward me.

"No, you will not." My voice is firm and brooks no argument. "I'm already mortified, and I can't take any more. Just don't."

I win, and we manage a ragtag return to the castle. By the time I'm alone with Zach in the apartment, I've gone from slow simmer to boiling cauldron. I sit on the bed, fully intending to take a shower, but I will deal with this nonsense first.

"What the hell was that about?"

Zach is stripping out of his regalia and stops with his shirt half raised. "What was what about?"

"Your he-man display a few minutes ago."

"My what?"

"Your chest-beating 'my wife' moment."

"You're not my wife?"

I narrow my eyes at him so hard he should catch fire. "If you play ignorant with me, I can't be held responsible for my actions. And that's not a joke."

He lets the shirt slide down and plants his hands on his hips. There are few men who wouldn't look absolutely ludicrous to be standing half naked, a Jacobite shirt kissing his bare thighs, and Zach is one of them.

It pisses me off.

"Paige, what the hell did I do?"

"You called me 'my wife.'"

"You've said that. What am I missing?"

"You freakin' claimed me like some kind of prize dog. We've been married almost three decades, and you have never, ever acted like a possessive child screaming, 'Mine.' You embarrassed me a thousand times worse than hurting my ankle."

"Well, excuse me if it threw me to see some strange man carrying you, *my wife*, across the grounds."

"Why should that throw you? I hurt myself. A friend was bringing me to our family tent. What did you want to happen? Was Leith supposed to build a travois from limbs and branches and haul me in?"

He looks at me, takes a breath, and shakes his head. "I am completely lost here. I was taken aback. I've never seen you in another man's arms."

"And you had to be sure and claim your territory? What was next? Were you going to pee on my leg and mark me?"

"Was I going to p—where is this coming from? I had to take a second to process the visual signals coming at me. The moment was a bit chaotic. Do you want me to apologize or something? I don't think I did anything wrong, but I will if that's what you're asking for."

Of course he doesn't know where this is coming from. He refuses to see anything that doesn't fit his paradigm of our relationship.

I push myself to my feet, limping toward the bathroom. I hold on to the doorjamb and look to where Zach is still standing, eyeing me like I'm a snake poised to strike.

An apt analogy, and I don't care.

"What I'm asking is for you to acknowledge that you don't want me, but you damn sure want to make sure no other man can have me." I lift my finger in the don't-interrupt-me signal. "I fell down. Another man picked me up and brought me home, basically. You somehow took that as an affront either to your manhood or your ownership, and I am more pissed off than I have been in as long as I can remember."

I force myself to take a deep breath, screwing my eyes shut so I don't let something slip I'll truly regret. "You don't want me. You've made that clear. But you don't get to say someone else can't by staking some kind of public claim on me. Not anymore."

My throat closes up, and I force away tears I refuse to shed in front of him, but a pressure cooker of anger's burned too long and too hot. I refuse to mince words at this last inning of the game.

"Zach, I've asked you to talk to me. I've pleaded with you to go to counseling. I've begged for us to go away and reconnect. You've said no to every single one. So you don't get to refer to me as 'my wife' when you've treated me like a *sister* for five goddamned years."

I hobble toward the shower, but there's no weakness when I look back.

"Just let me go."

I shut the door, and it's a study in awkward to maneuver myself into and out of the tub, but I manage. It's too much work to blow-dry my hair, so I wrap it in a towel, fight my way into a nightgown, and creep over to the bed. Two ibuprofen and a glass of water are on the nightstand, but Zach isn't to be seen. I take the pain meds and climb under the sheets, knowing he's already asleep in the guest room.

Same song, different castle.

I don't really care. I'm glad I don't have to keep space between us on top of being physically exhausted and sore. While I wait for the pills to kick in, my thoughts circle the day like a vulture spotting a carcass.

Leith has no way to know what he's healed, but his flattering attention has laid waste to my certainty I'd end up a lonely spinster. He's validated the part of me too-long ignored, and I appreciate the insight more than he will ever know.

I'm still confused on some things, but I have crystal clarity on one thing. From my nonfights with Zach, to my flirtation and kiss with Leith, to tonight's carnival show, none of it's about choosing between two men.

It's about me. I need to choose *me*. Decide what I want. What I need. Demand it.

And no one in my life is used to me being so baldly self-centered.

Acid climbs my throat at framing such a selfish thought, but I push away the flash of guilt with the iron will usually reserved for others.

As my muscles start to relax, my last thought, post grand declaration, is what do I do now?

Truthfully, I don't have a clue what my next step should be, other than to let my exhausted body go to sleep.

And pray I'll have an answer in the morning.

CHAPTER THIRTY-EIGHT

MINA – NOW

My hand is so sweaty when I go to answer the door, it slips on the knob.

"Lord, give me strength." I try again, this time successfully, and invite in the handsome man who's caused my sleep a mess of trouble these last few weeks.

"Mina, good evening."

"Evenin', please come in."

CT steps inside and offers me a bottle of wine while retaining a vase of stargazer lilies. With one hand free, he takes off a perfectly creased Italian fedora and puts it on the rack by the front door. He takes my breath away in his black slacks, sky-blue shirt, and summer wool blazer.

I might not know much, but I know fabric, and his jacket is a testament to fine tailoring. And it's on a set of broad shoulders and buttoned over a fit chest that still snags more than my set of female eyes.

"Those flowers are my favorite." I lead the way in and put the wine on the counter so I can move the candles on the side to make room for the lovely bouquet. "How did you know? Or did you guess?"

"I knew. A birdie told me."

"Fina has loose lips."

"It wasn't Fina."

I wait for him to tell me, but he smiles and holds his peace.

My stomach flutters, and I move to the kitchen, both to give my wobbly legs something to do and to check the pasta. "Everything's ready."

"Can I help?"

"If you'll grab the salad from the refrigerator and the bread from the oven, I'd appreciate it."

"I have long arms, but I may need to do those one at a time."

A blush heats my cheeks, but I know he's teasing me. I pray he's teasing me, but I've been played before.

I take the pot over to the sink where the strainer waits.

"What are we having? It smells amazing." His voice is a bit muffled from behind the stainless-steel door of the fridge, but his eyes are bright when he reappears with the ceramic bowl keeping the fresh greens chilled.

"Puttanesca with tagliatelle pasta."

His smile deepens. "I'm glad I guessed correctly and brought a white. Or is this an exam to see if I like anchovies?"

My stomach threatens a revolt. The dish is one of my favorites, and my recipe is amazing, if I do say so myself, but I recall tonight was indeed supposed to be a test.

"Well, do you like them?" I try to keep my voice pert. I don't know how to flirt, so I'm doing the best I can.

"I do. I was stationed in Italy for a year, and I nearly got kicked out of the Army for failing to pass my physical the next go-round. Seems I ate my weight in garlic bread."

"Tonight we're having focaccia." I've been so proud of myself, making a fancy dish, making bread most people around here have had only at Olive Garden. All to impress him, and now I look like a know-it-all, getting bigger than my britches.

I try not to let it show in my voice that I'd rather run to my room and cry than drain the pasta, but what's left of my gumption rises from the dead.

CT finishes the tasks I assigned and stands in the archway to my kitchen. Filling the space a little too completely, a little too comfortably, if you ask me.

"Would you like me to uncork the wine?"

"Please." I point over my shoulder. "I have stemware in the cabinet to the left of the stove."

I stay with my head down, arranging the noodles on the platter and spooning out the rich plum tomatoes, black olives, capers, anchovies, and of course, garlic-infused olive oil. Small plates of EVOO and cracked pepper wait for us to dip our bread in, once I get him to the table.

"Why don't you have a seat, and I'll be right there."

He doesn't argue, and once he's out of sight, I clutch the edge of the sink and take long, deep breaths. What was I thinking? While I spent the afternoon cooking, my hands and mind were busy. Now he's here, in my house, and I don't have enough spit to swallow a fly, much less a meal.

I will not repeat the disaster of my behavior at lunch, so I stand up, suck in my stomach, and pick up the hot pads. As long as I don't dump the whole thing on the floor, I can make it through this.

When I join him in the dining room undeserving of such a noble title, he's already poured water into the glasses and wine into the stems he collected from the kitchen.

"Mina, I believe you have the loveliest table I've seen in a month of Sundays, and everything smells incredible."

He pulls my chair out, and my heart flutters. Lord love a duck, a man with manners is a spectacular creature, and I and my dizzy stomach are not immune. He sits, we put our napkins in our laps, and as if he's been in my home a thousand times, he starts the rituals of a Southern meal. The salad is tossed and served, the dressing passed, the bread cut, the peppered oil dipped and enjoyed.

By the time I've had a glass of a delicious Pinot Gris and finished my pasta, I'm full and have laughed more than I could have dreamed. It turns out CT Nelson has lived in more places than I could find on a map, courtesy of the United States military. He's kept up a running montage of his many travels, and I have been rapt with attention and have asked questions nonstop when it became clear he doesn't mind.

The sun's sinking into the horizon by the time we clear the table, with him insisting he will rinse the dishes and put them in the dishwasher, and no amount of objection from me will stop him.

"My momma taught me a few good things, and one of them is, when a lady spends hours fixing you a meal, you can take five minutes to do the dishes. And I've lived by it ever since."

I lean my shoulder against the doorframe he previously filled and sip my second glass of crisp wine. It's a nice vantage point to observe him with his coat off, his shirt cuffs rolled up, his movements sure and efficient. I want to ask if he did the dishes when his wife cooked, but I know he was heartbroken when she died five years ago from breast cancer. I don't want my curiosity to bring him sadness.

When he takes the dishrag and dries his hands, I stand and indicate the last pour of the bottle. "Would you be interested in moving to the patio? The sunset seems especially pretty tonight."

He makes quick work of rolling down his sleeves, but he leaves his coat off and follows me out the door. Like the dining room, *patio* is overstated for my postage-stamp garden, but I don't mind. There's enough room on the concrete for a small table and two iron chairs, and I'm proud of my yard. It's neat, my flower beds are weed-free, and the ground crew keeps my grass cut and watered. Living on the castle grounds is a slice of heaven, but this piece is my Eden.

"That was a lovely meal and wonderful company." He tilts toward me, and I gently clink the rim of my glass against his.

"It's my pleasure."

And, shockingly, it is. I completely forgot all the questions I wrote out to ask, to get a bead on him, to see if the man I've known casually for decades has a monster hidden inside him needing a bit of coaxing to come out.

"Since I talked your ear off all evening, why don't you tell me about your house? It's lovely. I thought I'd walked into a villa I rented in Florence some time ago."

I flush with pleasure. "I do love it. My sister loves all things medieval, and I got caught up in one of her magazines. It started slow. I bought a piece of marble at a garage sale one day, thinking, 'How do these people not know how valuable this is?' And then I found a table so ugly not even its mama could love it at the Salvation Army. Took that top off it, sanded the rust off the base, and found out how to seal it. When I attached the slab, it looked like I'd spent a thousand dollars on it. I got hooked, and, well, next thing you know, I've got Brian Steele over here helping me tear up carpet and put down tile."

I stop, suddenly horrified that I've got a severe case of jackhammer jaw. My stomach catches, and I try to hide my fingers in my lap.

Lord, here it comes. Here it comes.

CT tips his head, his brow frowning before he lifts it. "I can tell there's a whole story here. Don't stop now."

I clear my throat and take my last sip of wine, wishing the bottle was a gallon jug.

"Oh, it's not interesting. I putter, is all."

The joy fades from CT's face. As I knew it would.

See, Fina? I told you.

He pushes his wine aside so he can put both forearms on the table. His strong hands and long fingers take up most of the surface.

"I wasn't planning on bringing this up tonight, but you went from lighting up the whole backyard to lock-jawed. If you made or refurbished, or whatever the right word is, all those pieces in your living room, you're a certified genius. You have a beautiful home, and it appears you did most of it with your own two hands. And our dinner would make an Italian chef toss a white towel in defeat."

He folds his hands together, then unclasps them to lay them flat on the glass top, looking out into my yard before back at me. He catches my eye, and I'm frozen.

All I want to do is run.

See? See? I told you.

"I know why you stopped."

Huh? I want to ask, but I shake my head. It's automatic.

"You stopped because something crawled up out of your memory and said you were talking too much."

"How can you know such a thing?" I try to be brave, to sound challenging. What I sound like is a mouse with a voice box.

"I know what happened, Mina. My second cousin was sheriff in 1980 and had been deputy sheriff for years before."

Every organ but my heart shuts down out of pure preservation. I close my eyes, drop my head, and pray that when I open them, he'll be gone. *Lord, let him go home. Go to his store and his life and please, stop bagging my groceries.*

My prayer is a failure, as evidenced by him still sitting patiently in the chair not quite big enough for his broad shoulders when I open my eyes again.

His mouth goes tight for an instant before he speaks. "I know Trey did not kill his daddy. My cousin hated those gossipy biddies for the rumors tearing through this town when Trey came running in from the deer blind. That boy was hysterical. Nobody believed for a second he shot his daddy on purpose, except for the few evil creatures who can't keep their mouths shut."

I can barely breathe. I sure can't talk.

"But I will tell you one thing, and you can think badly of me if you wish, but if Trey had shot Roylee on purpose, my cousin might've given him a reward, because there is no man born in this county who needed to see the pointed end of a bullet more than that son of a bitch."

My eyes widen at his language. I've never heard CT utter a curse word in any context. Ever. I'm not insulted. Not at all.

I'm…touched.

I still can't talk, though. I want to. I want to express my appreciation. For the companionship over dinner. For doing the dishes. For being kind and sweet.

He takes a deep breath, letting me find an ounce of balance.

"I'll take my leave, since I've said too much and spoiled our evening."

"You didn't." Two words.

A start.

"I did. You got a look in your eye like you were waiting for me to slap you." He blinks too quickly as if he got something in his eye. "You tore me in two."

He stands, and I follow, lagging behind him as he slips on his jacket.

"I would never lay a hand on you." His voice is low, raw, vehement. "I've never hit a woman in my life, and I'll go to my grave with my record standing firm. Moreover, I can't conceive of a time where I'd raise a hand to a woman in any situation. I don't like having to tell you I'm not such a man. Anyone who would do that isn't a man at all."

At the door, he takes his fedora off the rack and pulls the brim between his fingers. I shadow him outside, wanting him to go.

Wanting him to stay.

He stops on the bottom step. "You took me straight to Italy, and I've loved that country my whole life. Thank you again."

"I didn't know. It's...something I like to make."

"You can invite me over for anchovies any time."

Somehow, some way, a smile finds its way to my mouth. I don't say yes.

But I don't say no.

He turns, and God as my witness, I don't know how I manage to say, "Isn't a date supposed to end with a kiss?"

His body angles toward me, the fedora halfway to his head.

"I didn't think you'd want one."

I suck in enough oxygen and cast all blame on two glasses of wine. "What if I do?"

The fedora travels the remaining distance, and he sets it on his head at the angle he's perfected. I expect his smile to be sweet. Or teasing.

Instead, it's a bit shy of devilish.

He gives the brim of his hat a tug. "When you figure it out, you let me know."

He walks to his car, and I race inside, shutting the door and locking it, leaning against the dark wood I stripped and stained myself. I put my hand to my chest, pressing hard in case my heart actually manages to knock itself through my ribs.

I feel nineteen, not fifty-nine, poised on the brink of something wonderful. Angels of mercy, I don't want to be nineteen again, but for the first time, I wonder what a completely different fifty-nine might be like...

CHAPTER THIRTY-NINE

VIOLET – 1974

WHEN MY BROTHER calls and asks me to come meet his new baby girl, I about fall over. Gerome has no desire to see me much. My curiosity is cured, though, in minutes of my arrival. He has to leave on deployment, and Christina can't seem to find the wherewithal to take care of a newborn by herself. I expected the Barnesdales to be beside themselves to help with their first grandchild, but it appears they're still too angry with Gerome for soiling the innocence of their little Madonna to forgive yet.

My stomach started in a knot in Magnolia Bloom, but morphed into an entire web with each mile of my drive to Austin. Part of me isn't ready to think the word *baby*, much less hold one, but the time has come.

Gerome seems impatient, his hands stuffed in his pockets as he paces the front porch while I park. He hardly offers a hello before he leads me to the nursery.

"Christina's asleep. This is the baby."

He says it as if he's ticking off a feature on his new car, or like I might mistake the occupant of the crib to be a puppy or something.

I step closer, and all my trepidation melts away. I pick up the beauty swaddled in a pink blanket and nest her in the crook of my arm.

Gerome is walking toward the door, his mind clearly already en route to his new base. "If you've got this, I need to finish packing. Christina hasn't been up to it."

I'm not sure he even waited until I nodded, but it doesn't matter. I'm already in the rocker, settling in.

"Hello, Miss Paige Jeanette MacInnes. Yes, your daddy is a butthead for breaking the tradition, but you'll just have to deal with it." I brush my hand over her perfect head. I'm still mad at Gerome for choosing Jeanette. No matter how much I hated it as a child, Gavina made me understand why we give girls MacInnes as a middle name. Times are changing, sure, but it's still a novel thing for a woman to not take her husband's.

Maybe Paige will be the trendsetter in our family. For now, since it's apparent my heart won't wrench itself out of my chest, it's enough for the empty place in my soul to start to fill.

"Maybe you're just the thing I need to fix me."

Paige wiggles until she frees one arm, stretching it over her head, then settling back to sleep.

She'll be dark-headed, for sure, and though her eyes are blue now, Momma said Christina's hoping they'll turn green like Gerome's and mine. Well, like Gerome's. I'm sure I don't enter Christina's thoughts.

I do what every good auntie does and unwrap her to check all her extremities, kissing her knuckles and laughing when her toes curl around my finger.

I stroke her cheek as she dreams. "Welcome to Clan MacInnes, beautiful girl. You got here just in time."

CHAPTER FORTY

PAIGE – NOW

I AM FAIRLY certain someone has messed with the space-time contin-uum, or maybe everyone loses an entire week when they spend twelve or fourteen hours a day scanning decades of documents into a computerized management system. I'm well aware I've used the monumental task to keep my mind off my disastrous evening with my husband and the awkward day after until he left for Austin. I've orga-nized and cataloged until I'm bleary-eyed, but June has bid adieu, and it's nearly midnight on another Friday.

Pity? Party of one? Your table's ready.

At least I made myself join Ian and his family for dinner earlier. They've had a grand American vacation, as they put it. They're staying for the Fourth of July fireworks at the city park tomorrow, making a trip to the Dallas aquarium on Sunday, and then heading home on Monday. Truth be told, they're exhausted and ready to go.

Ian's still grumbling about not winning the caber toss...

I've also made a promise to myself that I'll finish the diaries, and even if it is half past twelve, I'm doing it tonight. I used Violet and her babies to keep my mind off Zach and how firmly I've nailed the door shut, but I left myself hanging. Stifling a yawn, I return to the turret, which has been my work zone, but is now my sanctuary.

Violet's entries become shorter in this volume. I can understand it's hard for her to write all of this down. It would be for me. When I reach the part where she explains how my father called her to help with my care after I was born, I wince despite being alone. It hurts to see the difference between what she's written and how inviting it was when she told the story. On paper, my father sounds like a jerk, and it cuts deeply that I'm not surprised.

I have to bookmark the page when I read, *Maybe you're just the thing I need to fix me.*

For just an instant, those ten words threaten to turn my relationship with Violet on its head. The left-shoulder devil laughs spitefully, telling me V needed me only as second-string backup.

Luckily, I'm surrounded by decades of warmth and love and memories, and I know I'm just raw from the seemingly relentless slices to my soul these last couple of months. I'm blessed I can look around this one room, one among many, and see the reminders of the woman who did everything in her power to make a lost and lonely little girl feel like she was the most important thing in the world.

"I'm so glad I got here in time, Violet. And I'm forever grateful you were here to catch me."

I hold the journal to my chest for a long time, just absorbing the words and trying to picture a baby me and a young Violet, alone in a nursery, meeting for the first time and starting a special journey very few people get to experience. I just wish with every fiber of my being she hadn't been afraid to tell me about Juliette and Noelle. I would have loved to have known them through her eyes.

There's a knock at the door, and before I look over, I know it's Leith.

"What're you doing up so late? I didnae expect you'd be here."

He's carrying the folders I made for him under one arm and a vase with the most beautiful arrangement of flowers I've ever seen in his hands. Thanks to my favorite florist in Austin, I'm fairly good at naming the mix. Gerbera daisies, green stalks of bells of Ireland, purple palm, blue iris, orange solidago. I stop there, my heart touched. The most adventurous Zach has gotten with flowers was pink roses instead of red. Or yellow—this is Texas, after all—but those were rare.

I stand and reach for the dark-stained box holding the display, a grin breaking out on my face. "Gracious. How beautiful."

"Aye. The delivery van came as I was coming in a short bit ago. I told Mina I'd bring them up to you. There's a card."

There's a—wait, these aren't from...

If I've ever wanted the floor to swallow me whole, the wish now has an exponent.

I put the flowers down, but I don't have to touch the white paper. From this angle, I can see the strong Z at the bottom of the note bleeding through the envelope.

Moving around my chair, I pull the card from the holder and drop it into the trash. I push the bin under the desk with my toe and move the vase to the corner of the desk. There's no need to read the message, but I do need to keep the beautiful bouquet as a reminder of the good things, the good times, the good points.

And a caution to not dwell on the bad.

I swipe my hands together to brush off the bits of greenery on my fingers and walk to the couch.

"Are you—"

I cut him off. "I'm fine. I'm bloody perfect. Floral delivery is done, so don't let me keep you."

Leith looks at me for a decidedly uncomfortable moment, his eyes roving to the trash can now out of sight. "I dinnae believe you're close to fine."

My breath is slow and deep, and by the time I release it, if what's on my face isn't a smile, it's not a frown. Or tears. "Actually, I really am okay. Better every day."

"I'll have to take your word. I guess, though, I should tell you I'm not here solely as a deliveryman. I have some news, but if now isnae a good time, tell me. I don't want to bother you."

Bother me? He's done nothing but rattle me from the moment he said my name at DFW airport. I'm sure someday, when I'm looking back on this year with any semblance of clarity, I'll be grateful for how Leith MacMaster shook up my world. He's made me think and react, forced me out of the zombie slog I was in for five years.

At the moment? Not so much.

Might as well distract myself. "What's up?"

"I've solved the mystery."

"Mystery?"

"I've been working on it the whole week. With the blueprints and the surveys and a few hundred measurements, I've figured out where the discrepancy is."

I lift an eyebrow.

"I've found a hidden room."

My foul mood is gone in a *poof*. "No kidding? Tell me more, Scooby."

"Scooby?"

My pout is only half kidding. "Really? No Scooby-Doo in Scotland?"

His face brightens. "Och, aye, but I wasnae thinking of ghosts and jinkies and Scooby snacks."

"I'm mollified, but we do have ghosts, you know."

"Och, wouldnae be a proper Scottish castle without one."

"We have three. Evajean and Alisdair lost a daughter when she was four, and you can hear her playing in the grand ballroom some nights when you're alone and the lights are dim. The second is a maid who fell down the stairs in 1880. She's made more than one guest flee the third floor. And then there's Seamus."

"Now there's a proper Celtic name. He has to have been a sheep herder."

I stifle a giggle. "Excellent guess. He's seen walking the hills, but only in the fall." I move a step closer, a magnet inside me waking when he's around. I take a step to the side, as if I meant to all along. "So what's the big reveal? I'm dying to know."

Leith puts his files down and moves to the shelves right inside the doorway. As beautifully crafted as they are, I've always thought them being so close to the door is unusual for a bookcase. I've always assumed it's to conserve space in the small room.

He clicks on a flashlight and looks in and around the shelves. I help him remove the volumes on the slats he seems the most interested in, and in a moment, he gives an excited shout.

Reaching in, he presses, grunts, then presses harder. He's rewarded with a click, and the unit shifts into the room a few inches.

I gasp and immediately dive into impatience as he carefully pulls the secret door open until there's barely enough room to slip behind it. I race to the desk and grab my phone, swiping on the flashlight app, and rush to follow where he's disappeared.

The opening isn't big. I have to turn sideways to squeeze in, but once past, the room opens up, though not by a large margin. We can't quite stand shoulder to shoulder, but it extends in some ten or twelve feet, narrowing until it's barely a foot wide. And in the light of our combined instruments, it's clear that paintings are lined up on the floor against each wall. The air is still, dank. Cobwebs hang from the ceiling in wisps, and dust is scattered over everything, including the floor.

Hoping nature has done minimal, and hopefully reversible, damage, I pull a drop cloth off one stack and look at the portrait of a young girl. I assume from her dress the period is around the turn of the last century.

"Shine your light here." I point to the bottom of the canvas and give a happy yelp to see a distinctive GMM in the bottom corner.

"I can't believe it. You found them. Mina and I talked about them not long ago, but to be truthful, I've always been afraid the family rumor of Gavina's paintings was wishful thinking."

"I didnae know what I was looking for specifically, and I almost missed it. The length of the exterior wall was eased out gradually, and it took near fifty turns around the turrets to realize this one is smaller. If I hadn't kept comparing each one, I'd never have made the connection. I would've dismissed it as not an unreasonable correction during the building process, but I couldn't let it rest."

"I wouldn't have noticed in a million years."

"You're not an architect. These are the things that drive us batty."

We spend the next hour pulling out all the canvases, only a few of which are framed, and wipe the worst of the dirt from the edges. I don't touch the face of the pieces, knowing I'll need an art restorer, at a bare minimum. When we're done, we stand in cobweb-adorned silence and stare.

"She was brilliant." It seems an inadequate summation of the talent before me. "I mean, I already knew that from the work in the armory and galleries, but this is…wow."

"Wow, indeed. I'm no artist, but I can tell these are extraordinary. I wonder why she quit painting."

I can't take my eyes off the canvases. I'm mesmerized. "In V's diaries, she mentions Gavina loved a young woman, her best friend, but if we despair how slow our acceptance of homosexuality is now, it barely existed at the turn of the century. The twentieth, I mean. Her lover married, as was expected, and moved away. Gavina married, too, but she divorced—again, at a time when such things simply weren't done. If I had to guess, it hurt too much to paint after she knew she could never have the love she wanted so terribly."

We sort out the portraits of a woman of stunning beauty. Young, vibrant, clearly the belle of her time, and Gavina had captured her in various themes. Solemn, contemplative, intensely sexual. All conveyed in the tilt of her head, the thrust of her chin, a pull of her lips, of full breasts straining against her unbuttoned shirtwaist.

Leith leans down to look at one of the signatures. "She painted these in the 1930s."

"From what V wrote, she studied in Paris from 1915 to 1935. But even then, she was against the crowd. Dadaism, surrealism, and cubism were cool at the time. She is clearly a classical painter. She knew Picasso and Ernst and Suzanne Valadon and Marie Laurencin. How well, I don't know. V mentions their names almost casually, but it's mind-boggling. To her, they were the cool kids on the block. I'm sure she fit right in, though her style was nothing like any of them."

"The world should see these."

"I agree."

Gavina might not have been able to show the world how much she was in love, was loved, but I can do it for her. The least I can do is honor her memory and her testament to passion. And choices.

Oh, Gavina. I didn't know you, but you're teaching me. My heart is aching because she couldn't have the life she wanted, and more, I'm sad she felt she couldn't pursue another chance later on. Gavina was a stunning woman, remaining beautiful and regal her whole life. I have to believe she could have had all the lovers she wanted.

But she chose not to.

And I can almost sense her beside me, telling me to pay attention. To learn. To decide what I want and pursue it with the passion she put into her paints and canvas as the only way she had to express what she felt so deeply.

"I have to protect them." I immediately start a mental list. "I need to find a preservationist, someone to repair the damage time has done. Then we'll have to find a proper curator. Research showings and galleries."

"Seems like your job became a lot more complicated."

"No matter what it takes, it's totally going to be worth it."

"Maybe it's a sign for a new career."

I give my head a wry shake. "I can't draw a straight line with a ruler. Whatever cosmic force put this in my path, it's not because I'm supposed to touch any of these beauties with a ten-foot paintbrush. When we find the right gallery, though, they might not fix everything, but they could be a nice reprieve in our budget for a few years."

"You cannae tackle it tonight, or rather, this morning."

"Let's put them back, then. As much as I love everyone in this town, I'm afraid of leaving something so valuable out in the open until we can insure them."

Our excitement is abated only a small degree as we replace the masterpieces and close the bookshelf, finding ourselves in the exact spot where this started.

My fingers reach out as if they have minds of their own and pull stray cobwebs from his hair. He goes still as the stone surrounding us, his eyes locking with mine, and I stroke the mussed locks off his forehead.

I drop my hand, but I don't step away.

"Leith." His name is a sigh.

"Aye?" His breath is a whisper.

"Can I kiss you?" He starts visibly, and I cough a laugh. "Sorry. Should've had a better lead-in."

"Believe me, I'm nae opposed. Surprised, aye. Objections? Nae."

As quickly as I made my decision, I jump to awkward. I shake my head and pull away. "I wonder if I have an entire gene sequence for awkward, because I seem awfully good at it."

"Can you dinnae not do that?" He brushes my chin with a touch so gentle I shiver. "Can you not take a step forward, then three back?"

"I honestly don't know. I'm on new ground here and don't know how to ask for what I want. I don't have any practice, and the sad truth is I'd kissed a grand total of three boys before I met Zach and haven't kissed another man since." I know my face is probably glowing like a nuclear meltdown, but I press on. "Except you."

"I'm nae apologizing for that. Ever."

"I'd be hurt if you did, but I'm embarking on a journey to find me, and I have no idea where it will lead. But before I leave, before you go home, I want to kiss you, free of guilt. And I want it to be a goodbye telling you how much I appreciate what you've done for me this past month."

"I havenae—"

"You have. You don't realize that your interest, your attraction, has been incredibly gratifying."

"I'm no rocket scientist, but I'm no daftie, either. I cannae be the first man to flirt with you."

"No, but I've always taken it in fun, usually fueled by too much alcohol and dancing. I've never thought for a second it was anything but harmless."

"I'm flattered, then, you believing me."

"I'm flattered you were serious."

"I still am."

I move closer until my breasts are pressed against the hard planes of his chest. Threading my fingers into his hair, I pull down.

His cologne teases my nose, the spicy blend fusing into a memory that will stay with me forever. He moves his head so his lips whisper over mine, teasing, learning.

I lean in, needing more, seeking more.

His arms glide around me and match my embrace. As he pulls me closer, tighter, his mouth more demanding, I eagerly meet him, our tongues clashing and melding. He leans me over his arm and leaves me breathless as he traces his tongue down the skin of my throat, nuzzling the place where my neck joins my shoulder. I stretch to give him maximum access, gasping when he sucks the pulse beating a mad tattoo below my ear.

Time expands and contracts. His mouth returns to mine, and I'm not sure who the aggressor here is. It's wanton and heady and glorious.

And I nearly cry when he pulls away, shifting so he can rest his forehead on my shoulder. Not letting me go, but withdrawing none-theless.

"Paige."

I stroke the too-long hair at his nape, knowing I should move away, but I can't.

He's the one who finds the strength to do what needs to be done, standing to his full height, then letting me go.

"That…was…the most amazing goodbye I've ever experienced. Are you sure…"

"I am. Please understand. This is so damned hard, but I'm not rejecting you, I'm choosing me. If I give in to this…" I run my hand over his shoulder and down his chest, "And believe me, I want to. But if I do, I'm repeating the past. I have no idea how to be…me. It'll take time."

"I hear you, but I cannae say other parts of me are so under-standing."

I refuse to look down. I already have a fever with no access to a fire extinguisher.

He tucks a strand of hair behind my ear and gives me the grin I'll remember as much as the cologne. "You have my number. I'm not sure where I'll be in six months, but if you call me, I'll come meet you. Anywhere."

"I'm not asking you to wait for me." Panic makes my voice squeaky.

"And I'm not saying I will. I'm promising to be your friend and be here for you. If the future brings something more, well, we'll see, won't we?"

"Do you like Tahiti?" I surprise myself as much as him with the question.

He shrugs. "It's nice, I suppose, but if it's a beach you're wanting to leave you breathless, I prefer Sipadan. And since you're a SCUBA diver, I'm surprised it isnae your top choice."

"Question out of left field. Sorry. I'm flattered you remember the diving. I only mentioned it once."

That's the thing, yet again he remembered an offhand remark. Filed it away. Made me feel seen. Special.

He holds out his hand. "Dinnae be worried. I'd love to show you Tahiti or the Grand Caymans or anyplace in paradise."

When I put my fingers against his, he pulls me in and envelops me in his warmth. It heals another tiny slice of my eviscerated heart.

This kiss is short. It's warm. It's deep.

And it's goodbye.

CHAPTER FORTY-ONE

VIOLET – 1976

AUNT GAVINA IS DYING.

Still sharp and feisty and full of fire, despite her body failing her. It fuels the flames of her anger. Not the dying part, but the loss of her mobility and sometimes her dignity. Nothing infuriates her more than to know she can no longer deliver horses, throw hay bales, or chase a tangle of puppies.

I'm sitting beside her bed, reading as she's napping, when there's a tap at the door. I open it to find Brian Steele standing there with a bundle of wood.

"I've brought more firewood for Miss Gavina." He gives the load in his arms a wiggle, stating the obvious.

I don't razz him. Brian's sweet, and he knows, like everyone on the estate, that G loves a fire. It's September, and we've had a lovely autumn weather snap, which is the only thing I'm grateful for right now. It's not really cool enough, but G stays cold these days, and I couldn't care less whether a roaring blaze is logical or not.

"She'll love it."

He kneels by the cast-iron rack next to the stone hearth, the firebox that's large enough for a small child to stand in never failing to impress. Not the first time you see it. Not the thousandth. Brian's done in moments and stands, dusting off his hands.

"That should keep you for the rest of the day." His eyes stray to the bed. "I'm sorry she won't make it to see the latest foal."

"Me, too. I believe she was hanging on for all she's worth, but even Gavina MacInnes MacInnes doesn't always get her way.

His eyebrow lift says, *That's true,* but his mouth says, "I'll leave y'all be."

He pauses, his shoulders set, his feet firm. His family owns the big feed store, and he divides his time between working the grounds here and the register at the sprawling enterprise that sells everything from Western wear to hardware to housewares to actual feed and hay. Steele's Feed & Supply has been a fixture almost as long as the castle, sitting just outside town on the way to Atlanta.

He's always been a quiet guy. All the way back to our high school days, he's had a calm, steady presence. We aren't close friends, yet we're more than casual acquaintances. Come to think of it, he's far more handsome now, growing out of teenage awkwardness into a handsome, still-quiet, dependable man.

"Is there something else? You can stay if you'd like." His pain is a harsh slash across his eyes. Gavina was a mentor to him, and I wish I could do something, say something to make this less awful. It seems all I am, though, is useless, more a burden than a help to anyone.

I'm afraid Gavina is becoming impatient with me, but is there a timetable on mourning? It scares me to know a new clock will start for G any day now.

"I wanted to say I'm always around. You can call down to the warehouse. I'll be happy to fetch anything you need."

I start to give him a stock thank-you, but the urge dies when he looks straight at me. Have I ever noticed how warm and brown his eyes are? And he has those long, dark lashes wasted on a boy.

A man. Brian Steele is a man, and he's definitely telling me he wants to get me anything I might need, and I know he's not talking about more firewood. A warmth flames in the center of me that's grown icy.

"I really appreciate it, but—" I stop myself short. "You know what? There is something you can do. Can you bring Miss Bitsy and the puppies?"

The twitch of his lips elicits the same response in me.

"Be right back." He touches the brim of his cap and leaves, and I find myself engrossed as he walks away.

Was Tidy right? Does he have a crush on me? It felt absurd when she said it on our last visit to the dock, but now I'm not so sure. I was so busy worrying over the sunburn I got and the new bruises on her arms, I was distracted.

I don't know how to process the information, but for the first time since I can't remember when, I want to smile.

I catch myself humming and realize I've read the same page five times without retaining a syllable. I'm...antsy isn't the right word. Fidgety? Is that different? I give up and head over to the kitchen and make tea, adding some crustless sandwiches and cookies. I'm sure G will be awake when I return, and maybe I can coax her to eat a bite.

I'm right. When I open the door and bring in the tray, she gives me her Gavina half smile.

"What had you caterwauling so loud an old lady can't sleep?"

"I'm fairly certain humming doesn't rise to caterwauling, but sit up instead of arguing with me. I've got tea and cookies."

"So now I'm blind as well as dying?"

"No, cranky and dying, so hush and let me fix your pillows."

She obeys, and we haven't finished our first cup when there's a knock on the door. A faint, but distinctive, whine eases the strain on G's face. There's nothing weak about Aunt G except her love of horses and puppies. She'd never admit it, but I'm certain G's entire skeleton turns to mush at wagging tails and plump tummies.

"Come in." I take the tea service to the dresser so it's out of harm's way.

Brian enters, Miss Bitsy straining her nose forward but not moving an inch because she hasn't been released. The two puppies, one in each of Brian's arms, are squirming and struggling to lick his chin.

I smell the crisp scent of the special soap Brian and the stable groomer use when the puppies inevitably roll in something we'd rather not examine. Bits is a diva and loves her bath and blow-dry, and right now it's clear she wants to show off her new do to Gavina.

Brian lets out a soft whistle, and Miss Bitsy immediately sits, her focus solely on him. She stays stock-still until he gives another whistle, then she jogs over to Gavina's side and waits again.

Gavina looks happier than I've seen her in ages, and she pats the bed so Bitsy will come up. It amazes me Bits knows to temper her natural energy. She climbs up carefully, her steps as light as if she were a rabbit instead of a thirty-pound dog. Gavina waits until the current queen of the pack stretches out, then smooths her thumbs over Bitsy's white muzzle and her black, feathered ears.

Bits gives Gavina's wrist a lick.

"Hey, my girl," she croons. "Did you bring me your babies to love on?"

As if Bits knows exactly what's been said, she turns her head to Brian, and I swear her face says, *Bring me my puppies, human.*

Brian obeys, carrying the wiggly mini Bitsies over. He hands one to me and the other to Gavina. He doesn't say much, but he's observant and smart, and no matter how tough G likes to think she sounds, we all know one puppy is quite enough.

Bits sniffs her pup when it's close enough, observing carefully as Gavina pets the squirming black-and-white bundle.

"He's Double." Brian shakes his head at the imp in my lap trying to climb my shirt before he head-tips toward Gavina. "She's Trouble."

I'm curious if the entendre aimed at the woman he adores is intentional.

"She certainly is." I make my response wry to include both human and canine and put Double on his back in the crook of my arm for maximum puppy-belly exposure. He tries to bite my hand every time I stroke up between his paws.

"Only two?" Gavina asks Bitsy, but Brian answers.

"We lost one."

Sadness washes over her, but practicality follows. "I know you and Doc did everything you could."

"This is her last litter, but these two are perfect."

Gavina has a hard rule that no bitch of hers is allowed to have more than three litters in her lifetime. The rule was supposed to be two, but Miss Bits went gallivanting once, and the resulting litter was decidedly pit bull in feature, and in my opinion, some of the best pups we've ever had.

The MacInnes border collies are famous despite Gavina's immovable stance that none of her breed are papered. She keeps a strict genealogy of the dogs to ensure a continuous line from the original collies Alisdair and Evajean brought over from Scotland, but she refused to play the money game on the backs of her animals. She makes sure each one is spayed or neutered before being sold or given away, because she can't bear the thought of any animal of hers being used in a puppy mill. The woman who presents the toughest exterior in Texas is actually the biggest softy in all 267,000 square miles.

I take my bundle and go to Brian while Gavina talks to Bits and showers Trouble with affection, if slowly. It appears a warm puppy is the perfect balm for pain.

"You're so nice to do this."

His face moves from pleased to pensive. "It's good to see her smiling. We won't have her much longer."

"I know." Double seems to have worn himself out and is sound asleep in my arms.

"The castle, the property, the town, won't be the same."

In one sentence, he captures my fear. I've not let myself consider a life without Gavina. It's not my aunt who's dying, but the woman who raised me—not my birth mother, but the one I chose.

I step closer, my side almost touching Brian's as we stare at G. I find comfort in his warmth. "She's proud as punch of the new training and vet schedule you have for the dogs and the horses." I put my hand over my mouth and lower my voice conspiratorially. "We won't mention the sheep."

Brian breathes a laugh. "It always tickled me she never liked 'em, staying with her horses and dogs."

The black-faced MacInnes sheep are as famous as our collies, but I have to agree with him. I love the sweet but near-brainless things, but not Gavina.

"I've lingered long enough. I should go."

He steps toward the bed, but I stop him. "I'll bring Bits and the puppies to you. Let's let her have them for a while."

I nod toward the trio, Gavina and Trouble fast asleep, Bitsy with her head on her paws but her eyes clear and alert.

Brian holds out his hands. "I can take Double with me. That'll be easier."

I transfer my sleeping load into his arms, the tip of Double's tongue making me snort. I control my laughter as I give one last stroke to his head and resist the urge to *boop* the little pink bit sticking out.

Instead of taking up my book, I wiggle until I'm comfortable in my chair and lock eyes with one of the best herders we've had to date. Bitsy looks at her pup, at G, then at me.

"I know. We're losing her. But thank you for sharing your babies with her. With me."

Bitsy holds my gaze, then returns her head to her paws, adding a heavy sigh. The trademark black feathers on her ears flicker once then go still.

"This is the magic, you know." G's hand unerringly finds the top of Bitsy's head.

"Pardon?" I meet her still steely green eyes.

"This." She cups Bitsy's muzzle and lifts it gently. "And all the wonderful people connected here."

She scooches over on her bed, careful not to wake Trouble, and pats the space she cleared. Like Bitsy, I don't have to be invited twice.

"I'm sorry I'm leaving you, but you're going to be okay."

I press my fingers hard into the bridge of my nose. I will not start crying. "I'm not, though. I'm still lost."

"You're not lost anymore. You're hanging on to fear. Now hush and listen." She pauses, biting her bottom lip, a gesture I'm not sure I've ever seen. "I'm the last person who should be giving advice on love, but I will tell you two things. You've had to make a decision no woman should, but don't punish yourself any longer. Take a chance on love again, and give it your all. But if all you have isn't enough, and they can't be proud to be with you, they don't deserve you."

I rarely defy her, but I can't stop myself. "I wish it were so easy."

Her look slips, and a lost edge creeps into her eyes. "Not one easy thing in the whole recipe. I told you on the balcony years ago, and I'm telling you again to get it through your stubborn skull. Don't make the same mistakes I did."

My laugh is watery, and I have to speak around a lump in my throat. "I love you so much. I don't want you to go."

"Love you more, girl. And everyone has their time. This is mine."

Trouble decides naptime is over and gives a dramatic four-paw stretch and a yawn that nearly cracks her jaw. Her mama gives her tail end a sniff and then licks her face, to which she scrunches up her nose and swipes at it with a black-socked paw.

Which sends both me and G into a fit of giggles, and Bitsy's tail wags in agreement. Indeed, Trouble is the cutest pup ever born, and she's glad we realize it.

"Let me take these two to the warehouse."

"Go, and don't rush. Brian can be coaxed into some interesting conversations if you catch him alone and give him an excuse. Besides, it's nonsense for you to waste your day sitting here with me when all I do is sleep."

"I want to be here."

She smiles and pats my hand. "I know you do, and you're precious for it, but you need to spend some time in the company of a gentleman to remind yourself you're still alive. And then you can get to your desk duties."

I settled into my training to take over as chatelaine from almost the day I decided not to go to New York. Ever since, G's body might not have let her keep up with all the moving parts of running an estate, but her mind remained sharp and invaluable in helping me believe I might, maybe, be able to do her justice.

I still have my reservations, but G seems to be content to give me the reins, or the keys to the castle, as it were. I shouldn't need any further sign I'll be all right.

I call Bitsy off the bed, then take Trouble from G's gnarled hands. Filled with energy after the nap, Trouble's mind is set on either beating me to death with her tail or licking the skin off me with her nonstop tongue. Bitsy won't stray an inch from my side, both by training and because she's not leaving her baby in human hands.

"You're worried for her?" I give a pretend frown and show her my wrist. "Those baby teeth are sharp!"

They say dogs can't laugh.

They're wrong.

I stop at the doorway and look back, but G's eyes are closed. I tamp down the fear trying to strangle me. She's the reason I could give up my babies. The reason I'm still breathing. She's led me through the dark, and now it's my turn to be her light.

And I will be. Until the end.

CHAPTER FORTY-TWO

PAIGE – NOW

IT TURNS out my baby sister can be a bit of a bossy wench. She showed up the morning after my big discovery with Leith and acted like I'm one of her butter bar lieutenants or something, and I'm supposed to hop to. She's free from her military service and, to my immense relief, has agreed to stay and help me hold the fort with Mina and Fina.

She helps me get Leith, Ian, and his clan to DFW and on their way home. It requires my Highlander and the estate Suburban, both packed to the gills with bodies and luggage to accomplish it, but we manage and return to a lovely and quiet castle.

We talk for hours about everything from the nitty-gritty of running the castle, to the finances, to the still-uncertain condition of the magic. It leads me to be as honest with her as she was with me on the personal front, and as I suspected, she hasn't been shy with no-nonsense advice.

When I told her about needing to be by myself and all the possible itineraries I've plotted into my app, ninety-nine percent of which are in Scotland, she looked at me like I'd grown two heads. She actually kicked me. It didn't hurt, but my baby sister kicked me!

"What are you waiting for? We're related to half the people in the entire country, and they'll all be home before you can get there. You know they were serious about you, me, any of us coming over any time."

Once I hashed it out in my head a gazillion times, it was clear to my dense self she was right. A call to Kase has her running by my house to express-mail me my passport. Since she's there, I tell her to grab the file by my computer and get it to Grady. He'll take care of all the legal stuff. I'm saved from asking Zach for any of it, because he's in Australia. Or is it Austria? I'd have to reread the text he sent me, but it doesn't matter.

What does matter is I book the next available flight into Glasgow. I wince when I type in my credit card and hit enter, but I count it as an investment.

In me.

CHAPTER FORTY-THREE

MINA – NOW

I'VE BEEN a scaredy-cat all my life, but today I'm stick-a-fork-in-me done.

Oh, I guess I'd have to go to confession if I were Catholic, because I'm still scared, but I'm more determined to not tuck my tail and hide under the porch any longer.

There's not a single thing on my grocery list when I drive into town and park next to a certain Cadillac at the Magnolia Market. I walk right by the buggies and straight toward the office.

I'm standing like I half own the place. Arms back. Head high.

Truth be told, it's false courage. Like my striped chambray shirt-waist I hemmed last night. I double-checked every last button and snipped every stray thread before pressing it with my favorite light starch. The crisp scent is better stiffening for my backbone than a shot of Jack Daniel's, and my undercover courage is aided and abetted by my brand new matching bra and panties. Those, and my Vara bow wide-heeled sandals I found at Trader Days over in Atlanta last month. Two swipes of a Mr. Clean Magic Eraser, and they were good as new.

I found a curling iron stuffed in the depths of the bathroom cabinet, along with an almost-full can of Aqua Net. I used the heat to smooth under my ends, wondering if I should wait until I have time to buy a box of Nice'n Easy to touch up this gray, but decide I'm facing down enough demons for one day.

After slipping on my pearl earrings and swiping on some rose lipstick from the back of my vanity, I finished off with a spritz of Perfect Peony perfume. In doing so, I have officially exhausted every last bit of my feminine wiles. I hope it'll be enough. If it's not, I'm not sure what I'll do.

I put the brakes on before the thought can gain speed and give a sharp knock on the door. In a move that's out of character, I don't wait for an invitation and lift the handle like I've done this a thousand times.

Which might be true in my mind, where I've practiced for three days.

CT jumps in surprise, then rises from behind his desk. "What a beautiful sight on a bright Sunday morning."

I have to make myself not let the flattery in his words or the sincerity in his voice derail my intentions. I let the door shut behind me. I might have faked a brave facade in the aisle outside, but I'm not adding any more to the public fodder.

"And good morning to you. I'm sure I should apologize for the interruption, but if you shouldn't lie on any day, it's certainly not the Lord's day."

"That requires me to be perfectly truthful and let you know I'd be delighted for you to interrupt me any time."

I give a giggle and feel featherheaded for it, but I push on. "CT, would you like to attend the nine-thirty service with me this morning? I know you normally go to First Baptist, but—"

"I'd love to." He takes a step to the left and pulls his suit coat from the carved arm of a rack behind his desk.

It wasn't supposed to be so easy. I had a whole speech prepared on how St. Andrew's isn't as big a congregation as First Baptist, but Harville is a wonderful preacher, and how today's sermon, according to the website, is on courage. Or wait, that was for me, not CT, but I'd lined up another ten other things on my notepad, ending with if he didn't want to go today, we could go next week.

Now I don't know what to say. "Okay, then. I can meet you there."

"Why don't we take my car and stop for a coffee at The Bagelry? We have time, and I'd love to split a kolach with you so we don't get peckish. After the service, if you don't have other plans, we could have a quick bite at Vivann's."

The entire last of my carefully planned speech vaporizes like dew on a July Sunday morning. Which I now realize, with no small irony, is exactly what today is. All I hoped for was church, and all of a sudden I've got three places to show off my pretty new ensemble. And I have the perfect accessory in a tall, handsome man in a navy blue suit and perfect black fedora.

A smile starts in my toes and makes its way to my face, pausing to wrestle with the nerves still trying to tie my intestines in a bow.

"It all sounds lovely, but I didn't mean to take up your whole day."

CT has slipped on his coat and snapped his collar into place. "I cannot conceive of a lovelier reason to rearrange my calendar."

Tucking my fingers into the crook of his elbow, he walks me out of the store, Bethanie's eyes hot on my back as we step through the automatic door. The next hours pass in a blur, and I'm in the pew with CT's leg pressed so close to mine I can't hear a word Harville is saying from the pulpit. As a general rule, I love his sermons, but today my thoughts are locked tight on the heat warming the length of my thigh.

I'm sure I'm busting through one of the commandments like the football team under Friday night lights.

I'm nearly causing a tornado with my church fan, but half the ladies in the congregation are waving away, too, so maybe no one notices. I know, though, I'm kidding myself. A sea of heads turned when CT escorted me darn near all the way to the choir loft. I thought for a moment he intended to take the front row, but he stopped three back. I almost fainted from not breathing.

Harville says something about joy and peace and confidence, and the three words ignite something, sparking a flame in a place I thought clean clear of tinder.

Before I lose the last of my bravery, I reach over and take CT's hand. His is resting relaxed on his knee, and it's not hard to slip my fingers into the little cave of his palm. I'm shaking a little, more or less a six or seven on the Richter scale, but as soon as his knuckles curl over mine, whatever I was afraid of washes away like a sandcastle at high tide. He clasps me like I'm a precious flower he's afraid of bruising, but with such strength he tells me he's not letting go.

Now, I've never been much of a singer, and it doesn't help I'm wobbly from a joy I'm honestly not sure I've ever felt, but I don't care right now. I'm happy to let CT's deep bass wash clear over me and overshadow my tinny tenor.

I find myself blushing when Harville winks at me when the service is over, and CT escorts me outside with as much pride as he escorted me in. The preacher's such a dear man. Fina's right that we need to spend some time planning how to help him.

As if I conjured her, I hear her voice. "Mina, we have a problem."

Fina's out of breath as if she ran all the way to town. I didn't see her at the service, but we've never been attend-every-week members, so I didn't think to look. She's clearly not dressed for church, and my stomach tightens.

"What's wrong?"

"We have to call Zach. Paige left for Scotland."

I frown. "We knew she was going."

She gives me a look. "She's gone today."

"Ohhhh."

"Our plan worked too well."

In front of CT, I'm too much of a lady to say *her* plan worked too well, or *I told you so.* We've meandered to the bottom of the steps, and the other congregants are chatting around us. It usually takes a good twenty minutes to clear the property, and today is no different.

I turn to CT and put a hand on his arm. "I'm so sorry, but I have to help my sister with a family matter. Can I take a rain check on lunch?"

"I insist. Is there anything I can do?"

"No, but you're a sweet thing for asking. Fina will bring me to fetch my car at the store later."

I step away, Fina giving a quick wave to CT and moving to the parking lot. Maybe Harville filled me with more of the Holy Spirit than I thought, because I turn back around, walk up one step so I'm only a bit shorter than CT, and right there in front of God and everybody, I go up on my toes and plant a kiss on his lips.

It's no soap opera heat-maker, but it might as well be from the gasps around me.

I hope my smile is more ladylike than the grin on his face. I give my hair a toss and reach across the small space between us to swipe a pretend wrinkle from his lapel.

Then I prance down the steps and follow my sister to her car like I kiss the man I have a surefire crush on every chance I get.

CHAPTER FORTY-FOUR

OPENING night at the Magnolia Moon, Tidy's new bar, is wall-to-wall bodies.

I'm so proud of her, and so sad Gavina didn't see the fruits of her labor with my friend, seeds she planted without me knowing. It seems Gavina paid the rent on a tiny apartment so Tidy could leave the man causing her nothing but pain. G also gave her the money to buy the vacant bar with enough left over to renovate it into a happening dance hall.

Neither one of them told me a thing. I would be insulted, but I've been too busy finding out Brian Steele may be a man of few words, but he sure knows how to do other things with those soft lips. The slightest memory has me blushing brighter than the Pabst Blue Ribbon sign lit up on the wall.

"What can I get you?" Tidy's at my end of the polished bar she found at an auction house and, between her and Mina, stripped and stained so beautifully I bet it's worth ten times her investment.

My old friend is back. A little sadder, a little wiser, but there's hope in her eyes. Something I haven't seen in a long time.

I understand exactly.

"A Dos Equis for me. Brian wants a Falstaff."

"Coming up. And you're mighty shiny tonight."

She pulls both beers and puts them in front of me. I hand her a twenty to start a tab. "I went to Trader Days with Mina last month, and she's infected me with the haggle gene."

"Keep it up, because that top makes you look good enough to eat."

A tall man in a pearl-snap shirt slips in beside me and leans an elbow on the lip of the bar. "I agree a hundred percent."

My blush refires, but I side-eye Brian and smile. "Careful, cowboy. You're looking mighty tasty yourself."

He gives me a grin I know is mine alone. Brian's an intensely private man, a lot like my Uncle T's Monroe in that he doesn't have a lot to say, but when he does, his words mean something.

And when he kisses me, and we tumble onto his big brass bed...

We're forging our own relationship. It's a bit unconventional, but I'm content with it. He is, too, and we're the only two who get a vote.

He dips his sexy black Stetson to Tidy, picks up our beers, and takes them to our table. The band doesn't start until nine, but for now, the jukebox is playing *What Goes on When the Sun Goes Down*.

He holds out his hand and leads me toward the dance floor.

"Come on. I want to show you off."

CHAPTER FORTY-FIVE

PAIGE – NOW

IT TOOK ten seconds upon landing in Scotland to understand my extended family's pride in their homeland. One breath and the Highlands claim a part of my soul. It's more than vistas so beautiful I don't want to waste time blinking. It's the *welcome home* from all my ancestors filtering through the pines and heather.

Goodness knows Texas has its shares of lakes and rivers, but we have no comparison to being dissected by so much water. A map of Scotland, especially the Highlands, resembles a pane of cracked glass with each spidering vein being a loch. Add an astounding number of little islands, and it creates a land of water and majestic mountains a Central Texas girl can barely take in.

But she sure could get used to it.

In the month and a half I've been here, it's been amusing and touching to be fought over by the myriad family members I've met, all of them wanting me to stay with them. I've done a fair bit of moving around, but once I met Maggie, she was immovable on my accommodations. My couch-surfing days were over, and I would stay with her until I left for home. End of discussion.

Some days, I'm not sure I'm leaving. Others, I miss home so much it's soul-aching. It's nothing short of astounding a woman who's never been away for more than a few weeks' vacation is now headed into month two of a sojourn in self-reflection.

Which brings me to Alyssa MacInnes MacMillan's great-granddaughter, who might be a witch. She's certainly an oracle. And at ninety-eight, Maggie is an absolute gem and still going strong.

"And where have you sailed off to now?"

Her strong voice and even stronger tea pull me back to the tiny front patio outside her home on the outskirts of the hamlet of Inchree.

"I'm back at the waterfall. Hiking through the Glen Righ forest is definitely a favorite, but the falls alone are why I've done a year's worth of healing in six weeks."

"Aye, it's magical."

"You, my dear Maggie, are magical. I'm certain you're a witch."

"I am named after one."

I know because we took a trip over to Dunning, and I have a picture of the monument to Maggie Wall. Whether she actually existed or not is debated, but the fact remains she's a testament to women who lived and sometimes died to defy the conventions of their time. As a descendant of generations of women who've put their thumb in the eye of those who would make them invisible, I'll give Maggie Wall a nod, even if she's a myth. And hope I can be as brave.

"You scared me, I have to confess, when you saw my cairngorm and told me things you couldn't possibly know, but you were dead right."

Maggie shifts a plump shoulder under her soft wool cape. "People have said I've had the sight since I was a wee lass, but I'm observant, is all. Comes with having more years than the Highlands have sheep, so this old witch needs to know what those letters from your man back home are doing to you."

I'm not remotely surprised she knows, although I haven't yet told her I did it. "See? Proof you're supernatural. I didn't read them until barely twenty-four hours ago when I went on my hike."

I let my eyes roam the hills and can all but smell the pine and lichen. I went by myself, the letters from Zach in my pack. I was stunned when the first one arrived, and I almost let my old hurt toss it in the trash. Then I told Maggie I was wearing the cairngorm at the time and how it went hot against my skin. I felt silly admitting it, wanting to pass it off as a rise in blood pressure, but she said no. The heat was a message from Alyssa.

So I put the envelope on the little desk by the little bed in the little room she's graciously given me for my stay. One thing I can say is, I'll never take the space in my home or our castle for granted ever again.

Zach's missives, handwritten on rich vellum, have arrived about once a week. Each envelope feels thicker than the last, raising my curiosity, but my hesitancy won out until yesterday. Mostly because I'm still dealing with my feelings for Leith. Even though we haven't spent much time together, he's shown me something more alluring than his romantic interest.

Friendship with a man. Something different than the amazing connection I have with Kase. Something I've never even considered before.

I like him. And he likes me. The person, the woman who's seen enough of life to have stories to tell. Some funny, some poignant, some embarrassing. Maggie offered wise counsel to not discredit my memories because Zach was there when they happened. To Leith, everything is new. Shiny bits to capture the attention. Zach hasn't viewed all my escapades, such as they were, from the outside. He's made many of them with me.

Maggie brings me back from my mental meanderings. "Do you believe him? His letters?"

"I believe he's trying. The first few covered going to therapy twice a week after our final break at the games. Each one goes deeper, telling me not to call him, because he's working through a lot of stuff, but wanting me to know what's going on."

"Does him not wanting to talk bother you?"

"Not at all. I wasn't ready anyway. His letters aren't pleas for me to come home or give him another chance or any blah, blah, blah.

They're a window into what he's going through without any promises of what the outcome is going to be."

A breeze brings a waft of soft, peaty earth. I was stunned to learn heather has little scent, nothing like what I imagined, but I'm not disappointed, because the purple-pink sea I've feasted upon with my eyes is more than enough compensation. Maggie says it's been an especially good year for the blooms, and I've decided it's a gift from Scotland just for me.

"How does your distracting Scot fit in?"

The question has burned up a fair share of my soul-searching.

"The time I've spent with him, although not a lot, has been...amazing. He's still funny. Still sexy as all get-out. But I'm finding what's more important is he's a friend."

"Maybe that's the greater gift?"

"I hope so. I can't speak for him. For me, I didn't dare get caught up in all-Leith-all-the-time, or I would miss the entire point of coming halfway around the world."

"Wise."

"We'll see, I guess. It would have been so easy to be distracted by the glitter of infatuation, and it wasn't painless to put on sunglasses and step away from the light. But it was necessary, and I'm proud of myself."

"Your Violet would be proud, too."

I take her fragile hand and lightly squeeze my agreement. What I now know is it's not V's pride I'd want, but her understanding. After reading her journals and discovering her secret life, my initial disappointment that I didn't know her as well as I'd thought has turned to a deeper, profound kinship. All MacInnes women have struggled, but what I'm finding is we share the same constitution. We don't always keep calm, but we do carry on.

And I'm forever grateful I share the genetic blessing of their grit.

Maggie's great-great-granddaughter arrives to take me to the pub. It blows my mind to count the lines connecting Lexi to Maggie, but ninety-eight years can hold a lot of generations.

"Ready?" Lexi's bright red hair is barely contained as she pops out of the driver's side. She's my age, and our grandchildren have birthdays within months of each other. I bonded with her the instant she showed me the display case of the lace she and all of Alyssa's heirs still produce. My dread's been replaced by confident relief. The lace I've seen in the castle, its role in the lore of the chapel and the magic I was so certain I'd destroy, is still lovingly made by dedicated MacInnes hands.

I wave goodbye to Maggie and hop in the little black Corsa, which she drives as if there's no such thing as a speed limit and brakes are an option to consider only at the last moment. She gets me to the tiny village whose name I can't pronounce, breathless but in one piece. With my sweater buttoned against the cool wind and fifty-degree temperature, I savor my first pint of Belhaven for the evening.

"Tell me where you've been so far." She isn't nearly as affected by her pint as I am, and I have to blink against the torches providing the perfect ambience in the alcove created by three sides of the tavern.

"In no particular order, to Glasgow. Loch Lomond. Glencoe. Isle of Skye. Inveraray Castle, of course, since my own is an homage to it. Loch Fyne. The tiny Onich Tearoom. I saw St. John's church, and if you come see me in Austin or Magnolia Bloom early enough in the spring, you'll want to call my beloved bluebonnets bluebells by mistake."

"Sounds pure barry. I'm glad we're giving you the proper tour."

"To be honest, I've stopped trying to figure out where I am. I have the details in my diary, and someday I'll plot it all on a map. For now, I'm too busy falling in love with all of you and having my breath taken away by the mountains and lochs and the villages and kirks. I almost don't want to go home."

"Stay. We'll adopt you."

"I do love it here, but I'm a native Texan, and I'll always be. I plan on visiting so often, though, so you may want to rescind your invitation."

"Och, nae. Cannae happen."

Our conversation's interrupted by roars of booming laughter at the next table over, where Ian and Leith are in a crowd of locals. I'm able to grasp the MacInneses and MacMasters have a long history in Ardgour, and someone starts a long, cursing rant regarding the MacLeans until the brogues fly fast and thick, and I can't understand a word.

I raise an eyebrow in Lexi's direction. She shakes her head. "That bawbag's my cousin Jamie. He turns into a right scunner if he gets more than a dram in him, and Lucifer bars the doors from the inside."

"You know, I love all y'all, but I'm leaving the histories and infighting, the lairds and loyalties, septs and clans, and all the rest to you. I'd have to re-enroll in UT and earn a master's degree to keep it all straight, and I'm too darned old for that."

"You're brilliant to stay out. There's no winning with those blooters."

We have to hold our thoughts as another round of shouts and slurs waft by, most including various slang for male genitalia. I have to confess, I'm impressed by how many words they also have for passing gas, fornication, and the marital status—verified or questionable—of the rival's parents.

I've never laughed so hard in my life.

I can see her mouth is moving, but it takes a second before I hear her question.

"So tell me how you're doin'."

"Truthfully, I thought it would take months to find me. Turns out, when you're willing to have a personal come-to-Jesus meeting, things can move pretty fast. I'm hardly fixed, or finished, but I've discovered I like me, and I'm not willing to return to being everybody's go-to when they need something."

Still, even with what I told Maggie earlier, it's hard to stay focused on my personal journey when I see Leith from time to time. He's staying with his oldest sister, who's as beautiful as he is handsome, but after the dinner I was invited to, where four of his seven sisters attended, I understand why Leith stays away. And I have a clearer picture of his commitment phobia.

He's been true to his word. He's been a good friend. I'd be lying if I said the maybes and might-be's didn't interfere with my meditation and soul-searching. I'm proud of me, though. I don't explore any of the tempting side trails my thoughts want to explore when I'm snared by his blue eyes and slightly crooked smile.

But I do think about them.

Lexi pulls me back into the conversation. "Good for you for reminding your family you're more than a mum."

"I haven't reminded them of anything yet. But I'm going to, I promise."

Another ear-busting round of guffaws and backslapping makes me smile, but it also makes me think of Zach. And his letters. And him not liking boisterous crowds. I'd forgotten how much I love sitting with him at an outside table at any of our favorite restaurants, the night quiet as we enjoy a beer or margarita. Or maybe the sound of a band wafting over. Mostly, just him and me. And the quiet.

And each other.

"I'm glad you've had time at the falls and the shores of our lochs. Water will move your soul. You cannae not be affected by them, or the mountains."

She's not wrong. I thought about me, and Zach, and Leith. And long marriages and new, fresh flirtations. I felt the sting and sometimes gut-punch of acknowledging my own shortcomings. More often, though, I see I'm taking baby step down the road to forgiving myself. All in all, I'm a long way from having all the answers I need, but I'm a damn sight farther along than I've ever been.

A tiny white car pulls up, far too close to our table for comfort, and I do a double take at the long body unfolding itself from the clown-sized vehicle. I blink, wondering if I've had more Belhaven than I thought.

It can't be.

"Zach?"

The table beside us went quiet with curiosity when the cab arrived, but now has gone dead silent. My voice sounds too loud in the stillness.

When the man turns and the flickering lamps light his face, it appears I'm not totally blootered. I leave the table, wobbly from surprise, not alcohol.

The driver pulls away, but stops at the end of the parking lot not a heck of a lot bigger than my front yard in Austin.

"What are you…here…how?"

"I'm here to talk to you, if you'll let me."

"You flew over four thousand miles to find me? And talk?"

I indicate the empty picnic table a few feet away. I wish I'd brought my glass with me, but maybe it's a good idea if the cool air clears my head a bit. He takes one side and I the other. He rests his arms, palms down, on the rough wood. I clutch mine against my middle.

He rubs one knuckle so long I'm afraid he'll reach bone before he meets my eyes.

"I love you."

I swallow. I nod because he deserves to know I heard him.

"I've loved you since I was seventeen. I've never stopped." He lifts his fingers off the table to stop me from responding.

"I've told you for twenty-seven years I'm not a complicated man. I'm intelligent, but I let you handle complicated. It was easier. I'm learning I was taking the chicken way out."

He jerks his fingers through his frustration-and-wind-tousled hair and massages his neck.

"I've been talking to a counselor. I told you that in the letters. And I read the book you gave me on vulnerability, but I have to tell you, it scares the shit out of me. I still have a few other issues to tackle with the therapist."

If I wasn't speechless before, I am now. It's one thing to read what he's up to. It's another to hear equal parts fear and determination in his voice.

"We've both changed, Paige. We're not kids anymore, hanging on to each other for dear life. Trying to pay bills and raise kids and stay above water."

"I hope that's a good thing."

"It is. But now the busyness is gone, and I no longer know how to be your hero. It's what I worked for. What I lived for. Now I don't know what you need, or if what I have is what you want."

"How about being my partner? I've never wanted Superman. I never needed anyone but you, and you went away."

"I said I wasn't complicated. I didn't say I wasn't a knucklehead or prideful or stubborn."

I give a sad snort. "You don't hold the patent on mistakes or any of those things."

I don't even recognize the guy sitting across from me. He's broken. Gutted. Laid bare. He isn't the man who's been a ghost in our house for five years.

"Can we walk?"

I realize the silence has gotten prolonged, and sitting and talking is torturous for him.

"Sure, follow me."

I head in the direction of the loch over the rise. It's not visible in the darkness, but you can hear the sea kissing the banks in an eons-old dance. Two huge boulders lie ahead, their white surfaces moonlight soaked. There's enough light to get there safely if we don't stray from the rocky path.

I stretch to my tiptoes and scooch onto the first rock. Zach barely has to try to join me on the surface I believe has borne witness to more than a few private conversations, and not a few make-out sessions.

In the barely relieved darkness, I go first.

"You're right. We were young, plenty in love, but too busy to dig into the depths of what makes a relationship. A marriage. And to whatever degree I made you think you had to be Tony Stark and Steve Rogers all the time. I'm sorry. That's horribly unfair."

He smiles, but there's a sadness, too. "I liked being your Captain America."

I have to take long, deep breaths before I'm brave enough to risk stroking my fingers down the side of his face. "And you always will be, when I remember the past. But I'd rather have Zach Peters."

He hops down and paces to the other enormous rock, bracing his hands on the cold stone. "The thing is, I'm afraid. Afraid I can't ever be your hero again. I want to be. I've always wanted to be. But the years have gone on and…"

"And we drifted farther and farther apart."

"I want to pull us together. I don't know if I've caused too much damage. I'll do whatever you want. But if you need complicated—"

"I don't." The tears I tried to hold back slip over my cheeks. I slide down and join him. "I don't need you to be me. God, one of me is more than enough."

His chuckle sounds watery, too.

"I didn't want complicated, Zach. I just needed you to try. To want to try. To be worth trying for."

"You've always been my moon. Ah, hell, I'm not good at saying romantic stuff, but you are the light and center of my soul."

I have to sniff, because of course in the midst of an amazing moment, my nose is running, and I don't have a tissue. Zach stretches out his arm and offers me his sleeve.

It's so Zach, I have to laugh. The sound is pure, if a bit broken. "I'm good."

We lean against the boulder, side by side, not touching.

I offer him a thought I had on one of my many walks. "Maybe it wasn't such a great thing for me to idolize you and for you to worship me."

"But I liked worshiping you."

He smiles the wicked, just-for-me Zach smile I haven't seen in a long time, but every fiber of me recognizes.

In one glance, he tells me he still has it. We still have it.

My moment with Leith was sweet, flattering, but I don't know him. Not truly. He's a good, decent man, but I don't know his soul.

I have a much better vision of Zach's heart. It's come from nearly thirty years of shared joy and pain, passion and tears, triumphs and sorrows.

He came forty-five hundred miles to throw one hell of a Hail Mary pass. The ball still wobbled, end over end, in the air, but he threw it.

"I need to get to the taxi."

"You're leaving? Tonight? Are you serious?"

"If I stay, I'll pressure you, even if I don't mean to. Which is the opposite of what I want. I don't fly out until tomorrow, of course, but I'm going home. In the meantime, I have a lot of reading and therapy left."

He starts down the path, turning and pausing until I join him. At the clown car, I stop him and cup his jaw so I can kiss him.

It's simple. No promises.

A thank-you.

He opens the door, and I put a hand on his sleeve. "I have a lot to consider. Coming here, what you've said, the letters…it's all amazing. But I'm scared. If I believe you, and you break my heart again, I—"

"I can only promise I'm trying. I can only tell you I love you and I want us to be us again. It might not always be pretty, as we…as I learn to be different. I know now time doesn't heal all wounds. It makes untreated ones fester." He reaches inside his jacket and takes out an envelope. "I almost forgot."

I open the seal. In the darkness, I can't tell much, other than being able to make out ITINERARY in bold black letters at the top of the page.

"What is it? It's too dark."

"It's a ticket to Tahiti. It has an open date, so…" His voice goes sharp and rough, and his breathing is fast before he takes a breath and clears his throat. "So if you're interested, give me a call, and I'll firm it up." He stops, licks his lips, and tries again. "Or, if you want, you can go by yourself. Or with…someone else. You can email the airline directly."

"Zach, I—"

"Don't say anything. Finish your trip. I know you have another month. But call me. Or text me. Any time. I'll be waiting."

He kisses my forehead, then crams himself into the seat, his knees jammed nearly to his nose. I back away so the driver can reverse out of the lot, and I stand there like a bampot, following the white box careening down the winding road, the headlights barely making a dent in the darkness.

Lexi eventually draws me back to the table and a fresh pint. No one asks me what happened, and I let the conversation and the beer flow again. Leith raises his glass to me, and I salute in return.

I have a lot to dissect, but for tonight, my head and my heart are full.

CHAPTER FORTY-SIX

EPILOGUE

SIX WEEKS LATER, I'm leaning on the railing of a balcony, looking at the lights of a completely different city, a completely different country.

Scotland will forever remain in my heart as the place my life changed forever. The place where I got to choose me.

I can feel his body before he joins me, pressing against me and wrapping his arms around my waist. The music of Paris drifts up from the street, the wind teases my hair and whips apart my red satin robe, exposing quite a bit of skin to anyone who might be able to see five floors up.

Warm lips kiss my neck, tracing every inch from my earlobe to my shoulder.

The shudder rippling through me has nothing to do with the chill in the air.

"I'm glad you're letting me help find Violet's twins. It's a heck of a story."

My head lolls against his shoulder. "I hope I'm doing the right thing."

"You are. It's what she wanted but couldn't ask for."

Turning around, I untie the belt barely holding my robe together and pull him against me.

"So what'll it be tonight?" He uses the tip of his nose to trace my jawline. "Captain America?"

"Put the shield away, Cap. All I need, all I want, is Zach."

# # #

Keep reading for a preview of MISTLETOE AND MAGNOLIA, Book 2 in the Magnolia Bloom series...

MISTLETOE AND MAGNOLIA

Chapter One
Kiki

For the record, I followed the directions to addiction recovery with GPS perfection. *Just go straight to hell and make a U-turn.* While the mushroom cloud has cleared from my field of vision, I can still see flames in my rearview mirror.

And I have one person to blame for my monumentally messed-up life.

Me.

Well, me and my charming frenemy, vodka. In the not-too-recent past, I could have changed my middle name to Tito's. Grey Goose would have been more accurate, and I might have passed it off as a cool call sign if I'd been an aviator instead of a public affairs officer. Turns out, the United States Air Force doesn't play games with DUIs, and they're not called career killers for nothing.

If there's one good thing about said event happening with my superior officer in the car, it's when said officer is related to a very powerful family who made sure the DUI turned into running a red light. I neither asked for nor deserved the reprieve from my bad decision-making, but the family's intervention had nothing to do with helping me and everything to do with protecting their handsome, future politician. His image in DC is informed by his current officer trajectory, so to no one's surprise, I was... invited to separate from the only career I've ever had or wanted.

While the events in question aren't late-night monologue-worthy, I, Major Rebecca "Kiki" MacInnes, was the disposable one in this scenario.

Which is the short version of the long story of why I'm on a balcony spanning the North and East Turrets of Castle MacInnes outside of Magnolia Bloom, Texas.

The sound of the double doors to my left opening interrupts my stroll down memory lane, and I still have to blink to remind myself I'm truly living here now. At the moment, my coffee and I are waiting for the sun to rise and beat up the currently pleasant temperature of sixty-four degrees. The low sixties might not qualify as fall in most places, but in East Texas, October temperatures were often a Yahtzee throw whether it would be sweaters or flip-flops... or both. We had many Halloweens either sweating behind our plastic masks or vying for a Michelin Man ad in puffy coats.

"Hey, Traycee. Have a seat." With a wave of my hand, I invite my new friend and ally to join me. The beautiful wrought-iron table between us has borne witness to many sunrise breakfasts and heartfelt conversations over the decades. If roughly twenty-five years is used to calculate a generation, this table has hosted six since it was brought from Galveston when my ancestors Evajean and Alisdair MacInnes established Magnolia Bloom. I'm sure it's heard more salacious dialogue than will be provided this morning, but maybe the castle ghosts will forgive me for preferring boring-but-sober over titillating these days.

"I couldn't resist the invite, even if this is crazy-early."

I check my watch to see it's already seven, as sunshine is not an accurate indicator of time in Alaska, my most recent, and final, duty station. I haven't reacclimated to my home state yet, either in time or temperature.

I give my head a wobble. "Early's relative, but my relationship with mornings is best described as 'there appears to have been a struggle.'"

"I hear you." She settles in and puts down her travel mug bearing the stylized MBE logo of her store, the Magnolia Bloom Emporium. She looks effortlessly comfortable in black leggings and a T-shirt positing the question "Surely Not Everyone Was Kung Fu Fighting?"

I rest against the high back of the rocker. "For the last fifteen years, I've either crawled out of bed at an ungodly hour, or didn't go in until the middle of the afternoon but stayed up all night. Add in my last assignment, and the Alaskan sun cycle adds a whole 'nother level of why 'daylight hours' is a debatable term."

Traycee's nose-wrinkle eloquently expresses her feelings about the subarctic. "I could handle neither the cold nor the endless-day-and-night thing. The only ice this girl wants is in her tea."

"When I got there in February two years ago, I wondered what fresh hell I'd fallen into. There's a lot of beauty in Alaska, but not, in my opinion, in the dead of winter. Still, I've been away from Texas so long I've forgotten when autumn actually begins in our beloved Lone Star State."

"I guess you've erased all those Halloweens and Thanksgivings in shorts, then. Weather Channel says we're going to have another week of low eighties before we finally stay in the seventies for a while."

"Which is as awful as seeing Christmas displays already going up."

"Eighty-one shopping days left."

It's my turn to grimace. "Of course you know."

"I do. Halloween gets a little more shine, then it and fall-slash-Thanksgiving are relegated to the edges. From here on out, it's all Santa, all the time. The fat guy in the red suit gets all the love in retail."

"I've always been on the purchasing side of this fence until now, so Fina's got her hands full teaching me retail and event calendars. Paige left the office in great shape, but with Mina's wedding on top of everything else, it's a little hectic."

"From what I've heard, it sounds like it's been an entire season of a soap opera around here."

"Not quite, but keeping all the moving parts straight takes a pen and paper sometimes. Aunt Violet was the matriarch of the clan for a long time, and my sister, Paige, felt overwhelmed trying to step in earlier this year, especially if you add in she thought her marriage was over. Mina and Fina aren't blood, but they were Violet's rocks, so they might as well be on our family tree. They were angels to Paige, and now me. Then, add the bonus material of finding out Violet gave up twins for adoption when she was still a teenager, and… whew!"

"You need to write a book about all this someday."

"No literary tomes in my future, thanks, but I'll take you down to meet Juliette soon. She's really sweet. But to wrap up, I don't think we're so different from any other family—"

"With a Scottish castle in East Texas."

"Point to you, but really, is there such a thing as a normal family?"

"Not around here." Her expression's amused with a hint of sadness lagging behind. "All joking aside, I'm really happy for Mina and CT. I've known him for years through our merchant association and think he's a super-nice man, but I didn't see it coming."

"I don't think anyone did, least of all Mina. But he's a doll, and Fina's delighted for her twin, but so much has happened so fast. Losing Violet, finding out she gave her girls Juliette and Noelle up for adoption, Mina getting engaged, end-of-year holidays… I think Fina's only got one nerve left, and it's stretched thin. Which is why I'm determined to get up to speed in record time."

"If there's anything I can do, all you have to do is ask."

"I'll take you up on your offer when I know what to ask for. Now, let's go down to the kennels, since you're really here for puppies and not me."

She laughs, as expected, but wags a finger at me. "Don't count yourself short. I'm here for you *and* puppies."

She stands and slides her oversized sunglasses onto her nose against the already blazing sun. We take our travel mugs with us, and I lead the way through the turret and down the narrow steps depositing us onto the east lawn. The manicured grass extends for some fifty yards down to one of the estate's three docks, places I have hardly had time to visit. If I don't soon, the water will be too cold, and my only choice will be our local hot spring, which isn't a horrible second option.

"Love the hair, by the way." I manage to keep the envy out of my voice at my new friend's style. Today, the not-shaved side of her head is woven in an intricate profusion of cornrow braids, each a surprising variety of colors.

"Spent all day at the shop yesterday. Have the migraine to prove it."

"Worth it, though."

"I'll admit it when the ibuprofen kicks in. Tara can do miracles for you, too, if you give her a chance."

"Soon."

I don't doubt Traycee's sister's talent behind the salon chair. When I'm ready, I'll happily trust her to work her magic on my wavy mess, but I'm still guilty of wearing reg hair. Becoming a regulation breaker doesn't happen in mere months of civilian life, as my color-coordinated closet and hospital-cornered bed will attest. Decades of combined ROTC and active duty have me hardwired to French-braid my mop into submission.

If I have to be honest, feeling tucked and together provides the illusion I'll be okay. Someday. Dealing with my separation from the Air Force still brings nightmares, and has been, bar none, the most painful thing I've ever done... sober. Even though I'd been on the wagon for a while, by the time the actual day came to execute the papers, it was a test of my ability to keep from coming unglued and driving straight to the package store before the ink was dry on the last signature.

Traycee scans the quiet scene as we walk, our destination a series of barns and sheds still hidden by a dense copse of pecan trees. "I could get used to this."

"It does seem like a fairy tale, but you know better than anyone the business side of running something this massive takes away a little of the patina."

"I'd hardly call the Emporium massive, but it's like the folks who tell me they want to be their own boss so they can take time off whenever they want."

I cut her a side glance. "Do you bother to tell them how idiotic they sound?"

"Nah, they wouldn't believe I haven't had a vacation day in three years, or how glamorous it is to unload and tag stock."

I've been in a business position for only a few weeks, but I already know to roll my eyes. "Oh, yeah, all that free time when you're self-employed."

A quietness settles over Traycee, but I don't interrupt the moment. I'm happy to be outside in the sunshine and know the peace invites the mind to wander. I was a little shocked the first time she walked into an AA meeting over in Atlanta. I mean, I know there addicts in Magnolia Bloom, but I didn't peg Traycee as one of us in the few times I met her. We've become fast friends and traveling buddies since Atlanta and Texarkana are the closest places for us to attend in-person meetings.

Her steps slow to a halt, and she turns to look at the castle. Our beautiful Scottish anachronism looks straight out of a postcard with the morning sun striking the bluish-green schist stone Evajean MacInnes had shipped from both her and her husband's ancestral homeland to complete her project. It took years, of course, but Evajean and Alisdair created something magical here. Something allowing a determined woman to soar at a time no one believed a female could be an amazing architect. Evajean and the groves also healed Alisdair's lonely and wounded soul, so the magic is hardly one-sided.

The first generation of American MacInneses began a legacy, establishing the mind-set that it doesn't matter what's happened in the past, you can make your future anything you wish it to be.

"I hope so."

"You hope what?"

I didn't realize I whispered my prayer aloud and feel the blood rush to my Scottish-white cheeks. "That I can live up to the MacInnes legacy. I'm not so sure most days."

She hooks her arm around mine and starts us walking again, the dry grass crunching under our shoes. "You gonna be fine, girlfriend, if you keep showing up."

"So they tell us."

"Paige believes in you. Fina and Mina." She stops again and takes her arm back, but puts a hand on my sleeve. "Me."

I cover her fingers, then break the contact. Her gregarious nature and generosity are sweet, but still hard for me sometimes. I'm not used to it. Not Traycee in particular. I'm not used to anyone looking at me with such kind concern, and it makes me itch to get back to my project car waiting in the extra stall in the mechanical garage. It's where I usually head for solitude, letting the 1962 Ford Fairlane I bought at an auction keep me absorbed and out of trouble. It's going to take a lot of TLC to get her in shape again, but that's what project cars are for. It's a far cry from the Porsche 911 I'm driving now. She took me nearly three years to restore.

Sensing my tension, Traycee changes the subject. "I miss Violet so much. She'd ask me over to pick up her latest quilts for the shop, but I know it was an excuse to give me a break from town. This is the first time I've been here without her."

Pain squeezes my heart. I now occupy the suite Violet lived in for almost fifty years. My older-by-a-decade sister occupied it for a few short months while she was negotiating what she'd thought was the end of her marriage. Now I'm the next MacInnes in residence to hold the keys to the castle, even though I feel guilty taking over Fam One. Occupying the apartment reserved for a direct MacInnes descendant feels like a duty I'm not fit for.

I'm qualified in the genealogical sense, but my years in the military mean I can actually count the number of days I've spent here. It adds to the intensity of my impostor syndrome every time I sit in V's office. But while I'm here trying to put my life back in order, I'll accept the mantle of temporary chatelaine of this incredible estate. I'm determined to be of service to my family and my program.

And I'm terrified. While my résumé shows an impressive history of dedication and determination, recent events give lie to my current facade. I'm grateful I have a chance to reinvent myself, but I constantly fight the certainty I'm going to fail so much more than myself. I hold an entire family legacy, with hundreds of lives dependent on our estate, in my still-shaky hands. Luckily, I'm not swimming in the deep end alone. I have Fina—and Mina, when we can pull her out of the clouds.

I steer my thoughts from the path of fear and doubt to pick up my conversation with Traycee.

"I loved V, too, but the truth is, you were closer to her than I was. I was hardly ever here. And of course, no one was closer to her than my sister."

"I only talked with Paige a few times while she was here, but she's a doll."

"She is, and I'm really excited we're getting closer these days. We're ten years apart, so it wasn't until recently we've connected as adults, and I have my fingers crossed I might get the chance to get to know my brothers, too."

"Brothers?"

"Twins in the middle. Paige was already out of the house before I was old enough to grasp my family's dysfunction, and the boys only ever needed each other, so in a lot of ways, I was an only child."

"Ooof, that's some classic birth order shit right there."

I wish I could say my nod is merely agreement and not a bitter acknowledgement of the truth. "We're such a ridiculous stereotype, we could be the poster child for several sections of the DSM."

"When you find out the shrinks have an entire manual laying out our crap, it kinda punches a hole in our belief we're terminally unique. Still, having the Goose out of the way has to be a big help."

I give a dry chuckle. "No doubt, but since my big sis is traipsing across Europe with her newly reconciled hubster, I appreciate you filling the void of friendly ears."

I'm utterly sincere. Having Traycee around makes me feel like I'm not trying to climb out of the addiction trench alone, and I hope I provide her with similar solace.

We pass the giant rolling doors to the kennels, eventually reaching the normal-sized entry, and I lead the way inside. We've barely made it five feet before a tall figure steps into the breezeway.

"Good morning, Miss Kiki, Miss Traycee."

"Hi, Brian. Traycee's here to pick up her puppy."

Brian Steele has been a fixture at this estate for as long as I can recall. When I learned he and Violet were friends and lovers for most of their lives, I felt a little volcano of *Hell yeah! You go, V!* bubble up inside me. It turns out Aunt Violet had a lot of secrets and semisecrets in her life none of us expected, but I'm glad for this one. She deserved whatever happiness she found with stoic Brian.

I don't know him well, another casualty of not being on the property much, but sadness hollows his eyes. My heart constricts for him, and I hope it's only the newness of grief making him appear less than healthy. Regardless, it's not my place to ask, so I keep my worries to myself. I'll ask Fina later if he's okay.

"Y'all come this way."

Traycee winks at me as we do as we're told, but it's easy to follow the yips and barks to our destination.

Moments later, we're standing in a small room with *Fancy* written on the erasable board attached to the wall. The area looks like someone from doggy day care heaven designed it. Fancy is resting on a long cushion, watching her five pups decide between numerous toys and balls to attack. We sink to the ground, and three boys and two girls swarm us, all with fat puppy bellies and lolling tongues.

Brian looks at the whole group with amused indulgence. "Your girl's ready, Miss Traycee. You all set up?"

"I am, and I got everything on your list. Plus, I have all the appointments made with Doc."

Her assurances have Brian giving his seal of approval. His reputation for his love of the MacInnes border collies is known far and wide, as well as the knowledge you'd better obey every single one of his instructions. Failure to do so has had him reclaiming puppies before, and he'd make sure every breeder in the state of Texas knows your name if you get on his bad side.

"Good enough, then. You two have fun, and I'll come back in a bit."

It's impossible not to obey with a pack of pure happiness demanding our attention. Not more than five minutes passes before it's clear one little girl has already claimed Traycee, and not the other way around.

"I think you've been chosen." I don't stop playing tug-of-war with the little boy who appears to be the alpha of the brood.

"I think you're right." She strokes the fur of the beauty with perfect markings climbing into her lap and putting her head on Traycee's arm. Apparently, she got all the calm genes, and my boy got all the rambunctious ones.

"You going to take one?" Traycee's dreamy voice confirms she's already in love with her little fluffy bundle.

Though tempting, I know better. I'll stick with Penny, our fountain dragon. Always patient, waiting for me to visit and stroke her beautiful nose. Willing to listen to all my woes. Never has to be walked. No vet bills. Stone mason invoices, maybe...

"Not right now. I'm lucky enough I can do this every single day if I want to."

I can't speak for Traycee, but I've had exactly as much sitting still as I can manage, even with a determined black and white floof trying to keep me entertained. With every meeting we attend together and every lunch shared, I'm getting closer to my quirky new friend, but I'm hell and gone from being comfortable with myself yet and don't have the extra mental space for the responsibility of a pet. Besides, I move too much to take one on.

"You finish up here and meet me at the castle."

Traycee is too busy falling in love to do more than wave goodbye and assure me she'll see me in a bit. I leave her and Brian to work out puppy details and return to my office with determined steps.

Time to distract my fear gremlin. Deflect the little bastard into getting some work done.

Do anything to stay on my path.

THANK YOU FOR READING!

I hope you enjoyed Return to Magnolia Bloom. If so, please leave a review on your favorite sites (Amazon, Goodreads, BookBub).

THANK YOU!!

Please sign up for my newsletter to receive my next free novella, updates, and information on all future releases at www.Paula-Adler.com, or find my author pages at all the usual places: Amazon, Goodreads, BookBub, Facebook

ABOUT THE AUTHOR

Paula Adler is a born and raised Texan with a traveling soul. She's Mom to the two greatest kids in the universe who make her proud every day. She and her husband defied convention and all naysayers to too young, and are still married over forty years later. They spend their time SCUBA diving and dancing. She's doing her dream...one book at a time.

For more information, please visit
https://www.PaulaAdler.com

Made in the USA
Middletown, DE
03 January 2021

30600261R00203